Get th
backstory of how
"Sta

FOR FREE when joining
Sam's VIP Readers' Group.

See details at the end of this book.

Published by DukeBox.life.
http://DukeBox.life.

For my friend, Glynis Shiell (1963 — 2018). Thank you for being in my life and know that you will always be in my heart.

To all my friends and family, make the most of this one wild and precious life!

"But I don't want to go among mad people," Alice remarked.
"Oh, you can't help that," said the Cat: "we're all mad here.
I'm mad. You're mad."
"How do you know I'm mad?" said Alice.
"You must be," said the Cat, "or you wouldn't have come
here."

Lewis Carroll, Alice's Adventures in Wonderland

PROLOGUE

Alice sat on a large, rough rock to the side of the beautiful white Camps Bay beach, dangling her feet in the crisp, cold rock pool. Here, emerging like a diamond from a stream, she found a rare moment of clarity.

Her past, a phantasm of places, faces, emotions and events, shimmered on the rippling tide before her.

How much of it was real? She could not tell. That did not matter, for how can we ever really know, when all our existence is filtered through unreliable senses and tainted minds? Or when the past is construed and re-told by people around us working to their own agendas?

Giving in, she allowed herself to let go, to let the tugging currents of her mind pull her in and drag her under.

> *There are worlds inside,*
> *worlds lost in my mind,*
> *where what I see,*
> *both miracle and tragedy,*
> *is really only part of me.*
> *Here, unfettered by my past*
> *and the shadows I have cast,*
> *I cherish feeling that I'm free*
> *while knowing that this cannot be.*

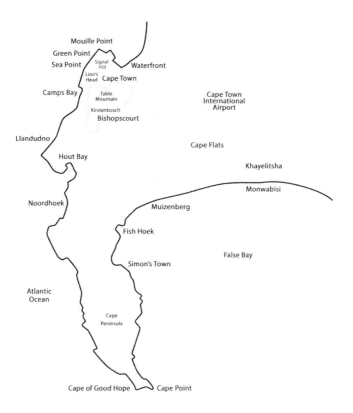

Mouille Point
Green Point
Sea Point   Signal Hill
Lion's Head   Cape Town   Waterfront
Camps Bay   Table Mountain
Kirstenbosch
Bishopscourt

Cape Town International Airport

Llandudno

Hout Bay

Cape Flats

Khayelitsha
Monwabisi

Noordhoek

Muizenberg

Fish Hoek

Simon's Town

False Bay

Atlantic Ocean

Cape Peninsula

Cape of Good Hope   Cape Point

PART I

SOUTH EAST ENGLAND, UNITED
KINGDOM

ONE

7 O'clock sharp, Toni and Lizbeth headed up in the lift of the small business co-op near Old Street in London that housed their respective offices. Their two weeks in the Maldives had been out of this world. So much happened, so much that was new, so much excitement. Toni stuck her hands into the back pockets of her jeans and leaned her tall sporty frame against the lift wall while she quietly admired the slight, beautiful, blonde woman dressed in a tight, navy, pencil skirt suit beside her and her heart swelled. She bit her lower lip. On one level she could not be happier. On another she felt an unfamiliar anxiety lurking. This had nothing to do with the holiday but everything to do with her dawning realisation — she never wanted to lose this beautiful woman from her life.

As Lizbeth glanced in the mirrored panel of the lift wall, she caught Toni's dark brown eyes staring at her in the reflection. "What?" she asked.

Toni shook her head. "Nothing." She leant over past

3

Lizbeth and hit the emergency stop button on the control panel. She turned and pulled Lizbeth into an embrace. "I just love you and..." she kissed Lizbeth deeply, "want to say thank you so very much for a super holiday."

Lizbeth smiled. "No, thank you. It was wonderful. I can't believe we saw whale sharks. That gave me a whole new perspective on what we think of as life, nature and what it means to be free in that wide ocean."

They kissed again.

"I don't want to go back to the real world," Toni said. "Shall we go missing for at least one more day?"

"Stop it, Toni!" Lizbeth smacked Toni's arm gently. "You know I'd love that, but you also know I am meeting with Judge Merchant today. I have to be here for that."

"She's an ex-fling. Can't you get her to come to your flat another time?"

Lizbeth frowned at Toni and was about to launch into the expected tirade about how that was years ago while they were still at university and had nothing to do with them meeting now, when she noticed the naughty twinkle in Toni's eyes. She pushed Toni on the shoulder in mock agitation.

Toni ducked in an exaggerated manner. "Okay. Okay. I was just teasing."

"No more teasing," Lizbeth said, and planted a peck on her cheek. "Besides, poor Lawrence must have drowned under all your paperwork by now."

Toni rolled her eyes and sighed. "True," she said, and hit the release button on the control panel. She had quite deliberately blanked out any thoughts about work, trying to enjoy the last few minutes of her first holiday away from the office in nearly two years.

The lift pinged and opened. They both stepped out and headed down the corridor.

Outside Lizbeth's door, Toni gave her a coy little kiss on the cheek and a wave as she continued on to her own office.

———

As Toni neared her office, she saw the door was ajar. About to rush in guns blazing, she realised it was just Lawrence, her young colleague and apprentice P.I., who had beaten her in despite the early hour. He stood in the middle of the perfectly tidy room — one she hardly recognised — holding the landline phone to his ear and scribbling in a diary. Except for her laptop and a little silver name plaque perched on the front edge, the rest of the desk was completely clear.

"Oh my God! Lawrence," she exclaimed involuntarily.

He held up one finger to his lips to show her to keep quiet. "Sure, Sir, I'll tell her. I know it is urgent and I'm sure she will be more than willing to help you out. You can speak to her yourself at ten this morning. She can be reached on this —" He listened for a few minutes, rolling his eyes back for Toni's benefit. "Oh, okay Dr McCroy, I'll let her know." He scribbled something on a Post-it note. "Ten a.m. sharp. Sure, she'll ring you." Lawrence put the phone down.

"This guy is desperate to see you. I'm not sure why. He won't say, but he's called over half a dozen times to check if perhaps you've come back early from your travels."

Toni advanced into the room and put her satchel on one of the spare client chairs in front of her desk.

"Wow, Lawrence! What happened here? Have I been burgled?" Toni remarked on the rather bare looking office as she ran her hand through her long dark hair.

He looked around the office with a smile. "Oh, yeah, I hope you don't mind... I tidied up a bit. You did say to make myself at home and asked me to do my best. So I did. I tried for a good few days to get the hang of your, er... filing system, but I found it a little too... unconventional, so I decided to modernise a bit," he said, looking pleased with himself.

"Where did it all go?" Toni asked, scanning the room.

"Since we're now in the twenty-first century, I decided to invest in a photocopier, and I enlisted the mind-blowing tech services of Three." He held out a hand rapidly. "Don't worry. I paid for it all out of my wages, not your petty cash, just in case you didn't agree. I figured either way it was a worthwhile investment to make my life easier." Lawrence leaned down, clicked on something on the laptop in front of him and swivelled it round so she could see the screen. "Here is a digitised archive of all your paperwork and notes, indexed by manual keywords, generic metadata, and OCR[1] identified search terms. Basically, any document you have that has text in it can now be searched for and found within minutes, and it takes up very little space. Oh, and you have access to all your records at anytime from anywhere in the world, since Three also installed your very own secure NAS server."

Toni's jaw dropped. Her brain couldn't quite comprehend what all that meant. "I trust the coffee machine still works the same way?" she asked. "Or do I need a Master's in IT to make a coffee now, too?"

Lawrence cleared his throat. "Yes, sorry, I probably should've let you have a cup of coffee first, before I launched into all of that."

Toni turned to the perfectly cleared trestle-table on

which the tiny coffee machine now looked lost. "Want one?"

"Yes, please," he said, joining her on the other side of the table. She poured them each a cup and handed him one.

"So?" Lawrence said stirring his coffee.

"So? What?" Toni carefully sipped the hot liquid.

"So? What do you think?" He waved his spoon in the direction of the office space around them.

She glanced around again. Then she slowly began to nod. "I just wish you had told me you were planning this. I could at least have done some of the sorting and tidying before I left."

"Phew!" Lawrence let out a nervous laugh. "Three and I got stuck in and we managed to clear it all over four nights. Well, she did most of it. You were right. That girl is a machine — she never sleeps." He shook his head. "I don't know how she does it. And, the OCR and metadata programme she wrote is a complete work of art."

Toni nodded in appreciation.

"And now as an unexpected bonus, we can both fit into this office at once."

Toni laughed. "True, it feels positively palatial. I was beginning to dread having to find somewhere bigger. Thanks!"

Lawrence nodded and his pale freckled cheeks flushed slightly.

———

After a quick catch-up with Lawrence, Toni rang Dr Magnus McCroy at the PhyCorp Institute. He invited her to come and see him at their offices so he could explain the details of a case that he said he was not at liberty to discuss over the phone. It all sounded a bit cloak and dagger, but she decided to take the bait.

———

Toni handed her ID to the armed uniformed guards. She watched as they cross-referenced her name to a list of expected visitors. Within seconds her ID was handed back and she was waved through the wide gates of the PhyCorp Institute. The property occupied a large estate in the middle of the Berkshire countryside. She steered her old banger along the long drive edged with a row of tall silver-birch trees. After four-hundred yards the driveway opened up to reveal an imposing stucco covered Georgian mansion, with large sash-windows. There were only six cars parked outside, which didn't seem many considering the size of the place.

Toni parked her car and headed to the main entrance.

Inside the lobby, a large, dark, oak reception desk formed the centre piece, behind a conversational arrangement of couches and chairs upholstered in a maroon and gold jacquard fabric which added to the opulent feel of the building. A middle-aged woman with dyed blond hair and nineteen-fifties reading glasses, sat behind the reception desk, staring at something on the computer monitor in front of her.

When Toni approached, the woman's face lit up as though she had been expecting her.

"Hi, I'm Toni Mendez. I'm here to see Dr McCroy."

"Of course," the woman said, still smiling. "Do you have an appointment?"

As if on cue, a tall, beautiful woman of Asian descent, possibly in her mid-forties and immaculately turned out in a turquoise silk dress with matching scarf, entered the lobby through a pair of somehow out-of-place, stainless-steel clad automatic doors with round porthole windows.

"Silvia, it's fine. I've got this," the woman said to the receptionist.

Toni could detect a slight accent confirming her hunch that this woman was either Indian or Pakistani in origin. The traces of an accent were, however, so faint that Toni guessed she had been educated in the UK, possibly Oxbridge, and probably lived here ever since.

"Toni Mendez, I presume," the woman said, holding out her hand.

Toni shook hands and nodded.

"I'm Sheena Mukherjee. Dr McCroy and I have been expecting you. Please follow me."

Toni fell in step behind Ms Mukherjee as she headed back through the out-of-place steel doorway and down a linoleum clad corridor that resembled a hospital — in strong contrast to the luxury of the reception area.

After Lawrence had told Toni about her appointment with Dr McCroy, she'd tried to do some research to prepare for the meeting, but all her searches came back empty, barring a very short industry description involving "mental health" and the physical address and VAT number on the HMRC database. Other than that, PhyCorp Institute seemed to have no digital footprint.

"Right this way, Ms Mendez," her escort said as she turned into another corridor, at the far end of which, Sheena Mukherjee opened the door to a small consulting room. Toni noticed the name plaque on the door read Dr M. McCroy.

As Toni stepped inside, she was greeted by a tall, well built, clean-shaven man in his late fifties. Unlike many men his age he had a full head of hair and he obviously looked after himself well. Over brown corduroy trousers and a beige shirt and tie, he wore a white lab coat.

"This is Dr McCroy," Sheena said.

He smiled and shook hands with Toni. "Please take a seat. Thank you for coming out this far to see us today."

Toni nodded and sat down.

The consulting room was very sparsely decorated with a stainless-steel table and four chairs around it. In the top corner, attached to the ceiling, Toni noticed a camera. Its light was red, so Toni gathered that the meeting was not being recorded at that moment.

Dr McCroy bent down and picked up his briefcase from the floor. It was an old-fashioned leather case with fake buckled straps. "Miss Mendez, we really need your help with this." He took out a cardboard pocket folder which he placed onto the desk between them.

As Toni stretched towards the folder, he put his finger on top of it and pulled it out of her reach. "This is a very delicate, highly confidential matter and you should only read the file if you are sure you are definitely going to take the case."

"With all due respect, Dr McCroy, I would need a bit more information to make that decision." Toni looked expectantly from Dr McCroy to Sheena Mukherjee who was still standing to one side leaning against the wall.

"It involves someone," he searched for the word, "close to me. She has gone missing in South Africa," he said. "And, I think she's in trouble. All we need you to do is go to South Africa, find her and bring her back to the UK."

Toni looked confused. "I don't quite understand, Dr McCroy, if this is a simple missing persons case, why not just call the South African authorities? Surely they can deal with that quite easily."

"Because, in some respects this is a slightly more delicate situation, which, if not handled correctly, could have dire consequences for me," he glanced up at Sheena, "personally and professionally," Dr McCroy said.

"Not to mention embarrass the organisation and affect our prospective funding," Sheena added. "We need this dealt with quietly and under the radar."

Dr McCroy nodded. "Alice is very important. It is imperative that, whatever happens, this needs to be kept out of the hands of the South African authorities."

Toni's curiosity was pricked, but she didn't want to ask too many questions. She didn't want to set the expectation that she would take the case, unless she was sure. But there were a few things that she really did need to know.

"Why me?"

"Ms Mendez, you come highly recommended by a trusted business colleague. You have all the right skills from your training and background, you can be discrete and more importantly," Sheena hesitated a few moments before finding the right words, "you are not bound by red tape, nor by any specific affiliations."

"By affiliations, you mean any law enforcement agencies?" Toni asked.

Sheena nodded.

"Ms Mendez, we believe you are uniquely qualified for this job and we are prepared to reward you very handsomely in advance."

Sheena Mukherjee placed a letter sized brown envelope on the desk in front of Toni. Toni picked it up and glanced inside. It contained a wad of fifty-pound notes, easily adding up to a grand.

"That is only the starting bonus," Sheena said. "We'll double your usual day rate, carry all expenses and double this sum as a completion bonus."

Despite the large cash incentive, which for Toni was certainly a drawing card, after everything that she had been through to build up her business so far, she was reluctant to get involved in cases of a spurious nature.

"I'm sorry Dr McCroy, Sheena," she nodded at each of them, "I really don't think that I'm the right person for this job and even if I was, I simply can't take off to South Africa right now. I appreciate the professional compliment you do me in bringing me out here but, I'm sorry if you've wasted your time."

Dr McCroy and Sheena shared a resigned look.

Toni got up and Sheena reluctantly walked her out to the reception.

"If you change your mind, Ms Mendez, please call me." Sheena handed her a business card. "That is my direct mobile number."

———

In her car, on the way back from Dr McCroy's office, Toni thought over her decision not to take the job.

They were offering her a lot of money for what seemed to be a simple missing person case. This in itself was intriguing and she couldn't really afford to turn away good money right at this stage in her business, especially considering the large credit card bill she would have to pay off, after her holiday. But South Africa wasn't merely a quick hop to the continent and she had just been away from work for two whole weeks. She really needed to knuckle-down and pick up the slack here in London.

Besides, while away on holiday with Lizbeth, Toni had taken a big decision, which now required some urgent action. With this in mind, rather than head back to the office, she cleared her diary for the rest of the afternoon and headed to her studio flat.

———

Toni opened her front door and paused before stepping inside. Since her flat had been ransacked during the Ransom-Evans case, at the start of the whirlwind journey that resulted in her and Lizbeth finally getting together, she had hardly been back there. Come to think of it, even prior to all that happening she used to spend at least three nights out of seven, at Lizbeth's.

Her flat felt quite alien now, like something from a distant dream, a different time. As she slowly advanced into the room, her mind flashed back to the night it had all started. She remembered arriving and finding the flat door ajar, the feeling of fear and shock, scrambling in the dark for Hillary her hockey stick in case the intruders were still inside. She remembered finding the big blood-red letters slapped onto her white walls and the weeks afterwards it took her to apply enough layers of whitewash to make them disappear. She grimaced at the irony. Obviously, the fates knew more about her then than she could even imagine at that point.

Without stopping to engage with any of the usual things in her flat, she headed straight for the little fridge-freezer in the corner. She was there for one thing and one thing only.

She lifted the flap to the freezer compartment that housed only one item, a small, white, plastic ice tray. She grabbed the tray and nudged it left and right to loosen it from where it had frozen in place. With a crunch it came away from the thick, frosted walls. She pulled it free and placed it on the side of the kitchen sink. She jammed the rubber plug firmly in the plug-hole, filled the kettle and switched it on. Then, just for safety, she grabbed a tea towel and placed it across the bottom of the sink over the plughole. Carefully, she turned the bulging ice tray on its head in the middle of the cloth. Once the kettle boiled, she poured the piping hot water over the back of the ice tray and listened to the satisfying cracks and squeaks as the ice melted and clunked onto the tea towel. She turned over the ice tray to make sure all the cubes had been dislodged and then removed it from the sink. She carefully poured the remaining boiling water over each of the ice cubes, watching them melt away rapidly, until she spotted the one she was looking for. She focused the rest of the hot water on that cube. Once all the ice had melted, she reached down and lifted from the water the little lump that remained, holding it up between her thumb and forefinger. It was a seven-carat rough diamond with no visible flaws, shaped in an oblong so it could be cut as a large oval gem, or two, smaller, equal-sized twins.

This diamond was the only thing she had from her mother. When she'd died, her father had got rid of everything else that reminded him of his beloved wife. The stone had apparently been passed down to her mother from Toni's grandfather, or so her dad had told her. When Toni first left home and entered the police force, she'd had the rock valued, intending to make sure her house insurance covered it adequately. Sadly, there was no way in a million years she could have afforded the astronomical premium demanded. Then one day, while she was drinking a whiskey on ice in the pub, as she drained the glass, one of the cubes slid down and bumped her on the nose, providing a eureka moment.

———

Lizbeth wasn't one for a big fuss, but on this occasion, Toni wanted to make things extra special. At first, she didn't have a clue how to achieve that. How does one set the right scene when asking such a big question? Then she decided just to keep it simple and honest.

On her way back to Lizbeth's, she stopped off at the grocery store and bought some fresh ingredients to make Lizbeth's favourite salmon Thai red curry dish. She called in at every florist she knew and bought up all their roses. She had never understood why people limited themselves to only red roses when trying to express the magnitude of their love for someone. Once home, she tied them all together in a huge bouquet of every colour and shape, attaching the rock in a small, black velvet jewellery bag to the ribbon around the base of the bouquet.

The rest of the afternoon was spent preparing supper and by 5 pm everything was ready. She had laid the table and opened a bottle of Lizbeth's favourite red wine to allow it to breathe. She had even contemplated changing the bed linen but stopped herself. That was really a step too far and a bit too close to the cliché of sprinkled petals on bed sheets — a thought she was embarrassed to admit to herself she had genuinely considered, if only briefly.

Toni paced about the house for the next hour and a half. On a number of occasions, she was tempted to text Lizbeth to make sure she would be on her way home soon, but she resisted. That would just irritate Lizbeth or alert her that something was up.

When Toni heard the key turn in the front door, her heart began to beat like a bongo. This was probably the biggest decision she would make in her life, but it felt right — as right as she could imagine it could ever feel. Even when they had their disagreements and niggling bits, Toni had never before experienced any relationship where she and her partner seemed so good together. She doubted any relationship could ever be any better than this.

"Wow! What's this for?" Lizbeth asked. She put her handbag and briefcase down on the kitchen stool and leant over to smell the roses.

"For you," Toni said, hanging back to allow Lizbeth time to admire the flowers.

"They are beautiful." Lizbeth beamed. She leant in to take in the full aroma of the bouquet. "Why am I so lucky today?" As she stood back to take another look, she noticed the little black bag and the small card that was tied around the stems.

She looked up at Toni with a quizzical smile. "What is this?"

Toni's heart was pounding and her palms felt clammy with nerves.

She sat down on the couch, patting the seat beside her to encourage Lizbeth to come sit next to her.

Lizbeth took the offered seat and cautiously opened the card. Then she read the message inside aloud. "I love you, please will you be mine?"

Toni had pondered long and hard and when she was completely paralysed with indecision on what to write she settled on the most simple, heartfelt, message.

Lizbeth looked a little perplexed.

Toni held her breath. This was not what she had expected.

PROJECT ALICE

Still Lizbeth said nothing as she opened the little black velvet bag and tipped the contents into her hand. The large rock landed soundlessly in her palm.

"Phew! Thank goodness!" Lizbeth laughed, relieved. "For a moment there I thought it was something silly like a ring."

"No, not yet," Toni said quickly, her smile beginning to fade as she tried to make sense of Lizbeth's reaction. "It's an uncut diamond. It was my mother's." Toni grabbed Lizbeth's hand and held it. "I want us to make it into two rings, one for each of us, to design our own. I figured that a relationship like ours is pretty unique so it is fitting that we make our own wedding rings rather than just buy conventional ones."

"Wedding?" Lizbeth said hesitantly.

Toni nodded. "Yes, Lizbeth Marie Du Cannon," Toni took a deep breath, "would you, please, marry me?" There was a long silence, one that felt like an age during which Toni waited expectantly.

Lizbeth took Toni's hand in both her own. "Wow."

"Wow?" Toni asked. "What do you mean 'wow'? I anticipated many responses from you, you being probably the most eloquent person I know, but not 'wow'."

Lizbeth got up off the couch and went to the kitchen. "This is a bit of a shock, that's all."

"Okay," Toni said uncertainly, getting up off the couch and following Lizbeth, "I can live with that."

Lizbeth poured herself a glass of water.

"Well?" Toni said again, rounding the kitchen table towards Lizbeth.

"Well," Lizbeth said. "Toni, you know I'm not really the marrying kind."

"I know. You've said that. You've said you don't believe

in the conventional. That's why I thought this," she pointed at the little jewellery bag, "would be perfect as an expression of our love."

Lizbeth took a deep breath, in that way she did when she was going to choose her words very carefully. "Toni, I'm truly touched that you thought of this, that you prepared this," she waved her hand towards the beautifully laid table, the food on the stove and the bottle of red wine standing ready with two polished glasses. "But, Toni, even though I'm mad about you and love you very much, I don't believe in marriage, never have —"

"But that is okay, we don't have to have traditional vows or a traditional marriage ceremony. We can do it whichever way you want."

Lizbeth sighed gently. "Toni, let me ask you this. Why do you want to get married?"

Toni looked confused. "Because I love you," she said plainly.

When Lizbeth didn't answer, Toni continued. "Because, I want you in my life till the day we die."

"And a rock or a ring or a ceremony is going to make that possible?"

Toni nodded. "Well, no not 'make it possible'. Marriage is a celebration of that love and commitment."

Lizbeth took a step closer to Toni. "It's so nice that you want to celebrate our love," she affectionately took Toni's hands in hers. "I really appreciate that, but not with marriage, Toni." Lizbeth put the little bag with the diamond on the kitchen counter.

"Okay, we can have a civil partnership," Toni said.

Lizbeth let go of Toni's hands and went to fill her glass, but this time she stayed by the sink. "No, Toni, not a civil partnership either. I'm pleased you see them as ways to celebrate love, but you must know that I don't. I see them as ways to combat our own insecurities, our fear that someone we care about, more correctly someone whom we want to care about us, might leave us. Marriage, civil partnership and even a ring," Lizbeth pointed at the bag on the kitchen counter, "are ways to stop people from leaving us, an attempt to shackle, to imprison. In my experience, the more you try to imprison someone, the more they fight for their freedom and if they don't try to leave you physically, you can be sure they will sooner or later flee you emotionally and mentally. The only way is to let people be free, and if they stay with you, you know they are truly there because they want it as much as you do."

Toni shook her head. She could not believe what she was hearing. None of it made sense. This was the last response she'd ever expected.

"Besides, Toni, you're still a babe in the woods. You've just discovered this new and exciting part of your life, your attraction to women. You can't pack it in now."

"But I'm in love with you," Toni said in protest.

"Toni, this, us, is but your first foray into this world and believe me we all fall very hard for our first." Lizbeth smiled at a private memory. "But also believe me, Toni, that's not it for life. It should not be. You should be going out there and spreading your wings. Meeting people, falling in love, breaking hearts and having yours broken a few times too. Then, if you still wanted to spend the rest of your life with me in it, then, I would believe you."

"Are you saying you don't believe me?"

"No, Toni, you are missing the point. Even then, we would not need a ceremony or a ring to prove that we love and care for each other. There is no need to try to own or put your mark on another person. That person will either be with you or stay with you or they will not. The choice is theirs as much as it is yours. At best formalities like that do not mean anything."

"How can you say it does not mean anything?"

"What would you say we are now to each other?"

Toni thought about it. "Lovers."

Lizbeth nodded. "Yes, we are friends, who are also lovers. How will that change by adding a ring and ceremony?"

This time it was Toni's turn to remain silent.

"It changes nothing," Lizbeth continued gently. "We don't need a ring or a ceremony to try to chain us together, to show the world we belong. We don't belong to anyone other than ourselves. We are together and will remain friends and lovers for as long as we both want that."

———

Toni had no idea what time it was. She and Lizbeth had finally retired to bed after a very emotional evening. Toni lay awake staring, unseeing, into the dark room. Her mind reeled from the events of the evening. For the last half an hour she had been acutely aware of Lizbeth's rhythmic breathing next to her, taunting her. How could Lizbeth fall asleep so easily after everything that had been said? Finally, Toni could take it no more. She got up.

The inside of the flat was dark and lifeless with the street lights casting zebra striped shadows on the walls and floor and draining all the colour and joy out of the sitting room and kitchen. The flowers and unused crockery were still on the table — now a derelict graveyard of Toni's earlier optimistic dreams. Toni wandered into the kitchen. She grabbed one of the unused wine glasses and poured herself some semi-skimmed milk from the fridge. It reminded her of her grandmother who'd believed that a glass of milk and a couple of cookies on a saucer could cure absolutely anything.

She sipped the cool liquid while staring out over the open-plan kitchen living room. As if watching ghosts, the memories of the past few months in this flat faded in and out of her mind's eye. She remembered that night she'd sat on the couch waiting for Lizbeth, scared stiff something had happened to her, and then, finally, Lizbeth stumbling home with Maxine. She remembered withdrawing into that dark corner of the sitting room and not being able to take her eyes off Lizbeth as Maxine had her way with her in the window, in plain sight of all the insomniac occupants of the neighbouring building. She felt her mouth go dry and her pulse quicken at the thought. God, she should have known then. How could she have been so blind to her own feelings for so long? Now, if she thought back, she'd always been in love with Lizbeth, since the day she first met her. She just hadn't realised that anything could be done about it. Thanks to Maxine, she'd figured that part out, eventually. She was very grateful to Maxine for making her see, but at the same time, if it hadn't been for Maxine, Toni would not be here now — her heart aching with the pain of Lizbeth's rejection.

Christ! Toni found it hard to even recognise where 'here' was. She was so far outside her comfort zone. Never before had she let anyone in, nor cared about anyone as much as she did Lizbeth. Never before had anyone made her feel so elated, powerful, almost omnipotent one minute and so entirely vulnerable and distraught the next, with nothing more than a smile or a frown. Worst of all was the thought of losing Lizbeth. She could not bear the idea of

Lizbeth ever choosing someone else over her, or saying she didn't want to be with her anymore. Toni had it bad, and the truth was she had no idea what to do about it.

She poured out the rest of the milk, rinsed the glass and stood it upside down on the drying rack. She needed time on her own, unclouded time, to think.

She picked up her phone from where it was lying on the coffee table from the night before. She scrolled to Sheena Mukherjee's number. She sent a text.

I'll take the case. Toni.

PART II

CAPE TOWN, SOUTH AFRICA

TWO

Alice waited for Magnus to come back to the suite for lunch. She knew he would be upset if she ate before he got back.

Margaret had moaned that she was hungry so Alice ordered an early lunch for her, gave her the insulin and then her medication to make her sleep. As a result, Margaret was out for the count, probably for the rest of the afternoon, slumped in her wheelchair, snoring softly.

Alice stood, looking out the large floor-to-ceiling window. The lunch table was ready and set behind her.

There came a knock at the door.

"Come in," Alice called, looking at her watch. It was 2.30 pm. "Oh, finally! I'm glad you made it." She turned towards the door. "I'm starv —" Gloria, not Magnus, stood in the doorway.

"Oh, sorry." Alice shook her head "I thought it was my husband here for lunch."

"No, sorry, Madam," Gloria said. She took a few more

25

steps into the room, placing the towels from under her arm on the bed and walked towards Alice, offering her a small silver tray she held in her other hand. "This is from Dr McCroy, Madam."

Alice took the envelope that was lying on the silver tray and opened it. Inside it was a handwritten note on the grey hotel stationery. She read it.

———

Honey,
Do go ahead and order lunch for you and Mother,
darling. I have been unexpectedly detained by work.
Enclosed find the tip.

———

"I brought you some more clean towels," Gloria said.

Alice refolded the note. "When did my husband give this to you?"

"He left it at reception this morning, Madam."

Alice turned back towards the window.

"It is such a lovely day out." Gloria said by way of making conversation. "You should really go and have lunch out. If you want, one of the porters could help take old Mrs McCroy downstairs for you."

Alice shook her head.

"Maybe you'd like lunch on one of the restaurant terraces? It is really something. All our guests talk about it."

"I can't take Mrs McCroy out," Alice said evenly.

"What about a little lunch for you in the hotel downstairs then? I could stay and watch over old Mrs McCroy for you." Gloria glanced over at the sleeping figure in the wheelchair. She took a few steps closer to Alice. "No one will be any the wiser. I'm used to doing babysitting like this and this is after all a respite hotel. It does not get safer than this!"

Alice stared out of the window and then at Margaret. The note in her hand made bile rise in her throat. It was a beautiful baking hot summer's day. She would have given her eye-teeth to be able to feel that warm sun on her skin. But Magnus wouldn't be happy if he found out that she had left his mother alone. Well, it wouldn't be leaving her alone, really, Alice thought. She knew from personal experience that Margaret was likely to sleep until way past 5 pm and Magnus would not be back before 5.30 pm.

She peered inside the envelope again and took out the two R20 notes Magnus had included for a tip for her lunch order.

She then slowly turned towards Gloria. "Actually, I think I will do that. Would you really not mind holding the fort for an hour? That would be most kind of you." She handed Gloria the money.

"Oh, no! I couldn't take that," Gloria said and gently pushed the offered hand back in Alice's direction. "I'm not really doing anything, just sitting here reading. You take it and go and enjoy a little drink on me out there with it."

Gloria winked. "Just give me two minutes. Let me go and get my tea and my book." Gloria left in a hurry.

Alice put on her outdoor shoes, grabbed a scarf, sun hat and her sunglasses to make sure no one would recognise her. Then she sat down at the table and, as she waited, she tried to bend her mind around the events that had led her to this moment of rebellion. She was about to do something, which, less than a week ago, she could not have imagined in a million years. She thought back to the confounding events of the past few days.

———

Despite not having slept very well during the overnight flight, Alice wheeled the still slumbering Margaret McCroy out of the Cape Town International Airport building. Alice's slight, sinewy frame was a lot stronger than it looked. She heaved her burden effortlessly into the lift and up and down the ramps on the way towards the short stay car park where their driver had parked the white limo that would take them to the hotel.

Dr Magnus McCroy and his PA, Nurse Rita Reynolds, a slim, stern looking woman with jet black hair and subtle cosmetic enhancements — perks of the business — followed right behind Alice.

The driver, a friendly, muscly black man in a navy suit, white shirt and tie, helped Alice to lift Margaret into the back of the limo. Alice was very glad she had decided to increase Margaret's sedative dose for the night, so that she was still soundly asleep. It meant Alice would have a slightly longer reprieve, hopefully long enough to enjoy the drive from the airport towards Cape Town, to their hotel. She had never been to South Africa, but since Magnus owned a respite hotel as part of his business, the MOD Hotel, in Camps Bay, she had heard a lot about it.

On the journey, no-one else seemed to pay much attention to the scenery. Magnus had his nose buried in a draft of the speech he was going to deliver at the conference dinner later that evening. Intermittently he read bits to Rita and they would discuss the finer points of inflection.

In the meantime, Alice was entranced by the alien

*beauty sweeping past her window as they made their way
along the motorway towards the city centre. The colour of the
light was so pure, the sky so blue. Table Mountain loomed up
ahead, covered by its legendary tablecloth, just as she had
imagined it. The warm, saturated, South African sunshine
even made the expanse of dishevelled shanty towns along the
Cape Flats look bright and full of promise. But nothing could
prepare Alice for the beauty of the Atlantic Ocean as they
crossed over Kloof Nek and descended into Camps Bay.*

*"Alice, focus," came Magnus's commanding reprimand,
pulling her attention back to life inside the limo. Due to the
sedatives and the jostling movement of the limo, Margaret
had started to drool a little. Magnus did not like to be
embarrassed in front of his work colleagues and it was
Alice's job to make sure Margaret didn't do that.*

*Once in Camps Bay, driving along the main seafront
road, the beauty and sheer overwhelming spectacle of the
place almost made her forget herself again. They passed a
number of shops and restaurants and a couple of beautiful,
large hotels overlooking the white sandy beach. Alice prayed
that one of them would be the MOD Hotel. Her heart sank
when she felt the limo turn away from the beach and head up
a side street, coming to a stop halfway up the road, outside a
modern, brutalist, glass and cement block of a building.*

*A cohort of fellow physicians and colleagues had
gathered in the lobby to sweep Magnus and his PA up to the
boardroom for a welcome brunch. Magnus was well-known
and well-respected in the field of plastic surgery. An army of
attendants were also on hand to help Magnus take his
suitcases to their room, but he turned them down, explaining
that Alice would handle it. That left Alice alone to
manoeuvre Margaret in her wheelchair and the seven Globe
Trotter suitcases, which Magnus had insisted they bring on*

this trip, up to their suite. Finally, a small, older, friendly-faced, black or coloured[1] woman, whose name badge read 'Gloria', took pity on Alice. Gloria's bubbly conversation felt like a tonic to Alice as they lugged the suitcases, and the sleeping Margaret, all the way up in the lift and along the slate-clad corridors of the MOD Respite Hotel to Magnus's suite on the second floor.

Once inside the suite, Alice sighed, relieved that they had finally reached their end destination. She parked Margaret in one corner of the minimalist room, positioning her chair so she could look out of one of the floor-to-ceiling glass windows when she awoke. Alice was a little disappointed that the view provided only a glimpse of Camps Bay itself. She'd been hoping to enjoy life outside vicariously, from the suite. The windows did however frame the wonderful mountains that formed the backdrop to Camps Bay.

It had been a long flight from London Heathrow, and Alice wanted nothing more than to lay her head down for a nap on the crisp white cotton sheets of the immaculate king size bed.

She suddenly became aware that Gloria was still waiting at the door and she felt embarrassed. Of course! "Oh, I'm so sorry, Gloria," Alice said. "Unfortunately, I don't have any money."

Alice caught the flash of disbelief as it swept across Gloria's face.

"Honestly," Alice said, "my husband keeps the money." She reached for her large handbag to show Gloria the contents, but before she could do that, Gloria gave a tired sigh that said, 'I've heard it all before' and turned to leave. "If you come back later, I'll ask my husband to tip you."

"Yes, Madam," Gloria said, bowing slightly as she backed out of the room pulling the door to behind her.

For a brief moment, Alice felt sad to see her go. She was the first friendly face Alice had seen in a long while. Her life wasn't really her own anymore, now that she was with Magnus and the full-time carer to Margaret. Magnus did not like Alice talking to other people, let alone going out and socialising. To be fair, with everything involved in Margaret's care, there was very little time for anything else, so she didn't often miss being sociable, but she did miss laughing.

———

Shortly after Gloria had left, Margaret awoke from her slumber. Alice washed her hands and face, checked her blood sugar levels and gave her the relevant dose of insulin and then called room service to bring up some lunch for them both. She knew Magnus wouldn't be back until just before the dinner in the evening.

After lunch, Alice gave Margaret her medication and prepared her for her afternoon nap. Margaret didn't like the palaver of getting in and out of her wheelchair all the time, so during the day she tended to sleep sitting in her chair.

While Margaret slept, rather than take the craved nap herself, Alice started unpacking. She needed to select her outfit for the evening's dinner. This was a very important event for Magnus. It was the opening night gala of one of the most prestigious annual medical conferences, which this year was being held in South Africa on Magnus's recommendation.

On his instruction, Alice had bought herself a beautiful, black, three-quarter length dress that complemented her trim figure without drawing too much attention to her angular frame. It had a subtle sequinned pattern over the left shoulder, down to the waistline on the front, along the top of the long left sleeve and over her left shoulder blade all the way down to the small of her back. The sleeve and those parts of the dress around the sequins were made from a see-through chiffon material. Her other arm was completely sleeveless and a delicate sequinned bow secured the dress just past her clavicle. It was beautiful and unlike anything she had ever seen. It was perfectly asymmetrical, casual and formal depending from which side you looked at it.

"You know you really don't need to dress up like that on my account?" Magnus said as soon as he saw her.

She kissed him on the cheek. "Of course I do. It's only right that the wife of Dr McCroy, leader in plastic surgery, looks her best for his key note speech at the conference opening gala." She smiled and twirled away again, enjoying the feeling of freedom and sexiness the dress gave her.

"I'm really sorry, honey. You can't come tonight."

She stopped short. "What do you mean?"

"I mean, who's going to look after Margaret?" he pointed at his mother in the wheelchair, out cold in the corner. "Who's going to look after her?"

"But Magnus —"

"Honey, if I had known you wanted to come, I would've organised a relief carer, but I thought you'd be too tired."

"So, what will you do? You can't go on your own."

"It's okay," he said, opening his cupboard and taking out the fine weave woollen suit that he had selected for this occasion. "I've asked Rita to accompany me. It is, after all, a work do and it will be convenient if she is there to arrange my diary. Saves me having to remember the details." Magnus quickly finished getting dressed.

Alice sat down on the end of the bed and stared out at the darkness descending over Camps Bay.

Just before he left, Magnus came to kiss her on her forehead. "You have something to eat and get some rest. You look tired."

———

At 2 am, Magnus finally came back to the suite. He stripped down to his boxers and crawled into bed next to her. Reeking of alcohol, he passed out, also snoring loudly within minutes.

———

Alice stared out of the large window in the hotel suite. Even the little she could see of Camps Bay beachfront made her wish she was out there, enjoying her freedom and loving life along with the hundreds of other tourists and locals.

She was so deep in thought that she didn't hear the door to the suite open.

"Oh, I'm so sorry, Mrs McCroy!" Gloria said quickly. "I didn't expect anyone to be in. I was just checking on housekeeping and delivering some more fresh towels, but I can come back later."

"No, it's okay," Alice said in a hushed voice. She glanced at Margaret who was sleeping, mouth agape, snoring in the corner in her wheelchair. She turned back towards the window. "You have such a beautiful country."

Gloria came to stand next to Alice. "We are truly blessed," she said. "The Twelve Apostles are truly awesome."

Alice followed Gloria's eye-line and took a moment herself to fully admire the beautiful mountain range that formed the backdrop to Camps Bay.

"They are beautiful in the evening. Most people sit and stare out over the sea, but I think the much better view is of

the mountains. My favourite is the early mornings though,"
Gloria continued. "That is when you see the crisp faces of the
Twelve Apostles."

Alice nodded, making a note to take a good look the
following morning.

"There is so much to do in Camps Bay, something for
everyone. There are often beach bonfires, picnics on the rocks
at low tide, and regular sports activities on the beach. In the
evenings you can have dinner and sundowners on the terrace
bars and there are sunset cruises that anchor in the Bay
almost every night. Most of the restaurants and bars have
specials on in the afternoon and a number of them have
wheelchair access." Gloria glanced at Margaret in the corner
and then checked her watch. "The Shanty has happy hour
between four and six in the afternoon."

Alice shook her head. "Sadly, Gloria, I couldn't possibly
take Mrs McCroy out. Dr McCroy would not like it, and I
wouldn't want to subject Mrs McCroy to any more
unfamiliar elements than are necessary. She is rather frail."

"Are you sure? I could help you take Mrs McCroy
downstairs, if you like. It really is a lovely warm day out. I'm
sure the vitamin D would do you both some good."

Alice simply shook her head. "Thank you, Gloria. You
are very kind, but I have to get on." Alice moved away from
the window as if to attend to some other business.

"As you wish, Mrs McCroy," Gloria nodded and let
herself out.

The soft knock at the door yanked Alice back to her reality.
Alice got up and went to open it. It was Gloria, looking
flushed like she had been rushing. "Sorry, honey. I got held

up in the staff room," Gloria said out of breath. She was carrying a large handbag and a cup of tea. She settled on the couch and took out a Mills and Boon, ready for an afternoon of babysitting.

———

Alice slipped out of the hotel. She walked down the road and stopped on the corner of Argyle Street and Camps Bay's main thoroughfare, Victoria Road. It was hot out. The sun on her skin felt like a warm embrace. She wanted to take her scarf and hat off but didn't dare in case someone recognised her or, God forbid, she got a tan — then Magnus would sure as hell know she'd been outside.

She turned and looked back at the hotel where it stood grey and stark, angular concrete and glass, like the brutal luxury prison it was, to which she would have to return in one very short hour.

Behind it, Table Mountain stood tall. The cable car was making its way up the side of the mountain, and due to the angle of her view, it appeared over a rise about halfway up and then disappeared again, just before it reached the cable station.

To her left lay the large mountainous lion that gave Lion's Head its name, basking in the sun with its head turned away, staring out to sea. She could just about make out colourful paragliders launching off its nose and using the thermal currents rising from its neck to wind their way down to the ground.

As she turned back around, she suddenly became aware of the stream of traffic in front of her, which at first seemed insignificant compared to the majesty of the rest of her surroundings.

She headed left along the near pavement towards the centre of Camps Bay. Soon she found herself in the middle of a gathering of hawkers who had created an informal mini-market along the pavement. There they had laid out their wares, ranging from knock-off sunglasses and reject branded clothing, handmade African fabric, copper, silver and brass ornaments and jewellery, to six-foot-tall wooden African animals. She thought the African animal jewellery was particularly ingenious. She could have spent her whole afternoon just browsing these stalls, but she dragged herself away and continued on to the pedestrian crossing that would take her to the beach.

The beach did not disappoint. Soft, pure white sand stretched from the promenade down towards bright azure-blue sea that pummelled the sand with powerfully crisp white waves. She longed to go and dip her feet, to feel the sand between her toes and the waves tug at her ankles, but she could not dare. She could not risk returning with sandy feet.

On her right, in a more secluded section of the beach that backed onto the rocks that elevated Victoria Road on its way out of Camps Bay towards Sea Point, she saw a small film-crew dismantling their kit. Clearly their shoot was over for the day.

Then she noticed two royal thrones that stood about twenty feet away from her on the side of the promenade facing away from the beach towards Victoria Road. This struck her as odd until she spotted another entrepreneurial hawker enticing a German couple toward the thrones for a posed photograph.

She continued down the promenade, along the long beach punctuated by periodic shower stations, where bathers either rinsed off salty water and suntan cream or just cooled off. Eventually her path brought her up to the far end of the beach where a large lifeguard tower watched over the swimming area and the coastline transformed into a rocky ledge.

She turned and looked back at Camps Bay and the route that she had come. It was awe-inspiring. It was busy. She tried to imagine having the freedom to spend as much time as she wanted out here. Then, instead, she focussed on drinking it all in, knowing that this would be her only chance to feel a part of it.

The strangest sounding screeching beep from the pedestrian crossing dragged her attention back to her immediate surroundings. She checked her watch. That walk had only taken her fifteen minutes. She glanced across the road towards the Twelve Apostles, which were now partly obscured by the line of terraced restaurants and two to three storey mall and hotels.

She remembered Gloria talking about the restaurants and, to be honest, the thought of a little drink in the warm, windless shade of one of the many terraces sounded very appealing.

She crossed the road. This side was a lot more cramped, as hundreds of visitors and tourists tried to make their way along the tiny pavement that separated a solid line of parked cars from the shop fronts all the way back towards the MOD Hotel end of Camps Bay.

About half way back towards the hotel, Alice saw a very inviting looking restaurant offering a seafront view, shade, large comfy looking cream couches, white cotton table cloths and tall, thin, condensation-beaded glasses of cold refreshments. The sign above it said: "The Sea Shanty". She wondered if that was the place Gloria had mentioned.

She opened her purse and checked whether she still

had the R40 Magnus had enclosed with his note, for her to use as a tip when ordering her lunch. Then, she took a deep breath, pushed her shoulders back and mounted the few steps up to the entrance podium of the restaurant.

Five minutes later, Alice sat quietly staring out over Camps Bay enjoying a little glass of cold Douglas Green Medium Cream sherry. She loved sherry. It wasn't something she had the opportunity to drink much, since Magnus didn't really allow her to drink. She remembered stealing little capfuls of the cheap stuff her foster mother used to hide in the kitchen cupboard behind the detergents, on the rare occasion her foster mother had left the house. Right now, there was the added advantage that the sherry happened to be the cheapest item on the menu and all she could afford.

Sitting there, she reflected on her experience. She had thought she would feel like a kid in a sweet shop. Instead she felt hollow, removed, like watching a movie with the sound off. This was not her life. She was watching others enjoy their lives around her. She was as much in a glass cage now as when sitting in her husband's luxury suite at the hotel, minding Margaret's dribble.

She drained her glass and started back to the MOD.

———

At 4.55 pm Alice rushed back into the hotel suite.

Gloria greeted her with a broad smile from her position, still on the couch.

"Thank God!" Alice said, wiping the sweat off her brow and trying to gulp in more oxygen after her brisk walk back to the hotel.

"All good," Gloria said, packing her book into her bag.

"If I didn't know better, I'd think she was dead." Gloria nodded towards Margaret.

Alice turned pale and rushed over to Margaret.

"Only kidding!" Gloria said, chuckling. "Sorry, that was a bit of gallows humour. Old Mrs McCroy is fine and still soundly asleep. Whatever cocktail she is on, it must be good." Gloria winked at Alice and got up.

"Did you have a good time?" Gloria asked.

Alice nodded. "Thank you. That was such a gift." Then suddenly Alice panicked. "You won't tell, will you?"

"No, it'll be just our secret." Gloria smiled. "Promise," she added. "Maybe sometime later this week we can do it again."

Alice took a few seconds to register. Her heart leapt into her throat. She could not dare to hope.

Friday - 6 October, SA

Magnus awoke late in a particularly good mood.

"I will order us brunch in the suite, darling. I had enough of being in the public eye yesterday and could do with some downtime before I have to see my clients later."

"That sounds lovely," Alice replied. Without being asked, she fetched the room service menu and brought it to him. He took the menu and scanned it. "I think we'll have fish chowder and some of the fresh bread, then grilled hake for the main." He handed Alice back the menu. She headed over to the telephone, dialled the room service number and placed the order.

"Oh, and choose a wine you would really like," he called back from the en suite bathroom where he had gone to shave.

Alice asked the person on the other end of the line to

hold for a moment, and an enormous joy filled her as she carefully studied the wine menu. "May we also have a bottle of your Ken Forrester Cape Breeze Chenin Blanc with that, please?"

Once the order was placed, Alice started to clear the dining-table that stood to one side of the suite. Magnus came out of the bathroom and headed to the table to take a seat to read the papers while he waited. He noticed her hands. "Why are you not wearing your wedding ring?" he asked, sternly.

"Oh, you know how lovely and big it is. The stones keep catching on clothes, so I took it off last night. I didn't want to have an accident with it, putting on that delicate dress."

"You had better put it on before you leave this room. It will be noticed."

Alice nodded meekly.

There was a knock on the door. Alice went to open it. She was pleased to be greeted by Gloria's smiling face.

"Good morning Mrs McCroy, I've come with a message for Dr McCroy," Gloria said.

Alice showed her in. She was followed by a young African girl, about fifteen years of age, whose name badge read "Deka", pushing the room service trolley.

"What is it?" Magnus asked without looking up.

"Doctor, Mrs Heaney asked me to let you know she will be ready for you directly after lunch."

As Gloria spoke, Alice wheeled Margaret towards the table, put the brakes on and took a seat herself. Deka decanted the dishes onto the table and started to pour the wine. Alice watched the gorgeous pale wine start to fill the crystal glass in front of her. It was not often that Magnus allowed her to drink wine, let alone choose it herself.

Deka had hardly poured half a glass for Alice when

Magnus held out his hand. "That's enough. She has responsibilities."

This suddenly reminded Alice of her promise to Gloria. So, when Magnus took out his wallet to tip Deka, Alice asked, "Could you spare another couple of tens, please? I didn't have anything to tip Gloria when she helped me bring the suitcases in."

Magnus looked annoyed. "Could you not even do that on your own?" he asked. Alice dropped her eyes to the table. In her peripheral vision she saw him take out a few more notes[2] and hand them to Gloria.

Suddenly, Margaret, who hadn't bothered to wait to tuck into her chowder, erupted in a huge coughing fit, spluttering soup and bits of fish all over herself and the table, and a few projectiles even landed in Alice's wine glass.

Magnus slammed his hand down hard on the table top with such force, making the crockery and cutlery bounce, that Alice was surprised the surface didn't crack. "Can you do nothing right?" he barked at Alice.

Gloria stepped forward with a tea towel and started to help wipe up the mess.

Magnus folded his napkin deliberately and dumped it on the table. "That's it! I'll have lunch in my office, in peace." He got up, grabbed his jacket and headed to the door. "After which I'll see my clients and then I have the big industry dinner. I hope I can rely on you not to kill my mother before I get back?" He gave Alice a disdainful glance. "Oh, do remember to come down and get Mother's insulin from my consulting room once you have cleared up this mess."

———

Alice arrived in Magnus's waiting room. It was heaving with men and women of all ages, all wanting to change something about their appearance or bodies. Their various needs ranged from face lifts, breast augmentation or reduction, tummy tucks and general reshaping to gender reassignment. Magnus specialised in breast implants and genital plastic surgery.

Right now, his consulting room door was closed. Rita Reynolds was there presiding over his domain. She acknowledged Alice briefly but not warmly. "Dr McCroy is busy with another client now, Alice."

"It's okay I'll just wait. He asked me to come down." Alice said and took a seat.

Alice knew she couldn't stay too long as she had left Margaret sleeping. All hell would break loose if Margaret woke up while she wasn't there.

Magnus's consulting room door opened. He stepped out with a client in her late forties. He was smiling his charming client-facing smile at her. As soon as the door opened Alice could feel the atmosphere in the room change, as the other women in the waiting room visibly started to jostle for his attention.

When Magnus spotted Alice sitting in among his clients, he smiled a bigger smile that was necessary and called out to her. "Hello darling. Just wait here a moment. I'll fetch the insulin." He disappeared back into his consulting room, leaving her to fend off multiple jealous stares from the other occupants of the waiting room.

"You're so lucky to have such a marvellous man for your husband," said one woman in a peach linen skirt suit. "He's so gentle and kind, with such a wonderful sense of humour. Not to mention those dreamy eyes and dimple chin..." The woman realised she might be overstepping a little and stopped.

Alice smiled as amicably as she could. "Yes, I'm very lucky."

By all accounts, Magnus was a good doctor. He really did believe what he was doing was for the good of his patients and Alice knew him to be a good man too. She was so grateful to him for what he had done for her. He had pretty much saved her life.

Her parents had been Eastern European refugees who arrived in England during the Cold War. When Alice was five, her mother and father were killed in a freak car accident which left Alice and her three siblings, a younger brother and baby twin sisters, at the mercy of the state. They had bounced around the care system for a while before they were settled with a Ms Margaret Delaney. There, as the eldest girl, it fell on Alice to help care for the other smaller children. A few years of unexplained chronic illness beset the household and she watched her brother and her little sisters suffer. The only silver lining at this horrendous time were the regular visits from the family doctor who was the kind, charming, and a little younger then, Magnus. He seemed to grow very fond of her and would sometimes make special house calls just to see her. Then one day in her late teens, he invited her out for the day. It was a nice day, Alice remembered. It was summer in England and they went to Hampstead Heath for a walk. The following week Magnus proposed. She remembered thinking how he and his world seemed so big and exciting — a doctor, with big dreams of travelling the world — so, she had gladly agreed to marry him.

After their wedding, they were intimate once or twice. She was not very good at it, or so Magnus had told her. As a result, the physical side of their relationship petered out very quickly. However, Magnus agreed to have Alice stay with him, living as husband and wife, provided she took over the responsibility of caring for his mother. This had seemed a small price to pay at the time. That, was seven years ago, now.

Magnus reappeared from his consulting room holding a plastic tray with a half a dozen insulin vials. Thank goodness, she thought, not a moment too soon! She took the tray, smiled, allowed him to kiss her on the cheek and made her way out of the waiting room.

"I'll see you later, my darling," he called after her.

———

Alice sat at the table doing a crossword, while Margaret had her afternoon nap in the corner.

The knock at the door surprised her. Magnus was not due back until early evening.

"Come in," Alice said.

Gloria appeared in the doorway carrying her large handbag and a cup of tea. "I thought you'd be ready."

"Ready for what?"

"For your stroll on the beach."

"Oh, Gloria," Alice shook her head. "That's very sweet of you but I can't. Yesterday was a wonderful gift, but I couldn't dare to go out again."

"Go on, honey. This is a chance in a lifetime so grab it with both hands. You're not here for long and you won't have me around again."

Alice considered it.

"I have it on good authority that Dr McCroy is otherwise engaged until much later tonight. It will be our secret."

Alice looked out the window to the sliver of beach that beckoned her from the other side of the buildings obscuring her view. In her mind's eye she visualised the rest of it, how beautiful it was and what it must be like to be able to go for a stroll on the soft sand or dip her toes. She so regretted not doing it when she had had a chance the previous day. She was so over-focussed on not giving Magnus signs of her deception that she had failed to even consider that she could get back in time for a shower, before he was due back to the suite. Today he was definitely going to be late, since he had another "early cocktails" function at the convention.

A large grin spread across her face and she rapidly folded away her crossword. "Thank you, Gloria. You really are an angel! I promise I won't be late."

Gloria plopped down on the couch. "It's a lovely sunny day out there, but it's a bit windy so don't lose your hat."

———

Alice headed straight for the beach, remembering to stop and take off her shoes and put them securely in a bag she'd brought with her for that exact purpose this time.

The feeling of the soft, fine, white sand beneath her feet was wonderful. Gloria was right, it was slightly windy, but not enough to put her off. The occasional gust of wind was just strong enough to whip the tiny particles into swirls around her ankles, which added to the magic.

As she neared the shore-break she could smell the distinct salty, fishy smell of the sea. She approached the shore's edge with anticipation. What would the water feel like? The wet sand felt cool beneath her feet. Then a wave approached and she braced herself. It was cold like liquid crystal.

She walked along the shallows, trying to absorb and commit every sight and sensation to memory.

For the first time, right in that moment, she felt really happy.

A little way ahead of her, a group of friends were heading into the sea for a swim. They are brave, Alice thought, almost giddy at the idea of the cold waves breaking over her entire body. She wished she was part of them, as she watched them happily squirm and shriek their way into the water.

She stood there for a while, watching and enjoying the experience, vicariously.

Once they started to come out, Alice checked her watch. She didn't want to lose track of time and there was still a lot to see and experience. She made her way back off the beach.

In front of her, on the other side of the main road, Alice saw a very large white hotel with balconies and sun-decks and what looked like multiple infinity pools on every level. That had to be the big, luxury hotel Magnus had told her was hosting the convention. As she got closer, she noticed the reception rooms behind the floor-to-ceiling windows and sliding doors were laid out for a large party, and there were about a hundred smartly dressed people milling about sipping champagne and nibbling at canapés. She realised that Magnus would be there amongst all those people. Her heart started pumping faster. What if he saw her? Her first instinct was to run, but there was nowhere on the beach side of the road to hide. On the side nearest the hotel, there was a high wall, and if she stood close to it, it would hide most of her body. She doubted Magnus would recognise a partial view of her dressed like this, in her sun-hat and glasses.

She crossed the road and, gripped by the same compulsion that makes passing drivers gape at a car accident, she studied the faces of the party guests mingling in view.

Then she saw him.

Magnus was there in the centre of a crowd. Always the showman, she thought. She could not help feeling a little proud of him. He had his back to her, so it was safe to observe him for a few moments. Then she saw the woman next to him lean forward and whisper something in his ear. In response, he leaned in and slipped his hand around her back to pat her bottom.

Alice froze. A light prickling sensation broke out over her scalp and neck. Her heart pounded in her ears. Did she just see that?

As the woman turned towards Alice, she recognised her. It was Rita!

On autopilot, Alice's legs took over and started propelling her away, away from Magnus and Rita, away from the luxury white hotel. It felt like her mind had shut down. She just needed to get away.

The small pavement was crowded with shoppers and holiday makers. Too many people. She needed peace. Just then, she passed a door bearing a sign that read "Entrance to The Mall". She went in.

It was quieter. She just stood there for a while, her mind blank. But then a security guard started circling. She realised that she must be looking a little suspicious, so she walked into the first shop she found. It happened to be a shop that sold only bathers and bikinis. Like an automaton, with blind eyes and a mind replaying the last few seconds of what she'd seen at the hotel, she pretended to browse the contents of the shop.

"Would you like that one?" A woman's voice startled her.

Alice suddenly registered the tall redhead in front of her. She looked like a bikini model, smiling, her hands folded and her stance a practised casual pose.

That's when Alice realised that absent-mindedly she had been fondling a turquoise and pink swimsuit.

If only she could feel those ice-cold waves crash over her now and wash away that clenching feeling in the pit of her stomach.

"Yes, actually, yes please." She handed the shop assistant the swimsuit.

The shop assistant took it, checked the label and with one expert glance assessed the fit before she took it to the cash register.

"That'll be six-hundred and fifty-two rand, please," the smiling shop assistant said, placing the swimsuit into a plastic bag with a wave curl for a logo on it.

Alice instinctively reached for her purse and took out her gold credit card. Suddenly the shop assistant's eyes opened wider and her smile became even broader. "Would you like anything else, Madam, to go with the swimsuit?"

Alice shook her head and was about to hand over the card when she stopped. If she bought the swimsuit on the credit card, which was linked to Magnus's account, he would know that she had been out and there was no telling what he would do. She could not cope with that as well.

She returned the card to its place in her purse. "Actually, never mind, I've changed my mind." As she left the shop, the protestations of the assistant followed her.

Not knowing where else to go, she headed back to the MOD hotel.

———

Back in the room, it was clear to Alice that Gloria could see something was wrong with her, but despite her urging, Alice kept the line that she was just tired after her unaccustomed adventure. Gloria finally gave up and left Alice in peace to prepare Margaret for the evening.

Later, once Margaret had fallen asleep, Alice lay awake. The day's events looped through her mind like a forgotten record player, its tiny needle dragging deep, painful cuts over her skin.

When Magnus finally came home, she once again pretended to be sleeping. She listened and watched him fumble with his clothing as he undressed and finally flopped into the bed next to her. She wondered if he had just left his lover's bed to come back to the suite. She lay there in the dark and felt her heart break. An incredible sorrow and loneliness flooded her, overflowing in a silent cry.

Later, she wondered why it had never occurred to her before, all those late nights working, those business trips away. She remembered, in the early days, how close they used to be, how happy and supportive their marriage was. Now he was more controlling and distant than she ever thought possible. It was like a slow-motion train wreck. She knew it was inevitable and there was nothing she could do about it. They were over.

But she couldn't possibly ever leave him. What could she be or do without him? She needed him. Even if there was only the smallest fragment of their relationship left, she didn't think she could survive without it.

As the sun started to rise, Alice finally drifted into a listless sleep and her mind carried her into the crisp cold seawater. She felt it washing over her body, tugging at her limbs, her hair, slowly pulling her under and numbing the pain eating at her soul.

THREE

Alice hadn't had the physical or emotional strength to complete the full routine with Margaret the night before, so after Magnus left for his morning's consultations, Alice put up the "Do Not Disturb" sign, and helped Margaret through the shower and got her dressed. When she finally finished, time was getting on. She assumed that it was now too late for housekeeping to come and do the room so she started to gather the dirty towels and empty the bins herself.

All the while, images from her dream kept tugging at her consciousness — swimming free, like she was flying through the ocean. It all boiled down to one question: How could she get money together to buy a swimsuit?

"Why are you doing that?" Margaret whined. "They have people to do that."

Alice tried to ignore Margaret and just get the chores done as quickly as possible. She was gathering the dirty crockery and placing it on a tray when there was a knock at the door. It was a young woman called Simone, from housekeeping. "I'm very sorry, Madam, I should've been around earlier but we are a little under-staffed today. One of my colleagues has left."

"Oh?" Alice asked, genuinely concerned. "Is that person okay?"

"Yes, Madam. You remember Deka? She used to do your room. She has left to go and get married and live with her new husband," Simone said, sharing her excitement for her colleague.

"That's very nice," Alice said, smiling. "Very exciting!"

"I want my lunch, now," Margaret shouted from inside the suite.

"Madam, I can come do the room later," Simone said hastily.

Alice smiled at Simone. "Don't worry, I've started to strip the beds and you can just bring me fresh sheets and towels later."

Simone looked very relieved. "I'm really sorry, Madam."

After lunch, as soon as Margaret had fallen asleep, Alice continued to strip the beds and remake them with the fresh sheets Simone had put on a chair outside the suite.

On clearing the last of the lunch crockery and the cups from morning tea from the coffee table, Alice caught sight of the R150 that Magnus had left out that morning, intended for tipping housekeeping and room service. She picked up the notes and considered them. An idea started to form in the back of her mind. She pocketed the money.

———

Around 3 pm there was another soft knock at the door. It was Gloria with a set of fresh towels under her arm. "Sorry, Simone forgot to deliver these earlier," she said.

Alice stepped outside into the corridor so as not to wake Margaret.

"Yes, about that. Simone said one of your girls has gone off to get married. I'm sorry to hear you are now short staffed."

Gloria shrugged. "Not much one can do about it. It happens."

"Do you know when you will have a replacement?"

Gloria shook her head. "We have started actively recruiting but because of the nature of this hotel it is difficult to find the right staff."

"So, I have a proposition for you."

Gloria looked surprised. "Oh?"

"How about I help you out during the afternoons while Margaret is asleep and do some of the rooms for you."

Gloria looked shocked. "Mrs McCroy, that would not be possible."

"Gloria, just listen. We both know that while Margaret sleeps, I have about three hours free. I can easily make up half a dozen rooms for you in that time." Alice did the maths in her head and six rooms a day at an average of about R40 to R50 tip per room would give her R1500 to R2000 in less than a week.

"Alice, that is very kind of you, but that won't work. Who will look after old Mrs McCroy? I can't do that every afternoon while you take up my staff's housekeeping duties."

Alice shook her head. "No, you wouldn't need to. I'll be in the building and can pop in every half an hour or so and check up on Margaret."

Gloria considered this.

"Honestly, Gloria, this would help me and it'll help you... just until you find someone new."

"How will this help you?"

"Well, it'd give me something to do in the afternoon, and if I can keep the tips, I'll make myself a bit of cash to spend in Camps Bay."

Gloria thought about this for a while. She glanced up and down the corridor.

"Please Gloria, you clearly need the help and I'd really like to do this. It's probably the only way I can manage to earn a little money of my own. It's an opportunity of a lifetime." Alice deliberately used Gloria's words. "Please, give me a chance. Like before, nobody need know. I'll be very discreet."

Finally, Gloria nodded. "Okay, but it'll be housekeeping only. There is no way I'm having you come into contact with guests. And only until I manage to find a replacement."

"Deal," Alice said, excitement bubbling up inside her.

Gloria huffed. "I'll come by tomorrow at two."

Tuesday - 10 October, SA

True to her word, Gloria arrived at Alice's suite at 2 pm. Alice had made sure that Margaret had taken her insulin and a timely lunch so that the sedatives had kicked in on time.

Gloria led Alice downstairs to the backstage area, as she called it. She showed her where the laundry room was and where she could lay her hands on fresh linen, towels and her own trolley with coffee, tea, bar and bathroom supplies. All the while, Gloria talked her through the dos and don'ts — presumably the standard, induction speech she would give to any new recruit.

Within half an hour, Alice headed back to her suite

with her very own room service trolley, ready to start in their own set of rooms.

By the time she had finished the other rooms on her wing, she had run out of fresh towels and needed to head back down to the laundry room.

She pushed open the large swinging doors and stepped inside. Industrial sized linen trolleys lined the side wall. She dumped the dirty towels and linen into one of these, then she glanced around the room in search of a supply of fresh towels to take back with her. On the other side of the room was a large trestle table with newly folded towels arranged in neat stacks. A couple of empty trolleys, which someone had obviously not stowed properly, stood between her and the table. As she pushed them aside and lent over to grab some towels, something caught her attention.

Under the table, in the corner and behind the empty trolleys, lay a small rectangular bedroll. At the foot of that was a bag with a couple of small items of clothing folded neatly on top. It looked like the tiniest and most bizarre little bedroom Alice had ever seen. Could someone actually be sleeping here?

Suddenly, noises started to come from somewhere down the corridor. Alice knew she had to get out of there. She grabbed the towels and left.

Wednesday - 18 October, SA

Just over a week later, Gloria managed to find a replacement housekeeper. She went to see Alice that morning in her suite.

"I've found someone," Gloria said softly. "Our little arrangement is over, and not a moment too soon." Gloria looked stressed.

"Did I not do a good job?" Alice asked, hurt.

Gloria shook her head. "No, it's not that. You were very good and it did help. I don't like the sneaking about. When I offered to look after Mrs McCroy for you that was simple and no real harm could come of it. For this, I could definitely have lost my job. I'm just glad I got a replacement before anyone found out."

Alice nodded. "Thank you, Gloria, for giving me the opportunity. I realise it was a risk for you."

Gloria nodded and was about to leave when Alice caught her arm.

"I wonder if I can ask you one last favour."

Gloria frowned.

"Could you look after Margaret for me for one last afternoon, today?"

Gloria shook her head.

"Please, Gloria, I just want to nip out one last time. I won't ask you for anything again."

Gloria hesitated. Then she sighed "Okay, but this will be the last time."

"Thank you, Gloria, you are an angel." Alice threw her arms around her.

Gloria gently pushed her away. "I'll be back at two. But you had better make sure you are back by five sharp," she said. Alice nodded and Gloria left.

"Who was that," Margaret asked, irritated. "So many interruptions! How can they call this a respite hotel?"

"It was nothing, Mum, just housekeeping wanting to know if we need anything," Alice said. Then she slipped into the en suite bathroom, closing the door behind her. She rummaged through her toiletry bag to find the small, drawstring tampon bag she had tucked away in the bottom. She fished it out, careful not to shake it. Inside it she had hidden the stash of notes and coins she had earned as tips. This was the safest place she could think that neither Magnus nor Margaret would poke around in. She carefully counted the money. R2 135.

———

As soon as the door to the suite closed behind Alice, Gloria closed her book. She sat watching Margaret for a few moments. Then she got up quietly and approached Margaret. She listened intently, making sure the old woman was fast asleep. She bumped the wheelchair a couple of times, pretending to be engaging the brakes.

She slipped into the bathroom and started to search through the cabinets. In the first cabinet she found a few packets of painkillers, sleeping tablets and laxatives, which she stuffed into the pockets of her uniform jacket. Looking a little further, in the next cabinet, she found a single, half used vial of insulin. She glanced over at Margaret and then put it back before she continued her rummage.

From the bathroom she went to the small bar fridge. She opened it and "bingo!" She picked up the plastic container containing a dozen new insulin vials.

Once back at the couch, she decanted her pockets and carefully placed the insulin into her large handbag. Then she sat back and picked up her Mills and Boon to continue reading.

———

Alice made her way to the shop where she had seen the swimsuit. The shop attendant was very pleased to see her, undoubtedly eager for her to spend money on the fancy credit card she had spotted on Alice's first visit.

Alice didn't have time for niceties. This was a very precious opportunity and she had to make the most of it. She bought the swimsuit, which luckily was still in stock, and made her way to the beach.

Once on the beach she realised she'd forgotten to bring a towel. She was not going to let that stop her. She had been dreaming of this. She slipped out of her sandals, threw off her sundress and headed past the rocks towards the sea.

The moment the sea hit her toes, shock-waves rushed up her body. She had no idea it would be this cold. She took a deep breath and pushed on into the waves. Each wave that lapped at her ankles, then her calves, then her thighs and eventually up onto her belly, was absolutely exhilarating. For the first time in a long, long while, she felt truly alive.

What was refreshing at first soon became numbing — a blissful stupefaction. But the current was strong, and without warning a larger than usual wave caught her off-guard. It toppled her and began to drag her under. It was too strong. Her instinct was to fight back to right herself but, for a fleeting moment, she considered what it would be like to just let go, to let the current take her. Would that not be an easier way to freedom?

Suddenly that quiet bliss was shattered. Confusion, anger and panic coursed through Alice's body and mind. Her body was numb but her lungs screamed. She realised there were strong arms wrapped around her. For a moment she thought they were pulling her further, deeper into oblivion. Her body reacted on instinct, causing her to kick, buck and lash out in every direction, but she couldn't free herself.

Eventually she broke the surface and felt herself being

dragged onto the coarse sand. She coughed and spluttered as her body fought to eject salt water from her air passages. Finally, when she could breathe again, she opened her eyes to find she had been beached like a whale in the shallows with the waves still smacking into her body. She looked around to see what, or who, was responsible for pulling her out. A few feet away was a woman bent double, coughing and spluttering as well, clothed in sopping wet long shorts and a T-shirt.

The woman turned to Alice. She had a beautiful face and her eyes seemed to look into Alice's soul. In that moment, Alice felt so ashamed.

"Are you okay?" the woman asked, still gasping for breath.

Alice nodded and started to get up.

In an instant, the woman was next to her, helping her up and half carrying her to a nearby rock where she could rest and recover. Then she trotted off. Alice was worried she was leaving, but then she saw her bend down and grab a towel from a clump of bags and shoes a little way off. Alice watched as she ran back with it and then draped it around Alice's shaking shoulders. She was shivering, from cold and shock.

The woman then began to chat to her very softly and kindly, like they had been friends for years. Alice learned her name was Lisa and she was an off-duty lifeguard. She had been playing volleyball on the beach when she saw Alice go under the water and realised she was in trouble.

Once Alice had stopped shaking and had almost dried off, she suddenly remembered the time.

"Shit! I'm so sorry, I have to go," Alice said. She got up and headed to where she had dumped her bag and sundress. She still had the woman's towel draped around her shoulders. "Sorry, here." She handed the towel back. "Thank you very much for saving my life today." Alice giggled at how odd that sounded but she meant it sincerely. She went to grab her stuff and headed off, glancing back once to wave at the kind stranger. She hoped she did not seem as ungrateful as she feared. Then she started running toward the MOD.

———

Alice got back twenty minutes later than she had promised.

Gloria was pacing and she had a panicked expression on her face. "What happened? I was worried!" she whispered softly enough so as not to alert Margaret, who was just starting to wake from her afternoon slumber.

"Long story," Alice said. "Thank you, Gloria, for staying —"

They both heard it — someone was at the door — and froze.

Alice dashed into the bathroom. As quickly as possible she stripped off her sundress and swimsuit, chucking them into the shower and closing the cubicle door. She wrapped herself in a towel, grabbed two other towels and ruffled them. Then she took a deep breath to compose herself and stepped out of the bathroom.

"Just these —" Alice said. Then she pretended to catch sight of Magnus who'd entered the suite by then. "Oh, hi! I didn't hear you come in."

Magnus's expression was on the verge of comical. Naturally, he was surprised to see Gloria standing in the suite with a half-naked Alice just popping out of the bathroom.

"Here you go, Gloria," Alice said and handed her the

rumpled towels. "It'd be very kind of you, if you would bring us two fresh ones later."

"Sure, Mrs McCroy," Gloria said without missing a beat. "Glad I could help." She took the towels and headed past Magnus to the door. She nodded her good night to Dr McCroy and exited swiftly.

Magnus watched Gloria go. Then he turned his attention to Alice. "I've made us reservations for dinner. I figured it would be nice to eat somewhere proper for a change."

"Oh, how lovely. I'll just finish jumping through that shower quickly then. Mum is due to wake soon."

Magnus nodded. "I'll wake her and give her the shot now, so that she is ready to eat when we get there." He stepped past Alice to fetch the currently open vial of insulin from the bathroom cabinet.

Alice rushed into the bathroom after him and turned on the shower tap, careful not to let Magnus see the discarded sundress and swimsuit which were still lying in the bottom of the shower tray.

He held up the vial and shook it. "Not much left in this one. I'll get a new one."

He pushed past her again and headed to the mini-bar fridge in the main part of the suite.

Alice got into the shower, relishing the strong, warm water washing over her. She hadn't thawed properly since her freezing near-death experience in the Atlantic.

"Where are they?" Magnus's voice boomed from somewhere inside the main suite. His tone instantly alerted Alice that something was wrong.

She turned off the shower, grabbed a towel and wrapped it around her before rushing out to see what the matter was.

"Where is it? The spare insulin?"

His words didn't make sense to Alice. "I don't know what you mean. They should be there," she said and took a few steps closer to see for herself.

"You know they have to be kept in the fridge."

Alice looked past him expecting to see the container of vials where she had left them. Instead, the fridge was empty, except for the usual mini-bar sodas and beverages.

"But —" Alice said, her temples prickling with shock.

"Where are they?" His tone was getting more and more dangerous.

"I don't know." She shook her head.

"You don't know?" He said in a slow, controlled, manner, that Alice knew he only adopted when he was struggling to restrain his anger.

Alice shook her head. "I really don't know."

"You don't know!" he repeated.

She heard the sound of the back of his hand connecting hard with her cheekbone before she felt it. The force of the impact knocked her off balance causing her to fall sideways and land hard on the floor.

What happened afterwards, Alice couldn't quite remember. It was all a horrendous blur. She did remember he was furious. He grabbed his jacket and wheeled Margaret out in her wheelchair, saying something about taking Margaret on his own and something about Rita, before the door slammed hard behind them.

Alice's world had imploded. She pulled herself onto the bed and collapsed in a foetal ball and began to sob.

———

The setting sun bathed the room in shades from orange to

ochre to a dark purple orchid around her, and yet Alice had not moved from where she'd collapsed onto the bed.

Even when she heard someone at the door, she still had no strength to move.

She closed her eyes and silently prayed that it was not Magnus and Margaret back from their dinner. She wasn't ready to face either of them yet.

Magnus had never before lifted a hand to her. Now that it had happened it had irrevocably changed everything between them. He might not have hit her very hard but, in that instant, something had broken inside her.

The door opened and Alice heard the light switch being flicked on. Suddenly the suite lit up in halos of yellow as the standing lamp in the corner and the two bedside lights sprang into life. These lights provided more ambient, atmospheric illumination, rather than flooding the room with brightness. As a result, Gloria only noticed Alice when she was almost on top of the bed.

"Blessed mother of Jesus!" She said and jumped a full step backwards. "You'll scare the life out of me." Then she caught herself. "I didn't realise anyone would be here. I saw Dr McCroy and old Mrs McCroy head to the restaurant and I thought you would be with them."

When Alice didn't move immediately, she took a step closer again. Finally, Alice pulled herself together and started to sit up. She shook her head. "No, I didn't go with them," she said softly, hoping her voice wouldn't betray her grief.

Gloria took another step closer and bent to see Alice better. "Are you o — oh my goodness! Are you okay? What happened?" In two strides Gloria was next to Alice.

Alice gathered her towel closer around her cooling body. "I'm okay."

"Who did this?" Gloria asked.

Alice shook her head.

"Here, come, let me help." Gloria went to the bathroom to wet a wad of tissues. When she returned, she dabbed it gently on Alice's cheek. She wiped away the dried blood that had crusted in the corner of Alice's mouth.

"This is none of my business, but Alice, you need to leave. This man is keeping you captive."

Alice took the wet wad of tissues from Gloria and sat up properly. "It's okay. He is not normally like this. He is just stressed this week."

"I have seen many things in my life and I can see what is going on here."

Alice shook her head. "He's my husband. I'm married to him. I took an oath."

Gloria shook her head. "God said one has to honour thy husband. But He did not say be a punch bag or prisoner, and He also said that a husband should love and not be harsh to his wife. This," she indicated the large welt forming on Alice's cheek, "is harsh."

Alice scoffed, "Even if I wanted to leave, Magnus would never allow it. He's too strong. I would have to run. And if I managed to do that, where would I go? What would I do?"

"My dear child, you are a bright woman. Don't doubt yourself. You will figure the rest out."

"You don't understand."

"Believe me I do."

Alice was about to argue but decided that it was futile.

"And the one thing I know," Gloria continued, "is that if I could get out, and survive, then so can you. It's always better to be free and figuring the rest out than to be captive and abused, with no way of doing anything to help yourself or those around you."

That night, Alice's mind churned over Gloria's words, the events of the past few days, as well as her history with Magnus and Margaret and the limited options available to her.

What was she going to do?

Eventually, the early pre-dawn light started to colour the ceiling.

Sunday - 22 October, SA

By 8.15 am the limo that was to take them to the airport had arrived. The driver was helping Margaret into the back of the car while the bellboys piled the mountain of suitcases into the boot. Rita was already in the car, on the phone, making arrangements for their arrival in London. Magnus stood at the reception desk settling some final details with the duty manager.

The lift pinged and Alice stepped into the grey slate and concrete foyer of the MOD Hotel, carrying her single suitcase and her large handbag.

"Oh good, you are here," Magnus said, falling into step next to Alice as she made her way towards the main entrance. "We need to get going or we will be late for the plane."

"I'm not coming," Alice said softly.

"What?" Magnus said absent-mindedly as he stopped walking, and he studied the expenses sheet the receptionist had handed him. When done, he resumed walking, taking Alice by her elbow. "Come on, the car is waiting. Rita is already inside."

"Magnus," Alice said again, more deliberately this time,

withdrawing her arm out of his grip. "I'm not going to come with you back to England." She forced herself to hold his gaze while her meaning sunk in.

"What are you talking about?" He asked irritated.

Alice put down her suitcase and her handbag. "I mean..." She regretted having to do this in public, but she knew that the only way that Magnus would let her go was if he had eyes watching him. "Magnus, I'm not going back with you." Alice fought to stay calm. Would she have the backbone to follow through with this?

Magnus still did not reply and his expression still seemed quizzical.

"I am not going home with you," Alice repeated.

Once again Magnus grabbed her elbow and tried to lead her towards the waiting limo. "Alice, we do not have time for a scene. As I said I'm sorry for my reaction the other day. You know I can't afford to go around losing medication or, even worse, become known as the doctor who supplies insulin to the black market," he hissed.

She pulled free. "Magnus, I'm not looking for a scene."

Magnus studied her intently. "Alice, you are in the middle of God-forsaken-Africa. You can't walk out of here. Where will you go? You don't even have a visa to be here without me."

"I know. And I'm sorry, but I know I have to do this."

"What about Margaret? Who will look after her?" he asked.

"I am sure you will have no trouble finding someone."

Magnus glanced around the hotel reception. Most people were very busy pretending not to have noticed their quiet altercation. "Okay," he finally said. He gave her a perfunctory kiss on the cheek, squeezed her arm.

Alice watched him walk out of the large glass doors

towards the limo. Without as much as a glance back to her, he got into the limo next to Rita. The limo pulled away. Through the rear window she could see Margaret looking back. A small bony hand appeared next to her face as she waved Alice goodbye.

Alice wondered if she should have said goodbye to Margaret. If she had done, Margaret would have told Magnus what was coming and she would never have had the strength to follow through. The other option she'd had, was to leave in the middle of the night without a word. To just run, but that would have been too cowardly and even more unfair on everyone.

FOUR

Alice had hoped she could stay on in the suite of the MOD hotel for a few days until she found her feet. But now, standing there in the reception, having just publicly embarrassed Magnus in his own hotel and feeling the hot gaze of his staff on her, she knew that would be out of the question.

She went, with as much dignity as she could muster, over to where her little suitcase still stood to one side of the marble clad lobby. She picked it up and with eyes cast firmly ahead of her she walked out of the cool hotel reception, through the large glass door and into the hot Camps Bay sunshine.

———

Alice found progress along the narrow pavement on the mountain side of Victoria Road quite difficult. Wheeled suitcases were not made to be pulled along uneven surfaces and, although it was still early, the street-hawkers had already laid out their wares, making the path even narrower.

She eventually found herself at the entrance of The Bay Hotel, where the upset from a few days ago came rushing back. She considered carrying on to find somewhere else to stay, but this was the only other hotel in the area that she knew. She continued along the brick driveway and headed for the large glass doors.

Inside, the lobby was cool and the floor's smooth marble allowed her suitcase to almost float behind her – a welcome relief. A smiling young man dressed in a blue blazer, crisp white shirt and matching blue tie greeted her with a broad, practised smile.

"I'd like to check in, please."

"Do you have a reservation, Madam?" He started searching his list before she had even answered.

"No, not yet," Alice said apologetically, thinking that this felt very novel. Magnus always dealt with these things. From now on, she would have to get used to doing this for herself.

The young man smiled at her. "In that case, let's make you one. Who is the reservation for, please?"

"Mrs A McCroy."

"When is it for?"

"Today," she said, and then thought better of it. "Maybe for a few days."

The young man nodded and smiled again. "That's no problem. Will Dr McCroy and Mrs McCroy also be staying with us?"

Alice could feel the prickling of her temples. She had hoped to remain anonymous. "No, it's just me," and then she swiftly added, "for now. My husband had to go back home unexpectedly, but he'll be back. I'm just not sure exactly when." None of that was entirely a lie, Alice thought.

"Yes of course," the young man nodded again. "I'll reserve you a suite in that case so that if Dr McCroy does come to join you soon, you won't have to move rooms again."

"Will that cost extra?" Alice asked, trying to sound nonchalant.

"Not at all, Madam." The young man glanced around to see if anyone was listening. Then in a lowered tone he said. "If Dr McCroy checks in, we'll only charge him for occupancy."

"Thank you, that's much appreciated." Alice noticed a bellboy advance across the lobby. He reminded her of a modern Charon crossing the Styx with his large copper trolley gliding behind him like a ghost-car. He picked up her suitcase and loaded it onto the trolley. Then he wandered off to attend the sliding door, clearly allowing her space to complete the check-in process.

"So, all I need from you is a credit card to swipe to cover the extras."

"Extras?"

"Yes, any extra charges to your room, like room service or mini-bar."

"Oh, sure." Alice said and fished out her gold card. She was very unlikely to have any charges to her room and if she did, she would pay Magnus back once she got a job.

The young man took the card and entered it into the card-reader. He held the little machine out to her.

She entered her pin number.

He smiled at her again as he waited for the system's data connection to relay the card information to the bank and pre-authorise the transaction.

A shrill double beep emanated from the machine. The young man's smile faded momentarily. He shook the machine and re-entered the information. "Terribly sorry," he said. "The Wi-Fi here in the bay is very unreliable."

Alice re-entered her pin and handed the machine back to him.

The handset beeped again. He shrugged his shoulders. "I'm so sorry, it has come back with the same error message. Do you happen to have a different card I could try? I'm really sorry about the inconvenience. As I said, we don't actually debit your account now, we just swipe the card to authorise the future payment at check out."

She fished around in her purse and got out another card which Magnus had given her 'in case of emergencies'. This would certainly qualify as an emergency, Alice thought.

The young man repeated the procedure and she entered her pin. Again, the machine loudly beeped its rejection. By now if felt like all eyes in the lobby were on her.

"One moment please," the young man said and picked up the reception phone.

Alice, in an effort to escape the spotlight, turned away and pretended to study a table display of wine and Proteas[1] on a nearby table in the reception. Above the wine stood a small A-frame backboard with the inscription "Save water. Drink wine," followed by something else about exchanging two bottles and somehow saving three hundred litres of water, which Alice did not quite understand. All that time she was acutely aware of the activity behind the reception desk. The young man sounded quite stressed. She changed direction and started to admire the various black and white photographs of famous guests, none of whom she recognised, on a large print hanging on the wall to the left of reception.

A few minutes later, the young man left his post and came rushing over to her. "Madam, I'm so sorry," he whispered and pulled a pained expression. "It seems your cards have been declined."

"That can't be," Alice said, panic tingling her temples again. "Did they say why?"

"No, Madam. The bank manager said that you can call him and arrange to have another card issued and delivered to you in five working days."

"Five —" Alice stopped herself. She swallowed. "Okay, thank you." She tried to smile. Then she suddenly remembered the cash she had left over from her earnings. "Do you take a cash deposit for the extras?"

"I'm afraid not. Only if you pay cash for the room upfront, but since you aren't sure how long you're going to be staying..."

Alice realised that this pre-authorising of her credit card actually served as a polite way to check up front whether the prospective guests were creditworthy. Her heart sank. Without these cards she certainly was not. All the cash she had left over from her little housekeeping endeavour would probably not even cover one night in one of the most basic rooms in a hotel like this.

"Okay, thank you. I'll just step out and see if I can get this sorted with my husband."

The young man nodded. "Good luck, Madam, and I hope to see you and Dr McCroy back here soon."

Alice grabbed her suitcase, which the bellboy had already removed from the trolley, and strode out of the hotel.

———

Victoria Road only offered three five-star hotels, all so exclusive that it was even hard to find their entrances. The streets further back from the seafront proved a little more promising. The hotels were smaller, but unfortunately no less expensive. It seemed Camps Bay was the place for boutique posh.

At about half past five, having had no luck in her hunt for accommodation, Alice found herself standing outside The Sea Shanty. Again, the large cream couches and tall cold drinks called out to her. She was exhausted and decided she needed to rest her feet. Maybe she could ask some of the waiters about cheaper hotels in the area.

A sullen looking waitress with short, dark hair, styled in a strange asymmetrical undercut, and a ladder of earrings up the outside of her ears, whom Alice recognised from her first visit, led her to the same seat in the front of the restaurant. Her table had a clear view of the beach in the distance and a handy secluded space next to the front railing, so she could stow her suitcase safely out of the way while she had a drink. The sun sat low in the sky, bathing her in its still strong, hot rays, which was made bearable by a gentle cooling breeze.

The waitress handed her the menu. Alice remembered the delicious little glass of sherry she had enjoyed previously, but she really did not want to spend any more money than she absolutely needed to. "Just some tap water, please," she said, "to start. I'm not sure what I'd like yet."

The waitress nodded, clearly disappointed. Twelve and a half per cent of nothing was still nothing. She disappeared towards the back of the restaurant.

Alice took out all the money from her purse, the entire

sum she had left from her earnings. She started to count it very carefully. In the middle of that, the waitress plonked a small glass of water on the table next to her. Alice politely thanked her and then started to recount. She had R771 exactly. That was not going to go far, certainly not around here, where the cheapest glass of wine on the menu cost R80, never mind the cost of somewhere to stay.

In the pit of her stomach she knew that the rejected credit cards were no coincidence. She could picture Magnus now, in the taxi, on the way to the airport, making a quick call to Clive, his personal bank manager. He more than likely claimed that he had misplaced his cards during his stay and needed them cancelled.

When the waitress dumped the fourth glass of water on the table beside her, Alice realised that despite the strong sunlight, time was getting on. It was around 7 pm and the restaurant section of The Sea Shanty was beginning to fill with dinner clientele. If she did not make a plan soon, she was sure to be homeless for her first night of freedom.

Then, Alice heard her name being called. She ignored it, as Alice was not an uncommon name and she was hardly likely to know people in South Africa. Only when the calling continued did she look round, and that's when she saw her.

———

Alice would never have imagined she could be so happy to see that face again.

Gloria waved, looking just as happy to see Alice.

Alice motioned for Gloria to come up and join her. Gloria's journey to the table caused an alarming disruption on account of the five large grocery bags she was carrying.

Finally, she reached the table and managed to pull up a
chair before collapsing into it. Then she dumped the large
bags haphazardly on the floor to one side under the table.

A butch-looking woman with a 70's style mullet,
wearing faded, ripped light blue denims with a white, plain
linen shirt untucked over the top, whom Alice had seen
hovering around the place before, came over to their table.

"Hello ladies," she said with a smile that did not reach
her eyes. "Are you having a good time?" The gravelly sound
of her voice surprised Alice.

"Yes, lovely place you have here," Alice said sincerely.

"Thank you. I'm glad you like my restaurant," she said.
"Judging by the amount of time you have spent here
drinking..." she pointed at the half full glass in front of
Alice, "...water, you certainly must love it a lot." The woman
glanced at Alice's suitcase. "Or, maybe you were thinking of
moving in?"

Alice felt her cheeks colour.

"I'm sorry ladies, unless you order something that
actually pays my waitresses, or you start paying rent, I'm
going to have to ask you to leave or start helping with the
washing-up."

Alice started to gather her things.

"That will be two glasses of..." Gloria turned towards
Alice, "Do you drink wine?"

Alice nodded, not sure what was going on.

"Actually, make that a bottle of your house white."

When the woman in the tatty denims didn't move
immediately, Gloria looked up at her. "Is there a problem?
Should we take our custom elsewhere?"

The woman looked at Gloria suspiciously, as if worried
that they would do a runner. The multiple grocery bags
around them must have convinced her that they were an

unlikely flight risk and she turned and disappeared into the back of the restaurant.

"What are you doing here?" Alice whispered, slightly side-tracked by the feeling of vegetables spilling onto her feet under the table.

"I'm on my way home but then I saw you and I thought I'd buy you a drink, honey. You deserve one after the spectacular morning you've had."

"Oh, you saw that then?" Alice said sadly. At the time she did wonder if Gloria was anywhere around.

The woman in denim dumped an ice bucket on a stand on the floor next to their table and placed a bottle of wine inside it and two glasses on the table.

"That'll be two-hundred and forty rand."

Gloria handed over a credit card. "Can we open a tab? Thanks."

Alice wondered how much Gloria earned. She was not quite sure exactly what Gloria did at the hotel. She knew she managed housekeeping in some way but was not certain of the full extent of her responsibilities.

While the woman poured them each a glass, Gloria continued in a stage whisper across the table. "Yes, I saw you this morning. You were spectacular and very, very brave." Gloria picked up her glass and held it up to Alice. Alice picked up hers and they clinked them together.

"I'm not so sure about brave," Alice said. "More like foolhardy."

"Of course, honey, very brave. It takes courage."

"What do you mean?" Alice asked, puzzled. "You were the one who encouraged me."

Gloria nodded and took a large sip of her drink. "Yes, I did. But what I had in mind was more, when you got back home, you should have a chat to the man and see if you two can work out a different, more respectful partnership. I certainly had no idea you would take it to the extreme and walk out on him in the middle of a foreign country. That takes balls!"

Suddenly, Alice felt completely overwhelmed. There was no way of holding back the tears. "What have I done?" she quietly asked.

"Oh, my poor honey," Gloria said, reaching out and resting a small warm hand on her arm. "You really haven't thought this through at all, have you?"

Alice shook her head and then swiftly wiped away a few tears.

"Do you have anywhere to go?"

Again, Alice shook her head. She took a deep breath and explained the situation with the credit cards.

"Do you still have some money left from housekeeping?"

Alice nodded. "But it's not enough for even one room anywhere here."

"Honey, you are looking in the Cape Town Riviera for cheap accommodation. It'll never work."

Alice stared into the golden yellow glass of wine. "It's the only place I know," she said in a small voice.

"Okay, on the way home I'll show you the local hostel. It's not much, but I believe it's clean, functional and the people are honest so they won't rip you off like this lot."

"Really, you'll do that?" Alice could not believe her good fortune. "That'd be so fantastic. How can I ever repay you for how kind you've been to me? Thank you."

"Here, now, since we bought this big bottle you are going to have to help me drink it. I'm a lightweight and don't really drink." Gloria picked up the bottle from the ice bucket and filled Alice's glass.

"So why did you buy a bottle?"

"For you, and just to show these hoity-toity fancy people not to judge." Gloria winked at her.

––––––

The bus ride to where Gloria lived in Green Point was a novel experience for Alice, one that took her back to her childhood living in Catford in London.

It was dark out and part of the road along the coast didn't have street lights. Even so, the roads were well illuminated by the outdoor lighting of the large hotels and luxury apartments. Alice thought Magnus was well off and had a particularly privileged existence in London, but nothing could compare to these.

When Gloria saw Alice's head turn at one particularly monstrous house, she said, "To think, one person lives in that house! And, half the year she's not even there, but swanning around in Switzerland or somewhere. At least thirty people could have shelter under that one roof."

Alice did not quite know how to respond. Instead, she focussed on the glint of the clouded moon on the sea beyond the opulent buildings, which seemed to cling to the cliff-edge on the sea side of the road.

Soon the scenery started to change. Gloria explained they were now in Sea Point. It was flatter and more spread out with more modest buildings lining the street. The roads seemed slightly wider and better lit, but busier and somehow more chaotic than any other she had experienced so far. Large white mini-van taxis dominated the traffic, cutting up other motorists as they darted out of side streets, and stopping without warning, sometimes in the middle of the road to drop off their passengers. One even started reversing in the middle of Main Road to secure the custom of a potential passenger over an identical taxi right behind him. Other motorists in the local equivalent of London hot-hatches[2], sounded their horns, yelled at their mates on the pavements through their open windows and turned up their music so the entire street could appreciate it. Large delivery vans double parked, blocking both lanes while they offloaded their wares. Yet, somehow, her fellow bus passengers and the other commuters seemed unfazed, as if all this chaos was perfectly normal.

Once they reached Green Point, the river of traffic divided around a large roundabout surrounded by wide grassy pavements on either side. A large green and white sign indicated that the spaceship-like white building on the far side of the roundabout was the Green Point Stadium. Alice had heard of it and was trying to get a better look when the bus pulled up at its next stop.

"This is us. My flat is a few blocks that way." Gloria indicated somewhere further along the road. "To get to the hostel you need to turn right here and then take the second left."

Suddenly Alice was gripped by fear. For the first time she felt like she was truly stepping into the unknown. Gloria shook her head and sighed, obviously feeling sorry for Alice, and offered to walk with her to the hostel.

———

Alice followed Gloria in silence, her mind looping around the question: "What had she done?" As they got further away from the main road, the streets got quieter. Alice could have sworn the air even felt thicker, more tense, more edgy.

"It's not far now," Gloria said as they turned the third corner down a small dark alley, well and truly away from the main drag.

Alice suddenly became aware of voices coming from somewhere ahead of them. It was only once she was about to overtake Gloria that she realised that Gloria had gone rigid and had slowed her step. Alice looked at her quizzically. "Where is it?" Alice looked around for any sign of a hostel.

"Shh!" Gloria warned. "It's just up ahead on the other side of the road," she whispered, having come to a complete halt while keeping her gaze nervously fixed ahead of them.

Alice peered in the direction Gloria was looking. Once her eyes had adjusted, she saw a group of youths in cargo trousers and dark, identical, hoodies with an abstract green and gold dragon logo on the back. Most of the youths had their hoods up and were gathered under a flickering street light that partly illuminated a concrete space outside a double garage. From the basketball hoop standing on one side, Alice deduced it was some sort of recreational area, but no one seemed to be playing basketball. Instead, there was definitely some other commotion going on.

Alice glanced back at Gloria. Her coffee coloured skin had grown ashen.

"What is it?" Alice asked.

"Keep your voice down." Gloria stepped backwards into the shadows.

Alice followed suit. "Who are they?" she whispered.

Alice felt Gloria's small hand on her arm. Alice wondered if she was imagining the clamminess of her touch. This was very unlike Gloria.

"Glo—"

"Keep it down. You do not want them to see you."

"Who are they?" Alice persisted as they both stared at the group.

"Come, let's go," Gloria said urgently.

"What about the hostel? How will I get there?"

"You won't," Gloria said. "You can stay at mine tonight."

They crept out of the alleyway, sticking as close to the dark edges as they could.

Only once they were three blocks away, did Alice sense that Gloria started to relax a little.

"Who were they, Gloria?"

"They are the Clicks. One of the most dangerous girl gangs in town. Believe me, you do not want to get on the wrong side of them."

———

Alice followed Gloria up a metal stairwell and along the second floor, dark grey concrete corridor, which was illuminated only by a couple of bare, flickering short fluorescent light tubes attached to the ceiling. As they neared the end, Gloria fished around in the large red faux leather handbag that clearly contained her entire life.

Finally, she retrieved a bunch of keys and slid a small Yale key into the lock of her front door and twisted it. As she opened the door the sound of sports commentary wafted out into the corridor.

Alice stepped into Gloria's flat and her eyes were instantly drawn to the American football game that was playing on the 24-inch flat screen TV fixed to the far wall.

"Hello, babe," Gloria said to someone in the room. She turned left into the small open plan kitchen area and dumped her heavy load of grocery bags on the counter.

Motion ahead of Alice caught her attention. A large,

well over six-foot-tall, black man with a shaved head, was getting up off the couch which was facing the TV. "Hey, Baby, been waiting for —" the man stopped dead at the sight of Alice. "Jesus, babe!" He scrambled to his feet. It was then that Alice realised the man was not only a giant but also naked as the day he was born. "Babe, Jesus! Really? You could warn a man." He frantically searched around for something to cover his not insignificant manhood. Alice had to suppress a giggle when he settled for the nearest item he could lay his hands on, which happened to be a comically small embroidered cushion.

Gloria looked up, oblivious. "Warn you about what?"

"About bringing strangers to my house."

Gloria huffed and picked up what Alice eventually realised were a pair of men's cotton trousers that hung over a breakfast stool on the other side of the small island kitchen counter. "First, this is my house. Secondly, Lekan I'd like you to meet Alice. Alice meet Lekan." Then she chucked the trousers at him.

"How do you do," Alice said, trying to look everywhere else other than at the big man who was now fumbling to put on his trousers.

"Alice is going to stay here a few nights, until she finds her feet," Gloria continued.

"What? Really? But babe —"

"No 'but babe'," Gloria said, grabbing a yellow striped polo shirt from the other breakfast stool and throwing it at him too. "So, I need you to go find another one of your birds to nest with for few days."

Gloria took off her shoes and stood rubbing one foot. Alice realised that Gloria had been walking all that way in a pair of red high heels.

"You can have the couch for the next few nights, Alice. I

can give you a towel for a shower, unless you already have one."

Alice shook her head. "It's okay." She started to head back to the door, "I can find somewhere else. I don't want to inconvenience —"

"Ah, ah!" Gloria reprimanded. "I won't have any of that." She took Alice's suitcase from her and gently nudged her back towards the main sitting room area where she put the suitcase down in the corner next to the TV.

Thankfully, Lekan was now fully dressed and was about to say something more in protestation when Gloria opened her arms and flung them around his neck, kissing him long and deeply.

This made Alice feel very self-conscious, so she turned and tried to busy herself by looking at the rest of the flat, without wanting to seem too nosy at the same time.

"There." Gloria said when she finally broke away for air. "That's just a little reminder. Now, you go be a good boy, babe," Gloria said, slapping Lekan on his bottom. "Say hello to Fumnaya."

"I'm not going —"

"I know you will. Now go!"

"I'll come get those in the morning," Lekan said, indicating something on the floor.

Gloria nodded.

Lekan glanced back at Alice and nodded awkwardly before he left.

"Sorry, I don't want to put you out," Alice ventured once it was just the two of them again.

"Nonsense," Gloria said, following Alice's gaze to the door. "He'll be fine. It'll do him good to go see what other nests are like, just so he doesn't count his chickens too quickly."

FIVE

That morning Alice woke up at 6.30 am. She decided to stay put in her temporary bed on the couch to avoid getting in Gloria's way while she got ready for work. About a half an hour later, Gloria came through to the kitchen to make coffee.

"Sorry I don't have much food in the house." Gloria poured Alice a large cup of black coffee. "There's some bread in the bin, which should be only a couple of days old.

What had happened to all the groceries Gloria lugged around with her the previous night? Alice instinctively scanned the kitchen. It seemed pretty empty, barring a slightly crumby breadboard on the counter, against the wall next to the bread-bin. She decided maybe the shopping had been for Lekan.

Suddenly Alice realised that Gloria had been speaking to her. "Sorry," she said, "I was a million miles away."

"Shame, honey, you must be tired. Please go back to sleep. You're welcome to stay here as long as you like."

Gloria washed out her coffee mug and placed it upside down on the drying rack.

"Thank you, Gloria. You've been so kind. I really appreciate this and I will repay you as soon as I've found my feet."

Gloria smiled and nodded.

"I don't intend to waste any time. I don't want to impose on you for any longer than I need to."

"Don't think of it as imposing. Think of it as me gaining a favour in the bank, if that feels better?"

Alice nodded. "For sure."

"So, what are you going to do today?" Gloria asked, grabbing a large red faux crocodile-skin diary from the kitchen counter and throwing it into her oversized handbag.

"I think I'll go back to the mall in Camps Bay, since I know it and I saw a few boutiques there that might need a shop assistant." Alice shrugged her shoulders. "I'm not exactly sure what else I'm qualified to do, really."

"Sounds like a good idea. You can do this."

Alice nodded. It was nice to know that someone had faith in her.

———

The first place Alice decided to try was the shop where she'd bought the swimsuit.

"Oh, hello again," the assistant gushed. "What can we get for you today? Need one of our luxury towels or one of our fabulous new towelling ponchos to dry off with?"

Alice shook her head. "No, nothing like that today, thank you." She hesitated for a moment, not knowing how to phrase the question. "I was wondering if you might need an additional shop assistant?"

The woman instantly recoiled, confusion clouding her face. "Staff? Or assistants? Why? Not to my knowledge. Who said we needed help?" She glared towards the back of the shop, where Alice assumed the owner or manager must be. "We don't need more than one," the woman said with an edge in her voice.

"No, no," Alice said quickly, needing to diffuse the situation. "No one said so, I was just curious as, you see, I'm looking for a little part-time, or full-time, work."

The woman, although she visibly relaxed, crossed her arms and pulled away from Alice. "Oh. Well, sorry, there are no vacancies here."

That was clearly the end of the conversation. Alice nodded and tried to smile through her disappointment in an attempt to break through the awkwardness. That did not work, so she thanked the assistant and left.

———

Alice tried every shop in the mall. Almost without exception, the owners and shop assistants she spoke to, initially looked a little shocked and then, once recovered, shook their heads politely as if they did not quite understand her question, or they dismissed her outright as if she were trying to sell them something cheap and nasty.

Finally, she reached the far end of the top floor of the mall. There was a designer furniture and vintage clothes store. Through the shop window, Alice caught sight of a flamboyant woman in her late fifties, with long, straight, silver-grey hair, thick 1950's black rimmed glasses and ample make-up, ringing up a long patchwork coat at the cash-register for her only customer. Good, it is harder to do this when there are more people about, Alice thought. She walked in towards the nearest clothes rack and pretended to study a steampunk-style silk shirt that was hanging a few feet away from the two women, in order to eavesdrop. All the garments in the shop were unique and perhaps as flamboyant, or rather as eccentric, as the older woman. Alice wondered if they had originally belonged to her. Then she overheard her explaining, very proudly, that her daughter was in the fashion industry in London.

That could be a link, Alice thought.

When the happy customer finally left, Alice approached the counter.

"Hello dear. How can I help you today?" Alice could feel the woman's appraising look over the top of those school ma'am glasses.

"Hello, my name is Alice. I couldn't help hearing you have a daughter in London —" The woman instantly launched into tales about her talented daughter, Lauren, and the career she had in leather underwear design for the stars.

Alice smiled inwardly. She couldn't help liking this woman.

When she eventually realised that Alice was probably not there to hear about Lauren all day, the shop owner laughed and said, "Enough about Laurie. Now what can I do for you?"

"Well," Alice started tentatively, "I'm also here, from London —"

"Oh, how nice." The woman almost couldn't stop herself from interrupting.

Alice nodded. "Yes, it is nice. But, actually, I wondered whether you could perhaps do with an extra pair of hands in the shop? You see I'm going to be in Cape Town for a little extended visit and would like to stay busy."

"Oh my, now that is a thing. It's amazing how the universe works," the woman said. "I was just saying to my sister, Frances, yesterday that I could do with a little help in the shop. I was meaning that she should get her bleeding arse down here and help out a bit more, but this would do as well I guess."

Alice's heart skipped a beat. Yes. Yes. Yes!

The woman looked her over again, "You seem very nice and you certainly will give the right impression to my clients." Alice knew she was not really talking about the way she looked, but probably referring to her English accent.

"That's fantastic! When would you like me to start," Alice tried to sound as calm as possible.

"Well, you could start as soon as I've seen your papers."

"What papers?"

"I'd need to see your I.D. book or, if you don't have one, being British and all, then your passport."

"Oh okay," Alice said. "That's no problem." Luckily, Alice had decided to keep her passport, the two redundant credit cards and all her cash, the little she had, on her. She reached into her little travel bag to get it out.

"And I assume your working visa is in order?" the woman said.

"Visa?" Alice asked, stopping in her tracks.

"Yes, you know. The stamp or piece of paper, I'm not sure what it is these days for Brits, which shows you have permission to work in this country."

Alice's heart sank. She had no such document. She had come on a six-month visitor's entry as Magnus's companion, which she was allowed on condition she wouldn't engage in any employment.

"Oh dear, it seems I've forgotten my passport at home, sadly," Alice lied.

"That's okay, you bring it in and we can get you started right away."

Alice nodded and tried to smile. "Thank you."

"No trouble at all. Nice to meet you. My sister wouldn't believe this coincidence."

Alice nodded. If only this woman was not being so nice, then she could justify the anger and disappointment she was feeling. From what Magnus had said, there must be hundreds of people working without papers, doing part-time or even full-time work in South Africa. How did they do it?

"See you soon," the woman shouted after her as she headed out of the shop.

Alice turned and waved.

———

After the lovely woman with the fashion designer daughter in London, Alice approached a number of other shops, albeit a bit more gingerly. She tried to choose businesses that looked like they needed help but might not place too much value on work permits. But she didn't really know how to judge that.

At one point, she even asked one of the street hawkers where they got their products from, thinking she might have to resort to hawking herself. At first, he mistook her for an enthusiastic customer, but when it became obvious that she was not about to buy anything, he started causing a commotion, accusing her of poaching in his territory. She had to make a hasty retreat into a nearby bar where she pretended to be a customer.

By 6 pm she had had enough. Her feet were aching, her head pounding, and she had run out of ideas. What was she going to do? She decided to go back to Gloria's and ask her for some advice.

When Alice got home the flat was empty. She collapsed on the couch. Frustration and despair brimmed over and tears started to flow down her cheeks uncontrollably. What had she done?

———

Alice awoke to the sound of the front door opening. It was Gloria returning from work. Clearly Gloria had not expected anyone to be sitting in the dark flat, and she jumped at the sight of Alice getting up off the couch.

"Goodness, child. You could give a person a heart attack." Gloria switched on the overhead light.

"Sorry," Alice said softly.

"What's the matter, honey? Are you okay?" Gloria dumped two large grocery bags and her handbag on the table and headed over to Alice.

Alice sat back down on the couch dropping her head into her hands.

Gloria sat down next to her and gently stroked her shoulders. The soft human contact was a bit too much for Alice and the floodgates opened again.

"What am I going to do?" she said, sitting back up and wiping her eyes and nose on her sleeve.

Gloria got up and grabbed a spare toilet roll from the bathroom and handed it to Alice. "Here, take this, honey, and once you feel a little better, you can tell me what is going on."

Once Alice had her emotions back under control, she told Gloria about her day.

"Oh, honey, I know it must be hard. This is all new for you and things like this are never easy. But you will find a job. You'll see. You've just got to be brave and keep on keeping on."

She knew Gloria had no more chance of assuring her future than she did, but somehow hearing Gloria be positive about her chances made it all seem a little bit better.

"Now, come, help me peel some carrots and vegetables for the stew. I thought it might do you and Lekan good to have a good hearty meal tonight."

Alice's ears pricked up at the mention that Lekan would be back for dinner. Obviously, his sojourn in another nest had been short lived. It was not her place to comment. She nodded, grateful for something to do that would take her mind off her dire situation.

―――――

It was well after 9.30 pm and Alice and Gloria had almost finished their stew when Lekan arrived. Alice didn't know what Lekan did for a living nor why he would be out so late and for some reason she felt it was better not to ask. But it was clear that working late like that was not out of the ordinary.

Lekan nodded a brief hello to Alice, kissed Gloria and took a seat at the kitchen counter. Gloria dished up a bowl of stew and handed it to him. He tucked in hungrily.

"Alice here has had a bit of a day," Gloria explained.

"Hmm," he grumbled shoving a large chunk of meat into his mouth.

"She went job hunting, the poor honey."

"Hmm." He nodded briefly.

"Seems no one is really looking, at the moment."

Lekan studied Gloria for a moment and then waved the back of his spoon at her. "Can't you get her a job at the MOD?" he said with a mouth still full of food.

Alice's ears pricked up. Now that was a good idea. Why had she not thought of that?

"That'd be marvellous," Alice said. "Maybe I can come do housekeeping for you. You said you needed staff and I already know what I'm doing."

Gloria shook her head. "No, that won't work."

Alice did not miss the stern look Gloria gave Lekan.

He simply shrugged and continued to shovel stew into his mouth.

"But why not?" Alice asked. "That'd be perfect. You know I can do it."

Gloria looked resigned. "I'm sorry, Alice, but I really can't. It would draw too much attention."

Alice was momentarily confused. "Attention?"

Gloria nodded. "Yes. Everyone knows who you are..."

Gloria did not need to finish the sentence. The unfortunate events in the lobby came flooding back to Alice. "I suppose you're right. I certainly did cause a scene." In hindsight she really should have told Magnus in private. She regretted that now, but she still doubted she would have had the strength to walk away from him if she had.

"There was one shop that was looking, but they asked for papers," Gloria continued to update Lekan, who nodded and put his spoon down in the now empty bowl. Then he began to dig a bit of meat out from between his teeth with his thumb-nail. "I might be able to get some ... wawers."

It took Alice a few seconds to register that he meant 'papers'. "You can?"

He nodded, looked at Gloria and sucked his thumb clean. "It'll cost though."

"What? How much?" Alice asked.

"Don't know but you know how these things are."

"Can you get her some?" Gloria asked.

He shrugged and nodded.

"Oh, that's amazing!" Alice felt like the world had lifted off her shoulders.

"And what about a job? Somewhere that doesn't ask too many questions?" Gloria asked.

Lekan shrugged again. "I'll ask Boytjie."

"Boytjie is an..." Gloria looked at Lekan as she searched for the word, "agent. He helps people 'in difficult situations'."

"He will help for commission," Lekan said, casually looking at Gloria.

"Oh, I will pay. If I can earn, I can pay," Alice said quickly. "What about the papers? You said they will cost?"

Lekan nodded again. "Yes, they might be quite expensive." Lekan looked at Gloria conspiratorially.

"Oh," Alice's heart sank.

"It's okay. If you don't have enough, I can lend you some," Gloria offered.

"Maybe she can help with —" Lekan started.

"Clearing the table," Gloria interjected, shaking her head at Lekan and handing Alice a plate.

Alice got up and took the plates to the sink.

"You could do with the help," Lekan pressed.

"Lekan, leave it! No! That wouldn't be appropriate," Gloria said sternly.

Lekan shrugged again.

Alice was dying to ask what they were talking about, but again she decided against it. It was clearly something between them and she certainly did not want to jeopardise the kind offer of help.

Shortly after dinner, Gloria and Lekan retired to bed. Alice was relieved. There was obviously some unresolved tension between them that made the atmosphere difficult around the kitchen counter.

Once in her makeshift bed on the couch, with the warm stew still sitting in her tummy, Alice could hardly keep her eyes open, even though Gloria and Lekan's muffled but excitable voices could still be heard through the closed bedroom door.

Wednesday - 25 October, SA

Two days later Lekan arrived home with a very official looking set of papers for Alice. She noticed that her name had been changed on the document to Alice McAvoy. Lekan explained that was a necessity to make sure Alice had deniability if the papers were questioned.

He also explained that Boytjie had managed to arrange a job for her through one of the staff at The Sea Shanty.

Alice could not believe her luck. The Sea Shanty of all places! At first, she was a little reluctant to go back there in case they recognised her, but she did not want to seem ungrateful, so she took the papers and asked what time she needed to report for work.

That night she could hardly sleep. Her tummy was a-flutter with nerves. She had never worked in a restaurant before. She knew a lot of youngsters did it quite successfully, but this still felt very new. What if she couldn't hack it? This was a lifeline. She could not afford to stuff it up.

Thursday - 26 October, SA

At 8.45 am she stood on the steps outside The Sea Shanty. She had put on her jeans and a shirt and tied her hair back into a tight ponytail, in the hope that it would make her look different.

When the waitress with the funky undercut and earrings came to seat her, Alice explained that she was there to start a new job. The waitress nodded and told Alice to come with her.

Alice followed her into and through the restaurant, to a door in the back that opened out into a short passageway. From the clanking pot and cutlery sounds that came from the doorway to the left, Alice deduced that it led to the kitchen. The waitress however turned right. A few feet on she stopped and knocked at an open office door.

"New recruit is here," the waitress announced, with about as much enthusiasm as a teenager on the way to Sunday school. She turned on her heel, "all yours" she said, and headed back past Alice.

Alice took a tentative step forward. To her left in the office she found the woman with the mullet hairstyle, faded and tattered designer jeans and cheese-cloth shirt who'd come over to speak to her and Gloria on that first evening they had a drink there together. She was sitting behind a light pine desk. In her hand she held a sleek, blue, metal, electronic cigarette which she puffed at slowly while she pored over what looked like a large accounting ledger under a bright halogen desk-lamp.

"Come in. Have a seat," she said, not looking up.

Alice stepped inside and took a seat on one of the hard, wooden chairs that stood in front of the desk. Alice glanced around the small office. The desk and chairs filled about a quarter of the room, while a dark grey filing cabinet stood ajar on the far wall next to a black metal coat stand that had a bright yellow fisherman's jacket hanging on it. Alice wondered how often one had the opportunity to use a fisherman's jacket in the restaurant business. To her right, and slightly behind where she sat, occupying most of the rest of the room stood a stack of large tomato juice tins, a tower of bags, each containing twenty-four rolls of toilet paper and some other surplus stock that Alice couldn't identify without leaning over to read the labels.

The woman finally leaned back, removed her reading glasses and looked up at Alice. Alice thought she saw recognition in the woman's eye for a brief second but then it passed.

"My name is Gerry and this is my restaurant," she said in her gravelly voice. "I believe from Boytjie you have some waiter experience already so I won't go through it all."

Alice felt a sudden surge of pressure behind her temples. What had Lekan told them? What experience was she supposed to have had?

"I will say this. I have two rules and as long as you follow them, we should get on fine. The first," she pointed at the tip of her little finger, "is don't be late."

Alice nodded. She could do that.

"The second is don't waste my time." Gerry sat back in her chair. "Think you can manage that?"

Alice nodded again, not quite sure if she had missed something vital that would make more sense of the last condition. Either way she couldn't really answer differently under the circumstances.

"Good," Gerry said, "now grab a uniform." She pointed in the direction of the tomato tins and toilet rolls, "and ask Lucy to get you collecting empties. Report back at the end of your shift and I'll let you know whether to come back tomorrow."

Alice nodded and got up to try to locate the uniforms. All she could see was a stack of white T-shirts in plastic covers tucked in behind the toilet rolls. She leaned in and grabbed one hoping it was the right size. She headed to the office door but then she realised she had no clue who Lucy was. "Um," she started to say.

"That walking colander of piercings who showed you in," Gerry said, having already turned her attention back to the ledger, a large cloud of steam bellowing around her head from her electronic cigarette.

Alice nodded and left.

———

Before she could ask, a somewhat indolent-looking Lucy pointed in the direction of the lavatories where she could change her T-shirt. Thankfully it fitted. When she came back out, she found Lucy standing near the bar clasping a tray to her chest and disinterestedly observing the half a dozen customers seated near the front of the restaurant.

As Alice approached, Lucy pointed over her shoulder in the direction of the kitchen. "That way."

Obediently Alice turned and headed towards the kitchen.

"But I wouldn't go in there right now, if I was you," Lucy called after her.

This naturally confused Alice.

"Trouble in paradise," Lucy said by way of explanation and then headed off to serve a customer.

A tall, pale, thin woman with bleached blond hair peeping out from under a chef's hat, above a long brow and large pointy nose, came storming out of the kitchen. Judging by the way she ripped her apron and chef's hat off her head and unceremoniously dumped them on the bar as she passed, she was clearly very angry about something. Close on her heels followed Gerry.

"Claire, come on —" Gerry stopped herself from saying any more when she realised she had stepped out into the restaurant. She slapped the door frame and headed back into the passage.

Lucy returned with a stack of dirty plates. "Take this to the back." In answer to Alice's questioning look she said, "Because any moment now I'm going to be called."

Lucy picked up the discarded apron and started putting it on. A voice Alice recognised as Gerry's bellowed from her office. "Luuuucy!"

Lucy rolled her eyes and pushed past Alice.

Alice followed her with the stack of plates.

"On it," Lucy called back, but rather than turn right towards Gerry's office, which Alice had expected, she turned left into the kitchen. From what Alice could tell, Lucy having to stand in as chef was a fairly regular occurrence and it was obvious Lucy knew what she was doing.

With one person down, Alice also had to work hard to satisfy all the customers. That meant that the afternoon flew by and, before she knew it, she had done her eight-hour shift and it was time to knock off. She went through to Gerry's office to find out if she would be kept on, but the door was closed. She could see under the door that the light was on and she could hear talking but when she knocked there was no answer.

Just then, Lucy came back in from her cigarette break. "What are you lurking in the dark for?" she asked.

"Gerry said to come find out if I'm good enough to come back tomorrow."

"She says that to everyone. Believe me if you weren't good enough you wouldn't have lasted beyond lunch time." Lucy disappeared back into the kitchen.

Alice clenched her fist and pumped the air. "Yes!" Then she straightened up and headed through the restaurant with a broad smile on her face.

————

When Alice arrived home, she discovered Gloria's flat empty. She assumed Gloria and Lekan were both working late. While making herself a cup of tea, she observed again that despite Gloria arriving home twice now with large bags of groceries, there was still nothing in the cupboards or in the fridge. She wondered what happened to all the food.

Then she had a brain wave. Now that she had a job and was pretty sure she would get her wages by the end of the week, she could splash out on some food to make Gloria and Lekan a nice dinner to say thank you for their help. She grabbed her purse and nipped out to the local supermarket, which was only a short walk back into Sea Point.

————

Forty-five minutes later Alice made her way back into Gloria's block of flats.

The bags of shopping were quite bulky and heavy. For some reason she had not thought about the practicality of carrying all her purchases all the way home. So, when someone, she assumed one of the other residents of the block of flats, held the outside door open for her, she was really very grateful.

"Thank you very much," Alice said, quite out of breath.

"You are welcome," a warm voice said.

Alice could've sworn the voice sounded slightly familiar, but she dropped the idea as soon as it occurred. She knew no one in Cape Town other than Gloria, Lekan, Gerry, Lucy and, fleetingly, Claire.

"Can I help you with that?" a woman's voice asked.

At that point Alice felt like she was about to drop the groceries altogether.

"If you could just take the top one and put it down for me, I will come and get it in a minute," Alice said.

Suddenly her load felt lighter and she saw the bag on top move, revealing a friendly face under a bright red peaked cap.

The face seemed familiar.

Not possible Alice thought.

Then it came to her. She was the lifeguard, the woman who had saved her from the freezing cold waves of Camps Bay that afternoon she went for a swim.

"Oh, my goodness!" Alice exclaimed. "It's you!"

"Hello, again." She was met by a very bright grin as the woman recognised her. "What brings you to this part of the world?"

"I'm actually staying here for a while," Alice said, unable to keep the blush out of her cheeks.

"Oh, how unlucky for you and lucky for us," the woman said. "I thought you were in one of the posh hotels in Camps Bay."

"I was." Alice nodded. "Then I decided to stay on a little longer."

"So where are you headed?" the woman asked, indicating Alice's heavy load.

"Oh, ah, I'm on the second floor."

"Me too. I'll bring these," the woman said and allowed Alice to ascend the stairs ahead of her.

Alice led the way up the short flight of stairs and along the cement corridor. The woman followed her all the way to Gloria's front door. Here, Alice fumbled around with the unfamiliar door keys. "Sorry," she said.

"Take your ease," the woman said, close behind her, unsettling Alice even more. Finally, she managed to open the door and put her bags down inside the flat. Then she turned back a bit too abruptly, not realising that the woman had followed her in. They almost bumped into each other. "Sorry!" They both giggled awkwardly.

"You are my life-saver a second time, thank you." Alice took the bags from the stranger.

"No trouble at all. I'm just next door anyway." The woman pointed at a blue door a few metres back along the corridor.

A slightly awkward silence followed.

"Okay, right. I'm heading home now," the woman said and headed out the door with a little bounce in her step.

"Thanks again." Alice said and was about to close the door.

The woman suddenly turned back. "Oh, in case I ever need to save your life a third time, can I ask your name?"

Alice blushed. "Sorry, yes, it's Alice."

"Nice name, Alice. I'm Lisa."

"Nice to meet you."

Alice watched Lisa reach her door, open it and with a little, almost gallant, tap to her red peaked cap, she disappeared inside.

———

"Oh, wow! Something smells lovely!" Gloria said as she stepped into her flat.

She immediately took off her shoes and put her handbag down on the floor near the door. She slipped her jacket off her shoulders and made her way to the bubbling pot on the stove. She lifted the lid and took a large sniff. "What's this, it smells amazing. I assume you have managed to find a job, or should I be worried about the police knocking at my door looking for a bank robber or shop lifter?"

"It's my personal pasta recipe. If I told you what's in it, I'd have to kill you," Alice joked back. She was pleased Gloria was in such good humour and it felt good to be able to do something nice to show her gratitude.

Fifteen minutes later they were both sitting at the breakfast bench, sipping cold white wine and enjoying the very tasty supper.

Alice became aware of a vibration emanating from somewhere in the flat. She glanced round to find the source. Gloria shoved the forkful of pasta she had been carefully winding and dipping in the last of the creamy sauce into her mouth. She wiped her lips swiftly. "Oh, that's mine," she said through the mouthful of food. She got up and rummaged around in her bag.

Alice tried not to listen too intrusively to the conversation. To be honest, there was not much to be heard, since Gloria was silent for most of it. Then Gloria fished around in her handbag and pulled out her red faux crocodile-skin diary and a pen. She clamped the phone between her shoulder and her ear and turned to a certain page. Finally, she said, "Okay I'll see you at nine-thirty".

She rang off, replaced her diary in her handbag and returned to the table.

"Problem?" Alice asked, noticing that Gloria's usual jolly disposition had clouded over fleetingly.

"No," Gloria said, checking her expression. "No, not at all," She took a swig of her wine. "By the way, I'll be late home tomorrow night."

Tuesday - 31 October, SA

The days had flown by since Alice had started working at The Sea Shanty. It hadn't taken her long to learn the ropes and she swiftly progressed from collecting dirty glasses to taking orders, to even sometimes managing front of house. Her rapid progress was probably also aided by the ongoing absence of the chef, Claire.

Alice had subsequently discovered that Claire was Gerry's long-term lover, and flamboyant spats between them like the one she glimpsed on her first day were not entirely unusual. According to Lucy, all bets were on peace being restored within a week or two and Claire being back, captaining the kitchen.

Gerry had a habit of sitting at the bar on a stool which was almost exclusively reserved for her. She would sit there and puff at her electronic cigarette while keeping a hawk's eye on the goings-on in the restaurant.

As the days went by, Alice started noticing that Gerry seemed to be paying her a little more attention than she did the other staff. At first, Alice thought she was just imagining it, but then she was singled out over all the other staff, including Lucy, who had been there for far longer than she had, to keep an eye on the cash register whenever Gerry needed to pop out.

Alice could sometimes feel Gerry's eyes on her when she thought Alice was not watching. Once or twice she even caught Gerry staring at her. There was something in Gerry's mannerisms, the way she engineered situations that would result in them needing to be in very close proximity that made Alice feel a little uneasy. Once Alice had become aware of this, she was careful to avoid being trapped alone with Gerry. It was not that she was scared Gerry would do something. It was more that Alice had no clue how she would deal with such a situation, and if it resulted in awkwardness, she knew it could cost her the job.

The other thing Alice had learnt quite quickly was that the slow periods in the restaurant were the most difficult to get through. By contrast to the meal times, the standing around with nothing to do produced a mind-numbing boredom that made time seem to stand still.

It was Tuesday morning. There were only two customers in the whole restaurant. Gerry sat on her perch, vaping and poring over the morning's newspaper.

Desperate for something to do, Alice had brought out the clean glasses from the kitchen and was busy stacking them behind the bar when she saw a person in a red peaked cap making their way up the stairs into the restaurant. After a moment or two Alice recognised her. It was Lisa, Gloria's neighbour.

Lisa smiled when she saw Alice and headed towards the bar. As she got close to Gerry, she stopped momentarily and greeted her with a cheerful tipping of her cap.

"Well, I never, if it's not the stud," Gerry said plainly. "To what do I owe the honour?"

Lisa smiled. "Nice to see you too, Gerry."

"Shall we grab a seat over there?" Gerry pointed at her usual lunch table.

"Actually, Gerry, I'm here to see one of your staff," Lisa said, glancing over at Alice who could not help blushing.

Gerry followed the direction of Lisa's eyes. "Oh, I see." She turned her attention back to the newspaper. "Well, you had better make it quick. I don't normally allow social calls while on shift."

"I know." Lisa said, keeping her tone light and friendly. "It'll only take a few minutes." Lisa carried on towards the bar, her smile growing as she approached Alice.

Alice raised her eyebrows in question, to which Lisa rolled her eyes and pulled a face.

"This country of yours is obviously too small for both of us," Alice said when Lisa pulled up a stool at the bar.

"Not at all. In fact, it took me a good few days to track you down."

"Track me down?"

Lisa nodded.

"So, how did you find me?"

"Oh, I get around."

A slight scoff came from Gerry's direction, showing that she was listening.

"People tell me stuff," Lisa clarified.

"I'm honoured. So, what can I do for you?" Alice said in her best waitress-like voice.

Lisa glanced around the bar until her eyes fell on the espresso machine to one side. "Since you probably need to earn your tips," Lisa shrugged in the direction of Gerry, "I should probably have a coffee, at least. Make it an espresso, please."

Alice put the espresso down on the counter in front of Lisa.

"I know you can't really talk now," Lisa said cocking her head in Gerry's direction. "So, I wondered if you'd come out with me some time? There's a beach party out there on Saturday night." Lisa nodded in the direction of the beach. "I was hoping I could persuade you to come."

Alice had been so busy with work and settling into life in South Africa that she had not set foot on the beach since Lisa rescued her that fateful afternoon. As for a party, she had not been to one of those in such a long time, she had almost forgotten how to be sociable or do something for fun. She tried out the idea in her head and soon found herself nodding. "Okay."

"Okay?" Lisa asked unsure.

Alice nodded. "Okay. I mean, that sounds lovely."

"Great," Lisa said, visibly delighted. "Saturday after work, meet me on the beach below the lifeguard station. I'll look out for you."

Lisa picked up the little espresso cup and threw the thick, darkly coloured liquid back in one swig. "I'll see you then," she smiled and placed a R50 note on the bar counter. "Keep the change." Before Alice could object, Lisa was already heading out, tipping her cap again at Gerry as she passed.

SIX

The next morning, Alice didn't have to be in the restaurant until 11 am. It was her turn on a late shift. She stayed tucked in bed, sipping her coffee until Gloria had left for work. Then she got up leisurely had a relaxed shower and relished having the flat all to herself.

At around 9.30 am she stepped out of Gloria's flat. At that moment Lisa's door also opened. Alice instantly smiled and was about to say 'hi' to her first new friend in Cape Town, but she swiftly stopped in her tracks, because just then, rather than Lisa, a tall, slender, beautiful blond woman stepped out of Lisa's flat. Alice spun round and tried to unlock Gloria's front door again. She was so flustered she dropped the keys with a loud crash on the hard cement floor.

When she turned back the blonde was far from gone. She was leaning into a sleep-tousled Lisa dressed in soft shorts and a baggy T-shirt. They were kissing passionately.

"See you later," the blonde cooed at Lisa as she

suggestively pushed herself off Lisa's torso. The blonde started down the corridor and then turned back, winked and blew Lisa a kiss, at which point she caught sight of Alice. She smiled at Alice and nodded a hello.

Lisa turned to see who had caught the blonde's eye.

Alice smiled and felt herself blush.

"Oh, hi," Lisa said, also looking a little embarrassed.

"Hi," Alice said. "Nice morning." That was *such* a stupid thing to say, she thought as the words left her mouth.

"Yes, it was — is, I mean." Lisa smiled, scratched the back of her head and closed her eyes as if to block out what just happened.

They both laughed awkwardly.

"Well, enjoy the rest of it," Alice said, as she slipped past Lisa on her way down the corridor.

"Thanks. You too."

When Alice had almost reached the door that led to the stairwell, Lisa shouted after her. "Oh, and see you at the party."

Alice nodded and escaped through the door.

———

The whole journey into Camps Bay, Alice could not get the image of Lisa and the blonde kissing out of her mind. It looked so... she had no words for it. She imagined what it must be like to kiss another woman — to kiss Lisa. She shook off the thought. She hardly even knew the woman. Why could she not throw off this sad feeling inside?

"Beautiful," she thought aloud. Seeing them kiss looked beautiful.

———

At work, there was thick tension in the air. Strained voices could be heard coming through Gerry's closed office door.

Lucy pretended to be busy monitoring the empty floor even though there was only one regular, sitting at his usual street table drinking coffee.

"What's going on?" Alice raised an eyebrow in the direction of Gerry's office.

Lucy shrugged a casual, disinterested shrug. "Still trouble in paradise."

Suddenly, Gerry's office door flung open and a flushed, furious looking Claire stormed out. As she burst past Alice and Lucy, she chucked her apron in their direction. "Let's see how long you last."

Alice looked at Lucy, more than a little confused. "Alice, a moment, please." Gerry's voice echoed from the office. It was not a request.

Alice panicked. Had she done something wrong already?

―――――

In the office, Gerry put down the phone and looked up. "Come in. Close the door, please."

Alice did as she was asked. The knot of nervous tension in the pit of her stomach was growing.

"There seems to be a staffing reshuffle," Gerry explained in a business-like tone. "I need you to help me cash up tonight. If that goes well, you can add that to your responsibilities, when I cannot be here to do it. An increase in responsibility like this will mean an increase in your wages." She paused briefly. "What do you say? You up for a raise or shall I offer it to someone else?"

Alice wanted to point out that Lucy had been working there for longer, but something stopped her.

"No, I mean, yes," Alice said quickly. "I'll be happy to do that."

"Glad to hear it." Gerry turned her attention back to whatever was on the computer screen in front of her. "That'll be all."

Alice felt a little bewildered. She headed over to Lucy who still stood at the bar with her arms folded across her tray.

"So, what does it feel like?" Lucy asked casually.

"What does what feel like?"

"Being the new flavour of the month." Lucy kept looking out towards the distant beach and sea. "I didn't take you for someone who'd agree to the terms so quickly." Lucy continued matter-of-factly.

"What terms?"

"Just watch yourself. The fall from grace can be a hard one." Lucy sighed and headed in to the kitchen.

"What terms?" Alice called after her.

———

The day passed pretty uneventfully after the rocky start. At 11 pm Alice watched everyone go home after their shifts, except Lucy who was still busy in the kitchen.

Gerry collected the cash trays and called Alice through to her office to start cashing up. Once in the office, Gerry made Alice sit in her chair at the desk. Gerry stood slightly too close behind her while explaining the cashing up process, the bookkeeping system and security and safety procedures related to handling and storing cash.

Alice was acutely aware of Gerry's frequent touches

that lasted a fraction too long. She found it quite hard to concentrate. Alice tried to keep her movements and responses to minimum to avoid giving the wrong kind of encouragement. She tried desperately to focus on the task at hand in order to get it done as quickly as possible and get out of there.

Lucy appeared at the door. "Right, this little chick is going to fly the coop and leave you two lovebirds for the night."

Alice went rigid. Oh my God! How was Gerry going to react?

For a moment time stood still. Then Gerry burst into a loud belly laugh. "You're such a card."

Partial relief at Gerry not taking offence and partial terror at being left alone with Gerry washed over Alice.

"You know me, always the card." Lucy winked and clicked her tongue.

"I'll come to lock up behind you," Alice said and jumped up, pushing past the slightly baffled Gerry.

Alice followed Lucy to the back door.

As she got to the door, Lucy stopped. "Good luck, I hope she makes all your wet dreams come true." She winked and left.

"Very funny!" Alice called after her. "Cashing up is hardly a wet dream."

"Don't say I didn't warn you." Lucy called back from somewhere in the night.

Alice locked the door. She took a deep breath and headed back.

In the office, Gerry had finished counting the cash and was stowing it in the safe. "That's great," she announced. "We got good takings tonight. Well done." Gerry looked happier than Alice had seen her in almost all the time she had worked at The Sea Shanty. "Fancy a drink to celebrate?" she asked as she headed out of the office.

"No thanks," Alice said quickly. "I'd better not. I should be going sooner rather than later."

"You got a hot date then?" Gerry locked the office door and led them out of the passage and into the main restaurant.

"No, my housemate is just expecting me, that's all," Alice lied.

That seemed to appease Gerry. "Okay, we can lock up if you would just help me switch off the lights." She flipped the mains. "Just wait there. I'll fetch you on the way out." Gerry headed over to switch off the final light in the far corner. Once the light was off, the restaurant was shrouded in pitch darkness. Alice thought she could hear Gerry moving around in the dark. Then suddenly it went quiet. Alice felt panic rise in her chest.

"Gerry, are you all right?" She called into the dark.

Suddenly Alice felt something on her neck. She let out a yelp and spun around, and in so doing propelling herself squarely into Gerry's arms.

"Finally, it's just you and me," Gerry purred, her breath sending tingles down Alice's spine. "I've been waiting for this all day. Now I am very all right."

Even though Alice felt it coming, she was powerless against the force of the kiss that Gerry planted on her lips. Alice froze. Panic rose up in her again and she pushed herself out of Gerry's arms.

"Gerry, I'm not..." She stepped backwards and fled from the restaurant onto the pavement.

Gerry followed. "I know you are friends with Lisa, but I felt the attraction, the chemistry between us, all day, especially just now in the office. You can't deny it," Gerry explained.

"Gerry," Alice shook her head. "I'm sorry. I like you. You are my boss."

"We can work that out," Gerry laughed, taking that as a good sign.

"Gerry, no, I mean I like you but I'm not attracted to you. I'm straight."

Gerry guffawed. "You are no more straight than I am a ballerina."

"Hello," a familiar voice said behind Alice.

Alice turned to find Lisa standing there, hands in her pockets.

"Oh, look! The cavalry has arrived," Gerry said, her voice dripping with sarcasm.

Alice felt her panic being replaced with relief, but before the thought had even flashed through her mind her heart sank again. Gerry would think she had lied about needing to go home to Gloria. It certainly now looked dubious. Nevertheless, she honestly could've kissed Lisa for arriving when she did.

"Hi. What brings you here?" Alice tried to sound normal.

"I gathered from this morning that you would be working a late shift. I found myself heading home via this way and wondered if you'd like a lift home — save you having to go on the bus."

"Thank you. That is very thoughtful," Alice said, glancing at Gerry. "I was just helping lock up."

"Okay, I'll let you two get on then?" Lisa said.

Was Alice imagining it? Did Lisa look a little disappointed?

"No" Alice said, a little too quickly.

"Yes," Gerry answered from behind her, almost in unison. Alice turned to look at Gerry and saw Gerry raise an eyebrow and throw a hand up in the air in frustration.

"I mean," Alice said again, "I'll be a few minutes if you don't mind waiting."

Lisa nodded, "Sure, I'll wait in my car. It's parked over there." She pointed at a red 1980's VW Rabbit Golf convertible parked on the opposite side of the road.

Alice turned to Gerry. "Is there anything else you need me to do... work-wise?"

Alice could see Gerry considering her response and then realising that she had been outplayed. Gerry shook her head.

"I'm sorry Gerry, really I am," Alice said softly.

Gerry looked at her long and hard and finally nodded.

"Okay, I'll see you tomorrow," Alice said before she turned and headed to where Lisa was waiting, leaning on the side of her car.

———

The ride home with Lisa was pretty quiet. For some reason Alice wanted to reassure Lisa that it was not what it looked like, but everything she thought of saying simply would have made it sound worse than it was. So, at the end of the ride she merely thanked Lisa for the lift, assuring her that she would see her at the party.

Alice crept into Gloria's flat as quietly as she could, unsure whether Gloria was working another late night or if she was already asleep in bed. Fifteen minutes later Alice lay tucked in bed on the couch, staring at the shadows cast by the street lights outside. Her mind churned relentlessly over the evening's events. She dreaded facing Gerry. She was pretty sure Gerry would fire her, for sure.

Friday - 3 November, SA

Thursday was Alice's weekday off, so she had a day's grace before she had to face the music.

Friday morning when she arrived at The Sea Shanty, she was very relieved to find that Gerry was not in the restaurant. Lucy seemed to have stepped into the breach seamlessly, managing the restaurant easily and efficiently. Alice wondered how often Lucy had had to catch the ball for Gerry like this. By 10.30 am a new temporary chef had been brought in and Lucy was back in charge of front of house as well as managing the whole restaurant.

During the mid-afternoon, when the restaurant was experiencing the usual lull, Lucy sidled up to Alice where she was keeping an eye out over the last three lunch customers.

"Honeymoon over so soon?" Lucy practically gloated.

"No honeymoon," Alice said.

"Ah gee! Sorry to hear that. I thought that by now Gerry would have truly popped your cherry."

Anger bubbled inside Alice. "Mind your own business," she snapped.

"No need to get snippy with me," Lucy said. "I did warn you." Lucy walked off to collect payment from a customer who was getting ready to leave.

At the end of her shift, there was still no sign of Gerry. She gathered Lucy had been in contact with Gerry, but so far no one had said anything about her needing to cash up again. On the up-side, neither had she been fired, yet. Alice clocked out and headed home.

Saturday - 4 November, SA

Saturday morning there was still no sign of Gerry. Again, Alice didn't have a chance to speak to Lucy to find out if Gerry had mentioned anything about plans to fire her, since Lucy was kept very busy standing in as manager of the restaurant.

By 6.15 pm Alice headed out from the restaurant to go meet Lisa. She really didn't feel in a party mood but knew it would probably do her some good. She needed to take her mind off the situation at work and it was about time she met a few more people. She was also quietly looking forward to seeing Lisa again.

Once on the beach it was easy to spot the party. A group of about thirty women had already gathered. A few were playing volleyball while the rest stood around a large open fire.

In the distance, anchored about two hundred metres from the shore, lay a large, exquisite, luxury yacht. Alice wondered if that had anything to do with the party at all.

True to her promise, Lisa must have kept an eye out for her, because she came trotting away from the crowd and up to Alice within seconds of her arrival. Lisa's cut-off jeans and red polo shirt to match her red cap showed off her sporty, boyish physique and made her look very cute, Alice thought.

"Hey, you made it." Lisa said, falling in step next to Alice. There was a certain level of reserve in her manner.

"I did. Was there any doubt?"

"Only a little. I thought you might be arriving with Gerry." Lisa looked hesitant. "I got the impression I interrupted something the other night."

"Yes, I guess you did interrupt, but I can assure you it was a godsend."

Instantly Lisa seemed to thaw a little.

Lisa led her past the volleyball nets. Alice did not quite feel up to such vigorous activity after the day she had had. She was still a bit nervous. As they neared the bonfire area, Alice saw some women sitting on picnic rugs, singing and playing guitars. However, it was the luxury yacht that intrigued her most.

Lisa caught her staring at the boat. "Isn't she beautiful? She is an Azimuth eighty-foot flybridge yacht. It's a custom model with an open galley, an on-board Jacuzzi and, as you can see, a stern platform." Lisa pointed to the low stern where a few people sat with their feet in the water. One of the women got up and dived into the sea, coming up within seconds and letting out a yelp from the cold. A small rubber dinghy with about six people on board was making its way in the shorebreak toward the yacht. On the beach near the dinghy a small gaggle of women gathered, waiting to be ferried to the yacht.

"Is that part of the party too?" Alice asked.

Lisa nodded. "It belongs to Sandra Dakota, a wealthy American entrepreneur who moved to Cape Town a few years ago. She runs sunset cruises in the bays. Every now and then she lends us the yacht for the evening. That way she promotes good will among the community and I guess she gets a bit of PR. Would you like to go check her out?"

For a split-second Alice wasn't sure whether Lisa meant the yacht or the owner herself. "Maybe in a bit," Alice said tentatively. "So, you like boats then?"

Lisa's face lit up. "Yes, I always have. I love the sea. I'm currently working as a lifeguard but I have my own boat in Hout Bay Harbour."

"Wow! That must be expensive."

"No," Lisa shook her head, "I help out the harbour master sometimes and in exchange he gives me free mooring." Lisa turned to look at the Azimuth in the distance. "One day I'll have one like that too."

1980's tunes that Alice vaguely recognised wafted across the water from the yacht. The more Alice squinted into the setting sun, the more women she noticed on the various decks and outside spaces of the yacht. A couple of women got up and squealed as they jumped off the flybridge together.

"The water must be freezing." Alice remembered how icy the water was the day Lisa rescued her.

"Come, let me introduce you to some of my friends," Lisa led Alice towards a little cluster of women huddled near the fire.

They were all very friendly and made Alice instantly feel very welcome. She got on particularly well with Andy, a shorter mousey woman with shoulder length brown hair and a naturally over-enthusiastic, inquisitive nature. Luckily, when Andy started prying into how she came to be in South Africa and managed to stay on longer, Lisa sensed Alice's reticence and helped to change the topic on to how they had been thrashed at volleyball earlier.

Alice noticed the blond woman she had seen coming out of Lisa's flat the other day standing in another group nearer to the fire. When Lisa turned to see what Alice was looking at, the blonde waved at Lisa. Lisa gave a very discreet wave and a smile back. Alice's heart sank.

"You don't have to babysit me," Alice said softly, "if you need to go talk to other people."

Lisa looked momentarily confused.

"I'll be fine on my own if you need to go to your

girlfriend." Alice nodded in the direction of the blonde, who was still staring at Lisa.

"My girlfriend? Who?" Lisa looked to see where Alice was looking. "Oh, Angelique." Lisa smiled. "No, she's not my girlfriend."

"I'm sorry. Did you split up," Alice said sincerely, also curiously feeling a wave of relief.

"No, it is fine. We were actually never together."

Alice didn't understand. To her they looked very much together that morning. She needed to ask, but Lisa clearly did not want to continue the conversation. While making small talk with Lisa's friends, Alice watched Lisa surreptitiously. She noticed a few other girls waving, smiling, some sharing knowing looks and some even venturing up to come say hello to Lisa. Lisa was very charming to all of them and it was impossible to tell if any one or all of them were potential new or current love interests. Alice was very relieved to find that Lisa made no effort to veer off from her side though. Occasionally she would smile and nod, but not very much more. It felt to Alice a bit like being out with a high school jock whom the entire cheerleading team drooled over but knew to be unattainable. But Lisa seemed shy and more than a little embarrassed about the level of attention she was getting.

"A few of us want to head to the yacht to see the sunset," Andy said. "You two want to come?"

"You mean you want to go and come back before it is too dark," one of her friends teased and tousled her hair affectionately.

Andy looked a little sheepish. "It's true. I don't relish the idea of going anywhere in that rubber bath tub after dark."

Lisa deferred to Alice to answer.

Alice nodded.

"Great," Andy said. "Let's go join the queue."

As they moved closer to the growing queue of women waiting for the dinghy, Alice noticed a number of heads turn in her direction. At first, she thought they were looking at something behind her. She actually even turned to see what it was. Then it became clear that they were looking at her.

"What are they looking at?" Alice asked Lisa quietly.

Lisa smiled. "You are a new face," she said, "and a pretty one at that."

Alice blushed. "No, seriously, do they always stare at new people like this?"

"Pretty much." Lisa nodded and laughed, making Alice unsure if she was winding her up or not.

While they stood there waiting together, Alice realised she was beginning to relax and to feel like she was starting to belong, to actually have a good time, for the first time since she had walked out.

———

Their little group was almost at the front of the queue. There were only two other women still ahead of them and the dinghy was on the way back to the shore to pick them up, when Alice suddenly heard a deep, familiar laugh behind her. "Hey, Rosa, did you save us a space?" said the gravelly voice.

Alice turned to find Gerry, with a woman flanking her on either side, heading down towards the queue. The redhead in front of Alice in the queue turned and waved at Gerry to join them quickly.

Gerry caught Alice's eye as she passed. She didn't say

anything, nor was there any warmth in her demeanour. Once she had joined her friends, Alice saw the group huddle together around Gerry, listening to something she was saying. A couple of them even turned and looked back in Alice's direction. This was followed by hearty laughter.

"Is something wrong?" Lisa asked.

Alice shook her head. After a moment's pause Alice touched Lisa's arm. "Actually, I'm really sorry; I think I'm going to go."

"No! Why? What's the matter?" Lisa glanced in the direction of Gerry's group.

The queue began to move.

"You coming?" Andy called back, when she saw Lisa and Alice hadn't caught up.

Alice didn't respond. Lisa shook her head. "No, you guys go. We're going for a little walk. We'll see you later."

"No, please, don't let me stop you from enjoying the party and seeing the yacht," Alice protested.

"It's okay. I see the inside of that yacht quite a lot."

Alice raised her eyebrows.

Lisa laughed. "Nothing like that. I crew for Sandra sometimes when she has a big corporate group."

———

Alice and Lisa walked back up the beach towards the bonfire.

"So, where would you like to go," Lisa asked.

Alice looked around at the growing groups of unfamiliar women.

"Can I be honest?"

Lisa cocked her head.

"I'd really like to get away from here. I mean. I like the sea and the beach. It's just..."

"Too many new faces, huh?"

Alice shrugged. "It's been a pretty full on week."

"Okay, well..." Lisa thought quickly. "I have an idea. How about we go back to Hout Bay and I can take your mind off your week by boring you with details of my boat?"

Alice was relieved that Lisa understood. She liked Lisa's company and wanted to spend more time with her, just away from the crowd.

———

Lisa's car was parked on Victoria Road in Camps Bay. The roof was down this time and Alice hopped in and buckled up. When Lisa turned on the ignition, James Blunt blared through the speakers. Alice just smiled at Lisa as she noticed the flush creep over Lisa's cheeks. She wasn't sure what Lisa was embarrassed about, but she found it quite sweet.

The drive south along the coast was beautiful. The road started at sea level and then steadily crawled higher until Alice imagined she could almost see all the way to Buenos Aires. The sun glinted off the ocean like a glass plate. Then the road descended again and ducked back inland, passing through a wooded coastal village before spitting them out onto the little shaded bay that is Hout Bay. A few minutes later, Lisa pulled up in the large car park of the harbour. She parked up and Alice followed her through a little gate onto the jetties. Lisa kept looking at her and smiling shyly, not what Alice expected at all. The few times she had seen Lisa, even in the corridor the other morning, Lisa seemed so confident.

A little way along the jetty, Lisa slowed her step. "There she is," she said with pride.

In front of Alice stood a smallish, bright blue and white power yacht. Judging by the windows, it had two levels, and on top was a small flybridge. The stern deck behind the cabin was covered by a bright blue canopy, and "Noreen" was written boldly on the side of the boat in matching blue ink.

"She's beautiful," Alice said genuinely.

Lisa stepped up onto the outside rim of the boat and opened the side canvas flap of the canopy. She held out her hand to Alice. "Come on. I'll show you around." Alice gripped her hand and stepped up and onto the boat.

Alice was amazed at how small and neat and well thought out the internal design was. Everything had a place and there was a place for everything — an adult doll's house. All the seats and soft furnishings were made from either a plain blue or a matching nautical pattern. The hard furnishings were varnished wood or glass, the reflections adding to the feeling of space. The windows were larger than Alice expected and through them she admired the beautiful red-orange sunset hitting the hillside across the bay.

Lisa stepped aside and quietly allowed Alice take a look around.

Alice stepped down three little steps onto a slightly lower level that contained the tiny galley and adjoining dining area. Just behind that was a small bathroom, not much bigger than an ordinary sized shower in its entirety. She admired the thoughtful design, where even the toilet-roll holder took the form of a cavity that receded far enough into the smooth surface of the cabinet below a small basin, to ensure it was not likely to get wet when someone had a shower.

Next to the bathroom was a tiny sliding door that led to the bow. Lisa noticed her looking at the door. "Oh, that is my bedroom."

Alice wanted to ask if she could look in but something stopped her. Somehow that did not seem appropriate.

"Come see my piece de resistance," Lisa said and headed back out towards the stern.

Alice followed her up a vertical metal ladder through a tiny hatch and up onto the flybridge. The three-sixty view of the harbour was breathtaking.

"I'll nip down and get us a drink and some cushions," Lisa said.

Alice nodded and continued to take in the view.

A few minutes later Lisa reappeared, passing up a bottle of J.C. Le Roux sparkling wine, two plastic champagne flutes and two pillows through the hatch.

The two of them sat and drank bubbles while Lisa told her stories about Hout Bay, the surroundings and her life in Cape Town. Once the sun had gone down and the air temperature sent a chilled shiver down Alice's spine, they relocated back downstairs into the surprisingly warm cabin. Eventually Lisa cooked them a linguine pasta, which they washed down with a bottle of Nederburg Shiraz from Lisa's little wine cabinet.

As the evening progressed, they spoke about past lives and past loves. Alice found Lisa really easy to talk to. Before she knew it, she was sharing stories from her childhood, her parents' deaths and about Magnus and how he rescued her from her foster home.

Alice had just finished telling the story of her shopping for a swimsuit in Camps Bay and how she had come to take a swim that first day they met, when she became aware of a strange choking screech outside the window.

"What was that?" She asked, looking quite alarmed.

"That is Fred," Lisa smiled. "He's my lodger."

Alice realised by the twinkle in Lisa's eye that she was up to something.

Eventually Lisa let out a little chuckle. "Seriously, that is Fred. He has taken to living on my boat. He is also my resident alarm clock and every morning around this time he wakes me up with a cough."

Morning? But it's not morning, Alice thought. She glanced at her watch and was astounded to see it had just turned 6 am.

"To be fair, Fred is not your average lodger, come I'll show you." Lisa went to the window where she pulled open the venetian blind. Alice stepped closer and peered out the window not seeing what Lisa was talking about, when all of a sudden, a three-foot tall seagull stepped in front of the window, making Alice yelp with fright.

"He does that sometimes." Lisa chuckled. "Sorry, I should've warned you."

Alice saw the naughty school-kid side of Lisa. She could imagine her utterly enjoying a cheeky prank a little too much. This inspired a rush of affection for Lisa that she couldn't contain. She leant forward and planted a kiss on Lisa's lips. For a moment she was lost in the sensation. Then she realised what she had done and she pulled away, mortified.

"Oh my God! I'm so sorry. I'm not sure where that came from. I... I'm sorry... I'm not... I mean, I'm not..." Every muscle in Alice's body shouted for her to run. What had she done? What was she thinking?

Lisa gently took hold of her hand to pull her out of the

frantic monologue. "It's okay," she said so gently that Alice
had to listen. "I assume you know I am like that. I'm not
offended though. To be honest, I do like you very much. I'm
quite flattered that you felt something, but just to reassure
you, I'm not going to jump your bones. So, you can relax."

Alice nodded, feeling exceedingly foolish after the
outburst and grateful that Lisa wasn't offended.

SEVEN

Alice found the intensity and constant interaction while working at The Sea Shanty hard. She didn't know how Gloria managed to keep such long hours. In fact, she had barely seen Gloria and Lekan since the evening they had dinner together before she started her job. Usually after Alice's shift, she would come home and fall, exhausted, into a dead sleep in her makeshift bed on the couch, only vaguely registering Gloria coming in at some later hour in the night. And, most mornings Gloria would be up and out long before Alice even awoke.

As a result, they had taken to communicating via little hand-scribbled notes pinned to the refrigerator with a small metal crocodile magnet. These notes included such things as reminders to pick up toilet paper or offers to get milk and other basic supplies, or invariably Gloria letting Alice know she was going to be late again and not to leave the lights on.

At first, Alice was grateful for the space and solitude, however with everything happening at work and with Lisa,

129

she really could have done with seeing a friendly face and having someone to talk to. So, when she found Gloria's note saying she was finishing work early that day and suggesting that they meet up for a drink after work, Alice was thrilled. Unfortunately, Gloria's note said to meet at "The Shanty", as Gloria like to call it, and try as she might she couldn't reach Gloria on her phone to change the arrangement. This meant she had to hang out at The Sea Shanty once her shift had ended.

To help her get through the wait she ordered a small carafe of chilled white wine with two glasses. She was about two-thirds through the carafe when Gerry swaggered up to her.

"So, I see you've been stood up by the gigolo lifeguard, hey?"

Alice hadn't dared to make contact with Lisa since Saturday. She couldn't bear the shame. In fact, she had slipped out of the flats extra early on her way to work, deliberately to avoid a chance meeting on the corridor.

"It's not what you think. I'm not waiting for —" The word froze on her lips as she looked up and saw Lisa walking up the stairs towards her table.

"Oh? Really? Not what I think, hey?" Gerry scoffed and headed back to the bar to survey the goings-on from a safe distance.

"Hi," Lisa said.

"Oh, hi," Alice replied, feeling exceedingly awkward. "What are you doing here?"

"I've not seen or heard from you since Saturday." Lisa scuffed the floor with her red North Star trainer. "I was passing by on my way and thought I'd stop by to see if you were okay and wanted a lift home."

Alice shook her head. "Thank you. That is very kind of you, but I'm okay."

Lisa suddenly noticed the almost empty carafe and two glasses. "Oh. I'm sorry. I'm interrupting." She lifting her hands in surrender and started to back away.

Alice shook her head. "It's not what you think."

"No, it's okay. I'm sorry I came —" Lisa looked hurt.

Alice got up and instinctively grabbed Lisa's hand. "No, it's okay." This halted them both. Lisa's eyes darted from the soft cool hands that gripped hers to Alice's level blue stare that met hers. "It's not what you think. I'm waiting for Gloria. She was going to meet me after work. But she's late."

Alice bent down to pick up her bag. The two of them walked out of the restaurant together. "Honestly, it is very nice you came to see me. I'm sorry that I've been avoiding you. I just feel like such a fool after my outburst on Saturday."

"I liked the kiss," Lisa teased, "the histrionics afterwards, slightly less so."

"I know, I'm sorry." Alice could feel herself blush.

Lisa smiled. "So, are you sure you wouldn't like that lift?"

Alice shook her head. "No, really. Thank you. Gloria just works around the corner, so I'll head over there to meet her. But maybe some other time," Alice asked, "If I promise no more histrionics?"

Lisa's face lit up. "Sure, let me know when."

———

As Alice approached the large square lump of cement and glass that was the MOD, her stomach clenched. The internal lights spilled out into the street through the large floor-to-ceiling panels. She could imagine some of Magnus's clients lazing in the luxury lounge, discussing the latest scandal on the Cape grapevine or the newest miracle anti-ageing cream. She really didn't want to bump into any of them. At this time of night, only a skeleton crew would be on duty, so she made for the tradesmen's entrance, which she had used to slip in and out of the hotel undetected.

The events of the morning when she walked out on Magnus came flooding back.

Was it the right decision? It was a pointless question. She had well and truly cast those die. She guessed he did love her once and she really was grateful for everything he had done for her in the past. If she'd had the strength to do it differently, she would have.

Then she thought back to seeing him with Rita at The Bay Hotel and anger crept through her veins. She could not have stayed!

As she rounded the corner and was about to head down the single-track road to the rear service entrance, a white minivan passed her and turned into the MOD premises. It gave her a bit of a start because its headlights were off. She doubted the driver would have seen her coming from the shadows if she'd inadvertently stepped out in front of it.

She took a few cautious steps forward.

From her vantage point she saw and heard the scream of metal on metal as the large slatted service entrance garage-door began to open. The van did a two-point turn in the small yard, to back up to the entrance. As it neared the building, the movement of the van triggered motion detectors and a bright spotlight flooded the scrubby outside space, illuminating the row of commercial waste and recycle bins and two beaten up staff cars, 'jalopies' as they called them, probably belonging to people on the night shift.

She squinted into the light to see who was behind the wheel of the minivan. There was something familiar about the shape of the person. The driver side door opened, briefly triggering the van's cabin light. It was Lekan!

What was he doing here?

A movement in the garage entrance caught Alice's attention. Gloria!

Alice stopped and stepped deeper into the shadows along the wall of the service road.

She watched Lekan go around the van and open the back doors. There was a sense of urgency and tension in his movements. The angle of the doors partly obscured her view, but she could still see enough of Lekan and Gloria hurriedly loading bags and boxes of stuff into the van.

Once done, Lekan closed the rear doors and got back into the driver's seat. To her surprise he didn't set off immediately but seemed to be waiting for something. Within moments, Gloria reappeared at the service entrance with a young girl, who looked about twelve. She reminded Alice of Deka and Simone. She had a small suitcase with her. Alice remembered seeing the little makeshift bed in the laundry room. She watched as Gloria and the girl hugged a heartfelt farewell before she was ushered into the passenger side of the van's cabin. Lekan gave Gloria a cursory wave and pulled away, heading back towards the access road.

Alice reacted quickly, dashing back to the main road and taking cover behind a large milkwood tree. She waited there a long while after the van had disappeared out of sight. Then, she hurried down the road, away from the MOD and back into the hubbub of Camps Bay.

———

Alice sat at the kitchen counter in the dim light created by the few down-lights under the kitchen cupboards. The tea she'd made to calm her nerves had gone cold. Her mind was churning. What kind of trouble could Gloria be in? The stuff they'd loaded into the van looked mainly like large, nondescript bin-bags, grocery bags and a few cardboard boxes, the kind you would expect to be used for hotel supplies. They could be filled with anything.

As for the young girl who left with Lekan, why would she be going with him? If he was just giving her a lift, why involve her at the same time as loading the van? Whatever they were doing, it looked very suspicious. So why risk involving a little girl in such activity?

Alice heard a noise outside the door. It sounded like giggling and she could make out a man's voice. Alice looked at her watch. It was 2.23 am. She listened again and recognised Lekan's deep voice. Great! That was all she needed. She'd hoped to confront Gloria on her own.

She heard a key scrape in the lock and the door opened. She braced herself. Through the open door she could hear Gloria's voice, "Now go," and a giggle. Her words were muffled as if said between kisses. "Shh, she's asleep."

Alice could see Gloria, silhouetted by the fluorescent lights on the corridor, wave and blow a kiss towards Lekan, who was somewhere out of sight.

As Gloria turned and closed the door, she caught sight of Alice and visibly jumped with fright.

"Oh, goodness, child! You will scare the living daylights out of me!" Gloria said, laughing. She put on the main kitchen light, which flickered briefly before bathing the room in its harsh fluorescent glow. "What are you still doing up?"

Alice didn't smile back.

Gloria looked at her, puzzled. Then it dawned on her. "Oh God! I'm so sorry. I completely forgot. I was held up at work." Gloria lifted a grocery bag onto the corner of the kitchen counter.

"I saw you," Alice said simply.

Her reserved tone alerted Gloria, who stopped and looked at Alice suspiciously. "What do you mean, you saw me?" Gloria said, clearly trying to sound indifferent.

"I saw you," Alice said, "stealing from the hotel."

Gloria stopped what she was doing and gave Alice a long hard look.

"When you didn't come to The Shanty," Alice continued in the same emotionless tone, "I suspected you'd been caught on another late shift. So, I came to the hotel. I thought maybe, if you weren't too busy, we could have a cup of tea and catch up between your duties." Alice let the words hang in the air for a moment. "I didn't want to be seen in the main lobby so I came around the back."

Gloria lowered her head and sighed. She turned and leaned back against the kitchen sink. She crossed her arms and took a deep breath. "Listen, Alice. It's not what you think —"

"I saw you Gloria! I saw you and Lekan load the van. It was obvious."

Alice nodded. By now tears had started to roll down Alice's cheeks. The one person she could rely on, her one and only rock had crumbled. She sniffed and swiftly wiped a tear from her cheek.

"Okay," Gloria said. "Good."

Alice felt confused.

"We did load the van... with old food and rubbish."

Alice looked up at Gloria. "Why would you steal rubbish?"

"Because... the powers that be would rather waste food than see starving children eat."

"What do you mean?" Alice wiped the tears from her eyes.

Gloria went over to her large red handbag and fished around inside. Finally, she pulled out her purse and opened it. From one of the large sleeved pockets she pulled out a battered, stained piece of paper, which she handed to Alice.

It was a photograph.

Alice wiped her eyes and sniffed. She took the photo from Gloria and studied it. Smiling back at her was a group of about twenty to twenty-five children, dressed in tired, mismatching, tattered clothing, either a size too small or too big for the bodies adorned. Most of them had bare feet and some of the older ones held the littlest toddlers and babies on their hips. They were all very thin and quite grubby but their smiles were bright. As Alice looked closer, she recognised a couple of the faces, Deka and Simone, and the young girl she saw get into Lekan's van earlier.

"Who are they?" Alice asked. "And, please tell me the truth."

"They are my kids."

Alice tapped the photo against the palm of her other hand and shook her head.

"I don't mean 'my' kids. I mean, I'm responsible for them. I run a little shelter in the township."

Alice considered this for a moment. "Okay, so what does stealing have to do with them?"

"Lekan and I, and a few other workers who help us, relieve hotels and restaurants of old food and bedding that are destined for waste." Gloria said matter-of-factly. "We rescue those supplies before that can happen and use them to clothe and feed these children." Gloria pointed at the photo in Alice's hand. "They're all street children, orphans. They have no one, and nothing, and they have no money to buy food and clothes or bedding for themselves."

Alice shook her head again. "So why have you got to do this on the sly? Why don't the hotels just give you the stuff they are about to throw away?"

Gloria raised her eyebrows and sighed. "That would seem sensible, would it not? Instead the bastards are too worried about 'policy'. They claim leisure industry policy and some health and safety guidelines prohibit them from giving away any food, especially old food, past its official sell by date, in case the food is off and someone gets sick. They do not want to be held responsible."

"But surely these children would never take the hotels to court?"

Gloria nodded. "You and I know that. But apparently the hotels and most restaurants here claim to have inherited their policies from the United Kingdom and United States' hospitality industries. In those countries, the hospitality industry adheres to strict health and safety regulations because there they are likely to be sued, even by the homeless."

Alice could believe that about the UK and US.

"So, you steal the food before they have a chance to throw it out?"

Gloria nodded.

"And the same for the bedding?"

"Yes, basically, we use the old sheets to make the children clothes."

"What about food kitchens and charity shops?"

Gloria shook her head again. "We don't have such things here. Those are luxuries of the poor in England, not in Africa, which is why many foreigners don't really understand African poverty."

Alice looked down at the group of smiling faces in her hand. "So, where are these children?"

Gloria hesitated for a moment. "If you really want to know, how about I take you and show you on your next day off?"

Alice nodded.

Later, back in the dark on the couch, Alice lay awake. Maybe she was wrong to doubt Gloria so quickly. How could she have so easily thought the worst of her? Gloria had always been nothing but kind and generous to her. She should've known there was a good reason behind Gloria's actions and she felt quite ashamed of how quickly she had been willing to judge her.

Thursday - 9 November, SA

By 7.30 am Alice and Gloria were heading out of the flat towards Gloria's banged up beige Citroen.

Gloria drove them out of Green Point, skirting the edge of Cape Town city bowl and onto the M2, past Observatory and out to Khayelitsha, which Gloria had explained was situated on the Cape Flats, bordering False Bay.

"Khayelitsha means 'our new home'," Gloria said as she took the turn off to the N2. "It's spread over a large portion of the Cape Flats and divided up into various sections or parts, each separately named and each quite different once you get to know it."

As they headed further out of the city, the suburbs gave way to large open land and then, like a mirage ahead of her, a vast, unbelievably dense settlement of eclectic dwellings emerged, ranging from brick built, quite smart, large

PROJECT ALICE

middle-class houses with fancy Mercedes-Benz parked on brick-paved driveways, to tiny rickety wooden shacks with gaps for windows and corrugated iron roofs.

"Where exactly are we going?"

"To the Shelter." Gloria said. "We're almost there."

A few minutes later, a large cement building, surrounded by a high barbed-wire fence, came into view on the right-hand side. The name on the side of the building read "Khayelitsha High School".

"Do the children go to school there?" Alice asked.

"You'd think so, wouldn't you?" Gloria smiled ruefully. "It's a school, but no one goes there."

"Why? It looks very nice."

"It is. Or, it was supposed to be. It was sponsored by a Canadian philanthropist whose company spent thousands of rands on the building and state of the art science and computer laboratories. I think some of the kit in there is good enough to run a Google office. Unfortunately, he did not realise that most of these kids need food, clothes and a place to sleep, more than fancy equipment."

"Won't he sponsor some of that too? Surely people can understand that?"

Gloria shook her head.

"Can they do something else with it, like convert it into accommodation?"

"No. Once it had stood empty for a few weeks and the locals realised that there was some expensive kit in there, he just hired a few men with guns to make sure that vandals didn't get the stuff. Beyond that no one has been allowed in there."

Gloria slowed the Citroen and took a right turn onto a dirt track that cut into an even poorer part of the town. Like a surgeon's knife on soft skin, the car cleaved a slow,

139

cautious, red dusty line along the track, past a sea of scrap metal, aerials and rotting wooden pallets that were cobbled together with rusted nails and fishing line to form a mass of dilapidated shacks.

About four hundred metres on, Alice caught sight of a slightly larger construction in a natural clearing created by a perimeter of debris. The curious construction was made mainly of a large marquee tent that had been modified, abutted, propped up, elongated and reinforced with various wooden, metal and fabric additions, creating extensions on either side. Alice guessed the debris and bits of rubble all around were what remained of a building that had been plundered for scraps and recyclable components for the neighbouring structures.

As they turned off the track and headed along the side of the marquee tent, Alice noticed a little brown girl, no more than four or five years old, sitting on a small upturned bucket, sheltering from the hot sun in the sliver of shade that remained. The little girl, surprisingly, had shoulder length, straight black hair and big brown eyes. She watched them intently with an impassive expression as they slowly drove in, passing the side of the tent.

A sudden loud thud against the side of the car made Alice jump. A little boy had shot out in front of them and, at first, she feared the car had hit him. It was a huge relief to find the thud was caused by a football that had bounced against the side of the Citroen. As the boy recognised the car, his face cracked into the largest toothy grin Alice had ever seen. He whooped and shouted something incomprehensible back towards where he'd appeared from. Within seconds, a small football team of young boys and girls swarmed around the Citroen. They were laughing and chattering excitedly while jogging next to the car as Gloria drove it around to the other side of the tent into a barren dust-bowl of a yard. Once Gloria had parked, she got out the car and was instantly swamped by the children trying to hug her. Meanwhile, Alice received wary, curious glances.

"This is my friend, Alice, everyone," Gloria said. "Say hello."

"Heeelloooo, Aaaaaliiiice," came the enthusiastic sing-song chorus.

Alice smiled and said her own, hopefully friendly sounding, hello.

Alice noticed that the little girl, who had been sitting on the upturned bucket, was now clutching the side of the tent, partly hiding, partly watching the procession.

"Who is she?" Alice asked.

"Oh, that's little Masika. She's very shy and keeps very much to herself."

Alice smiled at the little girl and then followed Gloria and her human skirt of small people into the tent.

———

The tent was divided into three main compartments. The first one was the central one, around which most of the activity was focussed. This room extended the full width of the construction, with the exception of a small, narrow add-on room at the rear, which was the shower room.

The first thing that struck Alice was the wonderful exotic smell that permeated the space. It was a combination of sweet spices and wood smoke and made her mouth water.

Three teenage girls huddled around an island made from repurposed wooden pallets covered in cracked laminate that stood in the middle of the rear half of the room. They were chopping vegetables and singing softly to themselves. Their voices had an amazing resonance that made Alice smile involuntarily from inside out. In the front half of the room there was a collection of chairs and tomato boxes adorned with padding and old cushions, arranged around a number of large, upturned wooden crates which served as a sitting-dining area.

Gloria dumped her large red handbag in a small wooden shed that stood on the left against the internal wall. Alice gathered from its large metal padlock that Gloria unlocked and locked again vigilantly afterwards using a key she carried on a lanyard around her neck, that this must be where the most valuable supplies were stored.

One of the girls had got up to stir a large, black, three-legged pot over a small wood fire on the far side of the island table. She had a blanket wrapped around herself and Alice marvelled at how hot she must be in this heat.

Gloria joined her at the pot where the girl handed her a loaded spoon to taste. Gloria nodded and said something too softly for Alice to hear. This made the girl smile and take a little bashful bow before she went back to chopping vegetables.

Alice noticed that the blanket held something in position on the girl's back — a small sleeping baby. The baby looked so tiny. The girl saw Alice looking. She smiled but lifted her finger to her mouth and whispered something to Alice in her language.

"She says her baby has just gone to sleep." Gloria translated softly for Alice.

"Her baby?" Alice was shocked.

Gloria nodded.

"Right, let me show you the rest," Gloria said. It was clear Gloria did not mean this to be entertainment or a nicety, but rather a matter-of-fact, functional necessity to get through as quickly as possible.

Alice followed Gloria into the next compartment. This section was completely empty of children and the floor was covered, wall to wall, in rugs, blankets, and bed rags.

"This is where the healthy ones sleep," Gloria said. "As you can see we do not tolerate laziness." She laughed. "We encourage them to go out and play or work or read rather than mope around. Besides it is healthier that way."

Gloria headed back through the kitchen to the other main compartment.

As Alice stepped in through the door-flap, she instantly became aware of a different smell — disinfectant and bleach. In contrast, this room was minimalist, with the only items in it being ten camp beds, six of them occupied by small sleeping or resting figures.

"We try and keep them off the floor so they don't get a chill and also it is easier to keep clean."

"What is the matter with them?" Alice asked softly, stepping forward tentatively.

"Various things. These two have venereal diseases." Gloria whispered, as she nodded in the direction of two young teenage boys to one side. "Adisa has TB. Kofi and Kwame have AIDS. Sadly, they have both come down with pneumonia." Gloria let out a deep, sad sigh, then seemed to shake off the funk and pulled herself together. "As for Fumy, we're still not sure what's the matter with him." Gloria lowered her voice and stepped closer. "Oh, and in case it gets confusing, Fumy identifies as a boy. He hates it if people get it wrong."

Alice nodded and filed that bit of information away for examination later.

Her heart went out to these tiny, poorly beings.

One other camp bed was made up with a pillow and a blanket but was empty. She was about to ask who the occupant was, when little Masika came in and flopped onto it, still maintaining her inscrutable stare, which was intently focussed on Alice.

"And with her?" Alice asked.

Gloria looked up. "HIV," she said with a sigh and shook her head.

Alice tried to smile at Masika as she felt her heart breaking. Masika merely stared back.

"And this part you know already. It's where most of them spend their time." Gloria had moved on through a side door out of the tent and into the dust-bowl they had parked in. After greeting Gloria and her newcomer the children had dispersed, resuming their various activities scattered in small groups around the yard. Some were kicking a ball about. Two older boys were shooting hoops through a roughly circular metal hoop affixed to a long wooden pole that also served as the main electric mast feeding the immediate neighbourhood. Others sat around in smaller groups. One such group had gathered in the little shade the tent provided at that time of day and an older boy, who was sitting on a short stump, was reading aloud to them.

Alice took a few steps closer to see what he was reading from. Gloria said something to the boy. He stopped and held up the book towards Alice. Even though the language was foreign, she instantly recognised the images and the author: Enid Blyton in Xhosa.

"Do they all speak Xhosa only?" Alice asked.

Gloria smiled, suddenly looking very proud. "One of the first things I did when we started all this was to get an English teacher. Now they all speak enough English to get by." Gloria must have seen Alice glance down at the book the boy was reading. "We try to give them equal exposure, if we can, to good stories written in Xhosa and in English."

"Where is their English teacher?" Alice asked.

"During the last set of riots, Lindsay got spooked. So now I do what I can, when I can, if I can." For a brief moment Gloria looked incredibly weary, but this was obviously a wallow she would not allow herself to indulge in. She seemed to pull back her shoulders and stand tall once more. "Right, I need to do a few things to prepare for the rest of the weekend. All that food we brought over in the week needs to be cooked before it goes off. You can either come help peel potatoes or you can sit out here in the shade and read to the little ones. The books are all in the sleeping area, against the tent wall. I could get one of them to grab a selection."

Alice looked around at the seven little faces staring up at her expectantly. She nodded. Gloria said something to one of the little boys who was sitting on the floor. He got up swiftly and ran indoors. A few minutes later he reappeared, his arms stacked high with English books. The boy who had been reading got up off his stump and smiled as he bowed to Alice and waved at her to take his seat on the stump.

Alice felt a little self-conscious as she took his place. The boy with the armful of books passed her one off the top of the pile. It was Enid Blyton again, a 'Famous Five' title. She cleared her throat and tried to subdue the nerves bubbling in her belly. Who knew that she would feel nervous reading to a few small children?

"'George dear, do settle down and do something,' said George's mother," Alice started to read. Within a few minutes her reading had obviously caught the attention of the other children in the yard. They soon abandoned their own activities and came to join the group.

About two chapters into the book, Alice became aware of a small presence lurking to one side, shyly clutching to the tent wall. She realised it was Masika. Without interrupting her reading she stretched out her hand and to her amazement and delight the little girl came over and nuzzled into her side, partly resting on her lap.

———

In the car, on the way home with Gloria, Alice felt exhausted. For the first part of their travels back to Green Point they were both quiet, both absorbed in their own thoughts.

"So, do you still want to report me and Lekan?" Gloria broke the silence. "You have every right to." She kept her eyes on the road. "Technically we are taking what is not ours. As I said, it is all food and materials destined for the incinerators but still, it's not ours."

Alice stared out the window at the passing shanty houses made from spare rubble, women carrying buckets on their heads and a pack of wild, emaciated dogs attacking a bag of refuse.

"No," she finally said, softly. "I want to help you."

Another long silence followed as Gloria manoeuvred the Citroen into the fast lane past Mowbray.

"I saw you've made a new friend today," Gloria said.

At first Alice didn't know what Gloria meant.

"Little Masika has taken to you."

Alice smiled at the thought. "Yes, she is very sweet." She had read to the children for about two hours. They had sat riveted all that time. Most surprisingly, little Masika did not part from her side until it was time for her and Gloria to leave. Then it took two of the older girls to unclench her little hands from Alice's top. This almost broke Alice's heart.

"And you have taken to her?"

Alice nodded. "Yes, I think I have."

"Let me give you a little bit of advice," Gloria said quite soberly. "Don't get too close to the children and don't let them get too close to you."

Alice frowned. "What do you mean? Why not?"

"Just take it from me. Life in the townships is hard and some of these children don't always make it."

Alice stared at Gloria, her brain trying to make sense of what she was saying. "I thought HIV is no longer terminal. Is Masika going to die?"

Gloria shook her head. "All Masika needs is her medication. I just mean, you need to protect yourself. It's easier to face the bitter realities that way."

———

Once back in the flat, Gloria cooked the three of them a wonderful meal consisting of a portion of the delicious stew the girls had been making during the day, served with a large bowl of morogo, which she explained was the Tswana word for vegetable and a type of wild African spinach that the boys from the Shelter had helped her gather in the grassy fields on the outskirts of the township, and a large bowl of putu pap, a traditional stiff maize porridge.

So far, Lekan had always been a man of few words, to Alice at least. Perhaps it was the wine, or the relief that she was not going to turn them in, or maybe just the fact that they were trapped with nothing but each other's company while Gloria busied herself in the kitchen, but on this occasion, he was quite garrulous. Alice was surprised to learn that he was a law graduate. He had decided to quit because he thought South African law was too chaotic, too erratic and unpredictable due to the reliance on diverse common law with too many cultural influences, as well as being corroded by corruption. The profession lacked structure and rigour. Lekan professed to be a man who believed in making one's own destiny.

"To do that," he said, "you need to make sure you are in control of yourself and the little wagon on which you make your way through life."

Finally, Gloria put out three plates and some cutlery on the kitchen counter and invited Alice and Lekan to take a seat. He topped up their glasses and they tucked into the amazing meal. The stew was unlike anything Alice had ever tasted and it went really well with the putu pap. The tradition of eating the stew and pap with her hands, like Gloria and Lekan were doing, was just a little step too far for Alice. Gloria and Lekan simply laughed good naturedly at her trying to cut the food with a knife and fork, in that fond and slightly bemused way that locals all over the world do when foreigners are not instantly able to embrace their national peculiarities.

After the main course, Gloria cleared the plates and brought out a spongy, sweet Cape Malay pudding called Malva Pudding and ice cream for dessert. Alice was urged to try it but she found it far too sweet, so Lekan wolfed down the rest of her portion without needing to be asked twice.

About halfway through the dessert, there was a little pregnant pause. Alice noticed Gloria and Lekan's eyes meet briefly.

"So," Gloria began, "you said you'd like to help us at the Shelter. What did you have in mind?"

Alice shrugged. "I'm not sure. I thought maybe I could take up the slack with teaching the children a little English, or to read and write." Alice took a sip of her wine. She wondered how many glasses she had had already. She was not used to drinking. "It depends where you need help."

Alice saw Gloria glance at Lekan.

"The kids really took to you today so teaching them English would be great...." Gloria trailed off.

Lekan shook his head and took another large swig of his wine.

"Okay, now you two are scaring me. Say what's on your mind," Alice said. Yip, she was a little tipsy. She would normally never be that forthright.

"Well," Gloria said more cautiously, "English lessons are nice to have but what the children need more are food and supplies."

At first Alice was confused. Then suddenly, like a sack of potatoes, the penny dropped. She started to shake her head. "No way! That I will not do."

Neither Gloria, nor Lekan, said anything. They both just looked down at their dessert plates.

"You can't seriously want me to help you steal supplies?" She looked disbelievingly from one to the other. "I'm an illegal visitor. I shouldn't even be here without Magnus. If I get caught, I'll be instantly deported and I didn't leave my husband and struggle to build a new independent life to just have it all whipped away."

"A new independent life you might not have if people hadn't helped you," Lekan said into his wine glass before he took another large sip.

"Are you really going to play that card?" Alice looked incredulously at him and then at Gloria. "Are you saying

149

that you helped me so now I have to break the law and risk being deported for you?"

"Not for me," Gloria said. "For Masika and those poor children who have no one else."

Alice shook her head. There followed a long silence as she stared into her wineglass, rubbing the smooth glass beneath her finger and thumb while she thought back to the day's activities. She had gone with Gloria to the Shelter convinced that she would be coming home afterwards and ringing the police to report them.

She thought about those vulnerable children, who were one hundred per cent reliant on Gloria to feed and clothe them and provide their medication. In her mind's eye she saw those big brown eyes of Masika's watching her every movement, the tiny little hand that curled around her arm, the other dirty little faces looking up at her attentively as she read to them, the joy and exuberance with which every activity was instantly abandoned when they were called for supper.

"So, let's say, hypothetically, I did help you. What would I have to do?"

Gloria and Lekan seemed to both start breathing again and they shared a smile before Gloria jumped in enthusiastically. "Well, you see, as you know we get all our supplies from hotels or restaurants. The hospitality industry is very wasteful. They often throw things out based on a policy that dictates that they bin supplies long before anything is really fit for waste, especially in the bigger businesses."

Alice nodded. "Okay, I understand that, but how does it work? What would you want me to do?"

"In each of the businesses we work with, we need someone on the inside who has access and ideally control of the stock," Lekan said. "This insider lets us know when there is stock about to be thrown out and helps us gain access to pick up the unwanted goods."

Alice thought for a few seconds. "No," she said as she realised what Lekan was getting at. "There is not a chance in hell that I'm stealing from my place of work — not from Gerry Cox."

EIGHT

The flight on Wednesday night had been long. Although Magnus McCroy had offered to pay for her to fly business class, Toni couldn't justify spending that much of her client's money on luxury. Unfortunately, like most people, she always struggled to sleep in the cattle class.

At the arrivals gate of the airport, a young African man in a sharp suit and very shiny shoes held a little cardboard poster with her name on it. He was very friendly and Toni was grateful for his help with her luggage.

The drive towards Table Mountain, up to the top of the city and down into Camps Bay to The Bay Hotel took just over an hour.

The Bay Hotel was a large, sprawling, white and green complex, placed front and centre, facing the Camps Bay beach. It had a few long, single lane infinity pools on the various decks, around which all manner of guests could have snacks, meals and drinks, or just relax and enjoy the sun when the conditions for the beach were not favourable.

Her room was spacious, clean and looked recently decorated. Toni thought places like this probably indulged in regular facelifts to keep up the facade of luxury. She didn't have a sea view, but did not mind. After all, this wasn't a holiday and she suspected she wouldn't be spending much time in her room.

Dr McCroy had invited her to stay at his medical respite hotel, the MOD Hotel, where Alice spent her last few days before she disappeared. However, Toni would rather have drunk bleach than pose as one of his clients about to undergo cosmetic surgery for a moment longer than she absolutely had to. Besides, Toni had felt staying there would draw too much attention to her investigation.

Although Toni was not keen to stay at the MOD, she did agree to let Magnus arrange a complimentary facial and pedicure for the Friday morning, her first full day in Cape Town. Toni figured a facial and pedicure were perhaps the least intrusive treatments that would allow her the opportunity to chat casually to some of the staff and regulars to find out what they knew about Alice's whereabouts.

————

At 9.30 am Toni walked into the MOD Hotel. The tall lanky receptionist checked her in and within minutes a young woman wearing a white gown and with a long dark pony-tail, who introduced herself as Janine, the duty manager, appeared in reception. She explained it would be her pleasure to show Toni around the facilities.

The first stop was the changing room. Janine handed Toni a thick, fluffy white robe, a similar large, white bath-sheet and anti-slip towelling slippers. She pointed at another door leading off the changing room and told Toni to meet her through there, once she had undressed.

On the other side of the changing room Toni found Janine waiting for her in a large room with tables and high-backed comfortable chairs forming semi-private workstations with computer monitors. Along the edges stood a few large, shell-like sofas on which more casual laptop users could recline. There were ample electric sockets scattered on the floor and walls within easy access of each workstation.

"This is the tech room," Janine explained. "Feel free to use your laptop and mobile phone here as much as you want. The Wi-Fi is free and secure and Trevor," she pointed out a short, squat young man who looked like he had swallowed a gallon of steroids for breakfast, "is on duty to assist you with any tech needs. Please be aware that the rest of the spa is a silent and tech free zone. If you choose to read on a tablet or other hand-held device, those are permitted, but be aware the rest of the building is protected by a state-of-the-art Wi-Fi and signal jammer and should you be caught taking any images or recording anything, those devices will be confiscated. We take our guest's privacy very seriously."

Toni nodded.

Janine turned on her heels and led Toni further into the spa, through a large dining-room. A few tables were already occupied by guests in white robes sipping teas and coffees. "This is where lunch will be served from noon onwards," Janine explained. "From two pm we also serve afternoon tea. Rest assured there will be attending staff on duty all day in all of our breakout areas if you'd like to order refreshments."

The next room was a large, dark room, with small LED

floor lights illuminating the edges of a wooden deck that curved and twirled its way between low reeds and over a large mass of water. Once her eyes adjusted to the dim lighting, Toni realised the water was in fact a large fish pond that extended under the deck, more or less across the entire room. The wooden decking formed regular alcoves, which each housed a clutch of comfy sun loungers and pot plants, positioned to give the illusion of privacy.

"This is the Koi Room," Janine whispered. "It has been modelled on the Koi Room at the Sanctuary Spa in London. You are welcome to have a sleep or meditate here whenever you want."

Soft strains of Deva Premal combined with gentle trickling water echoed through the room.

"We provide headphones if you would prefer listening to your own music or exploring our large in-house selection of meditations and chants."

Next, the tour brought them to the pool room, which was complete with hot-tub, glacial-tub and a half sized Olympic pool. "The first lane is jet enabled so if you'd like a swimming lesson, it is easier for Jimmy, the in-house instructor, to assess your stroke."

Janine then led her into a short, wood clad corridor punctuated by regular frosted glass doors on either side. "These are the treatment rooms." She pointed at the second one on the left. "That is where you'll have your facial at eleven this morning. Please report to Maya ten minutes before."

Only then did Toni notice the small, older lady sitting at a short wooden podium in the corner near the door. Toni smiled and nodded at her.

Janine carried on a few more paces down the short

corridor. "The door up ahead," Janine said, pointing at the door at the end, "leads to the saunas and steam-rooms."

She stopped and turned ninety degrees to her right, facing down another short corridor which Toni hadn't noticed. This one also had half a dozen similar frosted doors leading off it. "These are the private breakout rooms," Janine said. "You can book one from Maya as well." Toni wondered why one would need a private breakout room when there were clearly so many relaxation areas already available in the spa. Just then, she heard a grunt coming from one of the rooms and the penny dropped. Toni felt herself blushing as she imagined what carnal pleasure the occupants could be enjoying behind that frosted door.

"If you need anything or have any questions just ask any of our staff, they will be very happy to help you in any way they can. Here is our treatment card." Janine handed her a waterproof paper menu. As Toni flipped open the cover she was greeted by a large photo of a smiling, impeccably dressed, Magnus with the large print letters below it, "Our Founder."

"Amazing man, isn't he?" Toni said.

"Yes, Madam, Dr McCroy certainly is, and we are truly indebted to him for creating this wonderful spa."

"Do you know his wife?" Toni continued casually.

Janine looked puzzled. "Sadly, not personally."

"Oh, that is a shame. I had hoped she might relax and rejuvenate in this wonderful spa more often or..." Toni was about to take a gamble, "perhaps you know how else I could get in touch with her."

Janine smiled a practised smile. "No, sorry, I have no idea how to contact Mrs McCroy."

Toni nodded and decided to leave it at that. She didn't

expect it to be that easy, but it was always worth a try. Then she had another thought.

"Sorry, I don't mean to push. I have a brief acquaintance with Mrs McCroy," Toni lied. "Perhaps you know how I can get a message to her?"

"Although I cannot guarantee it, if you'd like to leave your contact details at reception, then if possible, I'll be sure to pass on your best wishes and ask her to contact you," Janine said, clearly well versed in handling such requests.

Toni nodded. "I'll do that. Thank you."

"Enjoy your day with us today, Miss Mendez. If there is anything else we can do for you, please do not hesitate to ask." Janine smiled and headed back past Maya and out through the door.

———

It was just after 10 am. She had some time to kill before her treatments. Might as well, Toni thought. She entered the sauna and steam-room area. It was tiled with thick, anti-slip, rubber matting on the floor. There were four glass doors leading to two steam rooms and two saunas. On the side there were two large monsoon shower heads along the wall, each with a chain drawstring. A shiver ran down Toni's spine as she imagined the blast of icy water those showers would deliver. Toni disrobed and wrapped her white bath-sheet around herself, hanging the robe on a hook on the wall. She pushed open the sauna door and entered.

The room was dark and the dry heat smelled of herbs. It took her eyes a few minutes to adjust, but then she could make out the naked form of one other woman on the top seat directly in front of her. Toni chose the lower bench immediately to her left and sat down, side on with her back against the wood clad wall. She let the towel slip off her body and drape over the wooden bench under her. She closed her eyes and thought about how she was going to persuade the staff to tell her more about Alice. Judging by the curt and professional responses she had received from Janine, she doubted they were just going to volunteer information. Sometimes it did happen. There had been a few occasions when Toni had gone to an organisation and spoken to the staff who could not give up the dirt quicker, on account of being so happy and relieved to have someone to talk to about their troubles.

Toni became aware of a strange sound coming from the other side of the dark room. She listened more closely. It was little moans and sounded like heavy breathing. At first, she wondered if the other occupant of the sauna was okay, or whether maybe she was having some kind of fit. She was just about to ask when she recognised the distinct grunts of someone discreetly on the verge of orgasm.

Oh my God! Maybe the other occupant had not noticed Toni enter. She scuffed her feet on the wood and gave a little cough to alert the person to her presence. Since her eyes had now fully acclimatised to the dark, she could see the woman's one hand gyrating gently between her legs, while her other seemed to be pinching her own nipple. There was the noise again as the woman stretched out her legs. Toni could feel herself instantly blush in the dark.

A long deafening silence followed in which Toni sat, not moving a muscle, barely breathing. She had no idea what to do or what would happen next.

Then there was a longer, lower, moan from the woman as she came.

The woman finally sat up and swung her feet off the bench. She leaned forward resting her hands on her knees. Now Toni could see she had short salt and pepper hair. Her body was trim but muscular for her age and it was obvious she took good care of herself.

"Hi there. Sorry about that. I just had to... You know how it is." Her voice sounded deeper than Toni expected, with a slight accent, German or Hungarian.

"No problem, don't mind me," Toni said, not quite believing she was having this conversation.

"You see, I've just had a massage, and that always gets me going." The woman wiped the sweat off her face and sniffed a little.

"Massages can do that," Toni agreed, remembering the passionate ending to the last massage Lizbeth gave her. She was not sure if it would have the same effect coming from a random masseuse though.

"The thing is, I have been coming here for about five years. It's a lovely place."

"It is." Toni was not sure where this was going.

"They recently changed my masseuse to Lena. Well, Lena is..." she trailed off lost in her thoughts for a few moments, "quite something. The best masseuse I've ever had and incredibly hot!"

Toni stifled a giggle. That was the last thing she expected to hear.

"So, you see, I hang on for as long as I can during the massage and then when it is over, I usually slip in here to finish off, otherwise I can't think or speak for the rest of the day. Normally no-one else is in here this early."

"Oh, sorry, I didn't mean to intrude —"

"No, no you did not. It was just, I could not stop when you walked in, sorry."

"No apology needed," Toni said.

"Actually, I should thank you. You sitting there, and not knowing you from Adam, made it even more hot." The woman chuckled, which made Toni chuckle too. She could not believe the woman's candour.

"Well, glad I could help."

"So, what are you here for?"

"A day visitor. I have a facial and a pedicure in a bit."

The woman nodded. "Are you here on your own or with someone? You don't sound South African."

"Here for work." Toni avoided the question.

"Ah, what a shame! Cape Town, like so much else in life, is a better place if you can enjoy it with someone." The woman winked at Toni. "I'm Olya."

"Toni."

"I'd shake your hand, but right now it's probably better I go have a cold shower first."

"Yes, probably better." Toni laughed and nodded.

"Please let me treat you to a massage by way of an apology."

"Oh no, that is not necessary. No apology needed —" Toni said quickly.

"No arguments, Toni. I'll put your name down. If you won't take it as an apology then take it as a gift. A shared treat and if I see you again you can tell me how it was for you."

Toni had no idea how to respond.

Olya got up, grabbed her towel which she was sitting on, wrapped it around herself and headed for the door. "Nice to meet you, Toni."

"And you." Toni had no idea if the woman could even see her properly in the dark, let alone would recognise her outside the sauna.

———

As Toni had hoped, the pedicures were not a private affair. In fact, in the spacious therapy room, six reclining chairs were arranged in a circle with their heads at an apex. All six chairs were filled. The other five women seemed to know each other from being regular 'inmates', as it seemed the residents fondly called themselves. This was good news. It meant that the women would chat amongst themselves more readily and Toni only had to listen and intermittently throw in a comment or question to direct the conversation.

Soon Toni's patience paid off. One woman, Maureen, turned the conversation to Dr McCroy. At the mention of his name the other women instantly crooned almost in unison.

"Oh, he's a dish," the one named Pauline said.

"Have you met him?" the little, slightly chubbier member of the group, called Colleen, asked Toni in a conspiratorial fashion.

"I have, but only very briefly," Toni replied.

"He's so gentle and has such good manners," Colleen said.

"His wife is so lucky," Pauline said, a wistful tone to her voice.

"Have any of you met Alice?" Toni asked casually.

"I have," Colleen said with a nod. "She is a funny little thing. Not worth the hype."

"Really?" Toni said making sure she did not sound too interested. "What was she like? How did you meet her?"

"Oh, I met her here in Dr McCroy's consulting room," Colleen said, "only a few weeks ago. She is very plain and mousey looking, rather skinny and certainly does not fill a room with presence."

"Hmm! Pompous, if you ask me," a fourth woman, named Ingrid, who had not contributed much so far, said.

"No, I think she is quite shy, really," Pauline said.

"As for the way she embarrassed poor Dr McCroy in public like that," said a tall woman with a dark tan and shoulder-length, fine, bottle blond hair, whose name Toni had forgotten.

"Like what?" Toni asked.

"Oh, dear, did you not hear? She's left," the blonde said.

"Come to think of it, she is so ordinary," Colleen continued. "I could've sworn I saw her double in Camps Bay the other day. I know it couldn't have been her since she's probably gone back to the UK. After all what would a woman like that do here in South Africa."

"Where was that?" Toni said, making sure to guard her tone.

"Oh, I'm sure it wasn't her. This was a waif of a girl really, even more ordinary than her, if that were possible, in one of the shops in the mall. I think it was one of the more upmarket clothes shops. No, maybe it was the chemist. I'm not sure. Anyway, I bet she's run back to Dr McCroy by now, begging forgiveness! That is certainly what I would've done."

Toni was not about to enlighten them.

"He probably took her back as well." Colleen sighed wistfully. "He's so kind, so generous. This debacle is probably why he hasn't returned to South Africa yet. He has such a hectic schedule and works so hard. I know he's not back yet because I was meant to have my second consultation already, but they offered me a registrar so I asked for it to be postponed. I prefer to deal directly with Dr McCroy himself. After all, there is no great rush for me. I would rather have his expertise than have to talk to one of his assistants." The way she said "assistants" made it clear that she did not hold them in high regard at all. "And I —"

"So, what brings you here, Toni," Pauline cut in. "Is this your first time?"

"Yes," Toni said. "I thought I'd come and check out this place, for future reference, you know. I thought a little pedicure could not hurt."

"Well, you'd be surprised," Colleen said, launching into another monologue that critiqued every beautician and member of staff she had known in all her years of coming to the spa.

————

After her treatments, Toni went to get dressed. Coming to the spa hadn't been as fruitful as she'd hoped, unfortunately. She hadn't expected any of the guests or staff to know Alice's exact whereabouts nor to bend over backwards to share that with her, but she had hoped for a little more than a single, potential sighting by one guest who simply liked the sound of her own voice. She would have to widen her search. The prospect of wandering around Camps Bay with a photograph and asking if anyone else remembered seeing Alice, wasn't her idea of fun. But if that's what it took to find her, then Toni would have to make a start.

At reception she settled her bill. As she was about to leave the receptionist called her back. "Ms Mendez, one of our guests, Olya, left you this." She handed Toni an envelope.

Toni took it and walked away from the desk to open it. She had almost completely forgotten about Olya and the sauna incident. Inside were a note and a small card.

———

Toni,
Nice to meet you this morning. Once again, my
apologies for the intimate circumstances of our
meeting. I have notified reception that you are to
have a massage on me, so to speak, but in case that is
not quite your cup of tea, I also enclose a little
something that might interest you.

———

Toni looked at the card. It was a business card with the
name "Melinda" and a telephone number on it.

For a moment Toni couldn't make sense of the note.
Was Olya propositioning her? Her name was Olya, not
Melinda. Then the penny dropped. Could Melinda be a
call girl or some kind of escort? Why would Olya have
assumed she would be interested? Toni shook her head and
stuffed the business card and note in her jacket pocket.

———

The rest of that day and the whole of the evening the
business card burnt a hole in her pocket. Even Lizbeth
could tell that Toni was distracted when they spoke over the
phone. In the end, Toni cut the conversation short. She
didn't want to subject Lizbeth to her own emotional roller
coaster. The last thing she needed right then was to have a
long intimate conversation, which would invariably make
her crave Lizbeth even more with every cell in her body.
The point of taking this job and putting all those thousands
of miles between them was to achieve some distance. She

needed to sort out her own head without putting them both through the turmoil of her own confusion and whatever crisis she was going through.

NINE

Saturday morning Toni spent talking to some of The Bay Hotel staff to see if they knew anything about Dr McCroy and his wife. She discovered that APRASSA, the leading cosmetic surgery board in South Africa, had held a conference at The Bay Hotel, which Dr McCroy had attended on most days. She also discovered that Alice had made enquiries about a suite at The Bay shortly after the conference had ended. Beyond that they could not shed much light on Alice's current whereabouts.

Now, Toni sat nursing a non-alcoholic Rock Shandy in a little bar on the pavement just outside The Bay Hotel. She held a 'no alcohol on the job' policy, but right now she could have murdered something stronger. She had just managed to informally question a couple of the MOD Hotel staff members she recognised coming in to this little bar after their shift, but her mind kept wandering.

She pulled out Melinda's business card from her pocket

and fingered the sharp smooth edges. Maybe this was not such a daft idea after all. Maybe Lizbeth was right. Maybe she needed to spread her wings a little. If Melinda was what she suspected, this would be a way to gain more experience and distance from Lizbeth, which might help her acquire a healthier, more balanced perspective. She just couldn't imagine getting into bed with anyone other than Lizbeth. It would feel wrong, like she was cheating. But maybe it would be different with a professional. Maybe with a professional she could just do something for the sexual experience, no emotional ties.

One thing was for sure. If she was going to make that call, she needed something stronger. She drained her glass and caught one of the waitresses' eyes.

"May I have something cheap, local, but stronger, please," Toni said.

A few minutes later the waitress placed a short glass that looked like Coke in front of her.

"What is this?" Toni enquired.

"Klippies and Coke," the waitress said.

Toni took a sip and was knocked backwards in her seat.

"You asked for cheap, local and strong." The waitress winked at her.

Toni nodded her thanks. Then she took a number of large swigs, drinking down the South African brandy mix in one go. Once done, she threw the correct amount of money on the table and left, making her way to the quieter part of Camps Bay beach. Here she sat on a rock and made the call.

Sunday - 12 November, SA

Sunday morning Alice awoke at about 8 am. It was her day off from The Sea Shanty. Gloria hadn't been home since early Friday morning when Alice heard her leave before sunrise. She had texted her and offered to go and help out at the Shelter, but she had not heard back. So, she decided to enjoy the scarce luxury of a lie-in.

At 10 am there came a knock at the door. She wrapped her blanket tightly around herself and went to see who it was.

A familiar red peaked cap greeted her.

"Hi, sorry to disturb you." Lisa said, referring to Alice's blanket attire and obvious tousled look.

"No, it's okay. I was just relaxing since it is a rare day off." Suddenly she remembered her manners. "Do you want to come in? I can switch on the kettle."

Lisa shook her head. "No, thanks. That's very kind, but unlike some, I need to get to work. I've a short shift in Noordhoek at twelve and I wondered if you'd like to come with me to see the Noordhoek beach. Afterwards, I thought, we could take my boat out for a little spin, maybe round to Camps Bay or Clifton. We could drop anchor there for sundowners, if you'd like. Then I'll bring you back later tonight."

"That sounds lovely." Alice said without hesitation. The prospect of spending the day doing something different with some company was a welcome one. "Can you give me a few minutes to throw on some clothes?"

Lisa smiled. "Sure, I'll go grab my things in my flat. Just knock when you are ready."

———

Twenty minutes later, Alice and Lisa headed through Camps Bay, Hout Bay and all the way down to the five miles of wonderful white sand that formed Noordhoek beach.

Here Lisa grabbed a rug, a couple of towels, her sports bag and cooler bag from the back seat and they walked down to a temporary lifeguard post consisting of a high chair and a few flags next to a rubber dinghy.

"Clearly not your permanent office," Alice said.

Lisa smiled. "True, it is only when the currents are particularly strong that the lifeguard service monitors this beach. Usually these surfers take care of themselves."

Lisa proceeded to set up a little camp for Alice not far from her post. "Will you be able to relax here for a couple of hours, swimming, enjoying the sun and keeping yourself amused while I do my shift?"

Alice nodded happily.

"I've put a few things in the cool-box that I thought you might like, so do help yourself." Lisa smiled, grabbed her sports bag and headed towards the lifeguard station.

Alice settled down with a paperback she'd borrowed from Lisa's bookshelf, while she waited for Lisa to finish gathering the last few things for their day's adventures.

Lying in the African sun was thirsty work, Alice discovered, and in less than an hour she had finished three of the six delicious South African ciders from the cool-box.

Another hour later, the shadow and cold drops from a wet, ruffled and very cute-looking Lisa woke her.

"Hi." Lisa smiled down at her. "You ready to go? Sorry, I kept you waiting. There was a little body-surfer who ran into trouble as I was about to knock off."

"No problem," Alice said, gathering her things. It was only when she got up and the earth moved in an unfamiliar way that she realised she might be a little tipsy. She caught sight of the bank of empty bottles stuck head first in the sand next to her. Oops! Those ciders had gone down a little too well!

———

An hour later, Alice sat on the flybridge of Noreen holding on for dear life as Lisa pushed her throttle into full speed around the headland towards Clifton.

"Clifton consists of four little bays and traditionally, different demographics congregate on the different beaches." Lisa shouted over the wind. "I like to go to fourth beach most. It is also the most sheltered which is nice for a calm sunset. Is that okay with you?"

Alice made the okay sign. Quite frankly, at that point, she would have agreed to anything. As a result of the cider and the motion of the boat, she had to focus all her attention on not losing what little was in her stomach all over the flybridge. She thanked the gods when Lisa finally slowed the boat and let down anchor.

Lisa, seeing Alice looking a little peaky, helped her down onto the front deck and settled her on a soft padded mat in the bow of the boat. Then she disappeared back into the boat and reappeared a few minutes later with two more ciders and an assortment of salty nuts.

"Here, this should help," Lisa said, with a wicked smile.

Alice scoffed a handful of salty nuts and gingerly sipped the cold drink. Surprisingly, it did make her feel a bit better and she started to relax.

What began as questions about how Lisa became a lifeguard, soon progressed into Lisa sharing her earlier aspirations to join the navy force, like her dad. Unfortunately, life had not taken the right turns for that. Now her goal was to fix up Noreen to sell and eventually buy a bigger yacht and sail around the world. For that to happen, she had to continue to work as a lifeguard and earn her mooring fees doing chores helping out the harbour master.

It was clear that Lisa was a self-starter, Alice thought. She had a strong sense of respect for people who could decide what they want and then focus and commit to doing what it takes to achieve it. But even in that category there were two types of people in the world. Those who would do anything, whether scrupulous or not, to achieve their desires, and those, like Lisa, who had the moral fibre to never stray into the darkness nor lose their place in heaven in the process of chasing their dreams. She thought about her own situation.

"Will I stoop to becoming a thief?" Alice mused.

"Why are you a thief?" Lisa asked, looking shocked.

Alice realised she had spoken aloud. Flustered she got up. "Oh, never mind." She tried to think quickly to cover her tracks, but her thoughts felt heavy. Everything somehow felt unreal. She was clearly more inebriated than she had realised. "I.. I just feel like I have had to steal a new life," she finally said and turned a little too abruptly, intending to make her way to the toilet in the cabin to give herself space to regroup. Instead, her foot caught on the cleat behind her and before she knew it, she was airborne, hurtling towards the icy seawater.

The shock of hitting the cripplingly cold water gave her an instant, excruciating headache and her teeth would not stop chattering. She was vaguely aware of Lisa throwing something overboard and then strong arms wrapped around her and pulled her back onto the boat.

Lisa guided her into the cabin, ran her a warm shower and helped her into the small compartment. Alice stood, allowing the scalding water to wash over her, while shame flooded her from the inside. A few moments later Lisa returned with a large dry towel, a pair of thick dry tracksuit-bottoms and a long sleeve T-shirt.

Alice was still too cold to move. She was grateful for Lisa's help getting her out of her wet clothes and wrapping her in the warm towel. Lisa vigorously rubbed her arms and legs to encourage circulation.

Being this close to Lisa allowed shame to be slowly supplanted by something else. She recognised the feeling from the other night, when she had embarrassed herself with her own irrational outburst.

This time though, it wasn't a flash impulse that drove her, but a certain need that washed through her, then built steadily from somewhere in the pit of her stomach.

Lisa must have seen Alice's strange expression, and stopped what she was doing. The two of them stood looking at each other until Lisa smiled.

Alice leaned forward and planted a soft, almost imperceptible kiss on Lisa's lips. At first Lisa did not seem to react. Alarm bells started going off in Alice's head. But then Lisa moved forward into Alice, pulled her closer and started to return the kiss, at first gently and then with growing passion.

Suddenly Lisa pulled away, startling Alice. She met Alice's gaze. Alice felt naked and vulnerable under the scrutiny of those deep dark eyes.

"Are you sure you want this? You are quite inebriated —"

Alice cut her off by pulling Lisa to her and kissing her deeply.

It was a very strange sensation, Alice thought. She didn't know if it was down to the alcohol, but it felt like an electrical current flowed through her, starting at the point where her lips made contact with Lisa's. The current seemed to swirl up through her skull and then twirl and whirl down into her body, heating and making every cell buzz slightly, on its way to where it was earthed in the centre of her sex. The longer she kissed Lisa, the stronger the current grew and the stronger the current grew the more it compelled her to move closer. She felt like her soul wanted to crawl inside this gorgeous woman. She had to have her, to feel her, to taste her. She had never felt anything like this before in her life, not for Magnus, not for anyone. She wanted more but she did not know how. Alice felt Lisa was holding back — being a gentlewoman. Alice had to let her know what she needed. She pushed Lisa gently backwards out of the little bathroom, towards the bedroom cabin. As the edge of the cabin bed connected with Lisa's calves, she collapsed backwards onto the bed, breaking their kiss.

"Okay, and here I thought you were an innocent." Lisa's smile lit up her face.

Alice knelt on the bed, straddling Lisa's legs. Then she crawled up and along until she was straddling Lisa's hips. "You're partly right. I might be inexperienced, but I'm not innocent."

Lisa's sexy grin just made Alice's insides twitch even more.

Alice grabbed her own long blond tresses and swept them over her right shoulder to secure them before she bent down and gave Lisa another long, slow, deep kiss. She sat back up and grabbed hold of the hem of Lisa's tight T-shirt. She tugged at it, making her intentions known. Lisa sat up slightly, allowing Alice access to the garment. Alice pulled it up and ripped it over her head and flung it backwards out of the cabin.

Alice looked down at Lisa and noticed her eyes had darkened and a strange expression clouded her features as she stared back up, admiring the body towering above her. There were no more giggles, no more shy banter. What Alice saw was pure desire reflecting back at her.

Lisa's hands glided up over Alice's smooth, pale stomach as if she was touching something rare and mysterious. When she reached the fold under Alice's breast she hesitated and ran the tips of her fingers along the bottom edge as if to acknowledge a boundary was about to be crossed that would change them both.

Alice savoured the moment.

She was not ready to slow the pace and she really didn't want to think about boundaries or implications. She just wanted to feel. She wanted Lisa's soft hands on her, her lips on her skin, her body next to hers. She leant forward into Lisa's caress.

Lisa smiled hesitantly. She allowed her hands to continue their journey up in light touches over Alice's soft, smooth breasts. She sat up and planted soft kisses starting at Alice's solar plexus, moving up between her breasts. This time Alice resisted the urge to lean in, savouring the delicious torture. A few moments later, Lisa cupped one cool breast in her warm hand and held it gently closer as she took the nipple into her mouth.

Alice moaned at this and reflexively thrust her chest forward to extend the contact. When Lisa started to suck at the nipple, hard, the exquisite feeling surged through Alice. Her breath caught as Lisa's calloused palm scraped over the tender flesh of the other nipple, but a mighty surge raked her body as Lisa grasped and tweaked that nipple with measured force.

She could feel herself growing wetter and wetter with each divine caress. She was not sure how much more of the sweet torture she could endure. She needed Lisa to touch her. She needed her to be inside her. This might have been the first time a woman had touched her, but her body knew exactly what she wanted.

She bent down and whispered close to Lisa's ear. "Please..."

———

Toni headed down the Camps Bay main road.

The call to Melinda was rather brief. There was probably not much more to be said. After Toni had told her that Olya had given her her card, Melinda had taken over the conversation, obviously knowing exactly how these exchanges should go. They had arranged to meet at a restaurant bar in Camps Bay, which was where Toni was heading.

Suddenly Toni's palms started to sweat. Was she going to go through with this? She glanced at herself in the reflection of one of the shops as she passed. Oh my God! What would this woman think of her? Wasn't it only old, sweaty, middle-aged men who did this? It was Olya who gave her Melinda's number, so presumably Melinda must have some female clients.

Toni slowed her step.

Maybe she could just ring the restaurant and ask them to tell Melinda that she had been called away unexpectedly.

Melinda would not believe that. If this woman were a

professional then she must be used to every excuse in the book as people succumbed to their own cowardice.

Come on, Toni. Grow a pair, as Maxine would say. She wondered whether Maxine had ever hired a prostitute. She'd probably never needed to.

Finally, Toni took a deep breath. You only live once!

————

Toni entered The Sea Shanty to find it quieter than she had expected for this time on a Sunday afternoon. There were two older couples to one side, each clearly there to enjoy the Champagne Sunday Special being advertised on the A-frame sign on the pavement outside. On the left near the entrance sat a group of young women sipping cocktails, chatting and giggling gregariously.

Suddenly, a roar erupted from somewhere to her left. Toni realised it came from the sports bar above The Sea Shanty. Toni remembered that a significant rugby match was due to take place that afternoon. She did not particularly enjoy rugby so the details escaped her. The fact that The Sea Shanty was not offering a TV broadcast of the match might have accounted for the distinct lack of customers.

Toni scanned the restaurant further. There was only one person sitting on their own, on one of the soft corner couches.

That had to be Melinda. She was nothing like the image of Joanna Lumley in Shirley Valentine[1], dressed in a pencil skirt suit and greeting her with perfect diction, that Toni had imagined her to be.

Instead, she was stunning, with straight dark brown hair to her jaw line that shone in the sunlight. She wore a black jacket, jeans, high boots, white T-shirt over a ripped abdomen. There was not an ounce of fat on this woman. Clearly, she worked out, hard.

A dark-haired waitress, with more piercings than a pin cushion, placed a large aluminium ice-bucket and two glasses on the table in front of Melinda. Then Melinda noticed Toni approaching, She smiled, got up and took a few steps towards her. "Toni, I presume?" Her voice was calm and somehow reassuring. She threw open her arms in welcome.

At the same time, Toni, acting on awkward impulse, stretched out her hand. Melinda merely smiled and took the offered hand in hers and squeezed gently.

"I took the liberty of getting us a bottle of Prosecco. I hope you like it." Melinda gestured for Toni to take a seat on the corner couch next to her and, not bothering to wait for service, she began to pour two glasses.

Toni, still feeling like a seagull in the Midlands, took a seat. The sparkle of the golden liquid in the sunshine mesmerised her.

Once Melinda had finished pouring, rather than hand Toni a glass straight away, she picked them both up and slid into her seat on the couch next to Toni.

"Cheers. It's lovely to meet you," Melinda said, deliberately handing Toni her glass and keeping eye contact.

Toni wanted to panic. Relax! Be open to this, Toni inwardly chastised herself. You want to do this. That is why you called her.

They clinked their glasses.

Toni cleared her throat. "Look, I'm not really sure —"

"It's okay." Melinda rested a hand gently on Toni's

knee. "Let's just have a couple of drinks. Tell me a little about yourself. The rest will come."

Even that question was hard enough, under normal circumstances, Toni thought. She took a stalling sip of her drink.

"Okay, maybe start with what brings you to this lovely city of ours?" Melinda gestured at their surroundings.

"Work." Toni started talking about the investigation, nothing confidential, just in very broad strokes explaining she had been hired to find someone.

During that time the rugby match that was keeping the regular customers away must have ended, for The Sea Shanty started to fill up.

Halfway through the telling of her experience of South Africa so far, and two glasses of Prosecco later, a slender, dapper looking gentleman in dark trousers and a white shirt, with an expensive smile and even more expensive wrist watch stopped by at their table. "I apologise for the intrusion, I could not help noticing you two lovely ladies and I wondered if you might like another drink?"

"Oh, how marvellous!" Melinda said, clearly delighted. She raised her eyebrow slightly and smiled at the man. "Just perfect timing! Make that another bottle of Prosecco and maybe some nibbles on the side."

The man grabbed the empty ice-bucket and smiled, obviously thrilled at striking lucky.

"Oh, and please could you make us a reservation for two at the restaurant for seven-thirty pm," Melinda called after him, throwing Toni a wink.

The man stopped, and looked back at them. His expression morphed from delighted to that of a child who's just been told his dream Christmas gift had been given to him in error and was meant for someone else. "What do you mean, just the two of us? What about your friend?"

Melinda's smile did not waver, only a small sympathetic crease appeared on her brow.

Suddenly, full realisation dawned on the man. "I was offering you a drink. I'm not the waiter."

"Oh, I'm so sorry, I didn't realise." Melinda said, her tone sincere. "I'm a little unaccustomed to strangers interrupting my date," she glanced at Toni suggestively, "unless they're the waiter."

For a moment Toni thought the man was about to explode. Instead he clenched his jaw and banged the ice-bucket back down on the table. "You can get your own drinks."

"Thank you for the offer though," Melinda said to the man's back as he strode away.

Melinda raised her eyebrows at Toni and once the man was out of earshot, they burst out laughing.

———

By the time Alice awoke, the sun had gone down and the air had chilled. She tried to snooze a little more in Lisa's comforting arm. Lisa must have sensed she was awake because she stirred, kissed Alice on the forehead and gently extricated herself from Alice's limbs.

Alice pushed herself up onto her elbow.

Lisa picked up the soft tracksuit-bottoms and long-sleeve T-shirt from where they had landed outside the bathroom and put them and a fresh dry towel on the edge of the bed.

"You are welcome to have another warm shower and then put these on until we get you home."

At the thought of having to go home, having to part from Lisa, Alice felt a little bereft, but she pulled herself together and went to shower.

For some reason she felt a little self-conscious now, so she closed the door to the little bathroom, rationalising that she didn't want the shower to splash into the passage outside. The warmth of the water was a boon. Her body felt so relaxed and energised at the same time — a feeling of vitality and youthfulness she had not experienced in a very long time.

She thought back to the events of the day and what had just happened. Wow! Could that have been her first orgasm? If so, she suddenly understood what all the fuss was about. Out of nowhere, an inexplicable wave of fatigue, fear and loneliness hit her. She collapsed her head against the cold wall of the shower and allowed her tears to flow, diluted by the warm water pouring over her.

Ever conscious that self-pity was not a productive emotion and the fact that the water supply on the boat was limited, she didn't allow herself to indulge very long. She pulled herself together, dried off and got dressed quickly and went to find Lisa on the flybridge.

"Great, you've finished. I didn't want to start the engine and set off until you were out. It can be a bit choppy on the way back."

Alice was not sure how to be with Lisa, now. She couldn't help still feeling vulnerable and exposed. As a result, Lisa's business-as-usual tone cut deeper than it probably should have.

But when Lisa got up, to Alice's surprise, rather than get straight on with the business of heading back, she came over to Alice, put her arm around her and pulled her close. She kissed her softly on her forehead. "Are you okay?" she asked.

Lisa's warm body felt so comforting, so safe around her that Alice had to grit her teeth to stop herself from once again dissolving into a snivelling mess. Instead she nodded and hugged Lisa back.

"Good," Lisa said. "I'm sorry we had to get up so abruptly. It's getting late and it's easier to navigate back to the harbour while I can still see."

"I'm fine," Alice said nodding and tearing herself from Lisa's embrace. "Thank you for a lovely day."

"You want to have a go at steering?" Lisa asked guiding Alice towards the controls on the flybridge.

———

After the trip back to the harbour, Alice felt much better. It would have been hard to resist the rush of endorphins inspired by the thrill of steering the boat, while feeling Lisa's body, strong and warm, pressed up close behind her. And, once they were safely moored up, Lisa seemed a lot more relaxed too.

"I'm happy to take you home," Lisa said, "but you're welcome to stay the night on the boat with me, if you want."

Alice felt relieved that the earlier tension seemed unrelated to what had happened between them.

"That's very nice of you," Alice said. "But I'd better not. I should get home. I've not seen Gloria since Friday morning and I'd like to catch up with her, if possible, before the week starts and to find out how the boys are."

"Which boys?"

"Two of the boys at the Shelter are very sick."

"Oh, what Shelter?"

Suddenly Alice felt nervous. Had she said too much? Were people supposed to know about the Shelter? Surely it was not a secret. "Oh, it's very cool," she said. "Gloria and her boyfriend or partner, I'm not quite sure which, help out at a children's aid centre in one of the townships."

"That's great." Lisa was clearly impressed.

"You should come and see it sometime. Maybe we can take the children swimming. I believe Khayelitsha has a public swimming pool and its own beach," Alice said, trying to remember what Gloria had said. "Do you know about it?"

"That beach, Monwabisi, is in False Bay." Lisa shook her head looking serious. "It's one of the most dangerous beaches in the Cape."

This was news to Alice.

"Someone had the bright idea to build a wall in the shore-break to try to calm the cove and create a man-made tidal pool. Instead, they caused far more dangerous sea currents and more people die on that beach every year than anywhere else."

"Why doesn't someone do something about that?"

Lisa shrugged her shoulders. "Good question. We did try, as a lifeguard organisation. We needed to convince the authorities that the deaths were not due to people being unable to swim, but that there was a real danger. By that stage they decided that too much money had been sunk into the development and they could not possibly spend any more."

———

Lisa and Alice headed into their block of flats. "Um," Lisa said, looking suddenly shy and awkward, "I'm, ah," she hesitated again, "going into work at ten tomorrow, so if that is not too early or late, you'd be welcome to a lift."

"Thanks," Alice smiled, "that would be lovely."

As Lisa followed Alice up the staircase, there fell another awkward silence between them. Alice wondered what could be bothering Lisa.

"Listen, ah, about what happened —" Lisa eventually said, as they reached Gloria's front door.

Then it dawned on Alice. "Hey, it's okay. You don't have to say it."

Lisa looked surprised. "Say what?"

"You know, the 'about earlier, it was just a bit of fun' speech. I know you are seeing someone else." Alice thought back to the beach party, the suggestive looks Lisa got from a number of women, not to mention bumping into Lisa and the blonde kissing outside her door. Right then she was not sure how she felt about that, but she certainly wasn't going to be the new jealous girlfriend, no matter how good the orgasm was! She reached out and touched Lisa's hand. "Thank you. It was great. I still don't quite know what you did to me," she could not help giggling, "but it was mind-blowing. Don't get me wrong, I'd love to play again sometime, but don't worry, I'm not expecting a marriage proposal or anything."

Lisa raised her eyebrows and shook her head letting out a little laugh. "That's not what I was going to say at all."

Alice looked at her a long moment, trying to decide whether Lisa had just changed her tune.

Lisa took hold of Alice's hand. "What I was going to say is, about earlier...I hope you feel okay about it and," she took a small breath, "and as some of you Brits say, 'it really was a bit of all right'." Lisa winked and squeezed her hand, then she seemed to think better of her joke. "Seriously, it was awesome."

Alice felt touched by the sincerity in her voice. It seemed Lisa was going to make a habit of surprising her.

Alice nodded and gave Lisa's hand a little squeeze in return.

Lisa pulled Alice closer, wrapping her arms around her waist. "Thank you for an unforgettable day," she said and gave Alice a genuine, soft, almost languid, long kiss.

When she finally broke the kiss, Lisa smiled and without a word turned and started back towards her flat.

Was she mistaken or was there an extra little bounce in Lisa's normal swagger? Alice thought.

Half way towards her door, Lisa glanced back with a cheeky grin. "Hopefully, that leaves you wanting more."

Before Alice could respond, Lisa disappeared into her flat.

———

Three hours and a bottle of Prosecco later, Toni and Melinda still sat on the same couch watching the sunset over Camps Bay. They had been enjoying a relaxed but lively conversation that flitted from personal to politics, to nature conservation, to world affairs. Toni liked Melinda. She was a great listener and actually very easy to talk to. She obviously had a knack for making people feel at ease. Toni had not felt so relaxed with anyone other than Lizbeth in quite some time.

Half way through the third bottle, Toni found herself starting to tell Melinda about Lizbeth. She stopped, thinking better of it. There was a long moment's silence. Then Melinda put her hand on Toni's leg. Up to that point their interaction had been comfortable, with relaxed gestures and the occasional unnoticed touch, much as one is with old friends. This, however, felt different. Toni knew what it meant. She held her breath. The moment of decision.

Melinda leant forward and kissed Toni. Toni kissed her back. Her lips were soft and her breath smelled of the sweet scent of Prosecco.

By God! She needed to get laid, badly. Could she do this? Could she sleep with someone who wasn't Lizbeth? She felt the flame whimper. No, Toni, don't overthink this. Just go with it! You need this! But it was too late. The image of Lizbeth obliterated all the desire Toni felt for this woman in front of her in an instant.

Melinda gently rested her hand on the back of Toni's neck and tried to deepen the kiss.

Toni took hold of Melinda's other hand that was now making its way up her thigh and she slowly and firmly pulled away from the kiss. "I'm sorry," she said in a soft whisper.

Melinda sat back enough to meet Toni's gaze. "Why?"

Toni shook her head, not knowing how to explain.

"You know that the business side has already been dealt with, courtesy of your patron."

It had not even occurred to her up to that point that Olya would have paid for her, but Toni nodded.

"Then what is it?" Melinda looked confused and, if Toni wasn't mistaken, even a little bit hurt. "Is it me? Am I not your type?"

Toni scoffed at the irony and shook her head. "You are so my type, that is probably half the problem."

Melinda just sat and waited for Toni to continue.

"I can't, I was brought up in Croydon," Toni quoted,

remembering how she and Lizbeth had ridiculed that line in one of their favourite TV series.

Melinda frowned.

Toni shook her head and waved the idea away. "Don't worry about it."

"Believe me, you are my type." Toni said more seriously this time. "I really like you. I've had a lovely afternoon getting to know you." Toni grabbed her drink and drained her glass with a gulp. "That is perhaps the problem. Maybe we should have just got straight to business from the off."

Melinda still didn't speak.

"I'm probably silly, but it will feel too personal, like I'm cheating or something."

"Cheating?"

"Yes, I will feel guilty if I think about Lizbeth when I'm, you know, with you."

A little chuckle slipped out of Melinda's mouth before she realised Toni was being one hundred per cent truthful. Then she sighed and nodded. "I won't spoil the illusion and remind you that that is what I'm paid, very handsomely, for." She looked at Toni, searching.

Toni held her gaze.

Finally, Melinda nodded, picked up her handbag and took out a small note pad. "This is a great pity. I like you. And we could have had a wonderful night together," she said as she scribbled something on the pad and then ripped off the sheet of paper and handed it to Toni. "If you change your mind, you have my number."

Toni looked at the piece of paper. It was an address, not a telephone number. "What is this?"

"It is probably more what you are looking for." Melinda pulled the strap of her handbag over her shoulder. "It runs every third and last Saturday of the month, if you are still around. Just say Melinda sent you and they will take care of you."

Melinda got up. Toni followed suit. Melinda leant in and gave Toni a long soft kiss on her cheek. "Maybe see you again?"

Toni did not want the evening to end. Melinda was lovely and she was having such a nice time, but she was aware that Melinda was professional and if she was not going to do what she had come here to do, this was probably for the best. She nodded. Melinda squeezed her shoulder and gave her a last warm smile. Then she left.

TEN

Alice awoke early with a sense of euphoria and energy bubbling inside her. She felt alive. She remembered the exquisite events of the previous day with Lisa, and squirmed inwardly with delight. Between that, her new job and doing something worthwhile, helping Gloria, Alice felt as if she was finally starting to live her new life, starting to become master of her own destiny — this was exactly what she had hoped to do.

Thinking of Gloria... She still hadn't heard a word from her. She hadn't been home since Friday. Lekan hadn't shown up at the flat either and she was starting to get very worried.

Lisa dropped her off in Camps Bay at 10.30 am, which meant she had an hour and a half to kill. The last thing she wanted was to spend any more time at The Sea Shanty than she absolutely needed to.

As she strolled along the main road, she passed a hairdresser. Inside she saw a young woman sitting in a chair

189

facing the mirror nearest the window. Her hair had been dyed blue. A young man in shorts and a rather flamboyant, colourful cotton shirt was giving her a really funky looking, asymmetrical haircut with a shaved side, not unlike Lucy's. Alice watched for a few minutes and then, going along with the euphoric recklessness that she'd woken up with, she decided it was time. It was time to celebrate the new positive changes in her life and the new person she was becoming.

An hour later she stepped out of the hairdresser. Her long, straight, blond hair had been transformed into a short, fiery red crop with shaved sides. She could not quite bring herself to embrace anything as wild as an asymmetrical style just yet. Even that might come in time, she thought.

———

Alice got home just after 7 pm. There was still no sign of Gloria or Lekan. She had done a small shop on her way home, buying some soup and a fresh loaf of bread for them.

She had just put her pot of soup on the stove when Gloria walked in.

"Oh, my goodness, hello! You are just in time for soup. Would you like some?" Alice asked.

Gloria shook her head. She looked exhausted.

"Where have you been?" Alice asked, cautious not to sound like she was prying. "Are you okay?"

Gloria nodded, but did not say much. She proceeded to put down her bag and take off her coat.

"Can I put the kettle on for you?" Alice persisted.

Gloria nodded again and sat down on a stool at the kitchen counter.

"Alice, we really need your help with a food collection

and we need it this week," Gloria said in a serious voice, rubbing her eyes.

Alice looked at her, almost unable to believe what she heard. "Gloria I'm sorry. As I said before, I'm not willing to get involved in that. I'll turn a blind eye and help you with the English lessons, but I'm not doing that." Alice returned to stirring the pot. "And even if I did agree to help you, which I haven't done, I'd have to get the boss to trust me a bit more to allow me anywhere near the stock, let alone give me enough space and opportunity to sneak the stock out." Alice banged the ladle on the side of the pot. "I haven't even cashed up on my own yet."

"Alice, it can't wait," Gloria said, her tone serious, almost reprimanding, causing Alice to turn back from the cooker and study Gloria, who was now standing at the counter staring at Alice.

"Gloria, I can't, I need more time to settle in —"

The front door opened and Lekan came in.

"And, where have you been?" Gloria demanded from Lekan. "Why are you so late? Where were you?"

Alice poured her soup into a cup, grabbed a slice of bread, sat down at the counter opposite Gloria and started to eat.

Lekan sighed and took a deep breath. "Trevor's been taken into custody."

Alice noticed he also looked exhausted. She wondered what had happened to them in the last few days.

Gloria's voice hitched up an octave. "For what?"

"Shoplifting and vandalism," Lekan said, going to pour himself a drink of water.

Gloria smacked the table with a flat hand making both Alice and Lekan jump. "Why did you let that boy out of your sight? You knew he was going to get in trouble," she shouted at Lekan.

Alice had never seen Gloria this fraught before.

"We can't do everything, be everywhere and watch them all the time." Lekan said wearily. "There are only two of us."

"As for you." Gloria pointed at Alice. "You sitting there in your nice smart clothes, with your funky new haircut, feasting on a nice warm meal. There are thousands of innocent children going to bed starving tonight. And your priority is to 'settle in'." Gloria banged the counter-top hard with the side of her fist once more, before she stormed off into her bedroom and slammed the door.

For a long moment Alice and Lekan remained in silence staring at the closed door.

"What's with her?" Alice asked softly, once she had recovered.

Lekan shook his head and refilled his glass of water. "Kofi and Kwame died last night."

"Oh God!" Alice said. "Were you there?"

"No, I was at the police station." Lekan shook his head. "One of our main food sources fell through this weekend too. She feels she has failed the children. She's worried because we barely have enough food left to feed the little ones until the end of the week." He rinsed his glass and put it on the drying rack. He started to cut himself a large slice of Alice's fresh loaf. He must have felt Alice's eyes watching him. He paused for a moment. "Is it okay?" he asked. Alice nodded and he continued. Once cut, he stuffed big chunks of the bread into his mouth.

Poor Gloria, Alice thought, to have gone through that this weekend, and that while she was out swanning around on a beautiful beach, getting laid and having a lovely time.

And those poor children! Suddenly, Alice was no longer hungry. She stared into her soup. "Okay, I'll do it," she said.

"Wha—," he said with his mouth full.

"Tell, Gloria I'll do it."

Lekan nodded and continued to cut another thick slice of bread.

Wednesday - 15 November, SA

During the following couple of days, Alice focussed on preparing for 'the snatch', as Lekan called it. She had managed to secure a couple of the commercial bins outside behind the restaurant, in the little service yard. Whenever she had any free time and was pretty sure no one would be looking, she slipped into the supply room to sort through and identify as many out-of-date products as she could. These she either retired from the stock control system herself or asked one of the other staff to do so. When no one was looking she smuggled these products out into the bins and stored them under black bags filled with non-perishable waste, ready for Lekan and Gloria to collect on Wednesday evening after her late shift, when she hoped to be left alone to cash up and close up shop.

Alice thought that the hardest and most critical part of the plan would be to persuade Gerry that she needed no help and was competent cashing up on her own.

When it finally came to it, Alice simply declined Lucy's help and even Gerry seemed fine with Alice locking up on her own. That was almost too easy, thought Alice. Gerry probably wanted to avoid another awkward situation with her after what had happened the last time she and Gerry locked up alone together, especially since she suspected that Gerry assumed her and Lisa were now an item and hence all other bets were off. She could imagine Gerry would try to avoid any further bruising to her ego at all cost.

———

Come Wednesday, Alice felt much more on edge. The restaurant was quite busy, so at least the day and evening seemed to pass fairly quickly. The downside was that cashing up would probably take longer, but she figured that as long as the doors closed on time, at 11.30 pm, she could take all the time she needed to finish up, after Lekan and Gloria had been and gone.

At 11.15 pm Alice started circling. She had instructed a couple of the floor staff to start moving furniture and clearing and cleaning tables to give the last stragglers the clear message that it was time to settle up. Putting chairs on tables usually gave even the most thick-skinned customers the feeling that it was time to go.

As usual, this tactic worked like a dream. The restaurant was cleared, the doors shut and the floor staff sent on their way by 11.45 pm. So far so good, she thought.

Now it was a question of waiting for Lekan to call and say he was outside. She had given him the office phone number since Gerry didn't allow any staff to have mobile phones on the floor while on duty and she knew she would more than likely be in Gerry's office, cashing up.

At 11.55 pm Alice heard a knock at the service door in the kitchen. She cursed under her breath, wondering which of the floor staff had forgotten what. She resolved to get rid of them as quickly as possible. As she reached the door, she heard a key being slotted into the keyhole.

That could only mean one thing — Gerry.

Shit!

Alice plastered a smile on her face and greeted Gerry with what she hoped sounded like surprise and delight. "Hey, so glad it's just you!"

"Ah, yes. I, ah, forgot my jacket," Gerry said and nodded in the direction of the office. Alice stepped aside and allowed her to lead the way.

"Did everything go okay tonight?" Gerry asked over her shoulder.

"Yes, pretty much. Mitch and his boys," she said, referring to one of the regulars and his gang, "got a bit rowdy, as usual, but they left reasonably early. Other than that, I think business was really good tonight and we got some pretty decent takings. I'm just in the process of counting."

Once in the office, Gerry grabbed the bright yellow jacket that hung on the coat stand in the far corner. Curious, Alice thought. She had never seen Gerry wear that jacket and she was pretty sure it had hung in that same place, untouched, since the day she started working at The Sea Shanty.

"That's great news," Gerry said. "I have a few minutes. I can help you cash up quickly." Gerry moved in behind her desk.

Inside, Alice's world crushed in on her. Gloria and Lekan would be arriving any minute.

Without warning, the shrill ring of the office phone pierced the stagnant air in the office. Gerry reached for the receiver before Alice could stretch for it.

"The Sea Shanty," Gerry said.

Alice could hear Gloria's voice on the other end of the line. Then Gerry passed her the receiver. "It's for you." If Gerry was surprised that Alice was receiving a personal call in the office at that hour, she didn't let on.

"It's probably my lift," Alice said, praying that Gloria had not said anything different. Alice could hardly hear anything on the phone because her blood was pumping so loudly in her ears. "Hi," she said, deliberately not turning away from Gerry. "Oh, sorry I'm not quite ready yet. It's probably going to be too late for you tonight."

"Is there a problem?" asked Gloria, seriously.

"Yes, so let's abort the plan for tonight and I'll make my own way home when I'm done here."

Alice could hear Lekan saying something in the background.

"Are you absolutely sure we can't come around later?" Gloria pushed.

"No, it's okay. Really sorry. Thank you."

"Okay, if you're sure." Gloria rang off. A sinking feeling settled in Alice's stomach. She knew Gloria and Lekan would both be very pissed off. She had let them down. Then it dawned on her. There was an additional bigger problem. The stuff in the bin had to go before someone found it. But there was nothing she could do about that now. It would have to wait. She needed to finish cashing up and to convince Gerry that she was competent and professional enough to manage entirely on her own next time.

Luckily, Gerry did not look up from what she was doing. It seemed her new approach to Alice meant making as little eye contact as possible. Alice was relieved. Right now, she couldn't deal with Gerry's personal complications as well.

———

When Alice arrived home later that night, the atmosphere could've been cut with a knife.

"I'm really, really sorry about tonight. It was not my fault. It was my first night cashing up on my own and I should've known Gerry would come and check up on me. I know you really need that food. There was no way I could get rid of her. I'm really, really sorry!"

"We understand." Lekan sighed. "It's not your fault. No one is cross with you. It's just, as you know, we are getting desperate."

Gloria sat at the counter holding but not drinking a cup of tea. She seemed quite defeated with no sign of any of that anger and fight she had exhibited the other night. This surprised Alice. She expected Gloria to be furious. Alice was not sure which reaction unsettled her more.

"We took too many chances tonight." Lekan said, giving Gloria a meaningful look. "We came too close to getting caught. And that we can't afford! If something happens to us there will be no one to look out for those children."

"I'm really sorry I let you down". Alice did not know what else to say.

Finally, Gloria simply nodded. "Get some sleep. We'll talk more tomorrow." She picked up her cup of tea and headed towards her bedroom. Lekan nodded a good night at Alice and followed her, leaving Alice on her own.

Alice felt terrible. There was no way she would sleep now. She needed to get out. It was very late. There was nowhere to go, or was there? She could only think of one other person who might still be up.

———

Alice said a small prayer as she tapped softly on Lisa's door. She didn't want to wake her if she was already asleep. Then, she heard what sounded like giggles coming from the other side of the door and she instantly regretted her decision.

After a few long moments the bolt slid back and Lisa, dressed in nothing but a large grin and a long shirt and carrying a tin of spray cream, opened the door.

"Oh, hi," Lisa said, surprised.

"Who is it," a voice called from behind her.

"It's okay," Lisa called back. Then, she drew the door closer to her side and returned her attention back to Alice. "You okay?" Her brow furrowed as she realised that Alice was not in a good way.

"Oh God! I'm so sorry. I shouldn't have come. I did not know you'd... ah... have guests. It's okay." Alice turned to head back to Gloria's flat.

"Hey, wait!" Lisa grabbed Alice's arm. "Not so fast." She gently pulled Alice back to face her. "What's up?"

Hearing the concern in Lisa's voice was enough to open the floodgates. Tears started streaming down Alice's cheeks. Lisa pulled her closer, held her until her sobs subsided a little.

"Come in," Lisa said, softly.

"No, I don't want to ruin your evening."

Lisa squeezed her hand. "Please come."

Alice allowed herself to be led into Lisa's flat and made to sit on the couch. The main living area in the flat was empty. Alice gathered Lisa's guest she had heard earlier was in the only other room, the bedroom.

Lisa grabbed a box of tissues from the bookshelf and a throw from the armrest. She handed Alice the box and tucked the throw around Alice's shoulders. "Now you stay there. Don't move. I'll be back in five minutes and I will make you my absolutely irresistible speciality hot chocolate with extra cream and mini-marshmallows, and you can tell me all about it if you want, or not. Okay?"

Alice nodded and obediently wiped the tears from her face with a tissue.

Lisa disappeared into the bedroom, closing the door behind her. Alice couldn't hear what was being said but she gathered from the tone of muffled voices that the other person was not happy. Five minutes later the door swung open and a tall, long haired brunette stormed out, high heels in hand, still doing up her blouse.

Lisa followed her out. "Alice this is Yvonne. Yvonne, meet Alice."

Yvonne scowled at Alice. "Pleasure is all yours tonight, it seems," she said and stomped out the front door.

Lisa closed the front door quietly in her wake. "Sorry about that," Lisa said, turning her attention back to Alice.

"No, I'm sorry," Alice said. "I shouldn't have come. I interrupted your evening."

"It's okay. Don't mind Vonney. She'll get over it and I'll make it up to her. We've all had moments when we need someone and believe me it's not always at the perfect time." Lisa headed round the counter that formed the divider between the minimalist sitting room and the super white kitchen. "Right, one extra super-duper, irresistible hot chocolate coming up."

Ten minutes later, Lisa brought over the largest mug of sickeningly sweet but delicious hot chocolate with extra-small marshmallows and a large, long-stemmed teaspoon with which to eat it. She sat next to Alice on the couch and just watched her tuck in. When Alice finally put the empty mug down, she leant into Lisa and Lisa wrapped her arms around her.

"Feel better?"

Alice nodded.

"Do you want to talk about it?"

Alice shook her head.

"Okay," Lisa hugged her tighter.

Alice pulled out of the hug but then leant in and kissed Lisa gently at first, then more passionately. After a few minutes, Lisa got up and pulled Alice with her to the bedroom where she wordlessly made love to her until Alice fell asleep in her arms, spent and exhausted.

ELEVEN

The next morning Alice woke up still curled in Lisa's arm. Lisa was lying on her back, fast asleep. Alice watched and listened to her slow breathing. She looked beautiful, so innocent, so unlike the wild woman who came to the fore in the midst of passion. Lisa had a carefree confidence about her that Alice associated more with young men than with other women her own age. She admired that. Even Lisa's body was boyish with its toned muscles and androgynous shape, probably from all the physical exercise and swimming. She gently lifted the duvet and found herself a few inches away from Lisa's small right breast. She pushed the covers lower. Then she leant in and kissed the dark, sleepy nipple. When it slowly came erect, she took it into her mouth and sucked at it gently, occasionally flicking it with her tongue. When this still did nothing to rouse the sleeping Lisa, Alice had a new idea. She pushed the covers even further down and softly started to stroke and tickle Lisa's torso, covering as much of her soft skin as possible with almost imperceptibly light caresses. Alice was not disappointed. Very soon, Lisa's whole body erupted in goose bumps and she moaned. Alice persisted, eventually allowing her fingers to drift down to Lisa's neatly trimmed dark brown curls. She tickled Lisa's lower belly, hips and upper thighs, before she returned to dip between her legs, slipping her fingers between soft, silky and very wet lips.

When she glanced up at Lisa's face, she was happy to find that even though Lisa's eyes were still closed, a wide grin crinkled the corners of her eyes.

"I've not slept with Medusa, you know," Lisa said in a croaky, sleepy voice.

"What?" Alice said. "You haven't even opened your eyes, how can you comment on my bed hair?"

"No, no. Medusa. You know? The woman who turned everyone to stone."

"Ah," Alice smiled. "That's true. I can confirm you are not made of stone." She continued to run her fingers along Lisa's soft centre causing Lisa's hips to buck ever so slightly.

Alice grinned inwardly. She was pleased to be having the desired effect. She had been nervous to touch Lisa or initiate any lovemaking herself before this, for fear of not quite knowing what to do.

Lisa moaned softly and spread her legs.

Feeling encouraged, Alice carefully slipped a finger inside and Lisa moaned again, then bucked her hips forward once more. Slowly, Alice began to slide her finger in and out of Lisa, mimicking the movements she had made in Alice to such glorious effect the previous evening.

"Put your thumb up so that it touches my clit," Lisa said softly.

Alice did as she was told.

Lisa moaned, grabbed the pillow with her free hand and squeezed it.

Within a few minutes Lisa's breathing escalated to a moderate pant. Then her body stiffened and she arched and let out a low grunt as she came, drenching Alice's hand in a fresh wave of moisture. In that moment Alice felt simultaneously overwhelmed and supremely powerful — to be able to have such an effect, to give such pleasure to another human being. It felt to her like magic.

Alice started to withdraw.

"Stay." Lisa's hand rested on Alice's forearm.

Alice leant forward and rested her head on Lisa's chest and revelled in the sound of her rapid heartbeats.

I did this, she thought with pride. But it was not enough by far. For the first time ever, she wanted to find out more, to learn how to be a better lover, to give this woman every kind of pleasure possible.

"Come here maestro" Lisa said, pulling Alice up towards her.

When Alice looked up, she almost fell into the deep, dark brown eyes looking down at her.

Lisa kissed her deeply.

Then Alice finally collapsed on Lisa's shoulder.

"Lees, can I ask you something?"

"Hmm," Lisa murmured, pulling Alice tighter into her.

"Are there any lesbian sex clubs in town?"

Lisa smiled; her eyes having closed again. "Ouch. You suggesting I have been a pillow princess?"

Alice laughed. "No, not at all." If anything, the opposite was true. "I want to see more, learn more. I want to experience more. I'm afraid it's your fault. You have given me a taste and I think it would be good to explore a bit. I want to be a good lover."

"You are a brilliant lover," Lisa said, rolling into Alice and kissing her gently on her nose.

"No, I'm being serious."

Lisa opened her eyes to look at Alice. After some thought, she rolled onto her back and rubbed her eyes. "Ah, let me think. Sure, there is a sex club. I don't know what it's like these days, since I haven't been in a while, but I'll write down the address for you. But first," she abruptly rolled back towards Alice, pushing her over onto her back and coming to rest on top of her, "I have some unfinished business to attend to." She grinned fiendishly and started to crawl, kissing her way down Alice's body."

"No," Alice giggled and pulled Lisa back up so she could look her in the eye. "I don't want to go on my own. You'll have to come with me."

"You're right." Lisa smiled. "You'll need a bodyguard, huh?"

Alice nodded.

"Okay, I'll find out when the next one is."

Lisa started to crawl back down Alice's body.

Alice stopped her again.

"I'm afraid I need to get up."

"But it's your day off."

"I know, but I need to help out at the Shelter."

Lisa rolled off of her. "That's a bummer. I have the day off too."

Alice sat up and started to look for her clothes. Then she had an idea. "Why don't you come too, if you have nothing better to do?"

Lisa looked dubious.

"Seriously, if you come, we can take the children to the swimming pool and you can teach the little ones to swim." Alice beamed with excitement.

"Gloria would not want that."

"No, she'd be delighted. They need help. They'd love it if we kept the children busy and out of trouble for the day. And the children would love it too, I'm sure of it."

Lisa considered it.

"Besides, it'll give me a little extra time to frolic with you," Alice teased.

"Okay," Lisa finally said as she rolled on her side, propping up her head with her hand. "But you have to clear it with Gloria first."

"Great!" Alice jumped out of bed. She picked up Lisa's T-shirt from the floor and chucked it at her face. "But in case she says yes, you'd better get dressed. We need to be ready to leave in twenty minutes."

———

Within minutes of their arrival at the Shelter, Masika appeared and made a beeline for Alice. Alice bent down and picked up the unbelievably light little girl who was crawling into her heart faster than she could crawl into her arms.

Inside the tent, the wake for Kofi and Kwame had been held and the bodies removed. Alice quickly showed Lisa around but was very respectful of not intruding on the children. There was a very sad and solemn air about the place. No one spoke much. A few of the girls in the kitchen were singing a very sad song that brought a lump to everyone's throat.

Alice and Lisa helped Gloria change the sheets and clean the part of the infirmary where the two boys had been sleeping.

About midday, Lekan brought the minivan round and

he and Gloria corralled most of the children into it. A few of the older girls stayed behind to continue making the sparse meal for the day.

The swimming pool was not that far from the Shelter and Lekan said he would normally make the children walk but they had been through so much in the last few days. Besides, it was easier to keep track of such a large bunch in the minivan.

Lekan parked the minivan on Walter Sisulu Drive. When she came into Khayelitsha that first day with Gloria, Alice had not quite realised how vast and open the Cape Flats were. The sense of space, with its large bare sky, uncluttered by high rise buildings or even tall trees, was almost vertigo inducing. So much so, in the distance, over fifteen miles away, Alice could see the familiar silhouette of the sleeping monkey that formed the view of Table Mountain from there.

Thirteen children, ranging from seven to fourteen, piled out of the minivan and followed Lekan across the road with Alice and Lisa bringing up the rear, through the gate in the eight-foot fence to the entrance of the municipal swimming pool building. The building was nothing more than a simple large concrete and wood ablution block, ladies and gents divided in the middle by a short open passage.

As they arrived at the turnstile entrance, Lekan greeted the woman in the ticket booth with great smiles and much flirting. They spoke in their language so Alice was unable to understand, but it soon became apparent that their conversation included a lengthy altercation about Lisa and Alice. Eventually the woman got up, opened the side gate and waved Lekan, the children and, somewhat reluctantly Lisa and Alice, through into the pool area without requesting payment. Lekan thanked her with a kiss to her cheek and a suggestive pat on her bottom that made her face light up. She waved a reprimanding finger at him while trying not to look very pleased, before she returned to her place inside the ticket booth.

On the other side of the ablution block was a large, plain, rectangular Olympic-sized swimming pool and one smaller, curvy-shaped kiddies' pool. The surroundings, Alice could only describe as green concrete — plain, unadorned, cheap pavement and what would probably pass for grass during the rainy season but was now, as a result of the mid-November heat-wave, barely more than a red dusty expanse.

A wall of sound greeted them, as both pools teemed with bodies of all shapes and sizes in various outfits, ranging from greying underwear to bright bikinis and surf shorts. The few surviving patches of thinning lawn were almost completely covered with people.

Lekan led them to a small clearing on one side near the outdoor shower that stood on the corner between the Olympic pool and the kiddies' pool. He explained that from there they could keep an eye on the little ones in the kiddies' pool and allow the older children to have lessons with Lisa in the Olympic pool.

Alice had come prepared, wearing the swimsuit she had bought in Camps Bay under her shorts and T-shirt. Lisa disappeared into the ablution-block and came out a few minutes later in a pair of surf-shorts and a bright red rash-vest that Alice recognised as her lifeguard outfit. By that stage the children had stripped off to their underwear and Lekan was having a hard time herding them on dry land until Lisa was ready to take over.

Alice took four of the smaller ones, including Masika, to the kiddies' pool for a wade. The water was relatively warm but refreshing enough in the heat. Masika would not leave her side but the other little ones jumped and giggled and played very happily a few feet in front of her.

While she kept an eye on them, her eyes could not help wandering over to the other pool where Lisa was teaching seven of the older children effortless floating and correct breathing techniques that involved a lot of bubble blowing and laughter. Lisa was very gentle but firm with them, in a way that gave them confidence in her authority but allowed them to trust her tenderness. When Lisa swam a few proper crawl strokes to demonstrate, Alice was mesmerised to see how elegantly and effortlessly she glided through the water. Even when she mucked around with one of the oldest boys, swimming butterfly for him, she made it look like she was flying. She looked like she had been born there, equally at home on land and in the sea.

Everyone, including the two children sitting on the side with Lekan because they preferred not to swim, seemed to be having a lovely time in the sun. For a few brief hours the tragedy that had clouded their lives for the past few days was forgotten. Even Lekan had undressed to his boxer shorts and cooled off a few times under the cold outdoor shower. Alice wondered whether he could swim. She decided to refrain from putting him on the spot by asking.

Alice had no intention of actually swimming herself, but Masika would not let her go. Eventually, once the other three little ones had tired and had got out to go dry off, Alice took Masika deeper into the pool, holding her arms and pulling her through the water in a circle around her, eliciting shrieks and squeals of joy from the little girl.

Finally, towards the late afternoon, Lekan got up and started to motion for the children to get out, gather round and get dry. He handed out five towels and the children shared them to dry off.

Back at the Shelter, all the children gathered together in the dining compartment of the tent, chatting and laughing and sharing stories of their day's adventures, while Alice helped Gloria and the older girls serve up the main meal of putu pap and giblets from a large cast iron cauldron. Alice had noticed that neither Gloria nor Lekan took any food for themselves, so she and Lisa followed suit. When little Masika brought over a small, grimy handful of pap for her, she accepted it gracefully and pretended to feast on it until dinnertime was over.

After dinner, Masika disappeared, only to return a few minutes later with their copy of "The Lion the Witch and the Wardrobe", which she handed to Alice. Gloria saw this, nodded and urged her to go and read to them in the main sleeping area while she and Lekan got on with clearing away the dishes and tidying for the night.

Soon Lisa and the children were gathered in a relaxed circle, sprawled around Alice where she was sitting, reading to them. She was very conscious of Lisa's eyes on her the whole time. When it got too dark for her to see the pages in the natural light, Lisa got up and came to sit next to her, holding up the torch on her mobile phone so Alice could see better. For the first time in a long while, Alice felt like she was part of one big happy family.

Friday - 17 November, SA

Lisa had the morning off. Alice had left early for her shift at The Sea Shanty and then she was going to the Shelter to help out with the kids. Alice had been spending most of her free time there, teaching the children English. This gave

Lisa some time on her own to do some of the little repairs to Noreen that she had been putting off in favour of spending all possible free time with Alice.

But first, Lisa was just about to head out on her run from the harbour, along the beach and then up over Chapmans Peak when her phone rang.

"Hi, Stud," said the familiar, gravelly voice.

Lisa rolled her eyes. "Hey, Gerry," Lisa said, keeping her voice light. "What can I do for you?"

"Oh, don't worry, nothing you haven't done to me already."

Lisa cringed inwardly, knowing Gerry was referring to the one drunken night they'd had together. They'd both agreed afterwards that it had been a big mistake, but Gerry seemed to relish reminding Lisa about it at every opportunity. "All jokes aside, I thought you might want to know, a snoop has been around here asking questions about your new little girlfriend."

"Who?"

"Who do you think?"

"She's not —" Lisa stopped herself. "A snoop? You mean a cop? Or someone from immigration?" Lisa asked quickly.

"Lucky for you, she seemed a little more casual than that."

"She?"

"Yeah, a stunner at that."

"Gerry, seriously! Now's not the time," Lisa said. "Tell me."

"Okay, okay. No need to get snarky. I'm doing you a favour here. I called, didn't I?"

Lisa nodded. "Yes, you did," she said, trying to remain patient. Now was not the time to give Gerry reason to digress.

"Anyway, I think more of a peeper rather than anything too official, thankfully, for your sakes. Going by her accent, also not local."

"From where?"

"Sounds a bit like your Alice."

"From England?"

"I think so. I'm not an expert, but judging by the ivory complexion and pommy accent, she probably does come from that miserable place too."

"What did she want?"

"She had a photo of your little girlfriend, but clearly an early-days one, when she still looked like the prissy innocent she was, before she met you."

"Gerry –"

"Rumour has it she's been asking around everywhere for information about your Alice."

"Did she say why she was looking for her?"

"No."

"When was she there?"

"Yesterday. Luckily it was your Alice's weekend day off."

"Did you tell her anything?"

There was a pause. Lisa could hear Gerry take a drag on her vape. "Nah, she wasn't asking me so I didn't volunteer — skills from a life serving behind bars, so to speak." Gerry laughed at her own joke.

Lisa breathed a sigh of relief. "Thanks, Gerry."

"I wouldn't thank me yet, Stud. The Bay is a small place and this chick seems pretty switched on."

"Have you told Alice?"

"No, I didn't want to spook her. I thought I'd let you do that."

"Okay. Thanks for letting me know."

"Sure," Gerry said. "You owe me one."

Lisa rang off. Her brow furrowed. What could a P.I. want with Alice? Alice had told her the story of how she left her husband and the fact that she was in the country illegally. They had been thinking of ways to make her legal. That seemed a tall order. They could not even do the unthinkable and marry until Alice got a divorce. Even then it was touch and go that she'd be able to get a work visa. Her best bet would have been to find an employer to sponsor her. The problem was that most employers wouldn't take her on in the first place because she was already illegal.

If she told Alice that a snoop was on her heels, she would probably panic and do something rash. Lisa decided to keep the information to herself for the moment.

Saturday - 18 November, SA

Toni had spent almost every minute since her morning at the MOD following up on the potential sighting of Alice in the Camps Bay area. Unfortunately, every lead seemed to turn up empty. In the end she resorted to going door to door to every business, shop and restaurant showing Alice's photograph and asking if anyone had seen her, to no avail. It felt like Alice had mysteriously evaporated the day she walked out of the MOD. At first Toni didn't want to believe that it was possible for anyone to disappear like that without a trace, but eventually she had to face the facts. Alice had taken whatever resources she had and escaped deep into Africa. At least that is what Toni would have done if she didn't want to be found.

She was still following up on one or two more ideas she had, but it was time to contact Dr Magnus McCroy and prepare him for the bad news. This was not a task she relished and when she rang and was diverted to his voicemail her heart sank. She had hoped to deliver the bad news quickly and get it over with.

"Dr McCroy, it is Toni. Please give me a call back when you get this," she said into the recording. She didn't think it was professional to deliver the bad news via a message.

———

The address Melinda had given her led Toni to a palatial mansion imprisoned behind electric wires and high walls, on a steep road in Bishopscourt, an affluent suburb nestled just below the tree line, on the eastern side of Table Mountain.

Toni parked her hire car in gear to make sure it did not roll back down the sheer slope. The gradient was so steep she almost had to hoist herself out of the driver's seat.

She made her way to the large gated property. It was already dark and that part of the suburb didn't have many street lights. As she neared the security entrance spotlights sprang into action making her wince and she put her hand up to shade her eyes. She continued slowly towards the intercom built into the side of the gate.

She pressed the button. A thick Afrikaans accent greeted her through the intercom.

"Hi, I'm a guest of Melinda." Toni felt stupid as the words left her mouth. This was so far outside of her comfort zone, but she was there now, so she might as well push along.

The gates swung open with a mechanical whirr.

As soon as Toni stepped through the gate, she was accosted by two buff bodyguards. Refreshingly, one was female. The other was straining against the force of a rather hungry looking Rottweiler that was sizing Toni up for starters.

"Welcome," the woman said and pressed a remote control that made the gate close noisily behind them. "It's that way," she added and nodded in the direction of the one large door at the end of the drive.

Toni banged the large leopard-head knocker once against the heavy mahogany door. A few brief seconds later the door opened and a petite woman in a red silk dress showed her inside and offered to take her jacket. Toni declined, not sure if she was going to stay very long.

As Toni advanced further into the lobby she was greeted by a tall woman in a black tuxedo, who ushered her through large double doors into a spacious and richly furnished Victorian styled ballroom, complete with large crystal chandeliers, polished wooden floors, large gold and burgundy draped windows and matching wing-backed Victorian chairs, mini sofas and chaises longues.

Toni suddenly realised that, compared to the large crowd of people in ball gowns and tuxedos animatedly chatting, laughing and sipping champagne out of sleek crystal flutes, she was rather underdressed in her jeans, T-shirt and leather jacket. She was about to rethink her decision to come when a beautiful redhead in a very tight black dress and exceedingly high heels turned and smiled at her.

"That way," the redhead said, pointing further into another room. It was only as she stepped aside that Toni noticed the large black man dressed in nothing but a chain, collar and body oil, kneeling quietly at her side like a well-trained guard-dog.

The second room was darker and also packed with people, except they were all in various states of undress,

Toni thought initially, until she realised they were all in carefully crafted suggestive outfits ranging from classic bondage to steampunk.

Above the heads of the crowd, she noticed the top of four wrought iron posts with mauve silk drapes slung between them. This formed the top of a beautiful four poster bed which dominated the space at the top end of the room. She tried to see if anyone was on it but the crowds were too thick. She had to get closer. With her heart rate picking up as she moved forward, Toni gently but assertively navigated her way to the front, through the crowd who were jostling for positions, like fans at a music gig.

On the bed, on a maroon silk sheet, lay a naked woman. Her arms and legs were loosely tied to the four posts of the bed with maroon silk ties. Her hair was red, but Toni couldn't see her face as she was blindfolded with a golden silk scarf.

Standing on the far side, at the top end of the bed, was a dark-skinned woman in a long chiffon see-through gown, and partly see-through veil. By her demeanour and her confident movements, Toni gathered she was a dominatrix. She held a large colourful peacock feather, like a magician's wand, gently caressing the supplicant's body with it. The feather shimmered in the light as it moved. The effect of the feathery touches on the woman's body had caused the woman's nipples to pebble and periodically she arched her back in an attempt to gain more contact with the offending article.

When the dominatrix's eye met Toni's from across the bed, the crowd seemed to part between them and, as if she could sense fresh blood, she sashayed her way around the bed directly towards Toni. Without a word she held out the hollow shaft end of the feather towards Toni. Toni tried to protest but the crowd around her started to murmur and then to chant "save her, save her, save her." In order to avoid the potential riot, which Toni suspected a refusal would cause, she took the feather and stepped up to the bed.

Tentatively, Toni reached out and touched the peacock feather's barbs to the supine woman's abdomen, stroking the area just below her belly button. The woman arched off the bed as if a surge of electricity had just coursed through her body. Encouraged and intrigued by this, Toni continued to trace a trail with the feather along the woman's abdomen. Each touch caused a similar contortion and moan to escape from her victim, and these resonated deep within Toni. It was hard not to envy the feather its intimacy with the woman's beautiful body. Toni allowed the feather to roam freely across her whole body, down along her legs and back up to her neck.

Toni could feel her own body react to the evocative scene before her. The entire situation, the sight of the unknown woman, tied, vulnerable and totally at her mercy, without any idea of who her sweet tormentor might be and what she was going to do next, and the crowd of onlookers egging her on, sparked a surge of arousal stronger than Toni could have thought possible. It all was a heady mixture of adrenaline, lust and power.

From where Toni stood at the foot of the bed, she could see the woman's wet centre, glistening with arousal. She allowed her eyes to drink in the exquisite sight, to caress the suggestive, small, but beautiful black dragonfly tattoo that rested just inside the woman's hipbone. The crowd kept chanting around her. Finally, as if compelled, she knelt down on the bed next to the woman. She ran the fingertips of one hand up the inside of the woman's leg, past her knee towards her upper thigh. The woman moaned and thrust her hips up again. With that the crowd's chanting became more incessant. Toni knew what the woman wanted. Toni wanted it too — to give this vulnerable woman before her all the pleasure she could bear.

Instead, Toni bent down, and in a gesture she hoped would convey her heartfelt apology, she gently kissed the dragonfly tattoo causing the woman to gasp. Then she got up and handed the peacock feather back to the dominatrix who graciously accepted it.

Sunday - 19 November, SA

By Sunday afternoon, Dr McCroy had not returned Toni's call. She had thoroughly exhausted every lead or hope she had had of finding Alice. The only thing left was to enjoy the lovely African sunshine in the glorious setting of Camps Bay until it was time to go home. With that in mind, she decided to take herself off to the beach. She was not one to spend hours lying in the sun but she did enjoy a nice walk, especially when the mountains started turning red from the late afternoon sun.

The beach was quite busy with locals piling down to enjoy sundowners or a late swim in the sea. Toni made her way along the soft white sand towards the south end of the beach. Here a group of people gathered around the volleyball nets watching what seemed to be a locals' volleyball tournament. Toni stopped and watched for a while.

She was about to leave and continue on her walk when a distinctly British accent caught her attention. From where she was standing she could not see the source for all the heads and bodies in the way. Then finally the sea of volleyball supporters parted and she saw her. There, standing talking to a small group of women, was a woman with an undercut and bright red, dyed hair. Her looks and accent made her appear like a hippy chick from Camden and Toni was about to walk on, thinking just another Brit on holiday, when she heard the short mousey woman in the group call out her name.

"Ali, do you want a drink?"

The English woman shook her head, "No thanks, I can't keep up with you lot." Then she turned and continued to cheer for the volleyball team who had just scored an ace.

Ali? Could that be her? Toni watched her in amazement.

TWELVE

Over the following days, Alice and Lisa spent most of their free time helping out at the Shelter together. Slowly they were getting to know each other and the children better.

Simultaneously a deep, deep bond was developing between Alice and Masika. Everywhere that Alice went there Masika would be, either holding onto her arm or leg or waiting patiently within reach. In the evenings, Alice had to put Masika to bed and wait for her to fall asleep before she could leave.

After the long days at the Shelter, Lisa and Alice would go back to either Lisa's flat or her boat where they would talk, listen to music under the stars, make love or fall asleep in each other's arms. Alice loved the time they spent together.

All in all, her new life was really good.

Gloria was not floored for long by their initial failed attempt to collect supplies from The Sea Shanty and by the following Wednesday they planned and executed a perfect "snatch". Even though she still felt quite nervous, Alice managed to squirrel away some supplies into the bins, ready for Gloria's collection. Thankfully Gerry must have decided that Alice was trustworthy enough by now to be left to close up shop on her own, so once everyone had left, Alice cashed up quickly and was finished and ready when Gloria rang to say they were out back.

Alice kept watch while Gloria and Lekan swiftly loaded the minivan and in less than fifteen minutes she had seen Gloria and Lekan off, locked up and was heading home herself. There after they had agreed to make it a regular Wednesday evening occurrence.

Alice had deliberately not made any arrangements to see Lisa afterwards on a Wednesday, as she had no intention of having to explain why she would be later than normal or risking a conversation about her night. She doubted Lisa would want to have anything to do with this part of the operation.

Ethically, Alice had reconciled herself with what she'd agreed to do by making absolutely sure that the produce she put out for Gloria and Lekan was definitely past its shelf life. That way she was sure the restaurant would not lose anything. The added bonus that the waste removal company came to collect on Thursday mornings, early, long before anyone was in the restaurant, was a lifesaving godsend that she discovered the morning after their first failed snatch attempt. This meant that no one would think twice about some extra bags of produce being placed out in the yard and no one would be any the wiser if some of that waste was syphoned off for starving little children.

Alice was beginning to convince herself that what they were doing was more like being a modern-day Robin Hood than petty thieves.

In fact, she was feeling more confident all round, so much so that on this Thursday, her day off, she even agreed to take the children swimming on her own, just with Lisa. As it turned out, they had a wonderful afternoon full of fun, sun and much laughter.

Friday - 1 December, SA

Friday morning Alice arrived back at work as usual. However, she was thrown by the strange tension in the air. She instantly knew something was up. Gerry's door was closed and the staff were acting strangely. Everyone seemed to be walking on eggshells.

Alice found Lucy standing in her usual position propped up against the bar surveying the floor. "Hey, what's going on?" Alice whispered.

Lucy raised her eyebrows and checked her nails in her usual disinterested manner. "Seems the Boss has her knickers in a twist." Lucy said.

"I gathered. But why?" Alice asked.

Lucy shrugged. "Not sure. Something about some stuff's gone missing."

Alice's heart started pounding in her throat. "Oh, really! What sort of stuff?" She tried to sound casual.

"Seems she got the waste bill for the month this morning and it showed our waste quota has taken a dip.

Alice looked perplexed. "Is the fact that the bill is reduced not a good thing?"

"Not when you don't know what else has been going missing, or when your returns are offset on your purchase bill, like in the wine stock."

Oh my God! Alice thought. She had no idea. Why had Gloria not told her? She must have known!

"Plus, the waste removal company went on strike yesterday, so not only did they not collect but it's obvious that some of the return products have disappeared, including two crates of wine."

"Really, you get money back for the wine that is returned?" Alice asked. "I thought it was all destined for waste."

"You really have no idea about this business, do you?" Lucy shook her head and rolled her eyes. "We pay a specialised waste sorting and removal company. They take what we put out and then dispose or return as needed, depending on the products and the various agreements we have with the suppliers."

"Really, suppliers take back old food?"

Lucy nodded. "Yes, they recycle."

Alice couldn't imagine how that would work.

"Think compost. Or, for instance, wine farms find other uses for returns, like making vinegar, and old wine gets used in some household products and detergents," Lucy said. She pushed herself off of the bar and headed over to a customer who wanted to pay their bill.

Alice racked her brain over the events of the previous Wednesday night. She couldn't understand why there would be wine missing. She had been sure to only put things aside for Gloria and Lekan that the children would actually use, and wine was not one of them. Then she remembered. This week she had left Lekan on his own in the courtyard while Gloria came inside with her to help lock up quickly, so she could get a lift back with them. He must have seen the crates of wine standing out and grabbed them.

Suddenly, the office door flung open and Alice heard Gerry's ill-tempered voice call for her.

Oh shit!

———

Gerry's expression was implacable. "Please take a seat." She closed the door behind her.

"Is something the matter?" Alice asked.

"Yes." Gerry said. She took her place behind the desk. "It seems someone has been stealing from me."

"Stealing from you?" Alice's ears were ringing making it difficult to hear Gerry through the roar. "How so?" Alice did her best to steady her voice. "What have they taken?" She glanced in the direction of the safe.

"No, not money. It seems someone has been stealing waste from me."

"Waste? Who would want —"

"You'd be surprised. Actually, waste is very valuable."

Alice waited for Gerry to continue.

"More to the point, someone has been taking stuff from the yard and I was wondering if you might know anything about that?" Gerry looked Alice straight in the eye.

Alice held her gaze and tried not to blink. Just keep it together, she urged herself. Just breathe! Alice could feel her ears burning under Gerry's unflinching gaze. Alice shook her head. "No," she said. "Why would I know something?"

"Well, you locked up on Wednesday. I'm told that the wine returns were put out early this week and now they're gone. My first thought was that it would be the waste removers themselves, but lucky for them they were on strike this week."

Alice just shook her head.

"I checked my invoice from them and it seems my

returns are down by thirty per cent this month." Gerry paused, watching her closely for a reaction.

Alice looked shocked. "You can't think it has anything to do with me? What would I do with waste stock?"

"Not sure. But I can't easily see how else things would go missing like this. You're here on a Wednesday on your own, with enough time and opportunity to help yourself to whatever you want." Gerry said matter-of-factly.

Alice had to think quickly. "I wasn't on my own." Alice cringed inside. "Lisa came to collect me after my shift."

Gerry nodded, clearly recalling the previous time Lisa showed up at that inopportune moment. "Lisa was here on Wednesday?"

Alice nodded.

"And she would vouch for you?"

Alice nodded again. She swallowed. Then her heart sank as Gerry picked up the phone and dialled a number.

Alice tried to sit still and calm the rising panic that was threatening to overcome her.

"Hi Lisa, it's Gerry here.... Yes, sorry to ring you like this. I seem to have a bit of a problem that maybe you can help resolve. I just need to know if you were here on Wednesday night with Alice when she closed up for me?"

Alice could hear the slight hesitation on the other side of the phone.

"Yes, Wednesday night" Gerry repeated.

Alice held her breath. Please Lees, don't let me down, she prayed in her head.

"And she was here on her own?" Gerry pressed.

Gerry's eyes pinned Alice to her seat. Try as she might, Alice couldn't hear Lisa's response.

"Okay, thanks Lisa. Sorry to bother you. I just needed to know."

Gerry put down the receiver and folded her hands, interlocking her fingers in front of her on the table. "You're lucky to have a woman like that, Alice. Lisa and I have had our differences, and God knows I don't know what so many women see in her, but I know she has integrity. I'll give her that. She is not someone who'd lie."

Alice nodded, her mouth felt too dry to say anything.

"Sorry I doubted you," Gerry said.

Alice nodded again while she tried desperately to swallow.

"That poses another conundrum," Gerry continued. "I still have to find my thief. Do you have any ideas?"

Alice shook her head.

"If I don't find the person responsible, I'll have to fire all the staff and start from scratch. That is not a good prospect for me or for you."

Once again Alice's heart started to race. She could not afford to lose this job.

"I'm not the only one that has access to the stock, am I?" Alice said. "Who else had the opportunity? Surely it could have been one of a few people."

Gerry thought for a moment. Then she shook her head. "You're right. The only other person who has access, and would have had the opportunity, is Lucy."

Alice shook her head. "I find that really hard to believe. Lucy wouldn't steal from you. She is devoted to you and this job." Alice felt panic clench her throat. She hoped there was another way out of this. She had just wanted to divert suspicion off herself, not implicate Lucy.

"That is the only other possibility."

"Could this not be a robbery or the waste removers making a mistake on the bill?"

225

Gerry shook her head. "No, it has to have been an inside job."

"What about one of the other temporary staff? We all have access to the yard."

Gerry shook her head again. "The amount that has gone missing is too much to be surreptitiously smuggled out of here in broad daylight. It would have to have been someone with a key and access to the premises." Suddenly Gerry got up. "Okay, thanks Alice, you have been most helpful." Gerry opened her office door and Alice took that as her cue to leave.

"Call Lucy in here for me, please." Gerry shouted to Alice as she headed out to the floor.

————

About twenty minutes later the office door flew open and Lucy stormed out, untying her apron as she went. When she got to Alice, she chucked the apron at Alice. "Happy now?" she sneered.

"Lucy…" Alice called after her. She wanted to say something, to explain. She felt gutted. Had she just cost Lucy her job? Should she go and own up to Gerry? If she did, would she not also be blowing the whistle on Gloria and potentially jeopardising the well-being of all those children?

For the rest of the day Alice was frozen with guilt and confusion like a fly trapped in amber. Gloria would never forgive her if she ratted them out. What would she do if she didn't have this job? She'd have to go back to Magnus. This was her one chance of freedom. She had no idea how else she was going to stay in South Africa in the longer term. Waitressing was certainly not what she

226

wanted to do forever but for the moment, this job was her lifeline.

Could Gloria and Lekan get her another job, if she lost this one because of them? She was fuming with Gloria. How could they lie to her like that? They must have known how the waste returns work. If she could have, she would have marched right over to Gloria and given her a piece of her mind. But for the moment that had to wait. She needed to get through the day and then have time to think.

———

Alice headed home from work at around 7 pm. She dreaded bumping into Lisa. She knew she would have to explain the phone call from Gerry and she did not want to keep lying to Lisa, but what else was there to do?

First things first, she thought. She had to confront Gloria. She was absolutely livid. How could Gloria keep those details from her? She was putting her arse on the line for them. She honestly had no idea. She thought she could trust Gloria.

When she got home, she found dirty dishes standing on the kitchen counter, including used empty wine glasses. This was probably the wine Lekan stole. She could hear noises and giggles coming from Gloria's bedroom. For a split second she considered waiting for the morning, but her anger won through. What they had done was wrong. Stealing for their own pleasure was wrong!

Alice banged on Gloria's bedroom door.

"Hi," came Gloria's voice from the other side. "Shh," and another set of giggles. Then Gloria opened the door, clad in a white sheet pulled tightly around her body like a bath towel. "I'm sorry if we're making too much noise." The wide smile on her face faded rapidly as she took one look at Alice. She stepped outside the bedroom and pulled it shut behind her, waving two fingers to Lekan.

"Are you okay?" Gloria asked, realising Alice's demeanour was unusual. "What happened?"

"No, Gloria, I'm not okay," Alice said and proceeded to tell Gloria what had happened that morning.

Gloria sat calmly and listened to Alice relate the whole story. Then she sighed deeply. "I'm so sorry we didn't explain it all to you. I figured you knew enough to understand how much good your help was doing, and you could understand how much it means for Masika and those children. You knew the risks."

"Gloria, I never signed up to stealing from my employer! I thought we were just saving food from going to waste. I signed up to help the children, not for you and Lekan," she indicated the dirty wine glasses on the table, "so that you two could get drunk and have a happy night."

Suddenly Gloria looked stern. "Now look, Alice. Don't you judge me and Lekan one bit. You have no right. You have no idea who I am or what I do for these children or what other sacrifices I make for others. If I have a little glass of old, stale wine once every so often as my reward, that is not for you to judge."

"It is, if I nearly lose my job because of it!" Alice felt near to tears with anger.

Gloria swallowed and seemed to reassess. "Look, honey, the only people who gain from that waste are the big multibillion-dollar supermarkets and retailers. They can easily absorb the few rands we take from them each week to feed the poor."

"Gloria, you know as well as I do that I'm not a friend of the big supermarkets but stealing is wrong. If I get caught, I will be sent back to England. Not only am I working illegally, I'm also stealing from my employer." Alice rubbed her temples where a headache was pulsing through her eyes. "And it is not only supermarkets and retailers who are affected here. Gerry and the restaurants you steal from are also out of pocket — good, hard-working, honest people whom, I'm sure, if you asked, would be happy to willingly sponsor or contribute to the Shelter. That is if it's all legal and above board."

"Believe me, honey, we tried that," Gloria said, looking fatigued. Alice wondered how old Gloria really was. Until now she'd seemed to defy any age.

There was a long silence between them.

Lekan came out of the bedroom with a towel wrapped around his middle. He was oblivious to the sombre mood between them. "Hey, what are my pretty girls gassing about?" The smile on his face died rapidly as he saw the serious look on Gloria's. "What's going on?"

"Our operation at The Shanty got blown today," Gloria said.

"Ah, shit!" Lekan said and collapsed onto the couch. "What happened?"

"What happened?" Alice said, a bitter tone in her voice, "What happened was you betrayed my trust."

Lekan looked confused.

"I left you to load the supplies I'd carefully put aside, but you had to help yourself to more."

"I don't know what you are talking about," Lekan said, glancing from Alice to Gloria.

"The wine, Lekan. You had to go and help yourself to the wine."

"The wine was also going to waste," he said quickly.

"Don't give me that," Alice said turning around in her

seat. "As for the fact that you and Gloria lied to me about the waste."

"We did not lie," Gloria cut in.

"Well, you weren't entirely truthful, were you?" Alice fired back.

"Now listen to me," Lekan said, getting up and approaching Alice where she stood near the kitchen table. "No one comes into my house and calls me a liar." His big muscular frame towered above her. "You ungrateful missy! We take you in when you had nowhere to go, and this is the thanks we get."

"You did no such —" Alice was not about to back down.

"Okay, stop! Both of you." Gloria got up and stepped in between them. "This is not going to help any of us. Lekan, go have a shower, I will come to see you in a bit. Let me handle this."

Lekan just held Alice's gaze over the top of Gloria's head. Finally, when Gloria put a hand on his shoulder he seemed to stand down and slowly headed towards the little shower room that led off the main room of the flat.

Once the shower room door had closed Gloria continued. "I truly am sorry, Alice. We did not mean any harm to come to you by helping us. And as for what Lekan said... That is not how I feel. I'm happy that I could open my door to you and help you out."

Alice relaxed a little.

"So, what do you want to do now?" Gloria said.

Alice shook her head and took a seat at the kitchen counter. "I don't know."

Just then, there came a knock at the door.

Gloria went to open it.

"It's for you." Gloria said and backed away from the door, revealing a stern looking Lisa standing in the doorway.

"Hi Lees, now is not a good t —"

"It had better be a fine time," Lisa said, her voice clipped.

Alice looked at Gloria. Gloria shrugged her shoulders. "Seems you had better deal with that first."

Alice got up and stepped outside, pulling the door closed behind her.

Lisa took a few steps away from the door. "Do you mind explaining exactly what that was all about today? Why did I have to lie for you?"

Alice felt her forehead prickle from stress. She moved away from the front door, glancing back to assess the level of sound that could travel through the flimsy planks that separated them from Gloria and Lekan. She had a feeling this was going to be a fight and she did not want to share that with Lekan and Gloria. She gently took hold of Lisa's elbow and tried to lead her further down the corridor.

Lisa yanked her arm out of Alice's grasp. "I'm not going anywhere until you tell me what the hell that was about. I do not lie for people."

"Lees, please calm down, I will explain it to you, but can we please go into your flat and talk, rather than air our dirty laundry out here for the whole block."

Lisa hesitated for a moment but then realised that her door was only a few feet further on. "This had better be good," she said and led Alice into her flat.

———

Once inside Lisa's flat, standing in the middle of the light, sparsely decorated open-plan sitting room, Alice spoke softly and as calmly as she could.

"Gerry found out that some old stock had gone missing. She thought I might have had something to do with it."

"And had you?" Lisa asked, impatient to get to the truth.

Alice considered lying again. She desperately needed Lisa on her side. She needed Lisa's help. If she lied to Lisa now, and Lisa found out, she would never trust her again.

Alice nodded.

"You stole from Gerry?" Lisa's voice was raised in severe annoyance and disbelief. "And you've made me an accomplice?"

"I'm so sorry to have put you in that position. I had no idea what else to do. The whole thing just spiralled out of my control. I had no idea that Gerry would ring you."

"Oh, so it would have been okay had I not found out that you used me to cover up your lies?" Lisa said.

"No, Lees. I panicked. I'm sorry. I really am. It's not what you think."

"I'm glad you know what I think." Lisa's deep brown eyes almost bored a hole in Alice's heart as she coolly assessed her. At that moment the warm, caring, lifesaving Lisa felt a million miles away. Only a wall of ice was left.

Alice felt despair wash over her. She didn't know how to reach out to Lisa.

"Will you let me explain?" Alice tried to move closer to Lisa, to reach out to her.

Lisa turned and moved into the kitchen, effectively putting more distance and the kitchen counter between them. She flipped on the kettle. "You had better make it good."

Alice felt a twinge of hope. At least Lisa was willing to listen. She sat down at the kitchen counter and began to explain everything that had happened as honestly and openly as she could.

Lisa listened, silently making them both a cup of red-bush tea.

By now, Alice was sobbing with remorse, especially over causing Lucy to lose her job.

Lisa handed her the box of tissues. "Thank you for telling me the truth."

"Thank you for listening. I'm truly sorry to place you in that position. I am so sorry it all happened. I didn't want Lucy to lose her job, but I don't know how to make any of it right." Alice dabbed her eyes and blew her nose. "If I could undo all of it I would, believe me, but I really don't want to go back to the UK and to Magnus or even worse to jail."

Lisa took a long sip of her tea as she watched Alice over the top of the cup.

"I'll tell you what you do," Lisa finally said, putting her cup down and folding her arms.

Alice waited, hopeful.

"Firstly, it goes without saying that you stop smuggling stuff for Gloria and Lekan. You go to Gerry tomorrow and you explain the truth and you resign."

"But, Lees, my job —"

"You should have thought about that before you started stealing."

"Lees, I thought I was helping the children, and I didn't see any harm in taking what was already going to waste. You have to believe me."

"I do," Lisa said evenly. "If I didn't, my hands would now be wrapped around my telephone receiver and I'd be calling the police."

"What will stop Gerry from doing that tomorrow?"

"That is a fair point. She would have every right to do just that." Lisa nodded. "I'll come with you and have a word with her tomorrow."

Alice swallowed. "You would?"

Lisa nodded. "I understand you had no intention of harming anyone. I believe you were ignorant. But that is not an excuse for failing to do the right thing."

Alice nodded. "I know, but, even if you help keep me out of jail, what will I do if I don't have this job? Unless Gloria and Lekan can find me another job —"

"I also suggest that you stop all dealings with Gloria and Lekan. They might be doing something good for those children but I don't like their methods. I don't trust it. Someday they'll be caught and you don't want to go down with them."

"But Lees, I'd have to move out from Gloria's. Where will I go without a job? I'd have to go back to the UK."

Lisa looked at Alice for a long moment. "You can move in with me."

Alice almost spilled the remainder of her tea. "What? Move in with you?" Alice shook her head.

"Why is that such a bad idea?" Lisa asked. "You spend a large part of your time with me here or on the boat already."

"Lisa, come on get serious. You wouldn't want me around your place twenty-four seven."

"Why not?"

Alice sighed. "Because of all the others."

Lisa looked confused for a moment. "What others?"

"Your other women," Alice said, in almost a whisper. "Your other lovers. I know you are seeing other women, not just me. Don't get me wrong, it doesn't bother me, but I think me living here might cramp your style too much."

Lisa considered this. She stepped back around the kitchen counter and took a seat on the stool next to Alice. "Okay then. How about you stay on my boat until we figure out another plan?"

Alice was dumbstruck.

Saturday - 2 December, SA

Alice stayed over at Lisa's that night and the next morning Lisa drove her into work. It was Lisa's suggestion that she would talk to Gerry first and help set the right expectation. Meanwhile, Alice stood at the bar and tried not to look or feel like a child waiting outside the headmaster's office. Some of the staff eyed her quizzically, but she made it clear that an approach or small talk would not be welcomed.

Ten minutes later, Gerry's office door opened again and Lisa stepped out. "You're up," Lisa said softly and gave her arm a gentle squeeze.

When Alice entered, a stony-faced Gerry was seated behind her desk. Alice closed the door behind her, took a seat and began to explain: She had taken the stock destined for waste. She had no idea that Gerry would be out of pocket and it was with the good intention of giving it to the poor. When Gerry pressed her for information on her accomplices, Alice didn't deny that she had help but she refused to give Gerry any names. She did reassure Gerry that she'd make sure that they wouldn't steal from Gerry again.

"You are very lucky you have Lisa on your side, you know," Gerry said evenly. "She is a very convincing woman. If it was up to me, I would call the police on you, and have you deported instantly."

"Does that mean you're not going to do that?" Alice asked, hopefully.

"You can go count your lucky stars, because you just used up one of them to get you out of this pickle."

"Thank you, Gerry. I really am sorry."

"Now get out of here before I change my mind."

Alice got up. "Oh, just one more thing —"

"Seriously?"

Alice nodded as she spoke. "Please will you give Lucy her job back?"

Gerry rubbed her eyes with one hand and pinched the bridge of her nose. "Yes, I guess I'll have to do that."

"Thank you." Alice said, but didn't move.

"Is there anything else I can do for you?" Gerry said sarcastically. "Soon people will think I work for you."

"Yes, please can I have Lucy's address. I'd like to apologise in person, if I can."

Gerry considered Alice's request for a moment, then she pushed herself up from her chair and went over to the beige coloured filing cabinet and took out a file. She scribbled down the address on a Post-it note, closed the drawer and handed it to Alice. "Tell her she needs to be back in at 9 am tomorrow."

Alice nodded. "I will. And thank you, Gerry. I am really sorry."

Gerry nodded.

Lisa had been waiting patiently at a corner table near the bar. When Alice emerged from Gerry's office she got up and fell in step next to Alice as they walked to Lisa's car.

"Home to get your things from Gloria, or to the boat?" Lisa asked.

"I want to talk to Gloria, so it's pointless going there now. I'm better off going to see her tonight once she's home."

"Okay then, straight to the boat," Lisa said cheerfully.

"Actually, please can we make one more stop on the way?" Alice handed Lisa the Post-it note with Lucy's address.

Alice couldn't imagine where Lucy's home would be. She was surprised when their drive took them up and away from Camps Bay. She had assumed, considering the number of shifts and the long hours Lucy kept, that she lived locally, near The Sea Shanty.

As they hit the entrance of the Waterfront, Lisa turned the car right and headed up through the town. Until that point Alice had not seen much of Cape Town's city-bowl itself. It was similar to most other cities, with its tall buildings housing banks, insurance companies and large household names, which were clearly sign-posted in large letters on the outside. What made Cape Town quite spectacular was its setting, nestled in the crook of the most beautiful basin at the foot of Table Mountain with its magical cloud tablecloth.

As they headed south-east again toward the mountain, dodging careless minibus taxis bursting at the seams with passengers, the roads grew narrower and steeper. Soon they were headed up into a tree-lined suburb right under the mountain. Two large tower blocks dominated the area, towering above the trees, set between small but affluent looking terraced houses and tired-looking gated complexes. Lisa pulled into one long, private, brick road that provided access to ten small, identical, terraced houses each with a single car parking space outside. Lisa leaned forward, reading the house numbers on her side out loud, as they crawled along the road.

"Thirteen... fifteen... seventeen B... seventeen A must be here somewhere," Lisa said. She pulled up outside seventeen B.

Alice took a deep breath and got out of the car. As she

got closer, she realised that next to 17B's car parking space was a short set of moss-covered steps down to a small, dank courtyard leading to a navy front door. Next to the door she saw the small number 17A hanging by one screw. She trotted down the steps and rang the doorbell.

She heard the door being unlocked and as it swung open a wall of sound hit her. At first, she could not make out what it was. Then, as it seemed to pause and start up again with extra vigour, Alice realised it was a baby screaming. Before her stood a rather dishevelled, exhausted-looking Lucy holding a baby's bottle.

"Hi Lucy," Alice said, tentatively.

"What do you want? How did you get my address?" Lucy scowled. "Haven't I had enough grief?"

"I'm sorry to bother you," Alice tried to keep her nerve and speak as evenly as possible over the wailing of the child in the background.

"Get on with it, can't you see I'm busy. Jack wants her milk," Lucy pressed.

"I just want to say I'm sorry about what happened yesterday."

"I bet you are. So, here to rub salt in the wound?"

"No, actually I've come to give you a message from Gerry."

"Oh yeah? What does that cow want?"

"There has been a mistake —"

"You're damn right, firing me for no reason — for something I had nothing to do with— was a mistake. She can't just do that to people, not when they have two mouths to feed and an AWOL girlfriend."

"I'm sorry," Alice said earnestly. "It was my fault, not Gerry's."

That seemed to make Lucy pay attention. Alice could

see Lucy contemplate whether to ask for more information, tear strips off her, or just to let things go. Mercy came through. "So, what does she want?"

"Gerry asks if you would please be at work tomorrow at nine am."

Lucy looked perplexed. "What? So, I'm not fired?" The hope was unmistakable in her voice.

Alice shook her head. "No, you're not fired."

Within seconds her guard was back up. "That bloody cow needs to make up her mind. She can't play Russian roulette with people's lives like this."

"I'm sorry," Alice said. "So, you'll be there?"

"Nine am?"

Alice nodded again as Lucy sized her up.

"Yeah, okay, tomorrow."

"Thanks," Alice said. She turned to head up the steps. Halfway up she heard the door close behind her as a voice shouted over the sounds of the crying baby, "Ma, I've got my job back!"

THIRTEEN

Alice didn't feel up to much after they got back from
Lucy's. She was so tired, she could hardly speak. Lisa kindly
led her to the cabin, and told her to get some rest. That was
pretty much where she spent the remainder of Saturday
and most of Sunday. Although the last thing she could do
was sleep. Her mind was churning with one big question:
What was she to do now?

Finally, on Sunday afternoon, Alice decided she needed
to talk to Gloria.

Lisa offered to drive her over. She dropped her off at the
flat at around 6.30 pm and they arranged that Lisa would
pick her up again in two hours. Lisa had a few errands to
run, in preparation for Alice moving onto the boat.

As Alice was about to step into the corridor that led to
Gloria's flat, she saw the front door open and Lekan step
out. Alice didn't really want to have a conversation with
Lekan right then so she ducked back into the stairwell and

sprinted up the few steps to the next landing on the floor above. Here she waited.

A few moments later the stairwell door swung open and she heard Lekan talking to someone in his native language. What surprised her was the sound of a young girl's voice answering back. Alice peeped down, over the railing, and saw Lekan lead a young African girl down the stairs.

The girl was carrying a small suitcase. Alice didn't recognise her. She thought back to the night outside the MOD Hotel when she saw a similar young girl come out of the hotel and get into the minivan with Lekan. She hadn't recognised her either, not from the Shelter and not from the hotel, but it had been quite dark that night and she'd been watching them from a fair distance away. What was Lekan doing with these young girls?

She listened until they reached the bottom of the stairwell and she heard the main door open and close. Then she dashed down the steps, taking two at a time. At the bottom, she pushed the outside door open slightly. She peered down the street. She saw Lekan and the young girl head down towards the main road. Where could he be going? It was getting dark and the commuting traffic had already died down. She slipped out of the door and followed them, being careful to use the parked cars and trees as cover and keeping a healthy distance behind them. She had expected Lekan to be heading to his minivan, but instead she followed them across Green Point's Main Road towards the Stadium. They slipped through one of the side roads and headed towards Mouille Point. Here they headed through a small car park beyond which they crossed the road on to the Mouille Point promenade. It looked like they were heading for a bench next to a bus stop.

Alice stayed on the near side of the road, taking cover in

the shadows of the buildings around the car park. A few minutes later a bus appeared, making its way along the road towards them. Was the girl going to get onto it? Shit! What was she to do? Should she stay and watch the girl leave and then follow Lekan, or should she somehow try to get on the bus too?

She opted for sitting tight and just watching what Lekan did. Once the bus pulled away, surprisingly, Lekan and the girl were still seated on the bench, facing the road, in some bizarre pastiche of a scene from "Waiting for Godot".

Two of the customers from the small bar on the corner emerged into the car park and headed to their vehicle. When they saw Alice, they started to walk a little faster and looked around nervously. She realised she probably aroused suspicion, lurking in the shadows as she was. To avoid being reported to the police, she decided to go inside the bar to see if she could find a good vantage point from which to keep watching Lekan and the girl. The bar had a small outside veranda with a clear view of the bench. She chose a seat, making sure she was not too obviously separate from the other customers.

When the waiter came along, she quickly ordered a diet soda and paid for it immediately when it arrived, in case she needed to leave in a hurry.

Twenty minutes later, Alice started to get impatient. What were they waiting for? She was about to throw in the towel and give up when a large white limousine pulled up across the road. As soon as the limo stopped, Lekan and the girl stood up. The driver climbed out and opened the rear passenger door on the sea side of the car. At first, Alice could just see the head of a man appear. As he approached Lekan and the girl, he moved into view. He was a tall, thin

African man in a dark, expensive looking suit. He and Lekan shook hands. Then he bent down and greeted the girl. Alice watched as the girl smiled, dipping her knee and her head a little. The man gestured towards the car. The girl nodded and said something to Lekan, gave him a hug and then got into the limousine. Once the girl was in the car, Lekan handed the driver the girl's small suitcase and the man handed Lekan an envelope and shook his hand, before he followed the girl into the limousine.

Lekan waited until the limousine had disappeared down the road before he opened the envelope, peered inside and then stuffed it deep into his inside jacket pocket. Then, he walked off along the promenade towards Sea Point. Alice was uncertain about what she had just witnessed but she was as sure as hell that it was nothing good.

———

Alice ran back to Gloria's at a speedy trot, just slow enough not to arouse suspicion herself. At every crossroad she stopped and looked back to make sure that Lekan hadn't changed direction and was following her. She had no idea where he was off to but she really didn't want to have a confrontation with him.

When she neared the block of flats, she saw Lisa waiting for her in the car outside. Luckily, she was facing the other direction, so rather than waste time explaining where she had been, Alice dashed straight into the building.

Inside, she took the flight of stairs two steps at a time. It was only when she was careering along the corridor towards Gloria's flat that she remembered Gloria could well be home by then.

She had come there earlier hoping to talk to Gloria

about quitting her job and moving onto Lisa's boat and potentially about doing more work at the Shelter while she was jobless. Now, after what had just happened, Alice wondered if she should confront Gloria with what she had seen. Then she decided against it. Although it didn't feel right, she had no idea what she had actually witnessed. She needed time to think it through and maybe talk to Lisa about it.

Alice approached the door, slid her key into the lock, turned and tried to sound casual as she called out, "Hello, anyone here? I'm home."

She was greeted by silence. She stopped dead and listened for any sound of movement in the flat. When she was sure that she was the only person there, she breathed a sigh of relief and quickly started gathering her few things into her suitcase.

Within minutes she had packed and was about to grab her coat and handbag when she saw it.

Gloria's diary. It lay on the kitchen counter.

Alice froze.

It was very unusual for Gloria to leave her diary out like this. She never let it out of her sight.

Alice scanned the flat to check she had not missed Gloria in the bedroom or bathroom.

She slowly put down her things near the door and approached the counter.

This would be the ultimate invasion of Gloria's privacy.

But what had gone down tonight? What was Lekan up to? Did Gloria even know? Was she involved in it? What if Gloria was innocent? Well then, hopefully the diary would prove that. What if those girls were in real danger? That last thought clinched it for Alice. She had to know.

Her hands were shaking as she carefully opened the

diary. At a glance there were the regular entries she had expected, shift times, meeting notes, hair appointments. She flipped through the pages to today's date. It started off similarly. "10.00 - Monthly inspection MOD", "14.15 - Team meeting" with some notes on what to cover. Then Alice saw the evening entries. "Late shift with an arrow until 22.00" and a single name "Dikaledi" written at 19.30, which was circled and marked with a star.

Just then, a door banged in the outside corridor. Someone was coming. Alice panicked. She seized the diary and stuffed it into her handbag, grabbed her coat and suitcase and headed for the door. She braced herself as she opened the door a couple of centimetres. She breathed a sigh of relief when she saw it was Lisa coming out of her flat carrying a stack of blankets and towels.

She waited a couple of seconds and then followed Lisa down to the car.

"Hey, how did it go?" Lisa asked, concerned.

Alice shook her head. She scanned the street to make sure neither Lekan nor Gloria were approaching the building. "Can we go?" she asked and got into the car quickly.

"Did you talk to her?" Lisa asked.

Alice shook her head. "No, Gloria was not home and actually I would prefer not to see her right now. Can we go?"

Lisa nodded, started the car and pulled away.

———

In the car, all the way back to the boat, Gloria's diary burnt a hole in Alice's bag where she clasped it firmly in her lap. She tried to focus on being calm and looking normal. She didn't want to arouse Lisa's suspicion. But her mind wouldn't stop racing over the events of the evening. What had she seen? Who was that man in the limo? Why did Lekan take the young girl to him? Maybe the man was a relative? But it didn't look like the girl knew him. She didn't seem reluctant to go with him. But then one couldn't always see coercion. What was in the envelope? She was pretty sure it was money, but was that jumping to conclusions? Her head hurt. She rubbed her eyes.

"You sure you are okay?" Lisa asked softly.

"Yes, I'm fine," Alice said, trying to put a smile on her face. She wondered if she should tell Lisa what she had seen. She wished she could share it. But no, at least not yet, not until she'd had a chance to have a better look at the diary.

"Thank you for asking and for being so good to me. It's just been a big day."

———

In the couple of hours since Lisa had dropped Alice off at Gloria's, she'd returned to her boat to give it a complete spring-clean. She had bought a fresh yellowtail, prawns, shrimps and squid from the local Hout Bay fisherman's market and pre-prepared a wonderful, gourmet fish chowder according to her dad's favourite recipe. She had set the tiny dining table very smartly for two. In the middle of the table, she had placed a bottle of the sparkling wine she knew Alice liked on ice. As a final touch she had hung a handmade cork key ring with a newly cut boat key around the bottle's neck.

Once they got back to the boat, Lisa opened the Cava and poured them each a glass.

"My skuitjie is jou skuitjie,"[1] Lisa said. "Mi casa es su casa. Seriously, you are not my guest. I want you to treat this boat as your home for as long as you need it. I want you to feel free and independent of me, but if you need anything please do not hesitate to say."

They clinked their glasses together and Lisa kissed her deeply. Then, Lisa got busy heating and adding the final touches to the chowder.

The meal was delicious and Alice was touched by how much trouble Lisa had gone to in order to welcome her to her boat. The key on the cork key ring was a particularly wonderful gesture. In fact, the whole evening left Alice feeling a little overwhelmed and so grateful to Lisa for everything she had done for her, especially in the last forty-eight hours. She wondered if there was something she could do for Lisa, to show her appreciation better. The trouble was, Lisa seemed so together, so self-sufficient, she seemed to be lacking in nothing. Alice was having such a lovely evening with Lisa, she almost forgot about the events of earlier. It was only when Lisa led Alice to their little cabin and she walked past her suitcase and handbag where she had left them as they came on board, that her troubles flooded back. From then on, the events of earlier rested so heavily on her mind she was too distracted to make love to Lisa. Lisa took her reluctance to be remnants of fatigue after the momentous weekend she'd had. Gently, Lisa helped Alice undress and get into bed. Then she stripped off too and curled herself around Alice in a supportive, comforting embrace.

The moon shone brightly through the cabin window. On the few occasions she had stayed over on the boat previously, Alice had liked being bathed in moonlight. She felt it soothing, almost magical, and she had told Lisa so.

However, tonight, it felt a little too bright, like a spotlight pointing out her deception. It was so hard not to tell Lisa everything. She almost did after supper, but something stopped her. Not just yet. *As soon as I really know what's going on, Lisa will be the first to know,* she thought.

"You did well," Lisa said in the semi-darkness next to her. "This could not have been easy." For a moment Alice worried that Lisa somehow knew what had happened. "Having made a mistake, making it right is often harder than not doing the wrong thing in the first place. It will be okay. You'll see."

"Thanks," was all she said.

Ten minutes later, she was relieved to hear soft, deep, rhythmic breathing coming from a sleeping Lisa.

———

In the dark Alice finally allowed herself to think over the events of the early evening. She replayed the scene at the bus stop over and over in her mind. The whole scenario was baffling, but there was something specifically unsettling about how the man in the limo had acted towards the girl. Alice could not place it. The best she could do was to describe it as 'not innocent'. And yet the girl seemed to go with him willingly. What did Lekan have over that girl? The hair on her neck stood on end.

Very soon after she had met Lekan, she'd realised he was a bit of a wheeler dealer. He seemed to know everyone and was able to source almost anything at any time. She thought back to the papers he'd had made for her and to the mobile phone he'd procured for her. At the time she hadn't realised it, but apparently it was very difficult to acquire a mobile phone without a contract in South Africa. In fact, she had learned that it was almost impossible without proof of residency. Yet, Lekan did not seem like an evil person.

What about Gloria, and the diary?

What about the diary entry showing a name next to Sunday at 7.30 pm? It was around 7.30 pm when she saw the girl get into the limo. Was that the name of the girl in Gloria's diary? Gloria must be in on this.

Alice could not take it any longer. She had to have another look at the diary. She took hold of Lisa's hand, which was resting on her ribcage and gently moved it off her. Then she carefully wriggled down and off the end of the bed. Thanks to its solid wooden base, this didn't disturb Lisa. Just to be sure Alice stopped and listened for Lisa's continued rhythmic breaths.

She tip-toed to the sitting area where she had stowed her suitcase and handbag. She suspected she would not be unpacking much during her stay on the boat, even though Lisa had made a concerted effort to clear space for her. She gently eased open her handbag and took out the red diary.

It was too dark to read anything just by moonlight. She glanced around and realised that there was not a lot of privacy on a boat so small. She considered hiding in the shower room, but she remembered that the light and fan in there made a noise which would wake Lisa. It would have to be outside. She picked up her raincoat and wrapped it around herself, to protect her naked body against the night's chill and the eyes of any potential insomniacs on the neighbouring boats in the marina.

She grabbed Lisa's emergency torch from the kitchen cabinet and headed up to the flybridge.

She sat down and opened the diary on today's date and studied it again. Then, she flipped backwards a day at a time, casting her eye down the pages one by one, to see if anything stood out. Gloria was meticulous about keeping notes. She found the entry of the previous food collection from The Sea Shanty, along with a little sad face and the word "blown" written next to it. There were a number of other similar entries that she assumed were food collections from other hotels or restaurants. Some of them had qualifiers in the entries like "clothes", "sanitary pads", "meds". It seemed Gloria and Lekan had a reasonable network of suppliers for the Shelter.

One of the entries caught her attention: "Masika - Doc." There seemed to be a few identical annotations in a cluster around the past few weeks. She hadn't had another conversation with Gloria about Masika's HIV since that first day, when Gloria told her. A shiver ran down her spine. She hoped little Masika was just going for regular check-ups and that nothing had taken a turn for the worse. She made a mental note to go visit Masika soon. She knew her way to the Shelter on her own now, so she could go when Gloria or Lekan were not likely to be there.

Flicking further back through the pages in the diary, she came across the fateful date that she'd moved in with Gloria, the day she walked out of her previous life. She realised that was merely a few short weeks ago. On one hand it felt like she'd been in South Africa, living this turbulent new life, for years. On the other, it felt like only yesterday that she'd watched Magnus and Margaret's taxi pull out of the hotel driveway.

Alice fanned back a few more pages. Her eye caught a name she recognised: "Deka". If her memory served, Deka was the young woman who had been helping with room service in the hotel, to whom Gloria had introduced Alice. She remembered they were almost inseparable at the beginning, Deka following Gloria around like her shadow, and then suddenly she was gone.

Alice remembered Simone telling her that Deka had left and her asking Gloria about it. Gloria confirmed that she had left to get married and live with her new husband. It had seemed a bit sudden to Alice, but then she didn't know Deka, her circumstances and certainly nothing much about African cultural and marriage practices. She'd read somewhere that tribesmen paid for their wives with cattle. But even that, she thought, must be an out-of-date practice by now. Nevertheless, this entry with Deka's name in a circle marked with a star was definitely made around that time.

Then the thought hit her and she snapped the diary shut.

Could Gloria and Lekan be running some sort of matchmaking agency? But why would money exchange hands in a dating agency though, unless... could they really be involved in people trafficking? Alice snorted. She did not know Lekan well enough to judge whether he was capable of something like that. But Gloria? Could Gloria be involved in something that evil? Surely not? Everything she knew about Gloria pointed to her being a really kind and generous person, only looking out for the children... and even going to extreme lengths to do so. Alice doubted there was anything Gloria would not do for the children...but how could human trafficking be for the good of the children? The only way she could know would be to confront Gloria.

FOURTEEN

When her phone rang for the seventh time that morning, Alice plucked up the courage to answer. That proved one thing to her: Gloria was very keen to get her diary back. It was obviously very important.

"Alice, it's Gloria." There was a serious sense of urgency in her voice.

"Hello, Gloria," Alice said evenly.

"I see you've moved your stuff. Have you found somewhere to rent? I thought you might say goodbye."

Alice waited. Had Gloria not noticed the absence of her diary? "Yes, I have, thanks. I have taken advantage of your hospitality for too long already. I did come by last night to collect my stuff and to see you, but you weren't in."

"You're welcome. I'm glad I could help you out."

There was suddenly something different in Gloria's voice. She sounded distracted.

"Ah, listen, Alice. I think you might have something of

253

mine," Gloria said. "I think you might have picked it up by mistake last night."

Alice hesitated for a minute. She did not know how to play this. It was no use pussy-footing around any longer. "Ah, yes, about that, you mean your diary?"

"Yes, yes, my diary." Alice could hear the relief in Gloria's voice. "Do you think you could swing by the flat or my work later today? You know what I'm like. I'm completely lost without it." Gloria let out a nervous laugh.

Alice paused for a long moment.

"Hello, Alice? You still there?" Gloria asked.

"I saw him, Gloria."

"What? Saw who?"

"Lekan... and the girl, last night." Alice waited for her words to register.

"Sorry, Alice, honey, I'm not sure what you mean. Whatever it is can we talk when you bring my diary round. I really have to go."

"No, Gloria. I'm afraid it can't wait.

"Listen, Alice —"

"No, not 'listen Alice'. I need an explanation, and a reasonable one too, or this diary will find its way to the police and you and Lekan can answer to them." It was a gamble but Alice decided to lay her cards on the table. She had had enough of the cat and mouse game.

Now, there was a long silence on the other end of the line.

"Look, Alice. It's not what you think."

"What is it then?"

"Just trust me —"

"What, like I trusted you with the food collection, trusted you to turn me into a criminal, make me lose my job and almost get me deported?"

"Alice, you don't understand —"

"You're right I don't understand. You say everything you do is for the benefit of the children. Selling them to rich business-men in limousines can hardly be for their own good." That was another gamble.

"It is."

Yes! She was right.

"Alice, just bring the diary to me and I can explain everything."

"Not a chance."

"Just meet me, bring the diary and I will explain everything. If you still want to take the diary to the police afterwards, then I won't stop you. But at least you'll have the full facts to make a decision."

Alice considered Gloria's suggestion. Gloria was right, she didn't know what she had stumbled upon. All she had so far was guess work and assumption. Did Gloria deserve the benefit of the doubt? Hell no, but the children did. They needed her. If Gloria was locked up, who would look after them? Alice thought back to the girl getting into the limousine. Looking after them so that you can sell them off? Alice felt the rage build inside her.

"What use will it be, Gloria? You will just lie again."

"I understand why you'd think that." Gloria said, sounding remorseful. "How about if you speak to one of the girls themselves? If they can explain what is going on?"

Alice scoffed. "Yeah, right! I'm not going to walk into your trap."

"Seriously, it's not a trap. If I can arrange for one of the girls to meet you and afterwards you are still not happy, then you can take my diary to the police. You lose nothing."

Alice thought this over for a while. If she did not give Gloria the opportunity to explain, she would never get to the bottom of what was going on. She would never know whether turning in the diary was the right thing to do. "Okay, I will meet you. But it has to be in a public place."

"Okay. Good!" Gloria sounded relieved. "How about we meet at the children's playground on the Sea Point parade?"

"No, that is too isolated." Alice thought for a few seconds. She had limited options since she did not know very many places. "I'll see you at Erte, the small bar on the corner at the end of the Camps Bay mall. Meet me there."

"What time?"

"As soon as possible."

"I finish work at four."

"I'll meet you at four-thirty. And Gloria, if you don't show or if there is any funny business, I promise you, your diary will be in police custody before you can even say 'get me out of jail'."

"We'll be there." Gloria said and rang off.

———

Lisa had left the boat earlier that morning saying that she needed to take care of some chores for the harbour master, and if Alice needed her, she would be by the large warehouses near the main docks. And that is exactly where Alice found her, and about four other labourers, still power-blasting a stretch of shaded, mossy concrete, shortly before 3 pm.

Lisa was very pleased to see her and immediately rushed over towards her. The passionate kiss that Lisa gave her, in front of the other labourers, caught Alice completely off guard. Obviously being affectionate in front of her straight colleagues did not bother Lisa, but it was all a bit too much for Alice and she pulled away quite abruptly.

"What?" Lisa asked.

Alice glanced at the four men in blue boiler suits who had all stopped what they were doing and were openly staring at her and Lisa.

Lisa looked back to see what Alice was looking at. "Oh, them? They're harmless. They know about me."

"Yes, but they don't know about *me*." Alice said coolly. Lisa swallowed and nodded. "Okay, sorry."

There was a moment of awkward silence.

"So, did you just miss me, or do you need something?" Lisa tried to lighten the mood.

"Oh, yeah. Remember you said if I needed something, I should just ask? You probably didn't mean that so literally nor think it might happen so soon —"

"What? What do you need? You name it." Lisa said, smiling.

"Please, can I borrow your car?" Alice said.

"My car? I didn't know you could even drive!"

"I really need to go and see Gloria and get the last few things I forgot. And this place," Alice looked around at the harbour, "is very lovely but it is not the most accessible for transport links."

"That is true." Lisa said nodding. "I tell you what, I could be finished here in less than an hour. How about I take you?"

Alice shook her head. "I need to go there under my own steam. After what happened yesterday, I really need to talk to Gloria." That was not entirely a lie, she thought. "If you were waiting for me, it would add to the pressure." Also, true. "And I thought about asking you to take me and pick me up, like you did yesterday, but under the circumstances,

I really would prefer being able to get away as soon as it is over." The latter was also too accurate for comfort.

Lisa looked at Alice for a long moment. Alice inwardly braced herself for what was to come.

"Okay," Lisa said and fished out the key from her pocket.

"Okay?" Alice asked, surprised. "You sure?"

"Yes, why not?" Lisa said. "I said you could ask if you needed anything. Unless you don't really need it of course?" Lisa raised an eyebrow.

"No. I mean, yes. Thank you." Alice kissed Lisa on the cheek. "I promise I will repay you, somehow."

"Repay me by bringing Uriah back in one piece."

"Uriah, who is Uriah?"

"Uriah Heap. That's her name, and she's my baby."

––––––

Alice sat at a small table for four near the balcony, with her back to the wall, in the small bar called Erte, on the second floor of the Camps Bay mall. She inwardly congratulated herself for choosing such a perfect venue for her meeting. In truth, it was more luck than design. After all, how the hell could she have known what would be perfectly suited to a situation like this? It was so far from any experience she had ever had, or imagined she might have, she almost felt like an alien in her own skin.

From her seat, she could see out into the street as well as admire the calming sea view. Instead, apart from scanning the pavement downstairs occasionally to see if she could see Gloria arriving, she kept her eyes fixed on the single entrance to the bar that faced into the atrium of the mall.

Before she arrived, she'd bought a map of the area from

a little tourist boutique, and on her way into the mall she made a note of her exit routes out of the shopping centre. Although Erte was not far from the main doors, there was also a small side service entrance about fifteen metres in the opposite direction, just beyond the public toilets on that level. This led to a small flight of external stairs that came out a few metres from where Alice had parked Lisa's car.

Erte was further out of town than The Sea Shanty and situated near the main intersection along Camps Bay's main road, which meant that if Alice needed to get away quickly, she had a better chance of avoiding the notorious 'Cape Town Riviera' traffic.

She ordered a diet soda just to blend in. The last thing she felt like doing was eating or drinking anything. She checked her watch. It was 4.40 pm and there was still no sign of Gloria or Lekan. She wondered what she would do if they didn't show. Would she have the balls to go to the police? If she did, would she be drawn into this whole debacle and potentially risk deportation or worse? Maybe she could ask Lisa to do it? Lisa probably wouldn't. She'd more than likely insist that Alice do the right thing and go in herself.

If she did hand in the diary, how would she explain where she got it? The police were sure to look into her background, passport, visa etc. If she said she'd found it, the police might not take enough notice of it. They might assume it was just an innocent diary, hardly worth handing in as lost property.

Alice's thoughts were interrupted as Gloria sat down at her table. Gloria called a waiter and ordered the same thing Alice was drinking.

"Sorry we are late," Gloria said.

Alice glanced at the door expectantly.

"They are on their way," Gloria explained. "Where is it?"

Alice shook her head. "I didn't bring it."

"What do you mean? We had a deal!" Gloria spat.

"Not a chance, Gloria! The deal was I'd get to speak to the girl and find out from you what the hell this was all about and then I would decide what to do with the diary."

"Alice, you're making a mistake. You have no idea of the consequences." Gloria leant forward and lowered her voice. "Many young women's lives would be in danger if the police started snooping about."

"You put these girls in danger, not me."

"Alice, believe me, I'm trying to help these girls."

"Help? By selling them to rich men?"

"It's not what you think —"

"Well, then please explain."

The waiter brought over Gloria's soda. She waited until he had retreated out of earshot before she spoke again. "These girls grow up in the townships." She kept her voice quiet, occasionally glancing around to check for eavesdroppers. "They grow up without parents, without an education to speak of and as a result, without a future."

"Let me guess. By selling them off as teenage brides or concubines or something, putting a fat wad of cash in your pocket, you are giving them a future?"

"Stop judging me and let me speak," Gloria said.

Alice held up her hands.

"I care for them, teach them, educate them and prepare them for the world, to be good wives and mothers."

"Is that what you do at the hotel?"

Gloria nodded. "Yes, the hotel is a perfect place for work experience."

"Does the hotel know you do this?"

Gloria shook her head. "Not quite, no."

"I knew it!"

"Alice, the hotel and places like that don't care about young black or coloured girls from the townships. I did approach them through the official channels. Do you know what they said?" Gloria paused. "They said they do not want thieves and prostitutes in their hotel."

Gloria met Alice's gaze head on.

That is terrible, Alice thought, but that does not excuse Gloria for selling innocent young women either. "Go on."

Gloria took a deep breath in and let it out slowly. "Okay. The truth is this. Once the girls get older, old enough to start thinking about their futures, once they are well educated and mature enough, I do look for suitable spouses for them."

"I knew it!" Alice smacked the table. "You sell them!"

"I only find good men. I try to find men who will provide for them better than I can, rich businessmen and tribal leaders who are looking for young, educated wives. I vet them personally myself." Gloria paused. "I love these girls. They are like my own children. I would have nothing happen to them."

"Gloria, you are selling your own children!"

Gloria nodded sagely. "It is true, we do accept money from the men. A dowry, if you like. That does not go in my or Lekan's pocket. Every penny goes into the Shelter and into educating the other girls, giving them a future and caring for the poorly ones who will not have that opportunity. These girls are not only saved from a life in the townships where they will probably experience violence, or be raped, killed or die hungry or with AIDS. They are given a bright future, as influential women in society. They become wives to some of the most powerful men in Africa — the power behind the thrones."

Alice mulled this new information over in her head. If what Gloria was saying was true then this posed a huge quandary for her. If she turned Gloria in, it would prevent these township girls from having a chance in life, albeit one that was achieved outside of the law.

"If you turn in that diary and we are investigated, not only will you stop other girls from the Shelter from having a chance, you will also risk the lives of those girls who are now happily living their new lives."

"How?"

"Some of these men are high-powered business men, politicians, tribal chiefs, and they demand discretion. If it becomes known how they sourced their wives, it would shame them and their wives would pay. Many of them would be shamed at the very least, others deserted or cast out and some even killed."

"Shamed?" Alice asked.

Gloria dropped her eyes to her hands which were now resting on the table in front of her. "Believe me, Alice, you'd rather not know."

The air hung thick between them as Alice tried to imagine what Gloria meant.

"So where is the girl? Can I speak to her?" Alice looked around again.

"Alice, I need you to understand. The girls do not know the details of the operation — for their own safety."

"They don't know you get paid?"

"Oh, that they do know, because it is customary to receive a dowry," Gloria said. "What they don't know is that it is illegal and regarded as shameful for me to arrange their betrothals, purely because I'm not their true family. I don't

262

want them to have to carry that burden too. Just because a child lost her parents, why should she be denied a happy, prosperous life? They know that we try to give them an opportunity for a better future, like I gave you, so they can be the best they can be. There's no reason why they need to carry shame with them into their new lives. That is why I wanted to talk to you first before you met Ayane. You can turn me in, but don't make this girl suffer."

Alice nodded.

Gloria fished out her mobile and dialled a quick-dial number. "It's clear," she said into the phone.

Alice studied this petite older woman in front of her. She could not figure her out. There was something so unorthodox, so left of field, about her and the way she operated in the world. Every time she thought she understood Gloria or knew how she felt, morally and emotionally, about the things she did, Gloria would somehow manage to pull the rug from under her feet.

A few minutes later, Alice caught sight of Lekan crossing the road towards them with a beautiful, young teenage girl, whom Alice recognised from the kitchen at the Shelter. She was beautifully dressed in a traditional African bright orange robe. Her hair had been done. She was wearing a triple string of beads around her neck and large copper loop earrings.

When they got to the table, Lekan pulled out the chair for her and she took her seat in a very lady-like fashion. "Thank you," she said softly. Lekan smiled and then sat down next to her.

"Ayane, you know Alice?" Gloria said.

The young girl nodded.

"She would like to know about your new adventure you are going on tonight."

The girl's face lit up. "Oh, I'm so excited. Mama Gloria has arranged for me a husband."

"That's nice." Alice smiled at her. "Have you met your husband?"

The young girl shook her head. Her eyes were sparkling with joy. "No, not yet. I'll meet him tonight. It's customary in our culture not to meet our husbands until our wedding night."

Alice nodded. She had to work hard to suppress the dissenting western voices from her own upbringing that shouted warnings in her head. "And, how did Mama Gloria find this lucky man for you?"

"Oh, Mama Gloria has been working very hard and looking very far. She has interviewed hundreds of men across the world and chosen this one for me." The girl looked at Gloria adoringly. "I know Mama Gloria made the absolute best choice for me."

Alice nodded again. "Where are you meeting your husband?"

"Uncle Lekan is taking me to meet him tonight and then we are going to his homestead."

"Oh, where is his home?"

"He lives in Mozambique but travels the world." Her emphasis on the word 'world' expressed her awe and wonderment at its magnitude.

"How well do you know Ayane's new husband-to-be and his family?" Alice asked Gloria.

"Believe me, we know everything there is to know, and we have insurances."

Alice shook her head. It was probably best she did not know about the latter.

"O vok!" Lekan said.

"Language, Lekan!" Gloria reprimanded, but stopped abruptly when she saw Lekan's expression.

He had been scanning the main road while they had been talking. Now he seemed jumpy and agitated.

"What is it?" she asked.

"The Pote[1] are setting up road blocks."

Alice did not understand what was going on. "What?"

"I thought you said tonight was a clear night?" Gloria said to Lekan.

"It was, in Green Point and Sea Point. I didn't know to check here," Lekan said, giving Alice a scathing look before he returned his attention to the roads.

Ayane looked around, confused. "Mama, what's going on?"

Gloria took her hand and held it. "Nothing, honey. Don't you worry."

"What's the matter?" Alice asked.

"The police have set up roadblocks out of Camps Bay," Gloria said.

Alice peered down the road and sure enough she could see blue flashing lights and beacons on the road leading out of Camps Bay towards Hout Bay.

"I need to go and have a look down the road to see if the Sea Point side is blocked too" Lekan said and got up.

"Okay, be careful." Gloria said, touching the side of his arm as he passed.

"Why would that affect you?" Alice asked.

Gloria looked at Ayane and patted her on the back. "Go freshen up a bit for your husband."

The girl did what she was told and got up and headed to the toilets.

Gloria lowered her voice, but Alice could hear the panic

in it. "If the police stop Lekan and me and they get Ayane
—"

"Why would they stop you?"

"Let's just say that we have reached the Pote's radar.
And before you take that as a sign that you should turn us
in, let me just say that it is thanks to one influential and very
corrupt township entrepreneur who is upset he's not getting
his share of the dowry, or benefits on the side, from the
township girls, rather than a case of vigilant law
enforcement. The Pote really don't give a hoot about us or
the girls from the township. This is about the wad of cash
they will get for bringing us, and even worse Ayane, to him."

"Shit!" Gloria said and rubbed her face and eyes.

Alice had never heard Gloria swear. Suddenly Alice
became aware of the fatigue etched on Gloria's face.

Gloria sounded quite distraught. "I should never have
brought her out here. I really thought if you could just speak
to a girl and hear it from her you would understand and not
prevent these girls from having happiness." Gloria quickly
wiped a tear from her cheek.

What must it be like for a girl from the townships to
entertain dreams of world travel and far away romantic
places, Alice thought. She had been there. She was a little
orphan in south east London once, swept away on the
promise of a wealthy man with big dreams. She was lucky.
All in all, Magnus was a good man. In fact, in some ways
Magnus had been the best thing that had happened to her.
Up until recently, he had looked out for her, and taken care of
her better than anyone else had. She was grateful to him for
everything he had done for her, for showing her a different
life. Ironically, he was partly responsible for helping her
along the journey that brought her to that fateful day when

she decided to leave him. In her own way, she had been where little Ayane was today. Who was she to play God over whether this little girl got to embark on her own journey?

Not only that, because of her arrogance, she had single-handedly jeopardised this little girl's chance of a future, by leading them into danger. This was her fault.

"Will they specifically be looking for you and Lekan or a black man and woman travelling with a young girl?"

Gloria's tired eyes met hers "What does that matter?"

"It matters, Gloria." Alice said more harshly that she intended. "My question is: Would they find anyone else travelling with a young girl from the townships suspicious enough to pull over and take back to your entrepreneur?"

Gloria looked a little confused. "Well, there are usually general roadblocks looking for people who are over the alcohol limit or smuggling something, so they might still pull you over... but unless you've broken some other law, there's no reason why they won't let you pass."

"Even if there's a young girl in my car?"

Gloria nodded. Then she suddenly realised what Alice was getting at. "Alice, no! You can't do that. I won't allow it. If they do stop you and decide to detain you for whatever reason, it could mean that you were deported. I won't have you risk your new life here like that."

"Gloria, you said it yourself. If they stop you and Lekan with Ayane, all three of you will be taken to that entrepreneur guy and that will be very bad for you two and for Ayane. Regardless of what I think about the rest of what you are doing, I won't stand by and let an innocent girl's dreams get shattered, or worse, let her be brutalised on my account."

When Lekan arrived back and asked what was going

on, Gloria explained Alice's idea to him. "Please talk some sense into her."

"No, I think that's a brilliant idea," Lekan said.

Gloria looked up at him shocked.

"How will she know where to make the drop?"

"It's okay. If she gets Ayane out of here, we can rendezvous in Sea Point and we can take it from there."

Gloria thought for a few moments, then nodded slightly. "And what about the diary?" she asked Alice.

Alice took a deep breath. "I'll think and decide what to do about that later. Let's get Ayane out of here safely, first."

Gloria was about to argue but Ayane arrived back at that moment.

"Ayane, there is a slight change in plan," Alice said. "You are coming for a little drive with me."

———

Alice observed Ayane from the corner of her eye as they sat in the queue of cars stopped by the roadblock. Ayane sat next to her on the white faux-leather passenger seat of Lisa's car, which dwarfed this young girl on the verge of her womanhood. If she was nervous or anxious there was no outward sign of it. She sat quite still. Her hands folded on her lap in a seemingly relaxed manner.

Far too soon, they reached the front of the queue. Alice put the car in gear and pulled forward to the cluster of Brobdingnagian men dressed in their dark blue police uniforms standing in the road. One of them directed a bright torch light at her and then waved her forward with some crude semaphoric dialect. As she edged closer. Alice was alarmed to see that a number of the men patrolling in the background were armed with AK47s. What could possibly warrant such force at a time like this, in such a beautiful city? Alice felt her heart beating faster and her palms slipping on the steering wheel. Until her encounter that night with Gloria, on the way to the backpacker inn, Alice had assumed most of the stories about the violence and crime in South Africa had been a result of ignorant tourists wandering off course into particularly dangerous areas, or overreacting to otherwise run of the mill incidents, which are rife in most large cities the world over.

Alice wound down her window.

The uniformed officer with the torch bent down. "Evening, Madam," the man said from behind the blinding bright torch light. Then he swept the light over the rest of the car interior to Ayane, where it lingered on her before swiping back over to Alice.

"Evening, Officer," Alice said politely, trying to resist the urge to shield her face from the intrusive light.

"Can I see your driver's license please?"

Alice bent down and fished out her UK licence from her bag. Thankfully Lisa had told her that in South Africa it is mandatory to carry your licence. She concentrated on her breathing and silently sent out a little prayer to anyone who was listening that they didn't ask her for any other documentation.

"May I see your passport, please?"

Alice gripped the steering wheel tighter. "Unfortunately, I don't have it on me, Officer."

"How long have you been in the country?"

"A few weeks. I'm here visiting family and friends." Alice hoped that sounded convincing and quite normal.

"And who are your family and friends?"

"Gloria," Alice said. She had no idea what Gloria's

surname was. Even if she had known, she was not going to give them her full name, in case it raised a bright red flag.

"Gloria who, Madam?" The officer was getting a little impatient.

"Oh, Officer, I'm so sorry, I do struggle —"

"Hambanathi,"[2] Ayane cut in. "My English auntie has trouble with the Xhosa pronunciation."

"And where are you going now?" the officer addressed Ayane.

"I'm taking my... niece... home, sir," Alice said.

"Have you been drinking?"

"No, sir. Not a drop... yet," Alice said. "Been a long day so looking forward to the first one later." She tried to give him a colluding smile.

The officer bathed Alice and Ayane in the blinding torch light once more. Alice held her breath. Finally, he stood back up and waved them through.

She slipped the car into gear and pulled away far more calmly than the adrenaline pumping in her body made her feel, all the time keeping an eye on the roadblock in her rear-view mirror. She saw Gloria and Lekan in the car behind, being stopped and questioned. Seconds before the roadblock disappeared completely out of view, due to the bend in the coastal road, she saw Lekan stepping out of the car.

Shit!

———

The plan was for Alice to get Ayane to the Sea Point Pavilion. From there Lekan would pick her up and take her on to the meeting point, while Gloria would go back to the flat with Alice.

Usually, during the day, this part of the promenade was teeming with locals and tourists alike, all descending on one of the most popular swimming pools in Cape Town. Now, it was relatively quiet apart from the occasional gay man out cruising.

Alice parked the car.

"Thanks," Alice said softly.

Ayane looked confused.

"For your help at the check point."

Ayane said nothing but nodded slightly.

"Is that Gloria's surname?"

The girl shook her head. "It's mine."

"It's a beautiful name."

"It's my clan name," Ayane said. "It means: Walk with us." She turned and stared out over the deep, dark sea to their left.

Alice nodded not knowing how to carry on the conversation.

They sat in silence in the car, waiting. Eventually Alice tried to ring Gloria's mobile phone. It just rang.

When, after twenty minutes, there was still no sign of Gloria and Lekan, Ayane started fidgeting in her seat.

"Do you know what time you are supposed to meet?" Alice asked.

"Eight o'clock."

Alice's watch said it was 7.35 pm.

Ten minutes later, when there was still no sign of Gloria and Lekan, Ayane had grown positively agitated.

"Do you know where you are supposed to meet?"

Ayane nodded in the dark. "Between Green Point and Mouille Point at the bus stop."

Alice had a feeling it was the same place she saw Lekan and the other girl before.

271

SAM SKYBORNE

Alice became aware of soft sniffing noises coming from Ayane. She tried to look at her, but her face was shrouded in darkness. Alice's heart went out to this young woman. Her future and all her precious hopes and dreams hinged on the events of the next half an hour, all of which were entirely outside of her control.

Right there, Alice made a decision. She switched on the ignition of the car. Ayane looked at her with panic in her eyes. "Where are you going?"

Alice smiled at her. "I'm taking you to the bus stop."

"Really?" Ayane wiped tears from her cheeks and eye with her sleeve. "You know where it is?"

Alice nodded. "Let's hope so." She pulled out of the parking space and headed down Beach Road towards Green Point and Mouille Point.

———

On the surface, it seemed like an unusually calm night. The bright watchful moon cast an iridescent silver path on the water's surface, leading a trail directly to Alice and Ayane where they sat in the car in Mouille Point.

Alice felt the tension building in her neck and shoulders as the minutes ticked by. What was she even doing here? The day had started out with her adamant about putting Gloria in jail for this, and yet here she was, actually bringing Ayane to meet her suitor herself.

She glanced at Ayane to see how she was doing. The young girl sat silently staring out to sea. The only sign that she was in fact awake was her right hand rhythmically twisting a large ring around her middle finger. Alice could not quite see in the dark what it was. From the occasional gleam as it caught light from the street lamp as Ayane moved, the ring looked like some sort of creature stuck to her finger.

"That is pretty," Alice said, needing to break the silence.

Ayane turned and looked at her.

"The ring," Alice explained.

Ayane lifted her hand into the light and nodded. "It was a gift from Mama Gloria." She held out her hand to Alice. "I can't take it off. It is Odenkyem[3]. A crocodile — to keep me safe."

Alice took hold of the offered hand and had a closer look. It did in fact look like a crude, stunted lizard-like animal clasping onto Ayane's finger as if it was about to crawl up onto the back of her hand. "A crocodile?" Alice asked.

Ayane nodded. "It represents being able to adapt. The crocodile lives in the water but breathes the air. It can adapt to circumstances. Like me. I need to adapt."

"It's nice," Alice said.

"They're also strong and dangerous. When they bite you they can kill you."

Alice laughed, more from the shock of the vehemence in the young woman's voice. "Are you going to kill people?" She asked not expecting an answer.

Ayane shrugged. "I'd only kill bad people, if I have to," she said quite seriously.

Inside the dark silver body of the little crocodile it had a transparent glass gem or cavity. "It is very beautiful. It has a see-through belly," Alice said.

Ayane nodded. "That is where it carries its crocodile tears."

"So it can cry?"

Ayane nodded again. "Yes, when it's sad. Crocodile's

tears are poisonous. When the crocodile bites you, he sheds his tears and that makes you die."

Alice did not know what to make of this. She assumed it was part of an African tradition or myth. She made a note to ask Gloria about it one day.

Alice automatically reached out about to touch the crocodile's little square face and long snout with her index finger.

"Don't do that!" Ayane said, and pulled her hand away.

"Sorry," Alice said.

A large black Jeep with blacked out windows and a number plate that spelt out GCA PAPA, pulled up in the space in front of them.

Could anyone be any more conspicuous? Alice thought. If they don't want to be caught, it would help if Lekan could persuade the husbands to be a little more incognito.

"Stay here," Alice said. She got out of the car and walked up to the Jeep as she had seen Lekan doing at the last exchange. She had no way of knowing that this was the correct contact. For all she knew it could be another gay cruiser looking to get lucky.

When no one got out, she approached the front passenger window. Her heart thumped in her throat. She was about to rap on the window when it slid down slowly with a low-pitched electronic whirr revealing two large black men. The one in the driver's seat was wearing a black suit and the other a traditional colourful African robe. Both of them wore black framed sunglasses over which they peered at Alice suspiciously. Alice almost giggled at the cartoon pastiche of mafia bodyguard meets African tribal chief.

"Hi, I think you might be waiting for Lekan?"

The man in the colourful robe spoke. "And what if we are?"

"Well, he has been unintentionally delayed and asked me to meet you instead."

The man looked Alice up and down. "Why would he send a white woman to do a man's job? This is not safe."

This question took Alice aback a little, but she decided that now was not the time to question traditional, possibly sexist or racist views, so she just shrugged. "I think he didn't want to miss the meeting and I was the only option."

Then the man wound up his window, leaving Alice to stare at her own reflection in the mirrored glass. Oh no! Had she offended him somehow?

Two seconds later, both doors opened and the driver and the man in the colourful robe stepped out of the Jeep.

"Bring her," he said.

The driver came around the Jeep and took up a protective shadow stance a little way behind the man in the robe.

Alice rushed back to the car, to Ayane's door. She opened it. "Okay, it's time," Alice said, helping Ayane and her little suitcase out of the Golf.

Once Ayane was out of the car, Alice gripped both her elbows and crouched down in front of her. "Are you sure you want to do this?" she asked.

Ayane glanced at the Jeep and the two men waiting for her near it. Then she looked back at Alice.

"You can stay if you would rather not and I'll take you home." Alice stroked Ayane's arms reassuringly.

Ayane nodded. "This is my destiny. It's my new life. I am adaptable."

"Okay, but —" Alice reached past Ayane into the glove compartment of the car and retrieved a pen. Then she pushed up Ayane's long sleeve and wrote her mobile number on her forearm. "Write this number down somewhere more permanent and if at any point you don't want to go with him anymore you just ring me. Okay?"

Ayane looked from her to the dark numbers on her arm and back. Then she nodded. Alice stood up. She picked up Ayane's suitcase in one hand and rested the other on Ayane's back protectively as they walked towards the men.

As they got nearer, the man in the colourful robe took off his sunglasses and smiled such a warm tender smile at Ayane that lit up his face and transformed him from 'evil gangster hidden behind dark glasses' to jovial, almost muliebral, cuddly teddy bear.

"Lumela basali," he said to them both. Then he opened his arms as if he was about to hug Ayane. "U tlameha ho ba khosatsana ea ka e ntle."[4] Then, he thought better of it. "Oh, how rude of me," he said. "I'm Bulelani. Please, let me take you two lovely ladies to dinner." He pointed to his Jeep.

Alice shook her head. "Not for me but, thank you." She leant down and gave Ayane a hug. "Take care now and remember what I said."

Ayane nodded.

Alice stood up and stepped back out of the way, allowing Bulelani to escort Ayane to the Jeep. The driver opened the door and Alice watched as the new husband-to-be helped his new bride-to-be into the rear passenger seat and then scuttled in after her. The driver closed the door and came back towards Alice, reaching into his inside pocket. For a moment Alice thought the worst and was about to run when she saw his hand reach towards her with a thick white envelope. He waved it up and down a few times when she did not respond immediately. "For you," he said.

With shaking hands, Alice took the envelope.

The driver bent down, grabbed Ayane's suitcase and went to put it in the boot.

She stood frozen to the spot, until long after the Jeep had disappeared completely from view.

————

From Mouille Point, Alice headed straight for Gloria's flat. There was no one home. When no one arrived after a further half an hour, she decided to head on to the boat. It was really quite late now. She was surprised Lisa hadn't sent out a search party for her. She had been so preoccupied with meeting Gloria and the events that followed that she had not given Lisa a second thought. She had no idea how she was going to explain where she had been or what she had done.

When she finally arrived at the boat, the lights were still on and Lisa was lounging in the main cabin watching a movie on her iPad.

"Hey, so sorry I'm late. I lost complete track of time," Alice said as evenly as possible.

Lisa smiled. "Nice to see you. Very nice that you're back in one piece. How's Uriah?"

Alice put the keys and her bag down. "She is fine. Sorry! You must have wondered if I had been in an accident with your lovely baby."

"Well, I figured either you led her astray or she took you for a ride," Lisa smiled.

Alice felt her ears burn with guilt. "So how was your day?" She attempted to change the topic.

Lisa glanced around the boat. "Well, it is too dark now or I would say see for yourself, but I did a pretty good job on the decks and even in here. There is now a little more space in the closet next to the bedroom for some more of your stuff."

Alice was touched by this gesture. "That's very nice of you. You didn't need —"

"But I wanted to." Lisa got up and came to put her arms around Alice's waist, pulling her closer. "I'd prefer it if you could unpack and didn't have to clutter up the place with that thing," Lisa said seriously, pointing at the suitcase. Then a smile broke out across her face. She leant in and kissed Alice.

"More to the point," Lisa said, "How was your day? How did it go with Gloria? Did you tell her you've moved out and you won't be working at the Shelter anymore?"

Alice pulled away, using the excuse of getting a drink of water to put some distance between her and Lisa.

"We spoke, yes." Alice filled the glass.

"And?" Lisa prompted.

"Well, I told her I've moved out."

"And the Shelter?"

Alice pushed herself off the kitchen sink. "No."

Lisa frowned.

"No, I decided I'll keep working with the children."

"Al —"

"I want to do it for the children, Lisa. The Shelter is all they've got. I want to help them. I couldn't live with myself knowing I'm just lounging around on your lovely boat all day when I could be helping them."

Lisa shook her head. "Those two are not up to anything good, Al."

Alice didn't really like the shortening of her name, but she decided that now was not the time for that conversation. "Lees, I'm going to do it, at least until I get another job, okay." Alice's tone was firmer than she had expected. "I decided to start this new life because I wanted to do something worthwhile, something that made me feel good about myself and was more authentically me, and for now, working with those children is it."

Lisa was about to say something else when Alice cut her off.

"Now, I really need some sleep and I'd very much like to curl into bed with you and feel your lovely strong arms around me, if that is okay with you?" Alice held out a hand to Lisa.

To be honest, sleep was the furthest thing from Alice's mind. She knew Lisa meant well, but she really couldn't face more of this conversation, not until she'd decided what to do about the new developments of the evening.

FIFTEEN

Alice hardly slept at all. Thoughts of the previous evening's events plagued her, going around and round in her head. Had she done the right thing by taking that girl to Mouille Point? Could someone that young really know what was best for her? She thought back to her own past and how Magnus had presented as her only way out of a sad and oppressive life back then. Was he her only salvation in the end? Perhaps not. But what did save her, she knew, was having hope. Even though a life with him had not lived up to the promise, if she hadn't decided to make a change, she would probably now be a mere shadow of herself, or worse. Perhaps the same could be said if she had decided to stay with Magnus. Was her decision to leave him and stay behind in South Africa the right one? Who knew? Despite all the logic she could muster, in the end, she still couldn't help worrying about little Ayane.

Eventually, just before dawn, she gave up on sleep and got up to make herself a coffee. She was careful not to wake

Lisa and headed up the ladder onto the flybridge to watch the sunrise. It was a crisp, clear morning and the sea looked like liquid silver.

"Hey, you're up early." Lisa's voice made Alice jump. She turned to see a sleep tousled Lisa coming up the ladder. "I thought you might want a luxurious lie-in on your first free day." Lisa came over and kissed Alice softly on her head.

"Actually, Lees, this is not a free day. I need to get going in about half an hour."

Lisa checked her chunky diving watch. "It's six forty-six. Where could you possibly want to be this early?" Lisa stretched and yawned. "Even I don't have to be anywhere before nine today."

"I need to get to the Shelter," Alice said and took another sip of her coffee.

"Alice, I really don't think that is a good idea —"

"I know you don't." Alice held Lisa's gaze. "Lees, it is my decision. I know how you feel about Gloria and Lekan, and you might very well be right. And, I appreciate how much you care about me, but I need to do this. Those children, they need me to do this."

Lisa shook her head, then she leant in and kissed Alice on the nose. "Anyone ever point out how stubborn you are?"

Alice smiled. "I need your support on this, Lees."

Lisa nodded. She gripped Alice gently behind the neck and looked her straight in the eye. "Okay, but promise me you won't get involved in any more of their schemes and trouble. Okay?" Alice nodded.

"Promise?"

Alice lifted her hand to her eyebrow in a mock salute. "Aye aye, Captain Lees. I promise."

Lisa gave her a smacker of a kiss. "You got that right."

Then she headed back to the ladder. "Do you want another coffee?"

Alice nodded eagerly.

———

At the Shelter, Alice was instantly struck by the quiet, sombre mood. A couple of the older children were in the kitchen preparing breakfast. When Alice asked where Gloria was, the girl with the baby on her back nodded her head towards the infirmary.

Alice found Gloria sitting in the hard-backed chair next to Masika's little camp bed, fast asleep. Masika was also sleeping, but looking pale and restless.

Alice gently touched Gloria's shoulder to rouse her. "Oh, hi." Gloria's voice sounded groggy.

"What's the matter with her?"

Gloria shook her head. "Not sure."

"Should we call a doctor?" Alice kneeled down next to Masika and wiped a strand of hair away from her forehead. "She's burning up!"

Gloria got up. "Yes, the doctor said to give her those," she nodded towards a white non-branded packet of tablets, "every four hours and to give her lots of water and wipe her down to keep her cool. She's due one now but we will wait till she's awake."

"So, the doctor was here?"

Gloria nodded.

"And that's all he said?" Alice picked up the facecloth where it was resting on the side of an aluminium bowl of water. She dipped it in the water and wrung it out before gently placing it on Masika's little forehead.

Gloria rubbed her neck and tried to stretch her back.

"How long have you been here?" Alice asked.

"I came straight here last night. Thanks for taking Ayane."

"What happened to you?"

"We got stopped. Die Pote dragged us into the police station and kept us there till after midnight."

"Really? For what?"

"They were bored," Gloria deadpanned.

"Seriously, I was very worried. I went back to the flat afterwards to look for you, but when you weren't there, I had to go home or Lisa would have sent out a search party."

"When we were finally allowed to go, I got a message from Qaqambile[1] to come to the Shelter."

Alice noticed how ashen and tired Gloria looked.

"You need some rest. Do you have work today?" Alice asked.

Gloria nodded. "My shift starts at eleven."

"Okay, why don't you go home and get some sleep for a few hours. I'll look after Masika until you get back."

Gloria looked like she wanted to argue, but changed her mind. "Okay, I'll be back by nine tonight. If you need anything ring me."

Alice nodded. Then she remembered. "Oh, and then there is this." She reached into her bag and held out the white envelope from the driver.

Gloria looked from her to the envelope and back. Then she finally reached out and took it. She paused, tapping the envelope in the palm of her hand. "You did a kind thing last night, Alice. Thank you."

Alice pursed her lips and nodded just once.

Gloria turned and left.

Alice took up Gloria's seat, watching over Masika. She sat there for about half an hour before Masika stirred. When she woke up, Alice immediately leant over and helped the little girl sit up and take a few sips of water. She wiped her brow.

When she reached across to take a tablet from the white box, she found it was empty.

Shit! She was going to have to ring Gloria and hope that she had not gone to sleep yet.

Gloria picked up on the second ring.

"Hi. Sorry. I hope I didn't wake you."

"No, just making my tea. Is everything okay?"

"Yes, she's woken up and I'm about to give her medication but the box is empty."

"Oh dear. I forgot. I meant to get the new box from the pantry."

"Oh, okay. Can I get them?"

"You can. You'll need the key."

Alice suddenly remembered Gloria fishing the key out from around her neck, from under her clothes, on that first day she came to the Shelter. "Do you have one here?"

"Yes, it's a secret."

"Of course."

"Go to the kitchen."

Alice did as she was told.

"Make sure there is no-one in the kitchen, nor any trouble-making eagle-eyes watching you."

Alice nodded automatically.

"Now, see by the back door, the herb pots?"

Alice cast her eye to a small arrangement of home-grown herb pot-plants that stood in the sun on a little shelf made from tomato boxes near the outside door of the kitchen.

"Yes, I see it."

"It's in the parsley pot."

Alice peered into the small parsley pot and realised it was a pot within a pot. She lifted the inner one out and, in the bottom, she saw a small copper Yale key. "Got it." She retrieved it and put the pot back as she had found it.

"Okay, please put it back there without anyone seeing."

Alice went over to the pantry. She stuck the copper key into the large Yale padlock that secured a chunky metal hasp and staple that had been firmly screwed into the wood. Alice had only ever been into the pantry once before, briefly, to hold a torch for Lekan while he replaced the bare light bulb that provided the only illumination in the small room. Not only did it contain all the important food supplies and stores, but it also served as Gloria's office and was used to store everything of the slightest value, from the little spare cash they had, to important paperwork, to the first aid and medical supplies.

"The light is on the right," Gloria said. "It's a string you have to pull."

Alice felt around in the dark until her hand connected with a small string in mid-air around shoulder height. She pulled it.

"Where is the medication?" Alice asked, glancing around the room while she waited for the energy saving bulb to warm up and her eyes to adjust to the light.

"On the right, further in, you will see a shelf with the new kitchen supplies. Next to that are the medicines."

Alice looked around and soon located the medicines in their wholesale, white boxes. She headed over to them. She squatted down and pinching the phone between her ear and shoulder, she rifled through the smaller ones that had the same size and shape as the empty box Masika's tablets were in.

"They're the round white tablets," Gloria said.

Alice opened up a packet and checked that they were the ones Gloria described. "What are these?"

"Paracetamol."

"Is that all Masika needs?" Alice frowned. "Surely, with such a high fever and the fact that she's so poorly, she needs something more?"

"No, just those and her usual daily tablets. I do what the doctor tells me. She has been very good to us for years."

"Gloria, I really think we need a second opinion. It can't do any harm, especially with her condition."

"Alice, please can we talk about this later. I really need to have a couple of hours sleep before I go to work."

"Yes. Sorry. Of course. I'll keep an eye on her and let you know if there's any change."

"Thank you. And remember to lock up properly."

"Of course."

Alice ended the call.

———

She was about to get up to leave the pantry when a glint of silver and glass in another square, white shoebox to her left on the same shelf caught her attention. She pushed the lid open a little further. Inside she found a familiar looking plastic container housing six clear vials. She opened it and picked up one of the vials to read the label. It was insulin, the same make Magnus used to get for his mother — the same insulin she had injected Margaret with four times a day since before she and Magnus were married.

What were they doing here? They should be kept in a

fridge. Maybe Gloria was scared they would be stolen, or get into the wrong little hands, since the fridge was not secure. But what would Gloria be doing with insulin in the first place?

Alice tried to think if she knew of any of the children at the Shelter who had diabetes. She'd participated in a number of meal times with the children but couldn't recollect ever seeing anyone inject. Gloria would surely have mentioned it if any of them did so she could keep an eye on them, especially when they went to the swimming pool or were out and about.

———

Shortly after 9 pm, true to her word, Gloria pulled up outside. The children had had their supper and were all in bed, the younger ones fast asleep and the older ones reading or talking quietly amongst themselves in the sleeping area.

Alice sat alone in the dark on a stool at the main kitchen table, listening to Gloria's approaching footsteps. The small white shoebox and its contents shone brightly in the moonlight on the table in front of her.

Alice knew Gloria would head straight to the kitchen to stow her handbag in the pantry before she dealt with life at the Shelter.

Gloria pulled the cord that switched on the two suspended bare bulbs that formed the main source of light in the kitchen.

At the unexpected sight of Alice, Gloria jumped with fright. "Jesus Christ and all the saints in heaven, you will stop a woman's heart! You have to stop doing this!" She didn't wait for a response, but went straight to the pantry to put her bag away.

Alice sat very still and waited.

When Gloria emerged from the pantry, she noticed the box in front of Alice and paused almost imperceptibly, but caught herself. "What have you got there?" she said casually. She pulled the light chord, enfolding the pantry in darkness once more before she stepped out and started to lock it up.

Alice shook her head. "I don't know, Gloria." She spoke slowly, quietly and deliberately. "Maybe, you can tell me."

"What's with the riddles? How should I know?" She busied herself locking the padlock.

"I'll give you a clue. I found this in the pantry when I got Masika's tablets this morning."

Gloria turned around, looking cross. "I trusted you with the key and you went through my things? You have no right!"

"No, Gloria I didn't go through your things. I saw this because it was lying open near the tablets." Alice said, still keeping her voice even. "What are you doing with insulin? Who is diabetic?"

Gloria stepped forward and reached for the shoebox. "Just give that back."

Alice pulled it away, out of her reach.

"Gloria, who has diabetes?" Alice asked more firmly. "Which of the children has diabetes?"

Gloria sighed. "Thankfully, none of them."

"So, what are you doing with insulin?"

"Alice, we have talked about this. You know we take what we can get for the children. If we don't need it ourselves then we trade it for other things the children do need."

"Gloria, do you know how dangerous out-of-date insulin can be?"

"Those are not out-of-date," Gloria protested.

Alice picked up one of the small medicine vials. She checked the date. "You are right. But insulin has to be kept cold."

Alice didn't want to ask the next question, but she had to know. "Where did you get these?"

Gloria looked at the floor. "You know where we get most of our stuff."

"Gloria, look me in the eye and tell me you did not steal these from my room at the hotel?" Alice asked, slowly. Now that she had voiced her fear, shock crept over her like a chill.

Gloria said nothing.

"You... you saw what my husband did to me as a result, and you said and did nothing, and later pretended to be the Good Samaritan." Her voice broke. "Gloria, how could you?"

Gloria shook her head. "Alice, it's not what you think! I did not know you then."

Alice reached into the rest of the shoebox, moving aside a bundle of white tissue paper that was covering whatever else lay in the box. Four silver crocodile rings, like the one she remembered seeing on Ayane, lay neatly top-to-tail on a bed of tissue paper. She lifted out one of the crocodile rings to take a closer look. What would this be doing here? She thought.

"Alice, put that back." Gloria's voice was now more urgent. "That has nothing to do with you."

"What is this?" Alice turned the crocodile over in her hand. She put the ring on her middle finger as she had seen Ayane wear it. She took it off and turned it round and put it back on her finger so that it was now facing down her finger away from the knuckle. She studied the little silver creature and slowly curled her fingers, pulling them into a fist. As she reached the end of the movement and squeezed her fingers together, she heard a click and to her surprise the crocodile's little jaw had snapped open and something small and sharp protruded out the front like a long, sharp tongue.

"What is this?" she asked, horrified. Alice took off the ring in order to have a closer look and saw it was a needle.

"It's nothing," Gloria said and held out her hand. "Just give it back."

Alice pulled back out of Gloria's reach, still studying the ring in her hand.

Gloria grabbed the shoebox off the table.

"Ayane had one of these. She said it was a farewell present from you." Alice shook her head. "With a needle? Why? She talked about crocodile tears and... said if they were spilt... someone could die." Alice thought this through. Then suddenly the horror became clear. "Is that what the insulin is for? Gloria, what have you done? You're giving these girls insulin? For what?"

Gloria shook her head.

"Gloria, you either tell me what is going on here or I'll call the police, I promise." Alice reached for the phone in her back pocket. She held it up.

They stared at each other for a long moment. "I will do it, believe me," Alice said.

Gloria sighed with resignation. "It's for their protection," she said.

"Insulin for their protection?" Alice realised her voice was getting higher pitched and if she was not careful, she would attract the attention of the children. The last thing she needed now was to be interrupted.

Gloria nodded.

"Okay, well you had better explain," Alice said more evenly, still holding her phone in the air as a silent threat.

"I don't need to tell you about insulin." Gloria came over to the table and put the shoebox down.

"No, but you do need to tell me what it's got to do with Ayane."

Gloria pulled up a stool, the one she always sat on when she prepared food for the children. "I need to tell you a story," she began. "I was not always here in Cape Town, city of beauty and democratic equality. I was a very young arranged-bride too — not a happy one."

Alice rested her phone on the table and waited for Gloria to continue.

"My husband was not a nice man. He used to rape me, and his other three wives, almost every night... until I got pregnant. Why it didn't happen sooner, I often wonder. They say that when a woman's terrified, her body, or maybe God, prevents her from conceiving. I'm not sure whether that's true, but regardless there was obviously one time I wasn't scared enough. I must've become numb or something."

Gloria shook her head as if to clear away the painful memories.

"He was very happy, he was going to be a father. For the next nine months I was treated like a queen. He couldn't do enough for me, and once the baby was born, he doted on her. But soon after the birth, things returned to normal for me, and I started to expect him most nights. I knew my fate, but now though, it was easier. I was bigger from giving birth so it did not hurt as much, and I took solace in knowing how much he loved our baby. She was his princess. That made anything I had to endure okay. I didn't mind what he did to me, as long as little Tandy was happy and loved."

Gloria's unseeing eyes stared down at her hands.

"That was until my little Tandy turned ten," she

swallowed, her mouth dry, "when I found him giving her her birthday present." Her face contorted in anger and disgust as she recalled the events of her past. After a while she spoke again. "So, I did what I had to." She paused again for a long moment, letting her meaning settle between them.

She took a deep breath and continued in a matter-of-fact tone, as if on a different, lighter, conversation. "I took Tandy and we left, and came to South Africa, to Cape Town. My uncle had a job here in the fishing industry and he had always told me about how beautiful it was. I changed my name and made a new life for myself, but I couldn't look after her like she deserved. So, I had to put my little Tandy up for adoption. I was helpless then to stop what happened to her at the hands of her father, but the day I had to kiss her goodbye, before she went to her new family, I promised myself I would try to make amends and never, never, let that happen to another little girl again. I will make sure they are never as helpless as I was."

The long silence in the room felt heavy. Finally, Gloria raised her head and looked at Alice. "So now you know."

"I still don't understand what that has to do with the insulin?"

Gloria nodded slowly. "I give the girls each a ring and a vial as protection."

"You turn them into killers?" Alice said.

"No," Gloria shook her head. "I turn them into survivors. It's merely insurance. They know to only use it if things go wrong and their new husbands are bad men. It's just levelling the playing field and giving them a chance to fight back if they need to. Five of my girls are very happy, their husbands are wonderful, powerful and kind men. Three of them are either pregnant or now have healthy little children of their own, and they live as wealthy, respected wives in their communities. But there is always a risk. Until you know someone. You saw a couple of those men, and how small and fragile someone like little Ayane is in comparison. There's no way she could fight back against such a man if she needed to. Unless..."

"Unless she kills him?"

"Not necessarily." Gloria rubbed her eyes. "I know it's not a perfect solution."

"Not perfect!" Alice scoffed.

"My experience has taught me that sometimes you need to take risks if you want a better life." Gloria pointed at Alice. "You know that from your own situation too. I try to give these girls an opportunity for a better life but also equip them with knowledge, skills and the ability to fend for themselves. That's what every good mother tries to do. There's nothing wrong with that. You see?"

Alice shook her head. She didn't know what to see. She wished that she didn't understand. But she did. She understood too well that she lived in an imperfect world, where some husbands do rape and beat their wives, where sometimes you needed all the edge you could get, just to survive.

Alice sighed, stood up and put the ring back inside the shoebox. She got up and went to return the shoebox to its position in the pantry. Then she turned out the light, locked the pantry and placed the key on the table in front of Gloria. As soon as she left the room, she heard soft sobs coming from behind her.

———

When Alice finally got home, Lisa was waiting for her on

the boat. Alice didn't feel like company and really just needed time on her own. Lisa seemed to sense that.

"Okay. I'm glad to see you're home safely. I'll go back to mine now and give you some space."

Alice nodded, grateful. "Thank you. It's not you. I've just had a bit of a draining day."

"Want to talk about it?"

Alice shook her head. "No, I just need some sleep."

Lisa took Alice by the waist and kissed her on the nose. "Okay. I'll give you a pass tonight." She gently took Alice's chin and lifted her head so that Alice would look at her. "But I can't say the same for tomorrow night."

Alice frowned. "What's happening tomorrow?"

"There's a big party on Signal Hill to celebrate the super-moon. It's quite a sight. I've seen it once before and it's amazing. As the sun sets in the West, the moon will rise in the East, it's really quite spectacular."

"And of course, what better reason for you and your hippy chick friends to throw a party," Alice teased.

Lisa smiled. "Busted! You're getting to know us too well." She playfully tapped Alice on the nose with her finger. "But it's actually not just us. This is a big regional event and there'll be a stage, DJs, stalls and refreshments and all sorts of weird from every major and minor community not only in the Cape Peninsula, but people will be coming from far and wide to see this."

"Sounds fun." Alice tried to sound enthusiastic. All she could think about was getting some sleep.

"It should be." Lisa slipped her fingers through Alice's jean loops and wiggled her hips gently. "So, do we have a date?"

Alice smiled and nodded.

"Cool. I'll pick you up at six." Lisa pulled Alice into a deep, gentle, kiss. "Now rest. You look exhausted."

Wednesday - 6 December, SA

Toni had one chance at this. She had to make it work. When Alice suddenly disappeared from The Sea Shanty, Toni knew it was time to make a move before she slipped through her fingers and disappeared for good.

She sat in the warm shade under the large canopies of The Sea Shanty sipping a cold beer. The restaurant was fairly empty with only a handful of customers. She had picked the time for her visit carefully. If she'd observed Gerry's habits well enough, which she was pretty sure she had done, she could bet on Gerry making her rounds in the front of house, checking in with the customers as she passed any minute now. Toni was not disappointed. A few minutes later Gerry meandered over.

"Can I get you anything else?" Gerry asked, collecting the empty beer bottle.

Toni nodded. "Yes, another would be lovely."

"Not working today?" Gerry asked, alluding to the fact that, unlike on her previous visits, Toni was indulging in alcoholic beverages.

Toni shook her head with a sigh. "No, sadly my case has gone almost as cold as your delicious beers."

Gerry looked concerned. "Oh, no. That's not good news. Wish there was a way I could help."

Toni looked up. "Well, actually there is." She let the words hang for a bit, noticing Gerry's subconscious glance towards the back of the restaurant. "I was wondering if you might be able to suggest anywhere nice to go in the next couple of days, maybe where there are a few nice people to chill out with." Toni raised her eyebrows conveying the unspoken message. "I might as well enjoy my last few days of being here in this lovely country with its gorgeous people." Toni made a point of allowing her eyes to drop down to where the top two fastened buttons of Gerry's shirt rested on her cleavage.

"Oh!" A smile curled Gerry's lips as she realised that Toni was flirting. "I might just be able to help you out. In fact, your timing couldn't have been better. There is a special super-moon party on Signal Hill this evening. Perhaps you'd like to come to that? Almost everyone in town will be there."

Toni smiled. That should work, she thought.

———

Alice had spent the day tending to Masika at the Shelter until Gloria arrived back at around 5 pm. She'd wanted to stay on with the little girl but Gloria had sent her home, telling her that there was nothing more she could do for Masika right now other than pray and hope. She instructed Alice to take some time off, rejuvenate and make sure she was rested and strong to take over from Gloria the following afternoon.

Lisa parked the car in an empty space along the road on the side of Signal Hill. Alice was pleased she had agreed to come out with Lisa although Masika was not far from her thoughts at any point. The last few days had been very stressful. She hadn't had much time or emotional and physical energy to engage with Lisa properly. She really needed to let her hair down and relax and reconnect with Lisa. It was a stunning evening and Signal Hill boasted probably one of the best views of Cape Town, Table

Mountain on the one side and Sea Point, Camps Bay and the sea on the other.

Lisa took Alice's hand as they headed up towards the car park where a large group of women had already started gathering. The organisers had brought in big metal baths of ice and water, stacked to the brim with cold beer and cider. To one side a spit braai was slowly rotating over half a large 44-gallon drum that contained a well-stoked fire. Alice was surprised that they were allowed to make a fire on the side of the hill, but she figured that perhaps they had received special dispensation on this occasion. She couldn't quite tell what meat was being roasted, but it smelled good and made her stomach grumble.

As they approached the crowd, Alice recognised a few of the women as Lisa's mates from the beach party. Some had brought camping chairs and were sitting in a little semi-circle, chatting and laughing. Just then, Andy turned and saw them approaching. She called out and waved them over. She reached into a metal trough filled with ice and drinks that stood behind her and pulled out two beers. She handed them one each. "Here. They're nice and cold."

There were a few new faces, to whom Lisa introduced her. They were very welcoming and were very keen to find out what Alice had been up to, where she had been hiding, working and living. So many questions! Alice tried to fend for herself as best as she could.

While she was engaged with the little crowd that gathered around her, she noticed in her peripheral vision a tall brunette whom she recognised as Yvonne, the woman Lisa had been entertaining in her flat the night after the first, failed collection at The Sea Shanty. Yvonne more or less dragged Lisa away from the group and launched into a series of agitated whispers. The rest of the group seemed unperturbed by this, so Alice tried to remain focussed on the conversation, which had thankfully moved off her and on to Andy's favourite topic: rugby. Unlike the rest of the group, Alice couldn't contribute very much but it was animated enough to distract her from what was going on between Lisa and Yvonne. However, she wasn't distracted enough that she didn't notice the commotion over at the entrance to the party.

Gerry and a tall woman with long dark hair had just arrived and were making their way up towards the group. Gerry was waving and shouting a greeting to someone on the other side of the car park. The woman with her was slender and had an athletic way about her. She moved with the grace and confidence of someone who knew how to handle herself, yet she seemed to be a little reserved, not shy, but slightly held back, as if she was new and did not necessarily know very many people, allowing Gerry to take the lead.

"Trust Gerry to make an entrance," Lisa said in Alice's ear, startling her. She hadn't realised that Lisa had re-joined them.

"All okay?" Alice asked, raising an eyebrow in the direction of Yvonne.

"Oh, that." Lisa nodded. "Yes, all fine." She shrugged her shoulders and took a sip of her beer.

Alice didn't want to pry.

By then Gerry and her companion had reached Alice's group. Close up, her companion was even more stunning. She had long, straight, almost black hair, tied in a ponytail. Unlike the rest of the group her complexion seemed paler, not unhealthy, but generally lighter with a fresh pink glow, as if she was foreign and had only recently experienced her first few measured bouts of the hot African sun.

Alice tried to figure out whether she and Gerry were together. If they were, then it was probably a very new thing, since there was no obvious hand-holding, nor any sign of the connection one sees when a couple is smitten with each other.

"Let me introduce you," Gerry said quickly. "Everyone this is Toni. Toni, this is Monique, Lisa and the rest," she waved broadly at the group, "you'll have to meet on your own, as the evening progresses."

Toni nodded her greeting. Her bright smile lit her chiselled features.

"Here, have a cold one," said Monique, a mousey blond woman with a partly shaved head and tattoos peeping out on her shoulders from under her vest top. She handed Toni a beer, clearly trying to make a good impression on the newcomer.

"Toni is here from London," Gerry offered.

That immediately intrigued Alice even more. Next to her, she felt Lisa go rigid.

"Oh, I love London, in summer," Monique said. "I went there a few years ago for the Olympics."

"Yeah, and she hasn't let any of us forget it," Andy quipped.

"That's nice," Toni said. "To watch or participate?"

The sound of an English accent was like music to Alice's ears. She hadn't realised how much she had missed it.

"Neither really," Andy cut in, throwing her arm around Monique's shoulders. "She was the physio for the women's soccer team.

Toni looked impressed. "That's pretty cool."

"Yeah and the players got many a rub-down," Andy teased. Those listening ooh-ed.

Monique blushed. "It was my job." She tried to play-kick Andy on the butt.

Alice turned to share her admiration with Lisa, to find she had disappeared. Alice glanced around. It was only then that she noticed Lisa and Gerry, a few metres away from the crowd. It looked like they were in a very serious conversation, verging on an altercation. Alice wondered what could have caused it. She hoped it didn't still have to do with her and the debacle at The Sea Shanty.

Alice returned her attention to Toni. It was great having another Londoner in their midst. Once the conversation had died down and all eyes were no longer focussed on Toni, Alice stepped closer. "Hi, I'm Alice," she said and offered her hand.

"Hi, Alice," Toni said, shaking hands gently and beaming her a breath-taking smile.

"So, what brings you to sunny Cape Town?" Alice asked.

Toni smiled. "I'm here for work."

"Oh, nice job that sends you to this lovely country."

Toni nodded. "I don't usually end up in such exotic locations."

"What do you do?"

"I am in information gathering," Toni said. That was her standard non-disclosure response. Telling people she was a private investigator often had a very unproductive effect on conversation.

"Oh, like a researcher?" Alice asked.

Toni nodded. "You could say that. What about you? What brings you out here?"

"Oh, originally a holiday," Alice giggled. "I liked it so much that I decided to stay for a bit."

"It's nice that you could do that," Toni said. "I'd love to

be able to go AWOL, especially in a beautiful place like
this. How long have you been here?"

"Not long," Alice said. "I'm still finding my feet."

Softly, softly Toni reminded herself. Now that she had
finally met the woman, she did not want to spook her.

"So, have you done all the sights?" Alice asked.

————

Alice could not quite remember what she and Toni had
spent the last few hours talking about. All she knew was
that she'd had a wonderful time. It had been so long since
she was able to talk to somebody who understood weather
with all four seasons in a day, ales and bitters as opposed to
only lagers and the inexplicable comfort of a familiar
accent.

At one point she was vaguely aware that Lisa was
hovering, clearly on edge about something and looking like
she was ready to leave. But, when she looked again, Gerry
had dragged Lisa off to join the group of women who were
climbing up Lion's Head to toast the rise of the super-moon.

When it was time to drive home, it was clear that Lisa
had had a few drinks and was well over the alcohol limit.
Luckily, Alice had been so engrossed in conversation with
Toni she'd hardly drunk a drop.

All the way back to the boat, Lisa hardly said a word.
Once they were home, she flopped onto the couch and sat
there sulking.

Alice could not take it anymore. "What is eating you
tonight?"

At first, Lisa refused to communicate, but finally she
blurted, "So, you're going to see her again?"

"See who?" Alice asked, switching on the kettle.

"Your new girlfriend."

"What do you mean, my 'new girlfriend'?"

"Oh, don't give me that! I saw the way you looked at her, the smiles, the little touches."

"What are you talking about?" Alice couldn't understand why Lisa was so upset.

"You know what I'm talking about — that Toni woman," Lisa spat, her speech slurred. "If I were you, I'd just stay away from her, I'm warning you now."

Alice was quite shocked by Lisa's vehement reaction. At the same time her pride raised its head. How dare Lisa speak to her like that! "I thought you don't do jealousy. You're the one who does not want relationships, who wants to be 'free'."

"I'm not jealous!" Came a somewhat petulant response.

"Well, you're behaving like it."

"I am not jealous!" Lisa crossed her arms. After a while she spoke again. "So, are you seeing her again?"

Alice did not see what the issue was. "Yes, as a matter of fact I am. She is also new in Cape Town and we are going up Table Mountain tomorrow to see what all the fuss is about."

"I knew it!" Lisa stropped.

Alice rolled her eyes. "Unlike you, I'm not about to jump into bed with the woman. She was nice, easy to talk to and friendly to everyone, that's all."

Lisa huffed. "I didn't see anybody else talking to her for two hours straight."

"We have a lot in common, coming from London."

"More than you think." Lisa snorted.

"What is that meant to mean?"

"Nothing."

"No, tell me."

"Don't come crying to me when your little dream is shattered, okay."

"Lisa, what are you going on about? If you know something I don't, then you have to tell me." Alice was getting very agitated with this cat and mouse game. "Lisa —"

"Magnus!" Lisa shouted back.

Alice felt a chill run down her spine at the mention of her husband's name. "What does Toni have to do with Magnus?" Her insides started churning.

Lisa took a deep breath. "I tried to get you away from her, but you wouldn't listen. Then all I could do was stand by and watch, hoping you didn't hang yourself."

"Lisa, tell me what Toni has to do with Magnus."

Lisa looked at Alice for a long moment. "She works for him." Lisa finally said. "She's a private investigator from London. Magnus has employed her to find you and take you back to him."

At first Alice couldn't make sense of what she was being told. Then she sat down on the end of the couch opposite Lisa and dropped her head into her hands. "And how do you know this?"

Lisa got up and came to sit next to her. She gently put her arm around Alice's shoulders. "I'm really sorry, Alice."

"You know this, how?" Alice said angrily.

"Gerry," Lisa said. "You know Gerry. Nothing remains a secret with her around."

Alice frowned. She suddenly remembered Lisa's reaction to Toni when Gerry introduced her. "You knew before!" Alice said in disbelief.

Lisa did not respond.

"Lisa! You knew who she was and you didn't tell me?" Alice was getting more worked up.

Lisa sighed. "Gerry called me last week and told me someone had been to the restaurant asking questions."

"You knew!" Alice said, exasperated. "And you didn't say anything!"

"I did try. You wouldn't listen, and then it was too late."

"I don't mean tonight. Before. You knew beforehand someone was asking questions? Why did you not say Gerry had called?"

"It didn't seem relevant —"

"Relevant? How does 'my husband has hired a P.I. to track me down' not seem 'relevant' exactly?" Alice said, her pitch shrill in disbelief.

"I didn't think there would be any way for her to track you down." Lisa shook her head. "I certainly didn't think Gerry would be stupid enough to invite her along to the party."

"Ugh!" Alice dropped her head back in her hands.

"So, what now?" Lisa finally asked softly. "What are you going to do?"

After a long while Alice sat back up. "Nothing. I'm going up Table Mountain. That's what."

Alice got up and headed to the bathroom. She needed space.

———

Ten minutes later, Alice came out of the bathroom after a quick shower. She found Lisa sitting on the far end of the couch near the stern of the boat with a packed rucksack at her feet.

"What's going on? What are you doing?" Alice asked, towelling her hair dry.

"I'm waiting for a taxi," Lisa said not making eye contact.

"What? Why?" Alice stopped what she was doing.

"I'm going back to my flat," Lisa said with steely resolve.

"Why are you doing that?"

"I love you Alice. I'm not going to sit by and watch you ruin your dream. If you want that woman more than you want me, than you want this," she motioned towards the boat and the space around them, "a new life, fine. But don't expect me to hang about, or bail you out again."

There was a flash of lights from outside.

"Lisa —"

"My taxi is here." Lisa got up and headed for the door.

"But Lees —"

"Oh, and don't worry, I, unlike most, am a woman of my word. When I said you can stay here for as long as you need, I meant it. You can also use my car for as long as you want, just return it in one piece before you shack up with your new squeeze." Lisa turned and stomped off the boat, almost tripping onto the jetty.

Alice considered running after Lisa. Even though the urge to do that was huge, despite being dressed in nothing other than her towel, she resisted. What good would that have done? Lisa was upset and she was drunk. They'd already had a volatile confrontation and more of the same wouldn't help either of them. She was better off collecting her thoughts, figuring out what to do next and then having a more sober conversation with Lisa tomorrow.

So, Alice put on her pyjamas and made herself the cup of tea.

She felt upset about Lisa jumping to conclusions and leaving like that and was angry with Lisa for not telling her about Toni in the first place. In her heart of hearts, she knew

Lisa had probably been trying to protect her, in her own way.

As for Lisa's patent jealousy, where did that come from? She really liked Lisa. It was not hard, considering how kind, helpful and supportive she had been. She had a lot to be grateful to Lisa for. She hadn't only been her one true friend, she had also opened her eyes to a whole new world of loving women. The truth was she had already fallen for Lisa. That was obvious by how hard she had to work to suppress her own surges of jealousy when she saw Lisa with Yvonne, and the other woman she had seen her kissing outside her flat. There were probably a number of other lucky ladies waiting in the wings that Alice didn't even know about. From the start, Lisa had made it quite clear she wasn't looking for anything serious.

Was it too much to hope that Lisa was more than just jealous out of pride — as a reaction to being faced with some competition for Alice's affection? Or could it be possible that Lisa felt the same? Alice didn't want to hope.

As for the party, it was wonderful to meet and talk to Toni. She had to admit that Toni had a certain irresistible charisma and was a very sexy and attractive woman. Anyone would be more than happy to be in her gaze, if only for a few short hours. And yes, she had enjoyed every minute. If she had the chance, could she sleep with Toni? She was gorgeous. But did she want to? No. She knew, sadly, her heart had already been claimed.

Sitting there now, in Lisa's boat, sipping tea at 3 am in the morning, Alice replayed the events of the previous evening. Knowing what she knew now about Toni, would she have avoided her? Should she call off the outing up Table Mountain? That seemed like the most sensible option under the circumstances, both for her sanity's sake and to keep out of Magnus's grasp. Toni did not know where she lived. Or did she? Her mind was foggy. She knew she'd told Toni that she lived on a boat, but had she said exactly where? She couldn't remember. She drained her cup. If she hadn't, she realised that Toni would get all the information she needed out of Gerry. Besides, she needed to know what her husband was after. There was no way she was going to return to the UK with Toni, but she wanted to know what Toni was going to tell Magnus? She had no choice. She had to go.

Thursday - 7 December, SA

At 9 am Alice stood outside the cable car station a few metres from the ticket office. She was still not sure she was doing the right thing. But, before she managed to change her mind, she saw Toni's striking figure heading towards her at pace.

As Toni neared Alice, a large, genuinely warm smile seemed to creep across Toni's face below the gold-rim Ray Ban glasses. Toni leaned in and kissed Alice on the cheek. "What a beautiful morning it is," Toni said.

Alice was determined not to let her guard down. She kept her cool. "Shall we get tickets?" she asked quickly and moved towards the queue that had already started forming at the ticket office. She wanted to make sure that Toni couldn't escape before she'd had a chance to find out everything from her.

While Alice waited in the queue, Toni excused herself. For a moment Alice panicked. Did she know Alice knew? Would Toni leave? Alice forced herself to stay calm. Probably Toni had just gone to use the facilities before they went up in the cable car.

A few minutes later Toni returned, carrying two ice-cream cones.

"It seems right to have ice-cream for breakfast in this heat, don't you think?" Toni said with a grin. "Hope you like vanilla and caramel."

———

The view from within the cable car was spectacular. The South-Easter, better known as the Cape Doctor, had cleared Table Mountain completely of its tablecloth and the city-bowl of its smog and fumes, leaving a crisp, clear view all the way around, over the city and miles out to sea. Even Robben Island looked like a big boulder, merely a little leap away.

As they neared the top of the mountain, Alice could see over into Camps Bay and even down towards the Hout Bay Area. The view gave a whole new perspective to her life. It seemed bizarre that a place that had become so significant to her could look so small and almost inconsequential from so high up.

At the top, Toni and Alice followed the crowd and took a scenic stroll around the decked area that surrounded the cable station. Periodically they stopped at the lookout points and studied the information boards which signposted landmarks, indigenous fauna and flora and occasionally provided snippets of historic information. They stood for a while admiring a small family of dassies[2] and the occasional brazen gecko sunning itself on the rocks.

Once they'd completed the circular walk that arced out from the cable station, Alice suggested they go to the canteen for a cold drink before heading back down. There was a surprisingly long queue in the canteen and all the food and drink was eye-wateringly expensive, but Alice didn't care. While Toni got herself a soda, Alice opted for a little bottle of wine even though it was still only 11 am. She needed Dutch courage for what was to follow.

Toni found them a table in the sun looking out over Cape Town harbour. It was idyllic, with the potential for being quite romantic, if that was what someone had in mind.

"You're very quiet today," Toni observed after they had settled.

Alice pulled her face into a smile. It was now or never. She just didn't know how to start. She had a big sip of her wine, her taste buds smarting at the cool sharp liquid. She cleared her throat. "So, I believe you —"

"I have something I need to tell you —" Toni said at the same time.

They both stopped abruptly and laughed nervously.

"No, you carry on," Alice said.

Toni seemed to search Alice's features for a moment. "Okay, well," she took a sip of her drink. "I have something I think you should know."

Alice waited, taking another sip.

"As you know I met Gerry at her restaurant. What you may not know is the reason I was there." Toni hesitated and took a deep breath. "I was there because I was looking for you."

"Go on," Alice said, with a slight nod.

"I judge from your reaction that you probably know this now, and I'm very sorry I didn't tell you last night. I probably should have."

Alice nodded. "You should have."

"And I guess that means you also already know that I

have been employed by your husband to come and find you, and try to persuade you to come home with me."

There was a long silence while Toni waited for Alice to respond.

"I would have preferred that you told me last night," Alice said, playing with the droplets of condensation on her glass.

Toni nodded.

"What have you told Magnus? Does he know you have found me?"

"No, not yet, exactly. I wanted to have the full picture and be sure of the situation first."

"But you are going to?"

"I will need to give a full report."

"And are you going to throw me over your shoulder and drag me back to him kicking and screaming?"

Toni laughed at the image. "My business is in intelligence, not muscle. I'm not a thug for hire. He's employed me, so I'm obliged to inform him of your current whereabouts, and ideally provide him with means to contact you."

Alice nodded, somewhat relieved.

"May I ask you a question?" Toni asked. "Why did you leave him and decide to stay here? I mean, South Africa has a lot going for it, but something tells me you did not stay simply for the great wine and sunshine."

Alice studied Toni, wondering whether she could trust this woman before her. Eventually, she shook her head. "It doesn't really matter."

"No, Alice, it does matter." Toni reached out and gently, with her thumb, stroked the back of Alice's hand where it lay palm down on the table. "I have a choice. I can either report back that I have found you, and leave you two to negotiate your return... or maybe if I understood a little more, I might be able to help."

"It's not so straightforward."

Toni nodded. "I realised that. That's why I'm asking you to tell me."

Alice took another large sip, drawing strength from the cool liquid in her mouth. "Magnus is not a bad man," she began. "He has a lot of capacity to care for his patients. I think he tries to do a lot for other people, for humanity and for his mother. He even did a lot for me." She trailed off, lost in her own memories.

"So, did you want to leave him?"

"Something that might have started off good and empowering grew disempowering, stifling, almost suffocating. But that is not the worst part of it all. For a long while now, I had accepted that as my lot in life — to fill the tiny gap that Magnus had made for me in his life. When I came here, I realised there needs to be more." She tapped her breast bone with her middle finger. "I needed to find me again, to be all I can be in this life."

Toni nodded.

"I'm not saying it is his fault. In this life, people tend to give one the respect one demands and I realised I was not demanding any. I didn't even know what I wanted."

"Do you know what you want now?"

Alice thought about this and eventually nodded slightly. "I don't know precisely, but I know maybe a little more. I'm not sure whether what I want is a life with Magnus as my husband anymore. I feel bad that I left him and Margaret the way I did." Alice confessed. "For all Margaret's cantankerous, and seemingly ungrateful behaviour, I realise she was also just doing the best she could in a difficult situation. She needed my help. Hell, I would even now be happy to give her my help, but as a carer, with boundaries, not as Magnus's wife. I shouldn't just have walked out on them like that." She took another sip. "I guess the reason I did it the way I did is because I feared I would not be heard, nor be strong enough to go through with it otherwise. I feared he would do what he has always done."

"Which was?" Toni spoke more softly. "Did he hurt you?"

"No," Alice shook her head, "nothing like that. I mean he did once or twice get a little rough when I was being stupid, but it's not that. He is a very powerful personality. He doesn't need to hit anyone to get what he wants."

Toni nodded. "How about if you have backup, you know, get help?"

Alice laughed. "Are you going to send me to some safe house, and get me a bodyguard or something?"

"No, if you say he is not physically violent towards you then I believe you. I meant like a lawyer, some kind of representation, to speak for you."

"There are people who do that?"

Toni nodded. "If you decide to come back with me, I can help you arrange that."

Alice thought about it. How would she feel being back in England, with Magnus? She tried to imagine talking to Magnus. Even with someone else there fighting her corner, she was pretty sure Magnus would not stand for it. He wouldn't willingly let someone else interfere in their marriage. She would have no chance.

She shook her head. "Thanks, Toni, but no. I think it's better if I just stay lost."

"You know, Magnus strikes me as a persistent man. If he hired me to come looking for you, he is bound to hire someone else or try to find you himself." Toni said, genuinely worried.

Alice nodded again "I know. Maybe I'll move on to a different part of this vast, lovely country. There are bound to be other towns in this beautiful place that will give illegals work, and a chance to start a new life."

"Do you really want to keep running your entire life?"

Alice shrugged. "If that is what it takes."

The two women finished their drinks in silence and made their way down the mountain on the next available cable car.

Toni walked Alice to her car.

"I am truly sorry for misleading you." Toni said. She took out her wallet and retrieved a pen from her inside jacket pocket. "Look," she said, scribbling on something inside the wallet. Then she looked Alice straight in the eye. "It's not my place to advise you about what to do with your life. So, I won't bring this up again, but," Toni held out a small, light blue card. "Here. It has my international mobile number on it. I'm staying at The Bay Hotel until Saturday, when I'll be flying back to Heathrow. If you would like my help to reclaim your life and your power, then come with me."

Alice took the proffered card and studied it. On it Toni had written "21.30 Saturday" and the date. She glanced back up at Toni. In her expression she saw genuine concern.

———

Alice headed straight to the Shelter from Table Mountain. Not long after she got there, the doctor arrived. While she had been waiting for Toni at the foot of the mountain, she had texted Gloria and insisted that she call the doctor for

Masika. Extra Paracetamol and honey water did not sound like a reasonable treatment plan and she wanted the doctor to take another look.

Dr Xhosa unhooked the stethoscope from her ears and put them back into her bag. She said something to Gloria in their language. It didn't sound like good news. The doctor picked up her bag and headed to the door.

"What is the matter? Is she going to be okay?" Alice asked Dr Xhosa. She saw the doctor glance at Gloria. Gloria shuddered as if to shake off the question and headed past Alice to see the doctor out.

Alice grabbed Gloria's arm. "Gloria, tell me! What's going on? What did she say?"

Gloria took Alice's hands in both of her own. "I told you not to get too close to these kids."

"What do you mean? What's the matter with her? She has a cold, right?" Alice asked, feeling the panic rise from her gut.

Gloria shook her head.

Alice turned to Dr Xhosa. "Please, Doctor, what's the matter with Masika?"

"She's a very poorly little girl," the doctor said gravely. "She has the TB disease. With her weakened immune system that is usually what kills them."

"But," Alice looked from one woman to the other, "I thought you said she will be fine as long as she keeps taking her medicines."

"That would be true if she were taking the right medicines," Dr Xhosa said.

Alice couldn't understand. She looked down at little Masika who was sleeping restlessly. Then she glanced at the saucer of tablets that had been standing on the tiny table next to her camp bed since the very first day Alice arrived at the Shelter. She thought back to how, since then, she had sat with Masika every morning and encouraged her to drink down every single tablet while explaining to her how it was necessary to keep her safe and healthy.

She took a closer look at the multi-coloured tablets.

Slowly, it became clear. Her heart started pounding in her ears. She turned to Gloria. "What have you done?" She asked in a venomous whisper.

Gloria shook her head. "I've done nothing. God is calling her home."

"Why?" Alice was almost beside herself.

"I'm sorry, I need to go," Dr Xhosa interrupted. "God speed, Mama Gloria," she said.

"Thank you, doctor." Gloria turned to walk out with her.

"Don't you dare!" Alice said sharply to Gloria. "Don't you dare walk away!"

Gloria nodded at the doctor apologetically to let herself out. Then Gloria sighed heavily and turned slowly back towards Alice.

Alice grabbed a handful of the tablets. "What are these? What are you giving her? Tell me!"

Gloria nodded. "Okay, Alice, but not here." She firmly took Alice by the arm and led her away, out of the infirmary.

Once they were in the kitchen and Gloria was sure there were no little listening ears nearby, she let go of Alice. "Alice, as you know we are a charity. Hell, we are not even a charity. Everything we give these children we have to beg, borrow or actually steal. The medication for Masika costs a lot of money."

"But you said you had her medication," Alice said. "You said she will stay healthy as long as she takes her medication."

"No, Alice. I said, 'all she needs is her medication.'" Gloria looked around, taking a deep breath. "You know, with the police clamping down, the new road blocks, the disaster with finding new supplies... We were lucky we managed to feed them this month."

Alice shook her head. She was not listening to Gloria anymore. "So, what have you been giving her? What has she been taking faithfully in handfuls every day?"

"Look, Alice —"

"Don't!" Alice warned. "What?"

Gloria rubbed her eyes. Eventually she said, "They are vitamins."

"Vitamins?"

"There is no money for the right pills. We have no money. The medication she needs costs thousands of rands a month. We can barely feed and clothe all the children. Almost everything we have, has been donated or we have sourced somehow, but as you can imagine people don't tend to leave this type of medication lying around where we can just help ourselves."

All Alice could think was that a little girl was dying. There must be a way to get her medication. She knew South Africa did not have an NHS but surely... "There must be something you can do!" She started to pace. "Can't we ask other charities to help or run a crowdfunder or something?"

"Alice, there are hundreds of children like Masika who die every day. We are already doing everything we can, using every hour that God gave," Gloria said. "Sure, maybe if none of us ever slept, we could possibly find a way to do a dozen other things that should also be done for these children. I can tell you for free that there is a lot we could, and need, to do with twelve-thousand rand."

"Okay, if you can't do it, then I will. I will raise twelve-thousand rand for her medication and show you it can be done."

"And then what? That's only one month's worth. Can you commit to raising that kind of money every month?" Gloria was now also worked up.

Alice's whole body was rigid with frustration. She couldn't take it any longer. She could not just stand around and do nothing while watching little Masika die a slow and painful death. She turned and marched out of the kitchen. To where? She wasn't sure.

SIXTEEN

Alice went to the Shelter early. She knew Gloria would have spent the night with Masika again and she was keen to see how the poor little girl was doing.

When she got there, she peeped into the infirmary. Masika looked peaceful and fast asleep. She went through to the kitchen. There she found Gloria and Qaqambile making putu pap and a soup from bones and chicken stock. Qaqambile had her hands elbow deep in the sink, washing the dirty bowls and cutlery. Gloria was stirring a large pot of soup. The delicious aroma made Alice's stomach rumble. She realised that, with all the tension of the past twenty-four hours, she hadn't eaten since the previous morning.

Gloria blew on the soup in the ladle and then had a little sip. "Right, I think this is ready." She refilled the ladle and poured some soup into a little mug. "I'm going to take this into Masika and see if I can get her to take her medication."

Alice shook her head. "I'll take it," she said. "You're

busy." A part of her understood why Gloria was keeping up the positive charade, for Masika's sake and everyone else's, including herself. Another part really wished she wouldn't.

"No, it's okay." Gloria tried to push past Alice.

Alice gently but firmly took hold of Gloria's arm. "Gloria, I will," she said calmly. "You carry on. You've probably been up all night with Masika. The other children need you too. I can do this." Alice saw a strange look in Gloria's eye. She was not sure exactly what it meant but then she could see Gloria relent, probably too exhausted to argue.

———

Alice entered the infirmary with the cup of hot soup and a teaspoon. She hoped the teaspoon would encourage Masika to eat more of the hot liquid.

She approached the little arrangement of camp bed, table and wooden chair which had been placed there for the purposes of watching over and caring for Masika. With an inward scoff, she moved the vitamin and paracetamol boxes over on the table so she could put the soup and teaspoon down. There were probably far more nutrients in that cup of soup than all the tablets Masika had been taking for the past months in the form of these vitamins, she thought. She sat down on the chair.

"Masi," she said softly. "Masi, my angel. You need to wake up. I have some soup for you that you need to eat so you can take your medication and get better." Her heart broke inside. Did this little girl know that all this medication was not going to make her better? Alice bit her bottom lip. Now was not the time to break down. She had to be strong for little Masika. She had to believe. The poor little girl looked so small, so frail, so peaceful. She was sleeping more soundly than Alice had seen her do in days. That was a good sign. Maybe there was a God who did not want this little girl to die either. Alice wondered if she still had such a high fever. Alice leant over and wiped Masika's fringe out of her eyes. Carefully, not wanting to wake her, she touched the back of her hand to the little girl's forehead. She felt cool.

Too cool.

Alice looked at her more closely. She was very still.

Too still.

Alice could feel an uneasiness building in her gut.

She leant forward and placed her ear nearer to Masika's little mouth and nose to feel her breathing.

Nothing.

Panic struck Alice. She took hold of Masika's shoulder and started to shake her. "Masika! Wake up. Masika! Wake up!" She was frantic now. "Gloria! Gloria! Come quick. Call the ambulance," she shouted.

Within seconds Gloria came rushing out of the kitchen, already dialling the emergency services number.

They would be there in forty-five minutes.

By this stage Alice was beside herself, crying. "No! No! It can't be. Not now!"

Gloria opened her arms and pulled Alice into a hug, cradling her head on her shoulders. "Shhh. It's okay, honey." She rocked her gently. "I'm sorry you had to find her. I'm sorry she is gone. It's better this way, honey. It is a blessing she did not have to suffer longer. Shh."

"I was going to get her the right medication. I was!"

Alice looked at Gloria. Where she used to see kind eyes, she now saw long suffering and a steely resolve and strength.

"You've got to believe me, Gloria. I was going to..." Alice's words trailed off in another sob and Gloria pulled her tighter into her arms and patted her back like she had done a hundred times to the children when they had suffered one of life's knocks.

————

Alice had cried all she could cry, for now. She had finally let go of Gloria, which allowed Gloria to get back to caring for the rest of the children. After all, they still needed to be fed and looked after.

Alice sat on the hard wooden chair and stared at the little lifeless figure in front of her.

She remembered the first day she arrived at the Shelter with Gloria, seeing little Masika for the first time, sitting on her upturned bucket in the shade, staring out at them with that guarded expression. Who knew then that she would burrow so deeply into Alice's heart?

Now, she would never again see Masika's smiling face and small form come running towards her when she arrived at the Shelter. She would never feel those little arms wrap around her or clamber up her body for a hug, or hear her squeal with laughter and delight like that day she and Lisa took them swimming.

The little figure lying there in front of her in the camp-bed looked so different now, felt so different — empty. How could Alice have mistaken this lifeless shell for her precious, sleeping Masika? This was not Masika. She was gone.

Alice's heart broke. The paramedics came. They marched in and went about their business with practised efficiency. Like long distance athletes, who had done this a thousand times, they paced themselves through their routine. After all, there was no longer any urgency — no time-critical need — no life still to save.

Finally, they lifted the tiny, empty shell onto a stretcher and carried her away, forever.

———

Gloria had to go with the paramedics, leaving Alice to clear up Masika's bed. Masika didn't really have any personal possessions, none of the children did, other than a few items of clothing. Even these were not personal in that they were recycled and passed on to the next child once they no longer fitted.

Alice stripped the sheets and blankets and folded the rest of Masika's clothes into a little pile. She made a mental note to ask Gloria what to do with them beyond that.

Finally, she took the cup of cold soup and the teaspoon back to the kitchen.

The kitchen was empty. Gloria had chased all the children outside to play after they had had breakfast. As Alice got to the sink, she saw that Qaqambile had left the plastic tub they used for washing dishes or bleaching cloths in the bottom of the sink, still containing a strong-smelling bleach solution. To make space to wash the mug, she drained the bucket. With a loud clank something fell into the bottom of the basin. Once the suds had cleared, Alice saw it was something shiny and metallic. She reached in and picked it up. It was a crocodile ring. It must be Qaqambile's. She was about sixteen, Alice guessed. She found it hard to tell the ages of some of the children. Either way, she was one of the oldest girls still living at the Shelter. She was obviously the next lucky bride-to-be.

Just then, Qaqambile entered the kitchen carrying a

glass. "Oh, sorry," she said. "I just wanted to get some water. It is very hot in the sun out there."

Alice nodded. She dried off the ring and put it on the table. "You forgot your ring." Alice smiled at her. She had to try to be stronger for the children, especially while Gloria was not around. She wondered when Gloria would get back.

After downing two glasses of water, Qaqambile wiped her mouth, breathless. "It's not mine, Auntie," she said.

A child's scream came from outside. "I'd better go and keep the peace," Qaqambile said and headed back out to where the children were playing Stockings[1] in the dirt.

Alice took the spare pantry key from its hiding place in the parsley pot to put the ring in the shoebox with the others until Gloria returned.

After hunting around a bit, she found the white shoebox on the top shelf. She took it down and opened it and saw the rest of the crocodile rings and the insulin vials. This little box still made her feel uneasy. But then, last night, after her conversation with Gloria, she had tried to imagine how she would feel, knowing little Masika had gone off with a future husband and he turned out to be mean and brutal. Would she not want Masika to have some protection? Of course, she wouldn't want Masika to go in the first place. She hoped for a better, more empowered future for Masika. 'Had hoped', Alice corrected herself and burst into tears.

Through her sobs she put the ring in the box, stowed the shoebox back on the shelf and locked the pantry.

––––––––

Alice stayed with the children all day until Gloria finally

arrived back from the hospital. She made Gloria a cup of tea.

"I thought you might like to know that the doctor said she died quietly and peacefully in her sleep." Gloria said between sips of her brew.

Alice nodded. "Thanks. That is comforting at least."

"Now, I think you should go home and get some rest."

"But —"

"No 'but'. You have been through a lot. I know how much she meant to you. So, I think you need to go home now, try to get some sleep and tomorrow, go do something nice, something that reminds you of life and the living."

Alice felt her tears well up again. She had been able to keep them under control all day while she was looking after the children. Now, with Gloria's kind words, her defences crumbled.

"Don't you need me tomorrow?" she asked through her tears.

Gloria shook her head. She opened her arms and Alice fell into them, taking comfort from the small woman's warm and soft embrace.

"No, honey," Gloria said softly. "I will handle it."

Alice moved away and tried to compose herself, feeling a little embarrassed at her lack of self-control.

"I've arranged for the wake tomorrow," Gloria continued. "Reverend Bentley will be here with some of the congregation. The community would want to pay their respects. So, you can take some time out for yourself."

Alice felt helpless and didn't want to leave Gloria to have to deal with the wake on her own, but it was clearly Gloria's wish. She nodded.

———

On the way home, Alice got caught in the Friday afternoon traffic into Cape Town. Normally she would've been irritated, but now every passing moment felt precious, even sitting in traffic. Nobody knew when it was going to be their moment. She felt lucky to be alive. She thought back on the events of the past few weeks, since making her decision to leave Magnus and remain in South Africa. It was true she had not felt so alive in a very long time. But alive also meant being more open, raw and exposed to both pleasure and debilitating pain. In the past few weeks she had experienced highs and lows she hadn't even considered possible before.

Back on the boat, it felt large and empty without Lisa there. She had hoped Lisa might have decided to surprise her by being there when she came home. She really didn't want to be alone right now. Alice fished out her phone and dialled Lisa's number. She let it ring until it eventually went to the answering service. She decided not to leave a message. Anything she could have said right then would have sounded pathetic.

She felt like a drink. She inspected Lisa's little liquor cabinet. The alluring, rich, golden whiskey that Lisa had introduced her to and loved so much caught her eye. She grabbed the bottle and headed over to the cupboard above the sink to get a glass. In the sink stood her coffee cup from the morning and glass tumbler she had used for water the night before. She rinsed the glass. The morning's events were looping in her head in an endless reel. Everything reminded her of snippets from the day — the coffee mug in the sink, the cup of soup, rinsing the glass, washing the cold soup mug afterwards, the plastic tub of bleach and the ring.

The ring.

Why would the ring be out? Whose was it? Other than

Qaqambile, the rest of the girls at the Shelter were all far too young to be wedded off. She meant to tell Gloria she had put it back in the pantry. She remembered finding the shoebox and replacing it. She remembered the glint of the insulin vials — five of them. Then something hit her. Five? She tried to think back. She was sure the day before, when she had the shoebox out and she confronted Gloria about it, there had been six. Why would one be missing? Could someone have stolen it? No, only she and Gloria had access to the pantry and Alice was sure Gloria would guard the rings and insulin with her life. It had to be Gloria herself. To whom could Gloria have given a vial of insulin? Why would the ring end up in the sink?

A terrifying chill crept up her spine as the thought settled in her mind.

No! Surely Gloria was not capable.

Then panic took over. She needed to do something.

She grabbed her phone and tried to call Lisa again. Still there was no answer. Who else could she turn to? There were only two people other than Gloria or Lekan whose number she had. One of them was Gerry and she was not going to involve her in this. The other was Toni Mendez. Alice still had the business card Toni had given her after their morning up Table Mountain.

She punched the number into her mobile phone. Within two rings, Toni picked up.

"Hi, Toni, it's Alice," her voice sounded shaky.

"What's the matter, Alice? Are you okay?"

At the concerned tone in Toni's voice, Alice crumbled again. She sniffed and tried to speak. "May I come and see you?"

"No, you stay put. I'll come to you."

———

Half an hour, two large shots of whiskey and many tears later, Alice let Toni on to the boat. She offered her a drink but Toni declined.

"So, what's up kiddo?" Toni said gently.

Alice blurted out nonsensical snippets through copious sniffs, tears and sobs.

"Okay, whoa!" Toni said and handed Alice a tissue. "Take a deep breath and begin at the beginning."

Alice did as she was told and started to tell Toni the story from the beginning, meeting Gloria, her days exploring Camps Bay and how she came about buying the swimsuit, and briefly how she ended up leaving Magnus. "That part I told you already." She continued on about how she helped Gloria steal food and supplies from The Sea Shanty, getting caught, deciding to move out of Gloria's flat, going back to collect her stuff and then seeing Lekan and the girl. She told her about sitting in the bar watching the girl get into the limousine that night, returning to the flat, taking the diary, arranging to meet Gloria and ending up taking Ayane to the drop herself. She explained how, when Masika got very ill, she had stumbled across the insulin and the rings. She explained that the rings had an injection mechanism which could be charged with, well, anything really, including insulin. She could see Toni was intrigued to know more about that, but she decided to omit the parts about Gloria giving it to the young girls, as well as how Gloria had come by the insulin. After all, those details did not seem relevant right now.

"The fact is, Gloria is the only person who had access to the rings and the insulin. There were six vials. Today I only saw five and today Masika is dead, very suddenly."

"From what you say, Gloria has certainly broken the law and done some dodgy things, but accusing her of murder," Toni said, "that is a whole different thing! From what you tell me, everything she has done so far is for the good of the children. Why would she now kill one of them? Do you think she is even capable of murder?"

Alice took another large sip of her whiskey. There was no way around it. She had to tell Toni the whole truth. "Because she has done it before."

"What?"

Alice sat down. "She told me a story of how her husband abused her, raped her. When she found out that his abuse extended to her little girl, she killed him and ran to South Africa."

"Where is the girl now?"

"Adopted."

"That is part of the reason she is caring for these children?" Toni asked thoughtfully.

Alice nodded. "...As some kind of penance."

"Okay, so she is capable of protecting herself and her child. That is still very different to premeditated murder, Alice."

"What I didn't tell you earlier is, the reason I know about the ring is because the first time I saw one it was on the finger of Ayane. Gloria had given it to her as a parting gift — that, along with a vial of insulin, in case her new husband turned out to be an evil man like Gloria's."

Toni stood stock still. "You mean, Gloria gives her girls the insulin and the ring so they could kill their husbands?"

Alice nodded. "Yes, she sees it as some sort of 'insurance' so they can fight back..."

Toni paced around the room. "My God!"

———

Lisa had explained to her boss, the harbour master, that her car Uriah Heap was currently indisposed. He had agreed to let her use the Bakkie[2] from work until Uriah got sorted. She was on her way back to her flat in Green Point after picking it up from the harbour when Alice had rung the first time. She was going to ignore her call, figuring they both needed time to think, but on seeing Alice's name flash up on her mobile screen the second time she decided to go see her in person. They needed to talk but Lisa did not want to do it over the phone.

She got back to Hout Bay shortly after 7 pm and was about to board the boat when she heard voices coming from inside. She stopped. She thought she recognised the other voice but could not place it. She went around the side of the boat to peep in through one of the portholes.

Her blood boiled when she saw it was the P.I. from London again. Lisa was about to storm in there and give the woman a piece of her mind for trespassing on private property when she saw how upset Alice was. Lisa stopped herself and listened. It didn't take long before she had heard enough!

Seeing Alice so upset, she wanted to rush onto the boat and envelop Alice in her arms and tell her it would be okay. But she couldn't do that now, not with Toni there.

She knew that Gloria and Lekan were trouble and she had tried her best to keep Alice away from them, but this had gone way too far. Lisa felt sick to her stomach. They needed to be stopped!

She glanced back through the porthole and her heart shattered.

Inside, Toni had stepped forward and taken Alice into

her arms and was holding her, while Alice trembled uncontrollably with grief and despair.

Numb with shock and fuelled by rage, Lisa fled back to the Bakkie and drove off with a wheel-spin.

———

"What should I do?" Alice asked sobbing into Toni's shoulder. "I know I should go to the police. But I'm scared."

Toni took Alice by the hand and led her back to the couch. They sat down. Toni rubbed Alice's back to calm her down and comfort her while she spoke.

"Alice, honey, you are right to be scared." Toni took a breath. She did not know how to best explain things to Alice. "If you go to the police with this, it will bring you into the frame."

Alice looked at Toni, confused. "What do you mean?"

"You had access to the key to the pantry. You knew about the insulin and the rings. Hell, from what you said, your fingerprints are on the rings and the box. You have not mentioned it but, by all accounts, I'm sure Gloria will find ways to connect the insulin to you too, knowing about Magnus's medical connections."

Alice thought about how Gloria got the insulin.

"I've never even got a speeding ticket before —"

"You have owned up to stealing from your place of work."

"But why would I want to hurt Masika?"

"There are people who will probably testify that you were very close to this little girl — an evil act of mercy." Toni let her words settle. "If you go to the police with this, they will pin it on you."

"But Gloria was with her last night."

Toni shook her head. "You found Masika. The person who finds a victim is always the number one suspect until proven otherwise."

"But Gloria is behind —"

"By all accounts, Gloria is a respected pillar of the community. A kind and generous woman who holds down a respected job in the hospitality industry by day, and in her spare time dedicates herself and her spare resources to care for orphaned children." Toni rubbed her forehead. "Who do you think they will believe if it comes down to it? If she is behind this, then she is very wise and very shrewd by the look of things. She has thought this through very carefully." Toni turned back to Alice. "And, that is not even mentioning the fact that you are here, and have been working, I might add, illegally."

"You think she did this on purpose? She planned this?"

Toni shook her head. "Honestly? I don't know. That is not the point. The point is you are squarely in the sights, if they ever suspect foul play in Masika's death."

Alice was stunned silent, desperately trying to take this all in. "So, what do I do?" she finally asked.

Toni got up and paced the room. "The way I see it you only have one option."

Alice swallowed and listened eagerly, relieved that Toni might have an answer.

"You have to go back and get the shoebox with the rings and the insulin."

Alice stared at Toni, blinking a few times, not believing she understood Toni correctly. "What?"

Toni came to sit next to Alice on the couch again. "Alice, listen to me. You have to go back to the Shelter and get the shoebox of insulin and the rings. As long as Gloria has them, she can pin this on you. Without the ring and the insulin there is no murder weapon and so no proof of the crime."

"But, Toni, that also means Gloria will go scot-free."

Toni nodded. "Yes, but the alternative is that you end up in jail for a murder you did not commit."

———

Back in her flat, Lisa paced to and fro. Her blood was boiling after what she had just seen and heard. She was furious with Gloria and Lekan for getting Alice into this mess — correction, these messes. She was even more furious with Alice for betraying her so easily with that P.I.

There was only one thing to do. She had no choice. She had to call the police. Gloria had to be stopped. Maybe then Gloria would leave Alice alone and Alice would come back to her. She picked up her phone.

———

Alice was in no state to drive and she certainly did not want to go to the Shelter on her own, so Toni offered to take her.

Toni decided it was best if they didn't park inside the Shelter's grounds. That way it would be easier to escape swiftly, if the situation needed it.

Alice got out of the car and headed into the Shelter. She couldn't see Gloria's car anywhere. She couldn't remember either whether it was parked outside when she had left the Shelter earlier. She suspected that under the circumstances Lekan might have given her a lift.

Alice was very pleased to see that all the lights were off in the tent. She wasn't surprised as it had been a pretty long day and she was sure Gloria would have encouraged everyone to have an early night in preparation for the wake the following day.

Alice tiptoed through the central area into the kitchen. Once inside she had to wait a few seconds for her eyes to adjust to the dark. She took her phone from her pocket and considered using it as a torch, but she couldn't really use a light of any sort, for fear of it being seen through the gaps in the canvas material.

It was a bright evening and by the moonlight she could make out the glint of the large padlock that secured the pantry.

She tiptoed to the parsley pot and felt around inside it for the key. She could feel nothing. She lifted the inner plastic shell containing the parsley plant out of its lime green, metal outer pot to have a better look inside. There was nothing!

Shit! Gloria must have moved the spare key.

What now?

———

Lisa ended the call. She had decided to make an anonymous call to the police, but she wasn't sure if they took her story seriously. However, if nothing else, she felt better for telling someone.

Then a worrying thought struck her. What if Alice decided to head back to the Shelter before the police got there? She had to tell Alice to stay away from the Shelter. She didn't want Alice to get caught up in this. She quickly dialled Alice's number.

———

Alice's phone lit up brightly with an incoming call. She'd had the foresight to turn it to silent, but could do nothing about the bright light shining out from the screen.

Shit! She silenced the phone as quickly as she could, but not before she saw Lisa's name flash across the screen.

Now she wants to talk! Alice thought.

She shoved her phone back into her pocket and tiptoed from the kitchen through towards the infirmary. She had a hunch that if Gloria had stayed over at the Shelter, as she suspected she might, she would be sleeping in there. Alice pulled the door flap to the infirmary aside. There she saw Gloria, fast asleep, still in her clothes with a single grey blanket pulled over her legs. There was no sign of her bag anywhere. There was also no way to retrieve the key from around her neck.

Alice was about to give up when she heard footsteps behind her. She froze. Two seconds later light flooded the little lobby area behind her. She instantly recognised the figure. It was Toni with a torch.

She motioned to Toni to follow her into the kitchen.

"I can't find the key," Alice whispered. "Gloria must've moved it." She pointed at the padlock on the pantry door.

Toni nodded, understanding, and pulled out a small leather pouch from her jacket pocket. She knelt down in front of the lock and in less than half a minute Alice heard the satisfying click as the padlock sprung open.

Alice patted Toni on the back. She opened the pantry and slipped through the door while Toni stood guard. Once inside she turned on the torch on her mobile phone then searched the racks for the white shoebox. She located it soon enough on the top rack where she had put it earlier that day. She grabbed it and headed out.

Toni locked the pantry door and more or less dragged her out.

"What's the rush?" Alice whispered.

"Can't you hear them?"

Alice shook her head. Then she listened. Sirens were approaching from the Cape Town side.

"Oh no!" Alice said.

"You're right. Get in," Toni said, opening the driver's door to the Golf and jumping in herself.

Blue and red flashing lights appeared at the bottom of the road.

"Shit! Too late." Toni said. "We can't go now. It'll look suspicious. We'll have to sit tight. Duck down!"

Alice did as she was told, hunkering down as far into the footwell of the red Golf as she could.

———

Two police cars pulled off the road outside the Shelter. Three uniformed men got out and headed towards the tent. The fourth stayed behind, presumably keeping watch.

Within minutes Alice saw the lights go on inside the shelter. She thought she could hear voices.

She was expecting them to drag Gloria out of the tent in cuffs at any point. It felt like they were inside for ages. Then she saw two of the police men come out and head to their car. A few seconds later the third followed with Gloria, who was surprisingly unrestrained and casually walking and talking with him.

Finally, the police officer turned and got back into his car. Gloria nodded and waved them goodbye before both cars drove off.

Alice watched as Gloria, looking frail and hunched,

wrapped in a long, oversized jersey stood motionless, staring at the cars disappear down the road. A part of Alice almost felt sorry for her.

Alice sat still, not daring to move until Gloria had gone back inside. But instead, as soon as the police cars had disappeared Gloria's demeanour changed. She fished something out of her long jersey pocket and studied it. Alice couldn't see what it was. Then, Uriah's cockpit lit up brightly as Gloria's name and image flashed across Alice's phone where it lay in her lap.

Alice froze. She didn't know what to do. She looked up at Gloria. To her surprise Gloria had turned and was looking straight at her in the car. Alice slid her finger across the screen and lifted the phone to her ear.

"Well played my friend," Gloria's voice sounded through the phone. "For a spoilt housewife you are cleverer than I thought."

"Gloria, how could you?" Alice asked, her voice almost a sob.

"Judging by the fact that the Pote did not find the shoebox, and you just made it out in time, I guess you were not dumb enough to call the Pote yourself, but know this: I still have the vial." Gloria allowed her words to hit home. "If you should change your mind and be tempted to try a stunt like this again, or feel the need to turn the shoebox over to the police, you should know that they will find the missing vial with only your own fingerprints and Masika's DNA all over it."

"But, Gloria —"

"But, nothing. Personally, I would prefer not to have to stoop to that level, as I would prefer never to see the Pote again, but if you force my hand, I will — and any future you might hope for here in South Africa will be obliterated.

And, in case you think you could claim the vials were stolen from the MOD, you are wrong. Don't you know your considerate Magnus never reported the theft in case it jeopardised his career and reputation."

———

Toni was not quite sure how to help Alice. From after she returned to the car, she had not quite seemed herself. She appeared to be in a bit of a daze, withdrawn and quite unresponsive. Toni guessed she must have been suffering from shock or severe stress after whatever she had gone through in the tent, since she left Toni waiting for her in the car. Toni considered taking a detour to a doctor on the way back to Hout Bay, but decided against it. Under the circumstances, it was more urgent to get Alice out of the country and safely back to the UK.

Saturday - 9 December, SA

Toni dropped Alice and Uriah off at the boat. With a heavy heart Alice packed up her suitcase and cleaned the boat. She tried to ring Lisa a number of times, without any luck. Eventually she left a message to let Lisa know that she was leaving with Toni on the next flight to London on Saturday. She really hoped to see Lisa at least one last time to say thank you for everything and to explain in person. She owed her that.

She resolved to get Toni to take them by Lisa's flat on the way to the airport. With any luck she would catch her there. Or perhaps she was at The Sea Shanty. Alice could picture her sitting at the bar.

Lisa sat slouched at the bar in The Sea Shanty. She stared into her Klipdrift. It was not a drink Lisa chose very often, except when she intended to get drunk and forget.

Gerry was drying glasses behind the bar.

"Are you going to mope all night?" Gerry tried to josh Lisa out of her funk.

Lisa hardly responded with more than a faint nod.

"What is eating you, Stud? Why don't you tell Gerry? She is a good listener. You know that."

Lisa looked at Gerry. The two of them had had a bit of a combative relationship, but Gerry was her friend and Lisa knew she'd have her back if she needed it. Now, she needed it.

Lisa shook her head. "I've been dumped."

Gerry started to laugh, then stopped. "You?" Her voice was tinged with disbelief.

"Yes, Alice has developed a thing for that P.I."

Gerry placed the glass she was drying on the shelf and then turned towards Lisa. She wiped her hands on the tea towel. "Lisa, you know me, I'm the faithful, perceptive bartender. Right?"

When Lisa did not respond she asked again, "Right?"

Lisa nodded and took a large swig of her brandy. The first swig of the strong liquor always burnt her throat.

Gerry moved forward and leaned on the bar in front of Lisa. "But on this occasion, I'm going to give you a bit of advice... whether you want it or not. The problem with you, with someone who has had everything so easy, is you have never had to work towards anything. You are intelligent, sporty, and good looking. Jeez, you hardly have to smile at a girl and they practically cum in their pants."

Lisa started to shake her head, not even smiling at Gerry's crude remark.

"So now, when things don't go your way immediately, or there is the slightest bit of adversity, you throw your hands up in the air and head for the hills to lick your wounds or," Gerry pointed at the glass Lisa was clutching, "drown your sorrows in the cheapest brandy you can find. Now, when it counts, you sit here feeling sorry for yourself...." She let her words settle. "For whatever reason, it might seem that Alice has chosen Toni, but everyone's perception of reality is subjective, so whatever that is, it might not yet be a done deal. If Alice is important, go out there and fight for her. She needs you, not some bimbo of a P.I. she only met a day or two ago. You, Lisa Lowe! Go! Show up! Show her what she means to you."

Lisa sat for a moment, dumbstruck by Gerry's lecture. She thought about what Gerry had said. And it actually did make sense.

"If you don't go now, you might miss your last chance."

Suddenly panic filled Lisa. What if it was already too late? That was a thought she couldn't bear.

She grabbed her keys and fled.

As she ran to the Bakkie she turned on her phone. Almost immediately a series of beeps indicated a number of missed calls and one new voice message. She listened to it as she started the car. As she feared, it was Alice saying she was heading to the airport. They were leaving on the 9.30 pm flight.

She shoved the car into gear and pulled away.

———

Alice and Toni barely spoke all the way to the airport. Alice had almost ground to a halt. Other than the complete numbness that had settled over her, she felt more or less incapable of doing or processing anything.

When they got to the airport, the taxi driver helped Toni to get Alice and their luggage to the departure terminal.

"Here." Toni sat Alice down on a bench near the entrance. "You stay here. If you give me your passport, I'll go drop the bags," she said.

Like an automaton, Alice reached into her large handbag and passed Toni her passport.

Toni took it, grabbed the two suitcases and headed off to the baggage drop counter, leaving Alice alone, lost, facing down her own demons.

————

As Alice sat on the bench staring into the middle distance, she suddenly thought she heard something. She listened again. There was nothing other than the usual airport din. Then there it was again. It was someone calling her name. How many Alices were there in the world? Thousands. Yet, something made her turn.

Then she saw her. In the distance, Lisa, running towards her. She had come!

Alice got up.

When Lisa finally reached her, Alice threw her arms around her. They clutched at each other, both conscious that this might be their last embrace. Lisa was the first to move, creating a little distance between them so they could speak.

"Stay with me," Lisa said simply.

Alice looked at her with tears in her eyes.

"You've been so good to me," Alice said. "But I can't stay, even if I wanted to, and believe me, I do."

Lisa shook her head about to protest.

Alice squeezed Lisa's hands to stop her. "I need to go back. I need to go and make myself free. If I stay now, I'll always be running from Magnus."

"But he can't find you. You can choose to stay, at least for a little bit longer. Nobody belongs to anybody, and we can belong to as many people as we choose. Choose me."

"And I'd have to run from the law. I'm an illegal immigrant. Someone will always be able to wield that over me. I'll never be free." Alice leant forward and took Lisa's cheek in one hand. "Thank you, Lisa Lowe, for being so wonderful to me. I will always remember you."

Lisa started crying.

"I'm so pleased you came and we had a chance to say goodbye." Alice swallowed hard. "Please, Lees. I need you to be strong for both of us and let me go, please," she nodded, urging Lisa to understand.

Lisa shook her head wanting desperately to argue.

"Please Lisa. Go."

She did.

PART III

SOUTH EAST ENGLAND, UNITED KINGDOM

SEVENTEEN

It was 2 am. The airplane cabin was dark and most of the passengers were attempting sleep as best they could. Some were reading, or passing the time watching movies. Toni had selected a rerun of Fight Club, from the meagre selection available. Although it was one of her favourite movies, she couldn't concentrate on it. Her mind kept drifting, looping over the events of the past few weeks.

She had also hoped to gain some clarity about what to do in relation to her own personal dilemma with Lizbeth while she was away. Instead, she'd been so busy she had hardly had a chance to think about it.

Eventually, she decided to give up on the movie and get some rest. She turned off the small monitor and tried to get as comfortable as possible in the small upright space of her seat. She glanced over at Alice who had fallen asleep leaning against the window. Just then something caught Toni's eye. In her sleep, Alice's top had ridden up revealing her soft pale side and there, peeping out over her low-cut

345

jeans, just on the inside of her hip bone, Toni saw the small dark dragonfly tattoo.

Oh my God! Toni gasped in recognition.

———

After they landed Toni collected her car which had been parked at the long stay car park at the airport, thanks to PhyCorp's deep pockets. Then she drove a somewhat defeated looking Alice back to PhyCorp and Dr McCroy's office. Toni gave her the contact details of organisations and people who she knew could help Alice in the time to come when she needed to separate from her husband, if that were truly what she wanted to do. For now, Toni was pleased that she had managed to rescue Alice from a potentially dire situation in South Africa and bring her back to England safely.

They sat together in the PhyCorp waiting room. Toni kept a close eye on her. It was really hard to tell what this woman was feeling. She looked far away, like her thoughts were in another world, another time. Toni had no idea what more to say. It was hard to think of everything she had been through and even harder to imagine what lay ahead.

A side door to the waiting room opened and the woman Toni recognised as Sheena, Dr McCroy's assistant from her first visit to PhyCorp, entered and headed over to them.

"Toni," Sheena nodded and shook Toni's hand, "nice to see you again." Then she turned her attention to Alice. "Hello Alice. I'm so glad you are back. Dr McCroy will be thrilled to see you. If you'd like to come with me."

Alice glanced at Toni for reassurance. Toni smiled at her and tried to convey all the calm confidence that she couldn't quite feel herself.

Alice turned and followed Sheena.

That was weird, Toni thought, as the heavy old doors of the main entrance closed behind her with a soft thud then a short series of clicks. She looked back, assessing the building as she walked away. The oddest and most low key "welcome home" she had ever witnessed. At the very least she'd expected Dr McCroy to come out and meet his wife himself. Perhaps some people were just too important for sentimental reunions. For a fleeting moment she wondered how Lizbeth was going to react to seeing her, after all her time away — she was hoping for a lot more warmth and enthusiasm. Dismissing the thought, she carried on to her car.

———

On the way back to Lizbeth's flat Toni picked up their usual pizza, a Hawaiian with extra peppers and half chilli, to share, with extra paper napkins.

When she got to the flat, Toni hesitated. It felt odd having been away for so long and she almost rang the doorbell. But she didn't.

"Hello, honey, I'm home," Toni called without thinking. It was a funny little habit that had started as a joke between them when they were still just friends. Now, the irony struck home.

The main area of the open plan flat was empty.

"In here," came Lizbeth's voice from the bedroom.

Toni busied herself getting plates and condiments for dinner while she waited for Lizbeth to come out.

A few minutes later Lizbeth entered the sitting room wearing her beautiful black and gold silk gown. She had let her hair down and was still slightly flushed from a recent bath.

"Oh wow... what a sight for sore eyes you are, Toni Mendez P.I." Lizbeth said with a broad smile. "Welcome back." She headed straight over to Toni and flung her arms around her in a fierce embrace.

Toni wrapped her arms around Lizbeth, and relished the feeling of her warm body melting into her own. It did feel good to be home, but Toni wasn't going to allow herself to relax into it just yet. They still needed to talk. Then, Lizbeth kissed her and Toni almost lost all her resolve.

"I'm starving," Lizbeth said, getting a whiff of the pizza. "I'll get the drinks, you can take the food through."

Toni did as she was told. She was feeling a bit nervous now.

Lizbeth followed her, bringing a glass of red wine for herself and an ice-cold beer for Toni.

The two of them settled on the couch as they had done every pizza night since the beginning.

"So, are you going to tell me about all your adventures in sunny South Africa?" Lizbeth asked.

"Not just yet, let's eat first." Toni said and prodded the pizza box in Lizbeth's direction.

"True, I can't quite think straight, my tummy is rumbling so loudly." Lizbeth flung open the box and helped herself to a slice.

Toni watched her take a bite and couldn't stop herself from smiling as pizza sauce started to trickle down her lover's chin, just as it always did. She wondered if there was anyone else in the world who could make that look so endearing.

Lizbeth muttered something unintelligible and dropped her half-eaten slice onto a plate.

"Pardon," Toni teased.

"Nawwkin," Lizbeth tried again through a mouthful, while she held one hand under her chin to make sure the juice did not dribble down further onto her lap.

Toni picked up one of the two paper napkins which had been rolled into tiny silver napkin rings that lay on top of the pile and handed it to Lizbeth.

Lizbeth turned over the paper napkin and discovered the diamond set into the silver band. Her eyes widened.

"I got pizza as a way to shut you up so I could explain something to you," Toni began. "As you probably realised after our last chat, I needed a bit of time to sort through some stuff in my head and my heart. And before you think I didn't hear what you had said about marriage, I want to reassure you I did — very loudly and clearly." She took the napkin and ring from Lizbeth and pulled the ring free, handing Lizbeth the napkin to wipe her chin. In that time, Lizbeth had managed to swallow down her mouthful and was about to say something.

Toni held up her hand. "Take another bite of that pizza if you have to but please hear me out."

Lizbeth kept quiet and remained sitting very still.

Toni took hold of Lizbeth's hand

"I have decided I want you to have this ring. With it I'm not asking for a commitment or a promise or trying to make a public statement of ownership. It is not intended as a mini shackle, but as a celebration of what you mean to me. Even if our friendship or relationship changes again in the future, I know you will always be special in my life and that is what I want it to mean." Only once she had finished her little impromptu speech did she dare to look up to see Lizbeth's reaction. As she did so, she caught Lizbeth wiping a tear from her cheek with the dirty napkin, smearing a new smudge of tomato sauce on her cheek.

Toni laughed, despite herself. She licked her thumb and gently wiped the smudge away.

Lizbeth took hold of Toni's hand and pulled her palm back up to her cheek, holding it there as she looked into Toni's beautiful watery brown eyes.

"Thank you," Lizbeth said softly. She leant in and kissed Toni.

Then she suddenly pulled away? "And what about the other ring?" Lizbeth asked.

"I'll hang on to that and wear it as a reminder not to string you up when you drive me nuts."

They kissed again — a hungry, unbarred, unrestrained welcome home kiss. Toni felt her passion rise like a tide that threatened to drown her. She needed to make this gorgeous woman, who held her heart, her own, and show her how much she had missed her. The chilling pizza lay forgotten as Toni picked Lizbeth up off the couch and carried her into their bedroom.

...RARELY AS THEY SEEM?

Hello dear readers...

For those of you who enjoyed this tale but still can't shake an uneasy sense of foreboding and who, like me, believe that things are very rarely as they seem, I have written an alternative ending...

TURN THE PAGE >>>

ALTERNATIVE ENDING

CHAPTER 17

It was 2 am. The airplane cabin was dark and most of the passengers were attempting sleep as best they could. Some were reading, or passing the time watching movies. Toni had selected a rerun of Fight Club, from the meagre selection available. Although it was one of her favourite movies, she couldn't concentrate on it. Her mind kept drifting, looping over the events of the past few weeks.

She had also hoped to gain some clarity about what to do in relation to her own personal dilemma with Lizbeth while she was away. Instead, she'd been so busy she had hardly had a chance to think about it.

Eventually, she decided to give up on the movie and get some rest. She turned off the small monitor and tried to get as comfortable as possible in the small upright space of her seat.

In turning to one side, towards Alice, who was seemingly fast asleep resting against the window, she accidentally kicked something on the floor. Toni leaned down to see what it was. To her horror she found that she had knocked over Alice's large red handbag and the contents were now strewn across the footwell.

Shit! She cursed under her breath.

It was dark and she didn't want to turn on the overhead light for fear it would wake Alice. She reached down into the dark and picked up the bag and began to shovel its errant contents back inside — a makeup bag, hairbrush, red faux leather diary, passport and a box. As she picked it up, she noticed it had opened partly, revealing the small glass vials inside. Toni glanced over to check Alice was still fast asleep. She was. Toni wasn't sure why she decided to look inside the box, but she did and as she did her stomach twisted into a knot and her breath caught. Inside were six insulin vials and the crocodile rings. Six? How did Alice have all six? That didn't make sense. From what little sense Toni had managed to get out of Alice after their return from the Shelter, Alice had been clear that Gloria had one of them at least and was using it to blackmail her.

Just then Alice stirred and Toni quickly returned the shoebox to the bag, stowing the bag as close as she could to its original position at their feet.

Toni leant back and closed her eyes to feign sleep. She needed time to think. Some things did not add up. Toni turned her head to the side to glance at Alice again. In her sleep, Alice's top had ridden up revealing her soft pale side and there, peeping out over her low-cut jeans, just on the inside of her hip bone, Toni saw the small dark dragonfly tattoo.

Oh my God! Toni gasped in recognition.

———

At PhyCorp, Toni did not have to wait long before Sheena Mukherjee returned after leading Alice off to meet with Dr McCroy. In her hand she had another large letter sized envelope which she handed to Toni.

"I trust this will be satisfactory. It includes double your rate, your expenses and a generous discretionary bonus. I also trust that the particulars of this case will remain confidential as per our agreement," Sheena said with a practiced smile.

Toni took the envelope and glanced inside. The money looked good. But something still did not feel right. Ever since finding the contents of Alice's bag on the airplane floor, something had been bugging her. She just couldn't put her finger on what. She didn't know how to articulate it or know which question to ask to get at the essence of her unease.

"Was there something else, Ms Mendez?" Sheena asked clearly expecting Toni to make her departure.

Toni shook her head. "No. Thank you."

"Okay, let me show you out," Sheena said and started towards the door.

"No, it's okay," Toni said. "No need. I know the way, I will show myself out."

Sheena smiled a blank smile again and nodded.

Toni headed down the long corridor that eventually lead to the reception area. She thought back to her previous visit to PhyCorp all those weeks ago. It struck her then, as it did now, that she still had no idea what PhyCorp really did. The building seemed too big to be purely a cosmetic surgery clinic.

The corridors were also too quiet. Come to think of it, other than the receptionist, Sheena Mukherjee and Dr McCroy, she really had not seen anyone else. Where was everyone? Up ahead of her, on the left side of the corridor, Toni saw large double doors.

Curiosity got the better of her and she decided to have a peek, to see where they led.

She tried one of the doors. They weren't locked, so she pushed through and cautiously headed down the passage, which took her into another wing of the building. As she went further, the sounds increased, until eventually she could hear a number of people — quite a din, coming from a door further up the corridor.

Toni tiptoed closer. When she peered in through the viewing window in the stainless-steel door, she was surprised to see people — patients, she assumed — dressed in gowns. Some were seated, strapped into wheelchairs and others gathered in groups around stainless-steel tables, accompanied by orderlies in navy uniforms. In the corner, one man was screeching and pulling at the window bars. A disproportionately small woman in uniform was desperately trying to calm him down.

What was this place?

Toni decided to venture a little further. She soon ended up in a bigger room, which had small consultation rooms leading off it. They were not unlike the one Dr McCroy and Sheena Mukherjee had seen her in that first time she was there. A fair number of these smaller rooms were occupied.

Then Toni noticed him. Dr McCroy sat at a small desk in one of them. He was alone.

She had to speak to him. Maybe he could shed some light on her unease. Perhaps he could explain the anomaly of the six vials.

Toni knocked on the door.

"Come," Dr McCroy called.

Toni stepped inside.

Dr McCroy did not seem to recognise her immediately.

"Dr McCroy, it is Toni Mendez. I am the P.I. you and your organisation hired to bring Alice back from South Africa."

"Ah, yes. Come in. Come in."

Toni did and closed the little door behind her. Once again, she was aware how small and spartan the office was. Dr McCroy was sitting at the little stainless steel table, writing notes. Toni tried to glance at the notes. It was in a strange hand — either a foreign language or some sort of shorthand, Toni deduced. In a place like that one probably had to be very careful with confidentiality. Sheena certainly was preoccupied with it.

"What can I do for you?" Dr McCroy asked.

"I just wanted to say thank you for your generosity."

He looked confused.

"As I said, you are welcome," Sheena's voice startled Toni from behind. She had not heard the little door open.

"Sorry to interrupt your work, Dr McCroy," Sheena said to him. "Ms Mendez, the public are not allowed back here unaccompanied. If you would like to follow me, I will show you to reception."

Toni made a show of not resisting. She nodded and turned to follow Sheena. She had to think quickly. As she got to the door she turned back to Dr McCroy.

"What is it you do here at PhyCorp exactly?"

Toni didn't miss his glance at Sheena.

"I mean, you led me to believe you are into cosmetic surgery, but none of the patients in the ward that I walked past to get here looked like they would be interested in face-lifts or tummy tucks."

The atmosphere in the room had changed. Toni glanced from Sheena to Dr McCroy. They were looking at each other seemingly assessing something or trying to decide what to do or say.

"You can either tell me or I can make it my business to find out in other ways. Believe me, you don't want that. I might not be subject to red tape anymore, but I still have a few contacts who love red tape."

Eventually, Toni heard Sheena close the door behind her. "You had better sit down."

Toni grabbed one of the stools that stood on the side of the room next to a set of sliding shutters she had noticed and thought odd when she first entered.

Just then there came another knock at the office door.

"Come," Dr McCroy called.

A slim, stern looking woman with jet black hair and full facial features entered, carrying a small pill bowl and glass of water. "Your tablet, Magnus" she said.

He nodded.

She entered and put the pill bowl and the water on the table next to him before she left, nodding at Sheena as she passed.

Toni sat waiting.

Dr McCroy swallowed down the tablet and then began. "Alice is not my wife."

Toni frowned. "Alice is not your wife?"

"No, in fact, Rita is." He nodded at the door indicating the woman who had just brought him his pills.

Toni frowned again, still unable to connect the dots of her unease.

"Our specialty is not cosmetic surgery as you guessed. It is a small niche field in psychopathy related to the prisons of the mind."

Toni swallowed. Of all the things she had expected him to say. That was not on the list.

360

"Alice is one of our inpatients. She was on a sojourn at our incarceration facility in South Africa when she somehow got out. It is unheard of for inmates to escape," he added the latter very quickly. "Our practice is fool proof, you understand."

Toni shook her head.

"PhyCorp is an organisation sponsored by the government, in fact a number of governments, to incarcerate their problem people."

"Problem people?"

Dr McCroy nodded. "Most of our inmates are in a class of high functional genius. They are incredibly bright, and in fact most of them are borderline if not fully psychotic, so much so that no ordinary state facility can contain them. That is where we come in. Our services are based on my lifelong work — on the premise that all perception, by its very nature, is subjective. And, all behaviour is motivated by our perception of reality. So, change the person's perception of their reality, and you will change their behaviour. In this particular project, freedom is as much an illusion as incarceration."

"In simple terms," Sheena interjected from behind Toni, "if you provide the incarcerated patient with the illusion that they are free, and they believe they want to be in that place, then they will not try to escape."

Dr McCroy nodded. "Yes, if freedom is what they aspire to. Some of our patients do not, but then we work to establish whatever construct will be acceptable to that individual."

"What? You mean that, basically, you use a person's genius against themselves, to create their own unique prison, from which they will never wish to escape," Toni said.

Dr McCroy nodded. "Precisely. In essence this is a foolproof method."

"So, what happened with Alice? Why did things go wrong?" Toni asked.

He shook his head. "The flight must have interfered with the medication which keeps her locked into the illusion."

"Let me get this straight," Toni said. "The MOD in South Africa is not a luxury spa, but an incarceration facility?"

Dr McCroy nodded.

"And you provide the inmates with the illusion that they are on some kind of spa vacation?" The pieces were finally starting to slot in place.

"Generally, the need for drugs is minimal beyond the initial stage, in which we need to create a consciousness that is open and hyper-suggestible to the illusion in the first place. After that the carefully crafted environment and trained staff are enough to cement the illusion. Even better, add to that the power of group psychology and it makes it almost impossible for the inmate to reject the narrative."

Just then a little beep sounded from an intercom Toni hadn't noticed in the wall.

"It looks like the interview is about to start," Dr McCroy said as he got up and pulled at the white shutters in the wall. As they parted Toni realised they obscured a glass window that looked into an adjacent room, not unlike the one she was currently in with Dr McCroy and Sheena. Only in the other room, she could see Alice sitting at a similar stainless steel table with another nurse.

"So, Alice, please tell me the whole story from the beginning, in your own time," Toni could hear the nurse say, through the intercom that Dr McCroy had just switched on.

Toni saw Alice take a deep breath and then she began. "Well, I didn't sleep very well in the plane on the way to Cape Town..."

———

A few hours later Sheena Mukherjee led Toni back towards the lobby of the PhyCorp institute.

"So, everything Alice just told us in there — the whole story of Gloria, Lekan, Lisa, the kids who she helped at the Shelter, that is all invented? I mean how can that be? I drove her to the Shelter myself. Granted, I never saw, nor met a Gloria. But I did see Alice with a large black man and I did find her at The Sea Shanty." Toni said, her head spinning as she tried to make sense of what she had just learnt.

Sheena shook her head. "No, it is not all lies. A lot of what she said would have a basis in reality, or at least it would be a fabrication that is not refuted by her experience of reality. Some people would have been real, with only certain details changed in her mind to fit her narrative. Others, like the Gloria character, I suspect we will discover to be an alter ego or one of her dissociated personalities."

Toni frowned. "Wow. Do you mean, she thinks of Gloria as someone else, but she actually is Gloria?"

Sheena nodded. "I know it is hard to believe what the mind is capable of sometimes — especially such gifted minds."

At that moment, Rita, whom Toni had last seen bringing Magnus a glass of water and a tablet in his office, came past them in the lobby.

"Good night, Vice Chair," Rita said.

"Good night, Rita. Enjoy your break!"

"Thank you," Rita said. "Hope he will be okay. If you need me, just call."

"After all this, and that sedative you just gave him, he will probably sleep until you get back," Sheena joked, good-naturedly.

"I know, I'll probably need to do the same," Rita said. She smiled and nodded at Toni before she headed out of the building.

Again, Toni's brow furrowed and she shook her head. Each time she thought she couldn't be surprised by something else in this case, she was proved wrong. "Let me get this straight. Rita is not Dr McCroy's wife?"

Sheena smiled back at her and nodded. "No, she's his handler."

"You mean he is also an inmate?"

Sheena nodded.

"And you are not his assistant?"

Sheena looked around and smiled guiltily. "No, I'm the Vice Chair of PhyCorp."

Toni's eyes bulged. "So... Madam Vice Chair –"

"Sheena, please. It serves us better if Magnus believes me to be his assistant and I don't believe rank is something to hide behind."

"So, Sheena, if Dr McCroy is an inmate himself, is it wise to put him in charge of Alice?"

"Contrary to what Dr McCroy has explained to you, the full remit of this project is not only to create the perfect subject illusions and incarceration, it is also about finding and utilising the inmates' unique abilities and skills — allowing them to be the best they can be. Magnus's skill is understanding gifted and aberrant psyches."

"How do you keep him under control or 'incarcerated'?"

Sheena Mukherjee smiled knowingly. "We don't need to do anything, other than making sure he has the occasional good night's sleep. His work is his own prison."

Toni nodded, but not for one moment really feeling like she understood.

"On that note. Toni, thank you very much for your services. We appreciate your commitment and diligence in helping us keep this very delicate situation contained and for keeping our people safe. You did a great job and in the unlikely event something like this happens again, we will be sure to call on you, if that is okay," Sheena said and stretched out her hand.

"One thing is for sure, if I can get my head around everything I have seen and heard today, this is going to make for interesting case notes."

Sheena nodded. "Yes. I'm sure about that. Perhaps you and Dr McCroy could collaborate on those notes. That way we can both have a fuller understanding of the events. But please, do be mindful of his specific realities in your future dealings with him."

Toni nodded, turned and headed out of the PhyCorp building, towards her car.

As much as Toni looked forward to dotting all the is, crossing all the ts and making better sense of this confounding case by producing a project report for PhyCorp, all of that had to wait for the moment. Right now, she had far more important things on her mind. She needed to make one very important pitstop on her way home...

PROJECT ALICE NOTES

My brief was to go to Camps Bay, South Africa, and retrieve Alice, whom I believed to be the wife of Dr Magnus McCroy, and bring her back to England.

This required me to:
A) Locate her
B) Persuade her to return with me to England
C) Bring her back under the radar

Alice (not her real name) is a high value inmate in a top-secret research programme, code named "Project Alice", which is being conducted by the PhyCorp Institute and funded by multiple government organisations.

The programme is based on the premise that all behaviour is motivated by a person's subjective perception of reality. By manipulating such perception, one can also control a person's behaviour.

Specifically, Dr McCroy's project aims to apply these

principles to the correctional services, to revolutionise the thinking and practice of incarceration of patients and prisoners who have been given indefinite terms of imprisonment. In particular, he is studying how to devise ways to make the inmates believe they are free and content, which would remove their desire to escape.

Dr McCroy's project falls within a larger study, which aims to use the same principles of perception manipulation to uncover and build on unique human abilities. Alice is one of the first individuals to be taken up into that study.

These notes have been prepared in strict confidence. They contain expert contributions from Dr Magnus McCroy who, in separate discussions with me, provided patient and programme background, as well as behavioural and psychological insights where relevant.

It was a challenge to find a form for these notes that best enabled an accurate and succinct record of the real events pertaining to this case. I finally settled on the following format: first, an explanation of the personalities and personas involved in the case, followed by a brief extrapolation of the events as I perceived them.

This report should by no means be regarded as a comprehensive account. Some aspects of this case still baffle me, but I have done my best to capture the essential elements.

Signed: Toni Mendez
Date: 15/12/2017

1. PEOPLE

Alice

In order to protect the true identity of the patient, she will only be referred to as Alice.

Doctor's Note:

The first crime is often the crime that triggers protracted acting out in later life.

Alice was first convicted of the murder of her foster mother and three of her biological siblings in 1998. Despite being a minor, she was given multiple life sentences and initially incarcerated at the category A, HM Prison Bronzefield, on "restricted status". However, the national prison organisation struggled to manage her and she was transferred to HMG specialist contractors, PhyCorp Institute, where she has been actively engaged in treatment since 2008.

Dr Magnus McCroy

He is Alice's specialist psychiatrist with specialised neuropsychology training and skills.

Doctor's Note:

Alice has formed a close attachment to me. She sees me as a strong paternal figure and depending on the particular situation, I manifest as either her husband or as a father figure.

Margaret McCroy

She is not a real person. She is the imagined persona of Alice's foster mother.

Alice came to England from Eastern Europe with her parents and three siblings when Alice was a little girl. Shortly after arriving, her parents died in a car accident and she and her siblings were taken into foster care.

Her foster mother was mostly wheelchair bound as a result of the repercussions of Type 1 diabetes.

While in foster care Alice and her siblings were drugged to keep them sedated and were repeatedly molested. Alice blamed her foster mother for allowing it to happen, and eventually Alice killed her by giving her an overdose of her own insulin. Afterwards, she killed her siblings. At her trial, Alice testified that her motivation for taking the lives of her siblings was mercy. In her uniquely affected mind, Alice believed it was her duty to rescue her siblings from living lives plagued and tortured by memories of their abuse.

In her constructed realities, Alice retained insulin as a preferred weapon of protection and her primary motivator is usually the rescue of children or individuals she sees as vulnerable.

Doctor's Note:

Alice manifests her foster mother as an active part of her life as a form of self-retribution — the personification of her personal guilt.

Rita Reynolds

She is a respected psychiatrist in the field of behavioural and cognitive analysis. She is also Dr McCroy's handler and pseudo wife.

Alice tends to construe Rita as Dr McCroy's assistant and naturally sees her as a rival for his affections.

Gloria Lamine

Ms Gloria Lamine was Alice's personal handler at the MOD, a PhyCorp Institute facility based in Camps Bay, South Africa.

Alice used her own amnesic sedatives, which she slipped into

Ms Lamine's drink, to drug her. This allowed her to use Ms Lamine's security key card, kept on a lanyard around her neck, to gain access to the rest of the facility, including the staff access areas, and ultimately enter and exit the facility undetected.

In classic dissociative disorder fashion, Alice took on the identity of Gloria once she had left the MOD.

Ms Lamine has been acquitted of all allegations of aiding and abetting Alice's escape and activities outside of the MOD and has been reinstated in her position as handler at the MOD after an internal investigation concluded.

Gloria lives in a small ground floor flat in Kloof Nek with her mother and her daughter's two-year-old son.

As for the suggestion that Alice earned money to fund her activities in Camps Bay and initial escape by doing housekeeping at the MOD, this is entirely fabricated. Inmates at the MOD are not permitted to carry money. Thus, it is believed that Alice stole clothes and money from the staff cloakrooms.

Olamilekan (Lekan) Zuberi

Alice met Mr Zuberi at the MOD. During the day he worked as one of the delivery men who brought supplies to the MOD on a regular basis. At night he used his work van to help round up homeless children and took them to a Shelter in the townships where they were fed and could sleep overnight if the weather was really bad.

According to Mr Zuberi, he and Alice met one day when Alice came out of the service entrance of the MOD and was heading into Camps Bay. He assumed she was one of the staff and they got talking.

On a whim he asked her out on a date and to his surprise she said yes. They met at The Sea Shanty where they ended up sharing a bottle of wine.

Under threat of being exposed as Alice's accomplice in all the crimes she committed, he admitted the following:

1. He and Alice had a sexual relationship.

2. Alice had come to live with him in his flat in Green Point for a while. During her stay with him, she had been fascinated by a young lifeguard who lived next door and often commented on what she believed to be a string of her female suitors.

3. He did organise fake visas and paperwork for Alice and put her in touch with Lucy who was his inside person at The Sea Shanty.

4. He took Alice with him one day to the children's Shelter. She got very fired up about what they were doing there and almost instantly volunteered to help with the running of it and care of the children.

5. Alice helped him to transport the goods they stole from the restaurants and hotels to the Shelter.

6. He also helped broker the transactions with prospective husbands for the arranged marriages.

In the matter of little Masika's murder, he maintains he is completely innocent and had no dealing in it.

Despite his hard-faced bravado he seems like a nice man who has a genuine regard and love for children with only their best interests at heart. I would find it hard to believe he had anything to do with the murder(s).

At the time of writing there is no proof that Alice had a hand in the deaths of the other boys who died at the Shelter, but it would fit her behavioural pattern, according to Dr McCroy.

Masika (Last Name Unknown)

She was a seven-year-old orphan girl.

According to Mr Zuberi, on the first night they went back to his flat in Green Point, he and Alice found the little girl curled in a dark corner near the garages outside a block of flats. Alice had insisted that they take Masika in. That is when he told her about his other occupation — rounding up homeless children and taking them to a Shelter.

That night Alice accompanied him to the Shelter for the first time.

According to the accounts given by the children at the Shelter and by Lekan, from the moment they met, Alice and

Masika formed a very strong emotional bond and whenever Alice was at the Shelter she was very seldom seen without Masika.

Background:

Masika's mother had TB and died while giving birth to her. Her uncle took her in. Because she was so little when she came into his care, he used to pre-chew food for her. At the time he had undiagnosed AIDS and thus infected her with HIV. When he died, she was left homeless and lived in the shadows in Green Point until rescued by Mr Zuberi and Alice.

Lisa Lowe

Miss Lowe was Alice's neighbour in the flat she and Lekan stayed in. She was a part-time life guard and has admitted to having a few girlfriends during that time. She testifies to having met Alice in the stairwell and occasionally bumping into each other in the corridor on the way to and from work.

She denies rescuing Alice on Camps Bay beach.

She claims never to have gone into the townships, nor to Noordhoek, nor any swimming pool with Alice. She has no knowledge of any beach parties, party on Signal Hill or any sex clubs.

She is adamant that there was never any relationship or sexual relations of any kind between her and Alice.

Doctor's Note:

It could be possible that Alice did feel an attraction for Miss Lowe and thus developed the fantasy of a relationship with Miss Lowe into her constructed reality, as some kind of wish fulfilment.

Gerry Cox

Ms Gerry Cox is the owner of The Sea Shanty and a number of other restaurants associated with the same brand. She has a long-term spouse, Claire Cox. They are happily married with two children and live in a house on Clifton Beach. Ms Cox denies all allegations that there was ever anything other than purely professional conduct between her and Alice or between her and any of her other staff members. She described as "friendly", her working relationship with her staff and would often host beach parties for them, as a way to build morale.

She admits to being impressed by Alice's evident aptitude for the hospitality industry and as a result trying to encourage her to rise up the ranks. This did not last long because after only a few weeks Alice handed in her notice and resigned from The Sea Shanty. Ms Cox confirmed that on the couple of occasions that Alice did work late, someone picked her up, in a red Golf convertible. On one occasion, she may have seen a black man in the driver's seat.

As an aside, Ms Cox did recollect seeing Alice and a rather "buff-looking black man" causing a bit of a stir one evening in her restaurant while having sundowners, a few days prior to Alice starting to work there. When Alice applied for the job, Ms Cox thought she recognised her, but didn't make that connection until I questioned her.

Ms Cox was instrumental in introducing me to Alice and allowing me to finally make contact with her at a community event on Signal Hill.

Lucy (Last Name Unknown)

I did not have the opportunity to interview Lucy personally as part of my investigation. Thus, not much is known about her circumstances or background other than she was a promising young graduate from a prestigious local hotel school, after which she started working at The Sea Shanty where she soon got promoted to sous chef and floor manager.

How exactly Lucy knew Mr Zuberi is unclear, but he admitted that she was his contact at The Sea Shanty and also the person who facilitated Alice getting her first job at the restaurant, without needing to present the relevant paperwork. Lucy has subsequently lost her job at The Sea Shanty on account of being caught stealing. It is unclear whether these accounts of theft were related to Alice's activities.

At the time of writing, Lucy is allegedly working as an apprentice at a boutique hairdresser in Camps Bay.

Other PhyCorp inmates interviewed

Not all of these "inmates" actually live on the MOD Hotel's premises. A few of them lead happy, well-adjusted lives and have successfully integrated into the local community — a fact which only came to my attention after my return to the United Kingdom.

- Olya
- Janine
- Pauline
- Colleen
- Maureen
- Melinda

2. FACT SHEET & EVENTS

The MOD

The MOD got its name from the Behavioural Modification Unit which was the small specialist team set up to initiate this programme within PhyCorp.

Alice used some of her own medication to sedate her handler, Gloria Lamine. She used Ms Lamine's security key card to gain wide access to the rest of the MOD facility over a period of time.

While in the MOD facility she posed as a new member of staff and used the service entrance to enter and exit unheeded.

She stole money and clothes from the staff changing rooms.

She stole insulin and medication from the dispensary.

During this time, she met and befriended Lekan Zuberi, who ended up becoming her lover and main accomplice once she had escaped from the MOD.

So far, no evidence has been found to corroborate her account of the near drowning experience.

The shop assistant at the swimwear kiosk confirmed that a woman matching Alice's description did purchase a swimsuit, but if someone did save her from the sea, it was not Miss Lisa Lowe.

Although I can't corroborate this, it seems most likely that Alice finally escaped the MOD by slipping out as part of the shift change on Sunday morning, 22nd October. That does coincide with the date on which Dr McCroy departed Cape Town to return to the UK.

Doctor's Note:

It is still not clear what precisely triggered Alice's abreaction to the paradigm of the MOD in the first place. Studies will continue as we endeavour to develop and perfect the programme.

Accommodation & Job

After she escaped from the MOD, I established that Alice tried to check into a couple of neighbouring hotels but the credit cards she presented were declined. We know that the cards which went missing from various staff members at the MOD had already been cancelled by that date. Probably as a consequence of this discovery, she sought out her new friend Mr Zuberi and agreed to go out on a date.

They met at The Sea Shanty. Mr Zuberi confirmed that one thing led to another and he suggested she could stay with him until she found her feet, an offer she gladly accepted. She ended up staying with him for a few weeks until she had earned enough money to get a place of her own.

Other than not having enough money, a lack of official paperwork was a problem in finding somewhere to rent herself. Over and above that, according to Mr Zuberi, Alice was not keen on tying herself down anywhere for too long. The perfect solution came along in the form of a boat for rent in Hout Bay harbour.

A couple of weeks later she moved onto the boat and bought herself a second-hand Golf convertible.

Mr Zuberi confessed to using his resources to help her get counterfeit paperwork, an unlisted mobile phone and helping her to secure a waitressing job at The Sea Shanty. Ms Cox reported that Alice was good at her new job and pretty soon was given more responsibility and higher pay. However, once Alice got involved in the Shelter, her mind was more preoccupied with that than with holding down her waitressing job and a few weeks later she resigned in order to dedicate all her time to the children.

The Recycling Operation

Once Alice started working at The Sea Shanty she became

obsessed, according to Mr Zuberi, with the tons of produce that the hospitality industry wasted daily.

She did initially try the official channels, and via formal letter, anonymously lobbied the MOD and The Sea Shanty to donate to the Shelter. She received no reply.

Soon she came up with the plan as to how they could redistribute some of the unwanted food and supplies.

She persuaded Mr Zuberi to help out, and they used his work van to transport their spoils back to the Shelter.

At first, they targeted the MOD and The Sea Shanty because Alice had inside knowledge. Thereafter, with Lucy's help, they expanded their enterprise to other neighbouring hotels and restaurants.

Unfortunately, neither Alice nor Mr Zuberi had heard about the recycling contractors and their plan was thwarted pretty soon as their inside contacts got caught. Alice herself did not get caught, nor did she own up to her involvement. She clung to the conviction that her liberty served the greater good because it enabled her to keep helping the children. So, even though they were limited to smaller enterprises that did not participate in the recycling scheme, they continued to loot what they could for the Shelter.

Arranged Marriage Operation

Mr Zuberi confirmed that Alice masterminded the arranged marriage operation to raise money for the Shelter as well as provide the older girls a way out of what she saw as an inevitably wretched township life. She believed this plan would give them an opportunity to do better for themselves.

Alice didn't only follow and observe Mr Zuberi to the first drop. She participated. Private CCTV footage from the bus stop shows her sitting on the bench with Mr Zuberi and the girl.

Mr Zuberi testified that the operation was entirely Alice's brainchild and mostly her doing. She had only asked him to help out as liaison to set up the exchanges in the first place, and then to help see them through more smoothly, since in African culture men are unaccustomed to dealing with women in business, let alone a white woman.

Regarding the Ayane drop, Mr Zuberi had agreed to bring Ayane from the Shelter to meet Alice after work, at a small quiet restaurant in Camps Bay, on the way to take her to the arranged drop. They were caught off-guard by an unscheduled road block in which Mr Zuberi was stopped and detained for a few hours.

Alice took Ayane to the rendezvous point.

When asked about the rings, Mr Zuberi confirmed that Alice gave each of the girls a "going away present", which she had specially made by a metal craftsman she met selling his custom jewellery outside The Bay Hotel in Camps Bay. Mr Zuberi had no knowledge of the noxious nature of the ring or anything related to insulin.

Doctor's Note:

The fact that Alice would enable the young women to protect themselves with insulin ties in with Alice's psychotic trigger. The fact that she regarded the rings and insulin as "insurance" suggests that she did not have murderous intent. In her mind she merely wanted to empower the women, to level the playing field and give them a way to protect themselves.

Alice has an ambivalent relationship with older men, on account of repeatedly having been abused by such figures. In her early teens, she allegedly confided in a seemingly kind doctor who made regular house calls to see her foster mother. Rather than rescue her, he started to abuse her himself. The doctor, however, soon lost interest in her, moving on to her siblings, after telling her that she was "not very good at it". This potentially could have triggered a deep-seated need to prove herself to older male authority figures.

Masika's Death

According to accounts collected from the children at the Shelter, when Masika became ill, Alice spent night after night by the little girl's camp-bed. On the Friday morning, just before dawn, after a series of particularly harrowing nights, with Masika suffering greatly, Alice used one of the crocodile rings to inject Masika between her toes with a lethal dose of insulin.

According to accounts collected from the children, Alice bleached the ring and then went home to shower before returning to the Shelter to cook the children breakfast after which she "discovered Masika dead."

In my opinion, it is also highly likely that Alice injected Kofi and Kwame in a similar fashion causing their deaths, but since it is not possible to involve the local authorities, there is not enough evidence to prove that.

Direct Contact Events

My personal account of the events that I participated in is as follows:

By prior arrangement with Dr McCroy, I was given access to the MOD. At that point I had no prior knowledge of the uniqueness of the facility nor the special nature of their clients. During my visit I interviewed a number of the clients and staff with a focus on gathering clues as to Alice's likely whereabouts. Unfortunately, most of the intel that I gathered amounted to not much more than vague, unconfirmed sightings.

From there I extended my circle of investigation to include the whole of the Camps Bay community and business and commercial centre, going door to door. It was my hope that someone might recognise her from the photograph Dr McCroy had given me for this purpose. Again, this endeavour turned out to be futile. I later learnt the reason no-one recognised her was because soon after leaving the MOD, Alice had dramatically changed her appearance, and the photograph I had been showing around bore very little resemblance to what she looked like by then.

More than ten days into the investigation I still had not had
any success in finding Alice, and I was about to abort the job
when, quite by chance, I saw Alice on the beach and
realised she had been hiding in plain sight all along.

Despite not having the necessary visa and paperwork she
had managed to secure herself a regular waitressing job at
The Sea Shanty.

From there I managed to follow and observe her enough to
learn of her involvement with Mr Zuberi, the location of his
flat in Green Point, the Shelter, her fondness for little
Masika, as well as observe a few of the recycling operations.

One of the leads from the MOD eventually led me to
uncover an underground organisation and network that
held "Special Adult Entertainment" events. I discovered
Alice and Mr Zuberi used this organisation and its network
to find potential suitors for their arranged marriage
operation. After following Alice and Mr Zuberi to a couple
of their meetings with the new suitors, I realised that the
rendezvous point rarely changed. As a result I was able to
liaise with a local cafe bar across the road and arrange to
hijack one of their CCTV cameras to record these
assignations.

I was not able to watch Alice 24/7 myself without rousing
suspicion, but I made a point of regularly frequenting The
Sea Shanty during her shifts.

On one such occasion, I deliberately engaged Gerry Cox
and enlisted her help to facilitate a meeting with Alice at a
local community event on Signal Hill. Ms Cox is very

protective of her staff and sees herself as more of a parental figure than a boss. I suspected Ms Cox was quite capable of calling the authorities on me, if she thought my intentions towards Alice were untoward.

Once I had made contact with Alice, I found our common origins were fertile ground for rapport-building. After only a few hours, she suggested we meet the following day for some tourist sightseeing together since we were both new to the country.

The following morning we met and went up the Cable Car to the top of Table Mountain. As mentioned, up to that point I had restricted all conversation to basic rapport-building, however the Table Mountain excursion presented a good opportunity to begin to persuade her to return to the UK with me.

All things considered, that engagement with Alice went well. Although she was understandably annoyed by my subterfuge and connection to Dr McCroy, I managed to gain her trust and it was not long before Alice herself sought me out for help.

Extraction

After Alice contacted me, I went over to meet her on her boat. She was very distressed. We spoke for about an hour, during which time she disclosed the full context of her predicament, which was very similar to the account she gave Sheena Mukherjee.

At that point, I had no reason to doubt her account.

So, once she had calmed down a little, I suggested we needed to retrieve the crocodile rings and the insulin. My intention was to prevent them from falling into the hands of the local authorities given that PhyCorp had asked me to extract Alice with discretion.

Alice was in a very emotional state and seemed very uneasy about entering the townships on her own. I offered to take her. I drove us to the Shelter based on her directions. I wanted to go in and help her, but she stopped me, suggesting it would be very hard to explain who I was and what I was doing there at that hour. So, I waited in the car.

She was inside the Shelter for just over half an hour and I was about to go see what was keeping her when I heard police sirens. I decided that unless it became critical, the prudent action was to lay low and observe. So, I hunkered down into the footwell of the car and watched.

I saw the police officers storm into the Shelter. I feared Alice would be arrested and taken away. If that happened, I had resolved to use my contacts to get her released off the record.

To my surprise, about ten minutes later, the police officers came out of the Shelter. Alice was engaged in conversation with one of the officers. I saw his team retire back to their vehicles, and within minutes he followed suit and they all drove off.

I discovered later, via my police force contacts, that earlier that evening the police had received an anonymous call informing them of a suspicious death, and tipping them off about a murder weapon in the pantry. I was able to listen to an extract of the call. The caller, who claimed to be an anonymous bystander, sounded very much like Alice herself.

When the police searched the pantry there were no rings or insulin to be found. I suspect Alice had removed and hidden them prior to the police's arrival.

Alice finally returned to the car, where I was still waiting. She seemed strangely distracted and withdrawn. I was not able to identify it at the time, however Dr McCroy has subsequently informed me that Alice would most likely have been suffering "an episode" — an altered state of consciousness. Apparently, to the observer the patient seems merely unresponsive and somehow dazed, however the patient herself would most likely be experiencing vivid auditory and visual hallucinations. That would account for Alice's description of Gloria's presence at the Shelter that night with the police, and the subsequent events leading up to the flight back to the UK: Gloria's threat to expose Alice, her recollection that we stopped off at Lisa's flat on the way to the airport and Lisa's farewell.

In reality, Alice remained in that unresponsive, altered state, until moments before we arrived at PsyCorp. Once we left the Shelter, I took her straight back to the boat in Hout Bay, where I helped her pack and lock up. We then returned the boat and car keys to the harbour master and I hired us a taxi to the airport which only stopped very briefly at The Bay Hotel so I could collect my things.

Doctor's Final Note:

In my professional opinion, patient Alice suffered a psychological break down, for reasons as yet unknown, resulting in the onset of an acute multiple personality episode. During this episode she assumed the identity of her personal carer Ms Gloria Lamine, and a composite personality based on her impression during a brief encounter with Miss Lisa Lowe. The reasons for this psychological break down are currently under investigation. At the time of writing remedial treatment has commenced. A full psychological analysis and progress report will follow.

NOTES & THINGS SOUTH AFRICAN

Chapter 1

1. OCR stands for Optical Character Recognition

Chapter 2

1. Generally, 'coloured' is used as an ethnic label for people of mixed ethnic origin, including Khoisan, African, Malay, Chinese, and white. In South Africa it is used to refer to people of mixed-race parentage rather than, as elsewhere, to refer to African peoples and their descendants. In modern use the term is not generally considered offensive or derogatory.
2. South African currency is rands. e.g. R10

Chapter 4

1. 'Protea' is the botanical name and the common name of South African flowering plants, sometimes called sugarbushes (Afrikaans: suikerbos) or Fynbos. Specifically, The King Protea was proclaimed South Africa's national flower. In local tradition, the Protea flower represents change and hope.
2. 'Hot hatch' is a colloquial term for small hatch-back cars, usually a young person's first car, that has been loaded with racing paraphernalia like under-car LED lights, 'go faster' stripes and oversized stereos. The drivers then tend to burn rubber down quiet stretches of road in the city or in disused car parks.

Chapter 9

1. Joanna Lumley played the role of Shirley's former school enemy Marjorie Majors.

Chapter 13

1. "My boat is your boat."

Chapter 14

1. 'Pote' is Afrikaans for feet. Also slang for white cops.
2. 'Hambanathi' means walk with us.
3. Symbol of adaptability.
       The crocodile lives in the water, yet breathes the air, demonstrating an ability to adapt to circumstances.
       http://www.symbols.com/symbol/denkyem
4. "Hello, ladies."... "You must be my beautiful princess/girlfriend." in Sesotho.

Chapter 15

1. 'Qaqambile' means brightness.
2. 'Dassie' is the common South African English name for the rock hyrax (Procavia capensis), or rock badger, rock rabbit, and Cape hyrax. The closest living relatives to dassies are the modern-day elephants and sirenians.

Chapter 16

1. 'Stockings' is a children's playground game using old stockings tied together in a continuous band and looped around two bystanders' legs. The loop was used as a framework around which to structure a chase, akin to long rope skipping. The person being chased performed various jumps and skipping patterns in and over the suspended stockings while in flight, challenging the chaser to replicate the patterns while in pursuit.
2. 'Bakkie' is a small pickup truck with an open body and low sides

IF YOU ENJOYED THIS BOOK...

Reviews are one of the most important ways for me to gain visibility and bring my books to the attention of other readers.

If you've enjoyed this book, I would be very grateful if you could spend just five minutes leaving a review on your favourite reader platforms (it can be as short as you like).

It really can make a huge difference.

Jump to your favourite reader platform now >>

Alternatively, send me feedback here:

mail@SamSkyborne.com

Thank you very much!

ACKNOWLEDGEMENTS

I'd like to thank everyone who has helped and been involved both directly and indirectly in this project. In particular, Anny, Ellie, Lily and my folks, Adri and Rob, thank you for taking precious time out of your busy lives to beta read, proof and sense-check for me. All and any remaining errors are entirely my own.

A special thanks to Alison for all your patience, help and support, and for endeavouring to make #MyOffice interesting and my product so much better.

A heartfelt thank you to the fabulous Judy OTHO. You were there from the very beginning and I'm so happy that you are still bumping along with me on this amazing journey, almost a decade later. I can not begin to thank you enough for all the ways in which you have supported and helped me.

And finally, thanks to my furry babies, for your kisses, cuddles and snuggles and for allowing me to stroke you when times got tough.

WHY NOT TRY...

http://SamSkyborne.com/Risk

"RISK: Three Crime-fighting Women Risk All for Love, Lust & Justice."

As if it's not hard enough 'coming out'.... Imagine being wrenched from the closet in the midst of a dangerous serial killer case by your new nemesis and your best friend.

Toni Mendez, an ex-cop turned private investigator in London, takes on a case... that will change her life.

OR TRY...

http://SamSkyborne.com/Simulation

"**Simulation: The Dawn of a Superhero**"

When passion runs too hot....

Of all the experiments, of all time...love still remains the most dangerous!

Samantha Fielding, an emotionally scarred ex-war hero, enrols into a top-secret scientific research programme for all the wrong reasons. Will she survive...and get the girl?

ALSO BY SAM SKYBORNE

Toni Mendez Series:

Starting Over (Free to Reader Group)

RISK: Three Crime-fighting Women Risk All for Love, Lust and Justice

Project ALICE

Standalone Novels

Simulation: The Dawn of a Superhero

Box Sets

Super Starter Box Set

Lesbian Erotic Shorts (L.E.S) Story & Film:

Cat Sitting: Lesbian Cat Custody Complications

Saying Sorry: A Queer & Complex Process

Short Stories

Unbroken (Free to Reader Group)

The Yellow Tandem

Milton

Stakeout

ABOUT SAM SKYBORNE

Sam Skyborne is the proud author of a number of award winning novels and currently lives & loves in London (UK) while happily going on writing adventures across the globe ... or even further afield, as far as the mind will travel.

Connect with Sam:

Private Facebook Reader Group:
Facebook.com/groups/SamSkyborneGroup

Facebook Page: @SamSkybornePage

Instagram: @SamSkyborne

Sam's online home: SamSkyborne.com

Or drop Sam an email: mail@SamSkyborne.com

FREE EBOOK! "STARTING OVER"

http://SamSkyborne.com/Starting-Over

Want to know how Toni & Lizbeth first met?
Join Sam's VIP Readers' Group and find out now!